The Jesus Spy

A Novel

ARTHUR JONES

Capparoe Books

Copyright © 2019 Arthur Jones. All rights reserved.

Published by Capparoe Books, Maryland, USA
ISBN: 978-0-9768751-2-3

Cover artwork by Carol Davisson

Visit the author's website: arthurjonesbooks.com

*For cardiac surgeon Dr James Gammie,
whose skill saved my life and
gave me these extra years,
And for cardiologist Dr Margaret Brennan,
whose persistence pulled me back from
a second brush with mortality—
Thank you*

MAIN CHARACTERS

Musan Deleig: Parthian prince, chief counselor and head of espionage to Pontius Pilatus
Jesus (c.1 BCE–c.33 CE): Messianic preacher, Nazarene carpenter

Pontius Pilatus (dates unknown): Prefect of Judea, 26–36 CE
Claudia Procula (dates unknown): Pontius Pilatus' wife
Formio: Pontius Pilatus' son, Pontius Cletus Formosus

Lady Lydia: Musan Deleig's mentor within Rome's imperial family
Marianus: Vasas' business associate and uncle of Caiaphas
Myrmid: Musan Deleig's deputy in all things, adviser and guard
S'veyda: Musan Deleig's chief assistant for trading activities
Talca the Saka: Musan Deleig's coordinator of Judea's espionage agents, enforcer of daily reporting
Vasas: Jerusalem businessman and Musan Deleig's boyhood friend

Herod Antipas (21 BCE–39 CE): Tetrarch of Galilee and Perea, son of Herod the Great
Caiaphas (c.14 BCE–46 CE): High Priest of the Temple in Jerusalem
Aelius Sejanus (20 BCE–31 CE): Prefect of the Praetorian Guard and Emperor Tiberius' chief administrator

Reigns of Roman Emperors relevant to the account:
Octavian/Augustus, 27 BCE–14 CE
Tiberius, 14–37 CE
Claudius, 41–54 CE
Domitian, 81–96 CE

Tenures of Roman Prefects in Judea relevant to the account:
Annius Rufus, 12–15 CE
Valerius Gratus, 15–26 CE
Pontius Pilatus, 26–36 CE

Black Sea
ARMENIA
Caspian Sea
ROMAN EMPIRE
Carrhae
Hatra
Cappadocia
Mesopotamia
Tigris
Tarsus
Dura-Europos
Syria
Cyprus
Euphrates
Damascus
Mediterranean Sea
Judea
Caesarea Maritima
Jericho
Jerusalem
PARTHIAN EMPIRE
Nile
Egypt
Arabia

Black Sea
ROME
Cappadocia
Syria
Mediterranean Sea
Judea

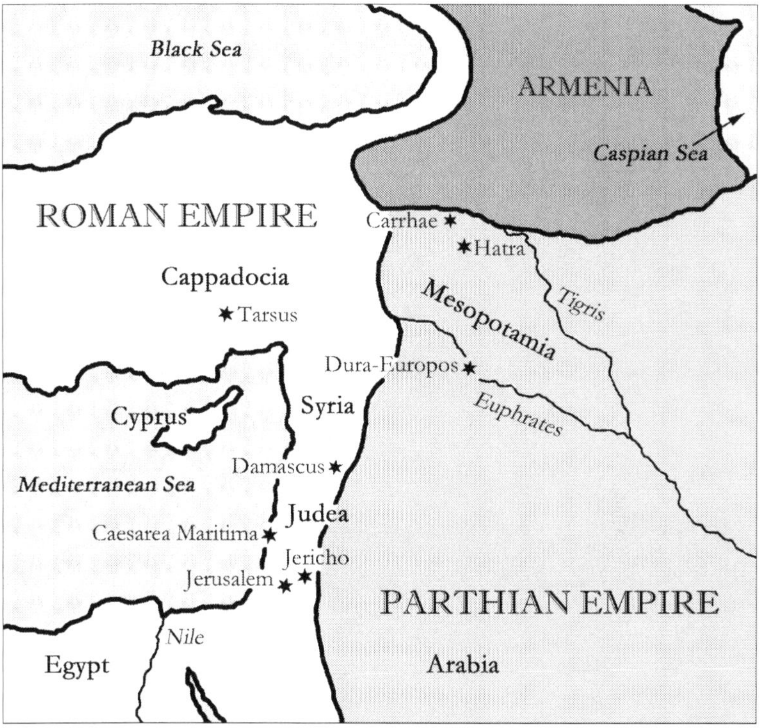

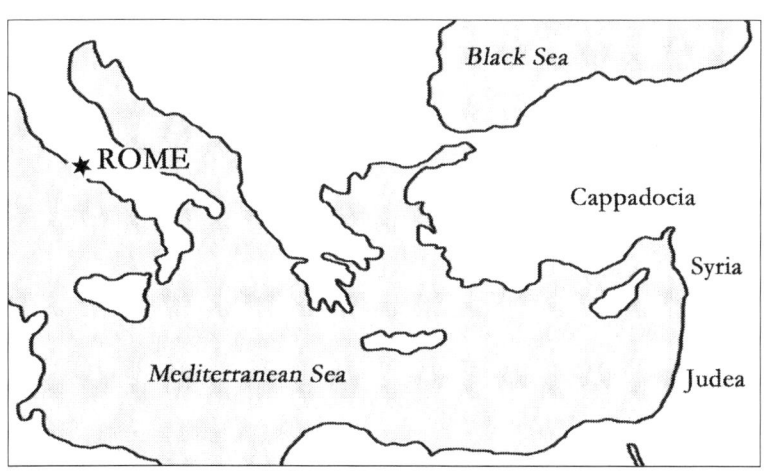

ONE

The black-shrouded rider halted and slid from his camel. He hobbled it and the one behind and walked the few steps to the crest of the escarpment. There, below, Judea.

It had taken twenty grueling days to cross the desert from Mesopotamia—dangerous long days, with cold nights. He was entering the Roman Empire through a back door, crossing over the border from the Parthian Empire at a point where no one would know who he was or question why he was there. Only his friend Vasas in Jerusalem knew he was coming. He intended to travel to the city at night to avoid notice.

He was an experienced desert traveler, but it had been foolhardy to cross the desert alone. He'd known the danger—had faced a difficult situation and lost a camel. Now, he was beyond tired. He stank worse than camel's breath—almost three weeks without bathing. No lice, thank Ahura Mazda, but biting flies had attacked several times and left sores. His current cravings were modest: fresh water, a wash, fresh clothes and a decent meal.

Once seen, Prince Musan Deleig of Parthia was never forgotten. At twenty-seven, Deleig was extremely tall, six-foot-four and slender, with a short, black pointed beard below a hatchet-edge profile—currently a shaggy black beard below a dirt-encrusted brow. Dark, bleary eyes peered with high curiosity, kindness and amusement from under the forehead overhang, eyes that switched from amused to alert in less than a blink.

The Royal Palace in Hatra, Mesopotamia, had not been his home for more than a decade, years he had spent in Rome, at the heart of power of the Roman Empire. But that was about to change. In four months, he would move to Judea—to become Rome's head of espionage in this subjugated nation.

He laughed at the idiotic turn of his life. "Head of espionage." The laugh-lines cracked the dirt caked on his face. He stepped back toward the camels and poured a handful of brackish water from one of the near-empty water skins. He wet his lips and rubbed the wetness on his eyelids and the facial dirt. It eased his dry eyes but made no impression on his grimy face.

He thought back to his introduction to spy-craft, when he was only six years old. What had those misguided elders been thinking?

"What are the six Ps of espionage, Musan?"

"Pierce, probe, proceed. Patience, persistence, preservation."

Spy training. He thought it was silly then, and standing here now, looking down on Judea, he considered it idiotic. Espionage wasn't a profession, something one could be educated into; it was a craft learned on the job. He'd early decided that his "governors," the best minds of Parthian royalty, aristocracy, military, academia and—such as it was—espionage, were hopeless at it, despite their determination to create a "peacetime" spy.

Thanks to Emperor Augustus' *Pax Romana*, Rome and Parthia, traditional enemies, were at peace. Through the reputation of his paternal grandfather, General Deleig of Deleig of the Royal Parthian Army, Musan would be sent to peace-loving Rome under the cover of completing his education. He would be accepted by some of the best Roman families—he was, after all, a prince and had social cachet. And while absorbing the best education the city had to offer, he'd be doing essential espionage work for the Parthian Empire. Or that was the plan.

His governors knew his fluency in Latin, as well as Greek and Aramaic, which were spoken in the palace. They saw that study, whether of history, geography, languages or diplomacy, came naturally to him. Imagination was a prerequisite, and he had plenty of that.

The governors hadn't realized they might create a precocious entity they could not control, Deleig mused as he surveyed the sweeping, surprisingly misty expanse of Judea below. The swath of treetops painted the valley a deceptive green, despite its general sandy dryness. He could see no trace of the River Jordan or his destination, Jerusalem.

He needed to get his load to Jerusalem, to the house of his boyhood friend Vasas, and then head back to Rome. Four months from now he would be back in Judea in his official capacity, but now he was on a mission of his own.

Deleig momentarily luxuriated in the thought of bathing, and of dining sitting down, with wine. But the past insisted on intruding. Like a favored taste on the tip of the tongue, it was back again. Memories, the traveling entertainment of the lone journeyer.

Suddenly he was grinning at himself. What the governors did not realize was that they could not penetrate his mother's guidance: his subconscious sense of being a prince. The daughter of a king, his mother had drummed royal protocol and a princeling's privileges and perquisites into her youngest son. His grandfather was correct when he referred to his grandson's "effortless superiority"—his ironic detachment and sophisticated air. Musan, however, did not feel superior; it all came quite naturally.

It gradually became obvious to Musan that not one of his governors had ever been to Rome. Not one knew any of "the best" Roman families, and worst of all, none had first-hand, front-line experience in espionage.

When he turned thirteen, Musan decided he would change their approach to him through a rebalancing of power. In the group session on "Parthia's Confrontations with Rome," Musan asked the Royal Espionage Director, "If, sir, our espionage is as good as you say, why didn't we know that Marc Antony had befriended Herod the Great? I'm talking about Parthia's defeat at the Syrian Gates a half-century ago. At the time, you, sir, were Deputy Royal Espionage Director. You would have known, I hope, that Marc Antony was playing a shrewd game he ultimately lost."

Musan fastened his gaze on the director's reddening face. The man obviously had no ready answer.

The young prince had learned enough to know not to wait too long when he had the advantage. His diplomacy educators had taught him some things well.

"Had you any agents usefully positioned *outside* Parthia? Or was your work simply conjecture?"

The director, completely unnerved by the attack, said, "I ... I—"

"Couldn't get anyone close enough to find out what was happening in the enemy camps?" Musan interrupted. "And why didn't we know Herod's military power and prowess at that time was equal to Parthia's? Why didn't we have a clue that Herod, at Marc Antony's urging, was likely to be strong enough to push us out of Judea? Or that Marc Antony would name Herod King of Judea?"

Musan closed with his final, fatal dig. "You were in charge when Herod took over. Yet our own records reveal we knew none of this."

Musan had learned how to research. The governors were aghast, many wondering if they'd similarly been researched and were due for a cross-examination. The furious Royal Espionage Director, rebuked and embarrassed by a thirteen-year-old, left the room never to return to the sessions. Not only had Musan shown insight into the mistakes of Parthia's recent past, but he had also out-maneuvered everyone in the room.

Deleig saw himself as direct, but at twenty-seven knew he'd rejected the posturing of rank he'd exercised as a boy.

"Well," Deleig said to the lead camel as he pulled it toward him, preparing to move on, "perhaps I was a little cocky for my age?"

As the Royal Espionage Director left, the boy had faced the phalanx of old men and said, "You must admit, your teaching has taken hold."

His dismayed grandfather adjourned the gathering. He needed to have words with his grandson. Deleig remembered "the words" so well. His grandfather had said, "You don't attack adults in prominent positions, Musan. It is not gentlemanly."

Deleig recalled he'd replied, "All I did, Grandfather, was ask him questions he should have been able to answer promptly, but couldn't answer because he was a dolt, unfit for his task—a duck wearing an eagle's hat."

His grandfather was astounded, undone by an apparent effortless command of the facts.

Well, Deleig smiled to himself, he had shown them then—and two years later when he got to Rome—what he'd thought of their plan. They had not been happy.

He turned his mind to the task ahead. To get to the River Jordan he would have to get down the steep, mountainous terrain of Perea. For the next two hours, he rode or led the camels carefully down the tricky escarpment, sticking to tracks and avoiding major paths.

Finally, the foothills leveled out. He stared into the distance—a sign of habitation. At least it meant water, if only rainwater. The wind—the only sound—was strong, blowing in from the greenery ahead. His nostrils sniffed at the welcome traces of moisture in the air. How refreshing it felt. His eyes were gradually becoming less scratchy.

He looked down at his long, ungainly, filthy fingernails. He needed a personal servant's attention. He snorted. Some chance. His hair must be wadded like wet wool. He'd be lucky if he could find some animal-fat soap. The chance of a Roman oil-and-strigil skin-scraping cleanse was nil.

He gave a humorless chuckle. Body cleansing was the least of his challenges, more testing was to get in and out of Jerusalem, then up to Caesarea Maritima and away by boat to Rome, without being seen by anyone official who could send up the alarm—or who would recognize him when he returned to Judea officially. Caesarea Maritima was the Roman Empire's enormous artificial harbor, jutting into the Mediterranean midway up Judea's coastline.

Deleig needed to get to Vasas' house in Jerusalem with his load intact. To reach Jerusalem meant crossing the River Jordan and then going through or around Jericho. From Jericho it was sixteen miles to Jerusalem. He thought through his strategy again. Why was he so worried? Worried, or just eager? Eager, he thought.

The main purpose of this trip was to find a local, but not a Judean, to fashion into his second-in-command in his personal spy network, a second-in-command about whom Rome knew nothing. That had to be done now. It was important no one could connect Deleig with espionage when he took up his position as the Prefect's resident astrologer—his cover story—four months from now.

If challenged on his present journey, he planned to pass himself off as a silk trader, a desperate measure because clean and properly dressed, Deleig would appear far too sophisticated to trade anything but badinage with people as sophisticated as himself. He laughed, a wry cackle. There was nothing sophisticated about him in his present state.

His pack camel was carrying two huge bundles of silk. Deleig had had to shift the dead camel's load onto the other one, which now looked like it might not make it as far as Jerusalem.

He had a further deception. His own mount had a sacking cover over its back, dirty sacking so thin and miserable in appearance it would create no curiosity, a disguise as effective as poor taste. Within the sacking, sewn in square-inch pockets, was a fortune in gold and silver coins that he wanted to secrete at Vasas' house. Deleig had drawn on his own extreme wealth to fund an effective, personal spy network in Judea, beyond the allowances of the Empire's central government. A network he would establish before anyone knew who he really was. Theoretically trained in spy-craft, but relatively untested in the field, he needed to gain a level of control before anyone realized he was learning on the job.

If he could reach Vasas, he would feel safe. He had a plan how to find this man who would become his second-in-command, a man who knew the ways of the world—and Judea. Then? Escape back to Rome to brief Pontius Pilatus, who was soon to take over as the Prefect of Judea—and would be his boss.

TWO

The sun hadn't crested. Deleig calculated less than an hour until noon. He swung his camel to the right and rode up an incline. On the downward side, he saw a village of perhaps forty or fifty dwellings.

He moved at a slightly faster pace and headed for what appeared to be the most established house of the lot, modest though it was. As he approached, a gaggle of young boys ran out to meet him, shouting to him. He caught in a rural Aramaic patois the squeaky cries of welcome and who are you sirs.

Outside the house he dismounted and stood upright. The boys were impressed. In this village they had never seen anyone above six feet tall. At six-foot-four this was a giant before them.

Deleig reached into the leather purse on a strap strung across his body from his left shoulder. He fished in a particular pocket and plucked out a small handful of *rions*, small copper coins. These he threw behind him. The boys turned to run for the money.

Deleig caught two laggards by the shoulders of their shifts, produced two *rions*, gave one to each and handed each one a halter rope from a camel. In Aramaic he said, "Let nothing happen to these camels. A larger reward when I return." He removed a small bag of clothing from the pack camel.

His arrival and the boys' noise had attracted the residents of the most established house. They now stood at their door, a stocky older man and his wife, shawl across her face, behind him. The couple, unsurprisingly, appeared fascinated by this stranger in their village, not least because as he approached them two silver *denarius* coins were displayed between his right thumb and forefinger.

He asked if he might use their well, to wash, and if he could take a modest meal outside, for which he would pay.

The man had a round face with a long, wide nose, narrow lips and a too small chin within an unruly beard. He became effusive in his welcome, issued orders to his wife and led the tall man to the well. Deleig laid the coins on its low, mud-brick wall.

The boys had followed the stranger and gathered beyond the low wall that fronted the house. His host barked two words at the boys; they fled. Deleig didn't know what was said in the local patois, but was admiring of two words that seemed so useful.

The man, whom Deleig now regarded as his host, immediately set up a bucket at the well and began to turn the handle. Two rounds of sustained turning and the well ladles brought water to the top. The laden scoops spilled over into the bucket before descending back down.

Deleig waited, removed the one filled bucket and placed a second empty one there. He signaled the man to refill them when empty. He asked the man if the household had any animal-fat soap. The man shook his head, but offered an oil. Deleig accepted. The man said his name was Dari.

The man disappeared into the house and returned with a small jug. Deleig placed the second bucket of water by the first and, without shame or embarrassment, shrugged off his desert gear. He stepped away naked from the discarded thick black Bedouin woolen robe and the light, white cotton *thobe*, his shift, now gray and stained. He poured half the oil into his hair and beard and rubbed hard. He poured the two buckets of water over his head and naked body, washing himself with his hands.

He covered his body as best he could with the remainder of the oil and poured the second batch of water over his body. His host stopped turning the well and quickly glanced at the naked Deleig. Not circumcised. Must be Greek.

Deleig, drying quickly in the dry heat, left his desert clothes where they lay. From his clothing bag he removed and dressed in his Parthian hunting clothes: tooled leather jacket, with matching cap, cloth leggings and tooled leather calf-length boots. The cap he rested on the side of the well while he combed his hair with his fingers and then manipulated his overgrown beard to a point. He donned his cap.

His host was immobilized. This was an important man. A very important man. A woman's voice called from beyond the door.

Almost servile, the man invited Deleig into his home, but Deleig pointed to the rough table and bench not far from the well. He must not let the camels out of his sight. He insisted the man join him.

Reluctantly, or bashfully, the man did. He picked up the coins and seated himself on a worn box he dragged to the table. The wife served two bowls to Deleig, one of liquid, probably a soup, he thought, and one of meat, a chunk of bread alongside and a jug of water. Deleig stood as she placed the items on the table. He held up his hand to prevent her leaving and bowed to her formally. As he did so he pulled a silken shawl from his sleeve, a boyhood conjuring trick. He folded the silk with a flurry of fingers, draped it across her right forearm and sat down.

She was wide-eyed. Her head bobbed up and down several times as if she were inflicted with a nodding disease. She turned and ran to the house as if pursued by a devil.

It took a while, but as Deleig ate and supped, he finally had the man talking. Guardedly about his personal life, freely and unfavorably about the Roman occupation, the host went on to excoriate local officials, most wealthy men and even a preacher or two, as little more than robbers.

Unexpectedly, the host stood up from his box and dashed into the house. He returned with a jug of wine and two beakers, poured and kept on talking as they drank.

The man was older than Deleig had first assumed. He took a chance and asked, "What was life like under King Herod?" Herod the Great, who'd died thirty years earlier.

"Vicious. He was mad. Threw his wife out of the window. Killed a son he didn't like and ruled us the same way. He was Idumaean, a peasant, not a proper member of the Hebraic tradition."

Deleig pressed slightly harder. "I heard he knew what everyone was thinking."

"Had agents everywhere," the man said. "Look at the size of this place. We had two of his agents here, in this village. All people were doing here was trying to stay alive on poor soil and raise their families, same as my wife and I. My brother was one of his agents in Jericho, said it paid better than farming. My brother said he used to make up things to keep his bosses happy."

Deleig was suddenly excited but did not show it. "I'm going to Jericho. Your brother must be a good age. Is he still alive?"

"He's alive, older but livelier than me. Tell him Dari sent you," the host said. "His name is Pavi, he'll welcome you, he likes the

Greeks, says they're gentlemen, as you yourself are, sir." This latter was not said in a fawning manner, but as a genuine compliment. Deleig nodded his gratitude and smiled.

Dari was obviously smart, for he offered to draw directions on a scrap of old parchment. Deleig said it wasn't necessary. Instead, Dari found a stick and sketched a rough outline of the journey across the Jordan to Jericho in the dirt. He told Deleig where to find the ferry-raft and gave directions to his brother Pavi's house. Deleig repeated them. A house near the old aqueduct, between it and the tower.

As they sipped their wine, the men talked in generalities for a while. Suddenly Deleig was up and off, but not before he'd laid two more silver *denarius* coins on the table. "Not a payment, sir. Simply a gift to a good man and his good wife."

Good manners satisfied, the men walked to the camels. The two boys still holding the camels were delighted to see him. They were tired. "We watered the camels, sir," one boy said, shyly, "and refilled your water skins." Deleig congratulated and thanked them as if they were grown men.

He gave each boy a further two copper *rions*, "for the camels," and two more, "for my water skins." He attached his empty clothing bag to the pack camel and re-mounted. His desert clothes he'd left where they lay. With the briefest of waves, he was gone, urging the rested camels into a fast gait.

Twenty minutes later, the moment he felt he was out of sight, he slowed the camels to a walk. He estimated he had almost four hours before nightfall. Once night fell he'd need to be on the outskirts of Jericho. Unseen. How? He didn't know. Jericho would be his first test of operating in the dark of night. Not a test of skill, but of ingenuity. He knew this night there'd be no moon.

Finding the old Herodian spy, Pavi—that would be the test. At night on the outskirts of the city, out of sight. How would he manage with the camels? He didn't know.

He came to an outlook on the eastern bank of the Jordan. Here, the river was about sixty feet wide and not very deep. He looked at the river below. This answered his question.

River traffic. There'd be rafts. He could leave the camels on a raft moored on the river, hugging the western bank beneath a ridge, out of sight. Then he could search the city at night on foot.

He must be on a ferry before nightfall. He thought he was not far from the track down to the ferry landing and urged the camels to a fast trot. Within minutes he saw a ferry-raft slowly borne along by the river, one man aboard. Deleig raced ahead, stopped the camels and jumped down, still holding a halter. He ran to the edge.

"Halt, stop your ferry, I need you."

The approaching ferryman looked up and waved an acknowledgment he had heard. He cupped his hands and shouted, "Half a mile. You'll see a rope across a path."

Deleig waved back, remounted and moved at speed along the riverbank. Within minutes he saw the rope. He rode right up to it, slid off his camel and fastened the halter-rope to one of the wooden posts that held the rope slung across the path—to prevent entry or perhaps, he thought, to signal the ferry was not there.

He ran around the post at the river end and toward the landing stage. It looked as if it had been carved out of the riverbank. The wooden stage had been built using trees for pilings, hard and dangerous work in water that deep. Rough-cut planks had been used for the platform.

The ferry-raft slid alongside it, and the ferryman, with the ease of the years, stepped off. He fastened the stern rope by lopping it over a huge rock and walked vigorously ahead with the prow rope to secure it to a short wooden pole pounded in the earth alongside the landing.

The ferryman was broad-shouldered and muscular, with shoulder-length black hair. He was not tall, but held himself erect. His face seemed to jut from his head, and he would have looked permanently reproving had his short nose not turned up a little at the tip and had he not had smiling eyes. His beard was trimmed, as was his long hair. He wore homespun, sturdy sandals.

"Greetings, sir, you've come far, judging by the clothes you wear." His eyes held Deleig's. "We've not seen your like here before, welcome to you."

Unabashed by Deleig's obvious membership in some high social class, the ferryman offered his arm. Deleig smiled and grasped the man's right forearm as the ferryman grasped his. "How can I and the ferry serve you?"

Deleig gestured toward the carved-out area of riverbank and the landing stage he had walked onto.

"It took a great deal of work over a long period to provide this; it's impressive."

"Great-grandfather, grandfather, father and myself over a ninety-year period. Three of them on each side of the river. I'll be the last of the family—shiftless son is little better than an idler. I've kicked him out. His mother's furious with me. He sleeps in a shed, but she still feeds him. Ten more years and I'll sell it all—which is not the information you need, sir. And it is obvious you need some."

"What are you called?" Deleig asked.

"Elph."

"I have two camels atop," said Deleig. "What I need, Elph, is a secure place for them, and my baggage, for the night, somewhere safe to sleep—I've no objection to sleeping outside—a meal and a guide who can handle darkness. I could leave the camels on your ferry—and would pay for the services, of course. There is someone I have to see in Jericho but cannot myself be seen, hence the darkness."

"I've a landing on the other side closer to the village," the ferryman said. "Let's get the camels down, and we can go to my house for the meal. There's a man, Jericho born and bred, married to a village girl. Joseph. He could help you. Yes, Joseph could handle darkness."

Twenty minutes later the ferryman was again securing the raft, the camels impassive as the ferry bumped against the landing. Ten minutes beyond that, seated in the man's house, Deleig was supping soup, dipping bread into it and drinking water-and-wine, usually a Roman drink. Surely the ferryman did not mistake him for a Roman.

This man's wife was totally unlike the other wife he'd lately met. She came bouncing in from the kitchen, no shawl across her face. "Sit yourself down," she said. "There's plenty more. Now where are you from and what is the uniform you're wearing and why on earth are you riding around on camels? The whole village already knows—my neighbor told me ten minutes ago her husband had seen you with camels on the far side ..." And more and more she delivered all at speed, and with intensity.

Deleig gave up listening as the flow of words continued while he ate. The moment her husband returned, she disappeared, silence descended. Deleig rather liked this woman; his mother, too, was uninhibited. He thought she disappeared because her husband was on the premises, but no, she was back. With more wine.

"Elph," she said, "sit down and have a drink with our guest. He's too quiet for his own good—that desert travel will do that to you, and here's me never even been on the other side of the river despite my husband commanding its waters." She gave a big throaty laugh, her husband obviously enjoying her enthusiasms.

"Judith," he said, "this is a gentleman, a prince of Parthia if I'm not mistaken."

"A prince?" said Deleig, astonished he'd know.

"Broadly speaking, sir," the man said. "Royalty not implied. The boys from this area were all taken through Damascus to the River Euphrates on a four-month journey when we were fifteen and sixteen. This was just after King Herod died.

"A local wealthy man wanted a reason to visit Parthia, and we became his reason—he wanted us to see the Peace Line Herod had established along the Euphrates when he'd pushed the Parthians out. Great time to be alive, he splashed money around like it was an inexhaustible supply and arranged for us to be invited across to meet Parthians, just to display how peaceful we were.

"It's your jacket and those boots that give you away, sir. They're tooled leather, and the images are Parthian, or Persian, that double-headed regal bird motif."

Deleig was having difficulty in hiding his amazement that such things had occurred. That a ferryman in a remote Judean village had been to Parthia—and was so observant he'd understood the images.

Then Deleig realized he was conflating two actualities: that the Romans were Judea's occupiers but he was talking to Judeans, not Romans. Their actualities were different and the Judeans lived a life apart from Roman preferences and hostilities—as best they could.

Finally, Deleig said, "You are very observant. More than that. What is it about this area of Judea that produces such educated men of modest means?"

"Preachers. They came, three of them, long ago, and taught us some of our letters—not just preached. Both sides of the river in this area. They stayed because of the wealthy man I mentioned, all honor to him under God. So, I've men bringing up your bags; they can be stored in the house here. Joseph from Jericho is helping. Then he's coming in."

"Elph, your beard and hair are trimmed. Who does that?"

"Judith."

"Would she do mine, do you think?"

"Ask her."

When Judith next appeared, with two small plates of food and more wine, he asked.

All she said was, "Outside." Out he went and sat on an upturned bucket.

As she swished a cloth around his shoulders, Judith said, "That bucket must be uncomfortable to sit on."

"Not after sitting on a camel for three weeks, there's no feeling left in my backside," Deleig replied with a laugh as she cut away at his hair. She was fast.

That done, she asked, "How do you wear your beard?"

"Short and to a point."

In barely two minutes she had dealt with his beard. She said with a laugh, "Done, return to the table before that wine curdles!"

"Am I permitted to pay you?"

"Of course. Not just permitted, expected."

Deleig stood and reached into his sleeve, bringing out a yard of beautiful silk that he draped over her shoulder. He said, "The payment will be on the table." He wasn't certain it was good manners—perhaps a breach of local customs—for a single man to hand money directly to another man's wife. Perhaps he had his cultures confused, he thought.

Inside the house, he laid the silver coins on the table and said to Elph, "That's Judith's." Elph nodded with satisfaction.

The two sat in a comfortable silence. The door opened after a slight tap on it. The blessing on the house was offered by a tall man, thin-faced, earnest in expression, who nodded to Deleig. "Joseph, sir. At your service."

Without invitation he sat down at the table and Judith reappeared with another beaker and an extra jug of wine.

Joseph was not shy and asked, "What is it you are trying to do, sir, and how can I help you?"

Deleig marveled at how secure these two men—and indeed, Judith—were in themselves. He admitted to himself he'd anticipated some touch of subservience. They were proud of who and what they were, he thought, and that's their security. He'd be as bold.

"I have directions to the house of a man called Pavi. He lives between the old aqueduct and the tower."

"I know the area well," Joseph said. "What do you need?"

"To be taken there without anyone seeing me, and returning here, with him."

"That doesn't make any sense," Joseph said. "Why don't I go there and bring him back?"

"Because I don't think he would come. It will take quite some power of persuasion to have him accompany me. Though your idea is certainly the more sensible."

"Very well, sir, when would you like to go?"

"Once it is dark, please. Then, once I am at his house, I would like you to return here without me. I need to test this man's capabilities before entrusting to him the next two stages of my journey. Plus, I would like to introduce him to this incredible little group of people my luck has brought me to."

THREE

Twenty minutes into nightfall, with nothing to carry, not even a lamp, Joseph led Deleig out of the village and into the blackness, the starlight providing just sufficient illumination to follow the track.

They did not talk, but increased their pace. It was not long before they were passing down alleys between clusters of buildings on the southern outskirts, Joseph stopped Deleig and whispered, gesturing with his right arm, "The Winter Palace, the baths and fountains, the architectural beauty of Jericho, are all in that direction. They are well patrolled. Stay away from there when you return."

He started off again and signaled Deleig to walk behind him as he wove between buildings, avoiding populated streets. A little while later they were at the base of an old tower. Again Joseph whispered. "That is likely the house," he said, pointing to a deeper shadow in the darkness.

Deleig said, "I will inquire. Stay exactly here."

Joseph stayed put. A moment later he saw a chink of light as a door opened. Deleig appeared to have stepped inside. Within seconds two men were outside. Deleig whistled softly. Joseph took that as a signal to reveal himself. He walked to them to say he was heading back and disappeared into the night.

Pavi gestured Deleig back into the house, the door only pulled to, not latched. By dim lamplight Deleig looked at the Herodian spy. He was indeed elderly, that spying was a long time ago.

The stooped and wrinkled old man, a staff for support, looked the tall visitor up and down and said, "Whatever it is you're doing,

I'm happy to do it with you. For Dari. My wife's dead, the two girls, two boys, long wed and fled, and any activity for me becomes an adventure. Time is of the essence?"

Deleig said, "It is kind of you to receive me. I have cargo, not a lot, two camel sacks, that I want to get into Jerusalem to a friend's house without being seen. To do that, I must first get around Jericho unseen and on the correct road. I thought—I hope you are not offended, it is something of a test—I would have you take me back to the ferry. You know it, of course."

"Of course," Pavi said, "it's the only way to Dari's. We need the night. Two minutes and I'll get a bag and a lamp, unlit." He left Deleig standing by the open door, disappeared into a second room and rustled about. He came out carrying a small bag and a long staff as high as he was. The staff was shaped into a hook at the top, and Pavi saw Deleig looking at it with interest.

"I hang the lamp on it if I go out at night. The lamp and fire-striker are in the bag," he said. "See that large colored cloth?" He pointed to a colorful sheet of some sort. "Drape it over your head and stoop low as you walk—for the next ten minutes. Your height's your enemy here. Then you won't need it."

Deleig spread it over his head and shoulders and stooped down. "I'm ready."

Pavi held the door for Deleig to exit. "How trusting you are, sir," said Deleig to Pavi. "I do thank you."

"I trust Dari," he said, in a non-committal manner. "This way."

Despite using a staff and carrying a bag—he had refused Deleig's offer to carry it—the old spy made rapid progress around the city's edge, and they were outside it far more quickly than the inward journey with Joseph.

It seemed only a short time later that they were approaching the village through the band of woods around it.

Deleig touched Pavi's shoulder, quietly signaling to stop. He whispered, "There's a flickering light ahead, to the right, and I briefly heard voices. They heard our progress and doused their lights. Light your lamp, but turn around so whoever it is won't see you light it."

The man knelt down, not easily, took the lamp from his bag and with one strike of his fire-striker had it lit. He returned the striker to the bag as Deleig said, "Put the lamp on the hook of your staff. If this is what I think it might be, when I shout 'now,' lift the lamp as high as you can on the staff."

"Good," Pavi said, impressed.

With the lamp offering a dim route along the path through the trees, making an easier trail than mere starlight had afforded, they continued walking, Deleig slightly ahead. As they approached the end of the band of trees, whoever it was also now held a lamp.

Deleig stepped even further ahead of Pavi and said, "Who are you?"

There was the man with the lamp. Deleig could make out two others to the right. "You'll soon find out. Get him!" The two men moved forward.

"Now," called Deleig.

As Pavi lifted the lamp high on his staff, the men glanced up at it. Taking advantage of this distraction, Deleig took two large strides forward, cautioning himself about attacking too aggressively. He had to lessen the blow from his foot, which had once killed a man.

Deleig took one great stride, pivoted on his right foot, swung his left leg high and hit the nearest man in the temple with the sharp point of his boot. He brought his foot back, pivoted on it and brought up his right boot into the other man's solar plexus. As the second man doubled over, Deleig chopped his neck with the side of his hand, turning in time to see Pavi's lamp-less staff crack the head of the third man.

Pavi then retrieved his lamp and held it high for Deleig to look at the downed men. They were young, not one of them twenty.

The man hit with staff stirred. Deleig leaned down and grabbed his throat. "Are you the ferryman's son?"

The extremely alarmed young man nodded. Deleig slapped his face with his open hand and again with the backhand. He stood back and said, "Get up." The man struggled to his feet.

"You have a choice. I can knock you unconscious like your friends and like them, throw you in the river. That way the world will be free of you—"

"Na ... na ... no ... mercy ... don't kill us ... don't kill my friends," he stuttered. "Their fathers would kill me ... mine would—"

Deleig said to Pavi, "Bring all three fathers to see their cowardly sons. Sons who'd beat an old man and a guest in their home, and rob them. Scum."

"Oh no, not that, oh dear God I'm sorry," said the young man, quivering. "Don't blame my friends, it was me! Me! Blame me!

They're good people ... I did it to them. I've no money to offer you. I'll do anything you say ... They didn't want to."

"I can kill all three of you with my bare hands and toss you down into the river—faster than any of you can move." Deleig wasn't certain that was true, but he amusedly reasoned he had such an advantage he was not likely to be challenged. "Anything?"

"Yes, sir. Yes. Oh please, I didn't realize, I've never done anything like this."

As a stain exploded on the young man's front between his legs, Deleig could see he was wetting himself. He said, "Tomorrow, once we've left, go to your father, apologize for being a lazy, sullen little shit. Ask him to teach you the ways of the ferryman you rejected in favor of doing nothing. For the first time in your life, work."

Pavi couldn't contain himself. Annoyed, he exclaimed, "What? What are you doing?"

Deleig ignored him and kept going, "Be the loyal son, learn. Apologize to your mother, she's the one who's kept you alive. You disgust me."

He looked scornfully at the young man.

"If you don't do this," Deleig said very quietly, "if you run away, you'll be found and brought to me. Then I will kill you for tonight's work. That's how powerful I am."

"I'll do it, sir, I will, I will." The man was petrified with fear, trembling, sweating, soaking wet.

Deleig pointed to the two unconscious men. "Stay with the friends you callously betrayed," said Deleig. "They'll come around."

He gestured to Pavi. Deleig knew the way to the ferryman's from this point. The young man dropped to his knees. He said nothing. Then he looked at Pavi and said, "I'm sorry, sir."

As they started along the edge of the woods a furious Pavi forcefully grabbed Deleig by the sleeve and made him stop.

"Why? Why did you do it?" He was personally affronted.

Deleig, still speaking softly, said, "Do which of the things I did?"

"What would you call it," said Pavi huffily, "let that young thug go unpunished?"

"I lack a sense of enmity," answered Deleig.

"That's a coward's way out, isn't it? He deserves punishing."

"No, it isn't a coward's way out. I tackled the three of them. He isn't going unpunished," continued Deleig, calmingly. "Apologizing to and working for his father will be punishment enough. Why did I do it? He is frightened, scared to death with the realization of it all. He was wetting himself. I took advantage of it. I hope he is contrite. I've no proof he will be. He will apologize to his father. Will he remain here? I've no idea. One moment."

Deleig returned to the young man on his knees and said, "Get up, but stay here until I return. Understood? You're dead if you don't."

"Yes, sir," he said, scrambling to his feet. "I will wait."

Deleig caught up to Pavi and said, "He will be there."

As they started off again, Pavi wouldn't let the topic go. "For all your 'I lack a sense of enmity,' why did you forgive him when he was going to beat us and rob us? Possibly kill us."

"Because he didn't. The intention was there, I agree. Why? He did shield his friends; he said blame him, not them. Pavi, you are a Hebrew, I am a Zoroastrian. We both believe in the one God. We're not Romans with a pantheon of gods. Ahura Mazda, my God, as Zoroaster, our leader, called him, tells us the fight over good and evil, fought in the world, is fought in our heads."

Pavi laughed. "I just saw the battle over good and evil fought with flying feet. I'm eighty-one and thought I'd seen everything until I saw that."

"Nooo," drawled Deleig, "that was just a battle for survival—that we won. These three were dangerous, I agree. They would have harmed us, possibly grievously. They were stupid. Short of robbery, did you ever do one big stupid thing at somewhere around their age, whatever their ages are?"

Pavi laughed again, an easy laugh, but didn't answer. Deleig said, "If, when I return here, they haven't complied—or the ferryman's son hasn't—I'll tell the whole village. That's all."

"*All* is a lot," said Pavi. "They'll at least ostracize him—or his father will beat him to a pulp."

"Precisely. That's not my task."

The two travelers walked out of the woods into a party. The men and women were all outside. The moment Deleig and his companion were seen, two musical instruments came to life, and once a circle formed, dancing began. Elph came toward them.

Deleig made the introduction and said, "Quite a welcome."

"We all decided to wait to see if you'd come back, knowing you would. We've solved your problem for you, and all for the price of two camels. We'll tell you tomorrow. Tonight, we're reasonably incapable of sustained clear thinking."

He waved the wine beaker he was holding as he said, "Come for some wine and food. There are two palliasses set on the floor of the house near the entrance for you to sleep. So don't worry about bedtime. Dance if you like."

"Elph," Deleig said, "you and your friends are very kind, but I have a schedule to keep. What is your plan?"

It was, the tipsy Elph explained, to trade Deleig's two camels for two donkeys and a cart. Deleig could ride in the cart, mainly hidden by his baggage.

"Are two camels worth two donkeys and cart, Elph?" Deleig asked.

"As long as you don't want a very reliable cart, or two donkeys with long life spans, because the cart I've got isn't good for much and both donkeys use crutches," said Elph.

"Will the cart get to Jericho? To Jerusalem? Are the donkeys still lively enough for those few miles?"

"Oh, they'll last. We'll take a look at the cart and shove some grease into the wheel hubs. The cart should be fine. Come on, lads, let's do it while these two get some rest—most excitement we've had around here since one of King Herod's watchers was thrown into the river, and the other two ran away."

There was something about these men Deleig admired, was it their basic sense of right and wrong, of justice? Their open-handed welcome? He just couldn't decide.

He scrunched up his face and pondered. Why was he doing all this? Why indeed. During his winter sojourns in Dura-Europos, where his grandparents lived, his grandfather had brought in the "governors" and educated him. Educated him, directed him, cajoled him, practically bullied him into being a spy. He had been sent to Rome, at age fifteen, to spy for Parthia under the guise of seeking further education, which he certainly had received. Now look at me, he thought—about to become a spymaster for Rome. Turncoat or realist?

Upon starting his studies in Rome, Deleig had quickly realized that the Roman Empire, under Tiberius or any other emperor, was impregnable and unlikely to be defeated again for centuries, certainly not by Parthia. A half-century earlier, at Carrhae, the Parthian Empire had shown an impressive flash of supremacy: totally vanquishing Rome's 40,000 troops with only 11,000 of its own. But it would not triumph again.

On his first visit back to Parthia from Rome, Deleig had urged the royal officials, generals, and his "governors" to relinquish any claim to Armenia, to the north of their empire. He'd warned them, as intently as he could, that to lay claim would put Parthia at war with Rome again. He stressed he was in no doubt that Parthia would be defeated and thereafter be dictated to as little more than a Roman province.

They had scoffed. Offended, Deleig asked why they had sent him if they weren't prepared to believe his report. After all, he was the only one of them to have had access to the enemy in its seat of power, up close and in private. They had not been swayed.

As a consequence, he sent no reports home, and any espionage activities had been to secure his own safety in Rome. The shame of the defeat at Carrhae still weighed heavily, and the Roman elite were not necessarily happy to have a Parthian in their midst.

He turned to Pavi, seated on a bench. "Stay here, I'll be back." Pavi nodded.

Deleig retraced his steps back through the woods to the ferryman's son. He was where Deleig had left him.

"Lead me to my camels."

"Yes sir," the young man said, lit his own lamp and moved quickly toward the river. They went down the narrow path to the ferry-raft and the snorting camels, fractious beasts not comfortable spending hours on a floating platform.

Deleig untied the sacking from his mount, laid it on the bottom of the raft and rolled it into a length. He picked it up as if it were light—it was extremely heavy, probably forty-five pounds of gold and silver coins—and flung it over his left shoulder to carry it.

"Back—to the house. Up we go." Deleig, pretending his load represented an ease that was far from the truth. He felt his way mainly in the dark, following the dim lamp of the ferryman's son. Sweating profusely, aching down his left side, he made it to the top.

He eased the roll onto the ground as if it were a light package and said to the ferryman's son, "Go to your home and tell Pavi to come with the donkeys and cart. Embrace your father, apologize and tell him we'll swing by to say farewell. Go!"

The frantic young man raced toward home.

Half an hour later, despite the darkness, the surefooted, if slow, elderly Pavi trudged, lamp on his staff. One donkey pulled the cart; Pavi had its rope. Deleig was in the cart, folded up like a cricket between the bags of silk and a few empty sacks. A second donkey was tied behind.

The journey triggered no incidents or alarms on the outskirts of Jericho. It was not long before dawn when Pavi led the cart into a stable somewhere in Jerusalem. Deleig creaked his way out of the cart. Pavi creaked his way over to a mound of hay and said, "Shutter the stable door." Deleig did.

The one donkey was freed from the shafts. The other one had wandered into the stable, found a water trough and now added its stench to the general disgust of the stable, pissing where it stood.

Neither man dared sleep. After an hour, Pavi said, "I will find your man. His home is not a great distance from here. Sleep. We'll return at earliest light."

He left. Deleig could do nothing about the stable door to deter entry. He climbed atop the hay and fell asleep. What seemed like five minutes later, he was woken up by banging and rattling at the stable door. A voice cried out, "Musan Deleig! Are you taller even than when last we met!"

Deleig pushed the doors open.

It was brown, curly-haired Vasas, with the same boyish round face, merry eyes, stub nose, wide mouth with full lips and round chin. Contentment oozed from him.

"Vasas!" They embraced, arms around shoulders, back slapping, standing back for second looks.

"Great beard!" said Vasas. "And you are gigantic!"

"Beard, small chin, great height—can't help it," replied Deleig, with a laugh. "What are …?"

"Don't ask and I shalln't tell," Vasas said. "All I know is you need to come to my home unseen. I have a patrol of bodyguards outside by the carriage."

Deleig turned to Pavi. "Are you tired?"

"No," the old man said, with a smile, "I rode in style."

"I could not be more grateful to you, Pavi. None of this would have been possible without you. I presume you have no companions from your old ways and days here in Jerusalem, or you would have mentioned them."

"None, sir." The "sir" was a first. Deleig felt Pavi must suddenly be feeling out of his depth, given his present company. Deleig looked at the kindly, elderly Judean.

"The cart and donkeys are yours if you want them."

"I have no need, leave them here." Deleig opened his hand so only Pavi could see the three gold *aureus* in it. "A gift, not a payment."

Pavi looked directly into Deleig's eyes.

"You paid me in excitement and adventure that doesn't usually come to a man of my age. It was a pleasure to be of service." With that, Pavi turned away, tapped his staff on the sodden stable floor by the door and set off home.

Vasas, obviously accustomed to being in command, said, "I have a carriage outside, with two horses. And six of my private guards. What are we to take?"

Deleig said, "Two huge bags, sacks really, light. One roll of various metal pieces used in armor. Heavy. My clothing bag. And me!" he added, with a laugh. This, he thought, is a very fine moment.

Vasas nodded to a guard, obviously the man who commanded the squad, saying, "Put them in the carriage, Morden."

"Morden is my second-in-command, Musan." The two men nodded acknowledgments.

Vasas explained, "The carriage will take us to the market area south of the Temple. The roadway we'll be on almost disappears—it becomes a narrow alley that tunnels through a gaggle of buildings to the market square. I own all of the commercial buildings on the alley's left side. And I live there.

"All that can be seen of the building from the alley is the tall wall. There are no windows on that side, just a thick, iron-studded wooden door in the wall. The carriage, much to the annoyance of everyone else, will squeeze into the alleyway, and as it passes through, that door will open and you will rush inside with me. The door will close before anyone sees you.

"The only other access is at the far end of the wall, from the market square, but it's double-barred and extremely secure. My home is hidden by the bustle of the market, the activity of others. Might I say that is a fair description of my life, about which I will say no more for now. Let's get moving."

Vasas looked around the stable, gave a disgusted sniff and laughed.

"I've an old brown cloak to go over your shoulders as we go now to the carriage—though who'd see you on this disgusting back street who'd matter? You'll be surrounded by the six guards. Bend your knees as you walk so you're stooped below six feet. Relax. No one will see you. Thank Jupiter you told me about your height in your letter. Behind my door you are safe. Go!"

"Thank you, Vasas, dear friend," Deleig said as he passed him, humped low under the old brown cloak.

Friendship, such friendship, thought Deleig as he stumbled along, crouching within the cordon of guards to transfer to the carriage. All this kindness based on childhood companionship. He admitted to himself he would have done the same. How strange is the world, he thought, that these years later Vasas would do anything I needed, and I would do the same for him.

As his friend climbed into the carriage after him, Vasas shouted, "Go!" and the carriage moved into a crowded road.

He said, "I have plenty of accommodation, Musan. Whatever brings you to Jerusalem, make your home here, or make my home your private place. You will tell me a little about what you do, but not a lot. We're friends. Complete candor is not essential.

"With you in Jerusalem, I suspect I shall see slices of life otherwise hidden to me. You will amplify my shuttered and quiet life. I am a simple—and very successful—businessman. Little more, little less. Here for another two or three years, for ten years in all. Then back to retire in Parthia."

"Vasas! You're only twenty-six!" Deleig said.

"What better time of life to opt for indolence."

Vasas' plan worked perfectly. Guards, in front and behind, kept people at a distance as the carriage made its careful way along. The alleyway they eventually slowed into was so narrow it was dark between the two tall walls. There was no room for a passer-by. It stopped. A door in the wall opened, and Deleig quickly followed Vasas through it.

After an appreciative tour of Vasas' building and his quarters, Deleig was seated with a cup of wine on the edge of the fountain in the beautiful atrium garden. Two now empty platters alongside him. Vasas was seated in a wooden chair that reclined slightly.

"Two things, Vasas," said Deleig. "One, have you any interest in the highest quality silk?"

"I've been known to trade in it."

"That's what's in those two sacks—silk such as you have never seen. Yours."

"And the other? What's the second thing, Musan?"

"I need to ask your guards if they know where, inside or just outside Jerusalem's city walls, is the highest stakes gambling. Board games, preferably."

"You gamble for a living?"

"No, not in the sense you mean, though I shall be gambling—in a sense—once I move here."

"To do what?"

"Practicing astrology."

"You jest."

"Only partly."

Vasas signaled a servant and whispered something to him. The man left. The two friends sat in quiet harmony, lost in thought. A servant refilled Deleig's wine cup.

A few minutes later two of Vasas' guards approached from the section of the rectangular building Vasas had explained was the guards' barracks. Eighteen men lived there.

Deleig considered the rectangle, and Vasas' luxurious residence—not impregnable, but highly secure. What sort of businessman is he? Deleig wondered. He knew he would never ask. The two of them would, over time, reveal what seemed sufficient, and perhaps they already had. Two guards approached; he recognized Morden, Vasas' second-in-command.

Vasas said, "Morden, please answer my friend's questions. Frankly. You will not embarrass either of us—and your answers will be no reflection on yourselves. He simply wants detailed information."

"Sir," Morden said.

Deleig said, "You're a Saka, aren't you? From Sakastan?"

Morden replied, "A child of the steppes, sir."

"Surprisingly tall?" asked Deleig.

"As with yourself, sir?" asked Morden, politely.

"It happens, Morden, it happens," he said, laughing. Vasas was laughing, too, at Morden's retort. "I need to know where the highest stakes gambling occurs in Jerusalem, preferably board games, but pitch-and-toss or bones, if that's all there is."

"There are board games, sir. And very high stakes. I know of one place inside the walls, but an inn just outside attracts the wealthiest gamblers. At Temple holidays, when the thousands of believers arrive, the wealthy among them wants to teach a lesson to the city people. They've money to waste. Just as well, they rarely win. I don't gamble, but I love to watch. So does Jarak, here, but he plays a bit, too."

The second guard, Jarak, nodded shyly to Deleig.

"Let me describe the man I seek," Deleig said. "I need the most skilled gambler on those premises. A non-drinker. That's essential. Probably a loner, a misfit. A man who, over the long haul, always wins a great deal—and the regulars, knowing that, rarely or never play against him. He attracts the high stakes visitors like moths to a flame. They see the pile of money in front of him and want it. Visitors—and, occasionally, a high-ranking Roman soldier or two—lose their money to him."

"There is such a man, sir," Jarak said. "Not a drinker, not sociable. Dresses carelessly in old clothes. No one knows where he lives—he wins often enough they'd want to rob him. The only attempt to rob him was a year or so ago. He was attacked just walking out of the tavern. The attack resulted in two deaths, neither of them his."

"He's a Saka, too, isn't he?" guessed Deleig.

"Yes, sir. How did you know?

Deleig just shook his head and smiled.

"Vasas, is there a way I can interview the Saka gambler without him seeing me?"

"Yes, you can use the room I use. I'll show it to you later. You sit behind a silk curtain. Heard, not seen."

"You amaze me."

"Musan, *you* are amazing *me*."

"Good. I suspect you are not easy to amaze."

The conversation was light-hearted, and Morden and Jarak, too, were smiling.

"Morden, can you or Jarak bring the Saka here?"

"If he will come, sir. Not by force."

"Please leave your master and me for five minutes, then return."

The soldiers departed.

"Vasas, I'll be returning to Judea in four months as the head of espionage for the new Prefect. My initial role will apparently be astrologer to the Prefect's wife. Only gradually will it become obvious what I'm doing."

"A Parthian running espionage for Rome? What have you been up to? No, don't tell me. I will tell you that I am a moneylender at the highest level of Mediterranean society, north and south of the sea. Romans, Levantines, Greeks—yet that is the minor part of it. My real might is that I can transfer vast sums of money very rapidly around the entire area under the tightest security."

"Highly profitable?"

"I own two grain plantations in Egypt, three vineyards in Italy—when people can't pay, they default. In three years I return to Parthia to wed, raise a family and remain there for the rest of my life. My working days done. The income from my holdings will more than suffice."

He held up his hands to show his revelations were ended. Deleig showed Vasas his empty hand and then with his conjuror's fingers produced two gold *aureus* from nowhere.

"Vasas, I'm going to give the guards these two pieces to hand to the gambler. Your men are going to feel offended carrying this to such a man. In my mind it would be fair of me to give them something as a thank you. I do not want to offend you, however. What shall I do?"

"Do what seems normal to you. I'm grateful for the consideration you showed me. And Morden and Jarak."

They sat quietly until the two guards returned. Deleig held out the two gold pieces.

"This is for the gambler. He will come."

"Sir," said Morden, astonished at the amount, and possibly a little envious, "that is several years' income for a well-fixed man."

"Or a successful high-stakes gambler, though it might only pass through his hands, not always remain in them. Give him this. Tell him it is solely for speaking to me. He is under no obligation."

"Yes, sir, but it is still a great deal of money."

Deleig held out his other hand.

"This is my thanks to both of you for delivering the gambler to me."

There were two more *aureus* on display. He tipped them into Morden's hand. Morden, astonished again, expressed his thanks.

"The gambler only plays of an evening and late into the night, sir. I could report back late tonight, or early tomorrow morning."

"Late tonight, no matter how late, if he is agreeable. Otherwise it will be tomorrow. Thank you again, Morden, Jarak."

The men nodded and left.

Morning was well established when Morden reported the Saka had been located and was en route to the meeting place. It was a blustery day. Deleig, led by Vasas, made his way across the rear gardens. The fountain was only fitfully making its presence known. That must be attended to, he thought. He would never allow any of his fountains to splutter.

They entered the building through the doorway at its farthest end, close to the guards' quarters. At the end of a series of locked doors was a large room where Vasas had told Deleig he could conduct business without being identified. It had a street entrance from the bazaar. Morden would soon usher the Saka in through that entrance.

It was divided by a silk curtain, commodious on both sides, said Vasas. Tea and delicacies supplied, he said, because he was usually dealing with borrowers accustomed to the high life. Vasas left.

Deleig waited behind the silken curtain in the comfortable chair, knowing he could not be seen, only heard. He poured himself some tea. They would converse in Aramaic.

Morden and the Saka entered. The Saka sat down, and Morden left to guard the door. For the Saka there was mint tea with rock sugar, some nuts and crystallized dates. Set on a small table to the right of where the Saka sat was writing material. Vasas had seen to every courtesy. He wanted the Saka to fear his guards, but see Deleig as his security.

Listening to the Saka going through the motions of pouring the tea from the high-spouted brass pot into the delicate, Turkish-style, tall porcelain cup, Deleig sipped from an identical cup. He took a second sip.

"You are well?" Deleig asked.

"Your Highness is kind to inquire after someone who counts for nothing. I am, sir, and thank you for your inquiry. Your Esteemed self, you and your family are equally in good health and fortune, sir, I trust?"

"Quite so. Your tea. It is hot?"

"Enjoyably so, sir."

"I notice you speak as a man of some modest breeding."

"A simple man from simple people who learned from the world, not the camp, not the nomadic trail—the manners of the world, Your Highness."

"Why so far from your native place?"

"Possibly for the same reason as Your Highness, if I might be so bold, sir. Isn't departure always from three causes: no reason to remain, inadvisable to stay, or sent away?"

Deleig laughed—it was a clever and humorous reply.

"You are an entertainer under your grubbiness, wandering Saka."

"Perhaps, sir, it is bitterness, not humor."

"Perhaps so," Deleig agreed, "nothing can sour a man as much as a sense of destiny without a destination."

"You hear me as I am, Your Highness. A compulsive gambler whose money parts company with him before it has time to greet his hand. Whatever I might have been I am not and will not be. A harsh draught to swallow, but by swallowing it daily I have become accustomed to the taste."

"You are literate, you can read and write?"

"Greek and Latin additionally, sir."

"Very well, wandering Saka, here is what you will do for me and here is what I will do for you. I will buy your services for one week and your silence for life. The amount I offer is six *aureus*. For one week—once I call on you. Four in addition to the two you have. Those gold pieces are some ten to twenty times the best you could do at the gaming table in five to ten years—if you never lost. If I need you for more than one week, we shall make other arrangements—those must be mutually satisfactory. What I want from you is not life-threatening."

"Sir, you are indeed well informed. With an offer impossible to refuse."

"And impossible to betray. Be well advised, wandering Saka, the quality of my information is why I am speaking to you. Evidence of the quality of my accompanying threat regarding your silence will appear several times over the next few days. A knife whose blade and handle will become familiar to you after you leave here will, occasionally, appear in your line of sight. It is simply a reminder. You have my word that I will not use your services and have you killed, for the simple reason I may have good use for you in the future."

"Sir, the superiority of your explanation, and the clarity and precariousness of my own situation, impresses me. What would you have me do?"

"How long have you been in the city?"

"Four years, nearing five."

"You know many people without them knowing you?"

"In a sense, sir, yes. You read my character astutely."

"I'm seeking to establish an espionage service. I say that with you knowing any hint of betrayal means instant death. I want your trust."

"Mine you have, sir. One day you'll give me a test and that will prove it. I know that. Can I do this? Yes. You want me to locate good men and hire them as spies?"

"Not yet. I want us to meet again."

"Is there a way I can communicate with you?"

"Ask that question of the guard. You will contact him."

"How long will you want me? The money you've provided has bought me for a lifetime and longer, as my mother would say. Yet I will not stop gambling. It is how I keep my wits sharp, and from now on it will be how I collect both gossip and the information I need."

"I would be troubled if you'd said you would cease gambling. What is your name?"

"Talca, sir."

"Well, Talca the Saka, you and I will meet again shortly. You may leave."

"Thank you, sir. Good day and good health."

"Good day and good health—and may success dog your footsteps, and I don't mean at the card table."

They both chuckled. He heard Talca knock on the door to where Morden waited.

Deleig could hear Talca and Morden talking, heard locks opened. He stood to return to his rooms.

He'd started. Or had he?

FOUR

"Mamma," Musan asked, "why am I a prince and Grandfather Deleig is only a general? And why does he want to take me away from here? And if I'm higher in rank than he is, why can't I tell him 'no'?"

Musan's mother, Regal Princess Farida, daughter of Parthian King Phraates IV, held six-year-old Musan's hand. They waited in the grand entrance of Hatra's Royal Palace for the arrival of retired Commanding General of the Royal Parthian Army, General Deleig of Deleig, the hero, in his own words, of the Battle of Carrhae against Rome.

His mother said, "Because you are a young boy and he is your grandfather, and rank has nothing to do with it."

"But I don't want to go to Dura-Europos and live in the palace there without you and without Megga." His sister, Megga, who was five, was his closest friend and playmate. "Father won't be in Dura-Europos, will he?" His father was generally unpleasant toward him. At least his grandfather was nicer.

"No, your father will not be there. It is only for three months, Musan, and then you will be back with us. Grandmother and Grandfather have nice friends, and Grandfather wants to see to your education." She did not mention to her son that his father, General Deleig the Younger, favored their first son, Darius, a junior officer. He ignored his second, much younger son and had willingly ceded to his own father the matter of Musan's education.

"It will give Father something to do," General Deleig the Younger had told his wife, "and this stick of a child"—as he referred to Musan, who was thin and tall for his age—"might benefit from constant supervision." Princess Farida had no power to counteract the decision, and no particular reason to do so.

Musan did need an education, if only to offset his difference from his brother Darius. Farida thought Darius was best off in the military, where his meager learning, like his father's, would prove no particular impediment to becoming a general. Her own mother had ensured Farida received a better-than-rudimentary education.

Farida suspected her father-in-law was intending to live through Musan the educated life he himself regretted missing. Grandfather was a knowledgeable man who invariably invited educated visitors from all over to stay in the junior wing of the Hatra palace with him. And invariably, his guests were entertained by Farida and the two boys while the general was off doing something else.

Her father-in-law truly reigned supreme in Dura-Europos, the city southwest of Hatra on the River Euphrates. Consequently, what convinced her to be deaf to Musan's pleas was that the type of education her father-in-law outlined meant that the boy would never be selected for the military.

True, there was peace at present, but it would not last. Soldiers like her father-in-law and husband wanted to battle. Musan, educated, she reasoned, was more likely to enter royal service, possibly as a diplomat or regular emissary. His Greek and Latin were already excellent, for his age.

So it was that Deleig's mother agreed wholeheartedly to the Dura-Europos plan even though, in this household, her agreement counted for nothing. From now on, Musan would spend the winters with his grandparents in a city, like Hatra, that was an important stop on the Silk Road.

The next morning, the carriage made its way for more than two hours over desert scrub to the River Euphrates' landing stage. Musan carried nothing, not even a favorite toy. He soon regretted leaving his puppet behind for he had to listen for hours to adult chat. Then they boarded the river-craft for Dura-Europos.

To liven up Musan aboard the craft, his grandfather told him to leave the cabin and stand with the boat's captain as it made its way downriver. This the boy was happy to do. Even when called in for lunch, he ate quickly to return to the captain, to wave to the people who waved to the boat.

Once ashore in Dura-Europos, Musan enjoyed the short walk through busy streets no wider than alleys, through markets and open squares with wells, and along wider thoroughfares. He felt a little more excited about the place. In the palace, he was introduced to a dozen people whose names he immediately forgot, initially even that of Fefeel, the older woman who was to be his prime servant and would sleep in his room.

To Musan she was ancient, skinny, strangely dressed. She had hair and a nose like a witch and a very determined way about her that Musan wished he had not recognized so quickly. What she was determined about he had no idea.

No idea, that was, until the second night. He was fast asleep. He had gone to sleep thinking about his puppet and had decided he would learn how to make one. In the dark of night, with just a small one-wick lamp to combat the darkness, Fefeel woke him up and told him to put on his shawl over his shift and keep quiet. To encourage him, she wiped his face with a cold wet cloth.

Startled, half awake, he did as bid. Fefeel, whispering he must make no noise, but follow her, took the lamp, led the way out of their quarters and kept on along a corridor until they reached stairs. They climbed the first flight. There was a second flight. Musan felt his feet getting cold.

At the top of the second flight, Fefeel led the way out of a small door onto the palace roof. It was pitch black.

Musan immediately understood—she was working for his father and going to throw him off the palace roof into the river. That's why he'd been brought here.

He looked at the sky. An enormous cloud shifted. There was a moon. To Musan's amazement, there were also about a dozen women standing there. Fefeel directed him to a box to sit on, threw a blanket around his shoulders, put a cushion under his feet and told him to stay awake.

Sleepy, but curious, he watched. Fefeel signaled the women over. She was telling or teaching them things in answer to their questions. He understood both the questions and answers as far as the language itself was concerned, but he didn't know what the words meant. She periodically splashed water on his face or wiped it with a wet cloth. She told him it was to keep him awake because he was too big and too heavy for her to carry.

Over the next six winters, until he was twelve, he and Fefeel would follow this routine on any moonlit or starlit night. He learned everything from her as she taught, selling her skills in astrology, soothsaying, potions and other psychic-magical things. Without at first knowing the words, he realized she indoctrinated the women into believing she had magic powers and a soothsayer's skill. Perhaps she did. He believed none of it. It contravened everything he did believe in his Zoroastrianism, and his god, Ahura Mazda.

The words she used, the sooths she told, and sold, the potions she described became as much a part of his Dura-Europos education as anything he learned from the indoctrination delivered by "wise men," "important men," "palace officials," "military officials," diplomats, tacticians, language teachers and historians into whose company his grandfather thrust him, day-after-day, six-days-a-week for six winters.

For the first two years, the secondary education on the palace rooftop, about which Musan's grandparents knew nothing, had them wondering why such an energetic young boy occasionally needed a mid-morning nap. Musan arranged that nap by simply stopping what he was doing. He lowered himself to the carpet, folded himself into a ball and was immediately fast asleep.

His grandparents simply accepted it as an oddity. At night, that little dash of cold water on his eyes when he showed signs of sleep finally became unnecessary, and so did his mid-morning naps. But forever after, his sleep was always broken.

What he did enjoy on the roof was the occasional presence of the famed royal astronomer-astrologer, Teleucid. The astronomer would remove Musan from Fefeel's company, to have the two of them lay on their backs on a large rooftop divan.

Teleucid would explain the constellation that night and tell him about the stars, their positions and their shifting significance. He explained how Musan could use the stars to guide him across the desert. Musan loved it, even before he quite understood what Teleucid was telling him. By the age of ten he was an expert young astronomer, learned in celestial navigation. That early gift would last a lifetime.

With Teleucid he never needed his face splashed with water. Particularly because, occasionally, during the day, he also taught the boy a range of conjuring tricks.

Yet it was Fefeel who gave him his most useful tool. She told him a secret. It was that every chief cook in every truly major establishment on both sides of the Mediterranean was that area's most important soothsayer. That it would always be a woman. And that she would always be literate in her language.

If Teleucid gave him tools for surviving in the desert by navigating it by the stars, Fefeel gave him the tool for navigating his way through intrigue in every palace and major villa anywhere he could speak the language. The chief cook, she said, was the center to which all the servants' chatter flowed. She'd been one herself in this palace. It was the servants who heard and saw everything, even without always understanding it. The chief cook interpreted it.

A decided disadvantage for the "stick" of a boy as he rapidly grew taller—five-foot-eleven by the time he was eleven—was that because of his height, he was always treated as somewhat older than his years. Even scholastically. He felt he was growing up too quickly. That pressure forced him to spend more time alone so he would not be so much involved in adult talk.

Back in Hatra he continued in the Royal Palace to polish his Greek and Latin—and to leave his bed at night to study the sky. His most exotic language, a smattering of Khotanese Chinese, he kept current through any Chinese-speaking Silk Road travelers his grandfather invited to enjoy the palace's hospitality. More likely the travelers would be from Arabia one month, from India the next. But always, twice a year, arrived his grandfather's favorite visitor, Lin Ma from Khotanese China's outpost in the Saka region.

What young Musan gained from Lin Ma was more than conversational Khotanese Chinese. It was a different way of looking at the world because Lin Ma was a Buddhist. Equally, Musan enjoyed looking at Lin Ma's round face, jet-black straight hair, gleaming teeth and dark eyes, which contained a merry disregard for life's finer points in a manner Musan had not previously encountered.

Musan's own family—with the exception of his cheerful, educated, constantly active mother—tended to seriousness. Not so Lin Ma. Alternating between careful Greek and rapid Chinese, Lin breezily educated the attentive young Musan into the intricacies of Chinese and trading, as he told of the dangerous world beyond Hatra.

Lin Ma one day said, "Today you will learn trading." He asked Musan, "Have you any gold?"

"I don't know," the boy told him, innocently. "I've never asked."

"Ask the Esteemed General, your grandfather. Go ask him for gold, and come back to me. Tell him you are learning an expensive trade. Everything's secret for now."

The old general, who insisted Lin Ma billet his camel train in the sweeping grounds of the Royal Palace and sojourn in the palace with the family during his visits, knew the trader was teaching Musan more than Chinese. Consequently, while the grandfather's reaction suggested to Musan he was bemused by the request for gold, in fact he was highly amused by it.

The grandfather summoned a servant and told him to bring an item from another room. The servant returned with a small, nondescript box with a lid. General Deleig of Deleig removed a Parthian gold piece from it and said to Musan, "Ask the wily old devil how much money, how many of these, he wants."

Musan looked at the gold circle in his hand. He had never previously seen money. Off he went to Lin Ma. Lin Ma said the amount was ten. Musan went to his grandfather who told Musan that Lin Ma could have only eight. Musan relayed the message. Lin Ma said to tell the grandfather nine.

The grandfather agreed and said to Musan, "That is what trading is: agreeing on a price, but never paying the first amount requested, or demanded." Musan was amazed. So this was what adults did. He thought it entertaining to watch two men play such a silly game.

Lin Ma sold Musan three gold finger-rings for the nine gold pieces. Then he told him, "You must sell these for fifteen Roman gold pieces each. That is their value as rare, finely crafted rings from Khotan, carved by senior craftsmen whose products are sought by all the emperors of the East. At least one of them you must sell to someone you do not know."

The boy kept looking from the rings—resting on their beautifully finished silk purses alongside their decorated boxes—to Lin Ma's fascinating eyes, which seemed to hold him.

"Every ring you sell must have a story, Musan Deleig, do you understand?" He was peering intently at Musan. "Without a story a ring is an exquisite circle of carved and bejeweled or enameled gold. With a story it is a rare object of indefinable value, something worth far more than its costly price."

Lin Ma could tell Musan still didn't understand. He began again, holding a highly engraved gold ring with an amazing red stone. "Confucius," Lin Ma said with all seriousness, "was China's finest philosopher. This is the only ring of Confucius in existence—this ring I give you was his. It possesses a form of wisdom within it."

Lin Ma was now staring so deeply into Musan's eyes the boy was almost afraid. But Musan held Lin Ma's gaze. He nodded his head to show he understood and said, "Thank you."

"This ring will impart some of Confucius' wisdom to you, boy." Musan nodded, again.

Then Lin Ma, without taking his eyes away from Musan's, said, "And if you lose this unique ring of Confucius, I will go to a goldsmith I know in Khotan, and he will make me another only-one-in-existence Confucian ring. Now do you understand?"

The Khotanese gentleman was smiling, trying desperately to have the boy continue to look deeply into his eyes. Musan did that. He carefully rethought what Lin Ma had just said.

Musan could not at first accept the audacity of what the man from Khotan was telling him. Then he smiled back, nodding vigorously, as gradually it dawned on him what had just transpired. He burst out laughing, "Every ring must have a story even when it hasn't." Lin Ma clapped his hands.

Musan shook his head in wonderment. The world of adults, he decided, was, perhaps, very little different from the world of boys.

Lin Ma relaxed, pleased with himself.

The following half-year later, Lin Ma, returning to the East from his trading journey, took his usual stop at the Royal Palace. He demanded to know if Musan had sold the three rings. Musan went to his grandfather's box and returned with a kid-leather pouch. He showed him the forty-five pieces of gold he had earned from selling them.

Lin Ma smiled and nodded with pleasure. He then produced five new rings, all different. He demanded fifteen gold Parthians for each ring and refused to back down. That led to the grandfather and Lin Ma bargaining in person, finally shouting at each other as they did so.

Musan understood that trade could be a very serious business and was pleased with his grandfather when Lin Ma received only twelve gold pieces for each.

Years later Musan often wondered if everything had been staged for his benefit—his grandfather was quite as wily as Lin Ma. General Deleig of Deleig wanted Musan to use the skills he gained from Lin Ma and large amounts of money from the royal treasury. The grandfather had at his disposal sufficient funds to take advantage of the *Pax Romana* and build a Mediterranean-girdling family trading company of immense profitability.

Musan agreed, as he agreed to everything else.

The last time he had seen Lin Ma was the year he left for Rome. They had talked about Parthia and Rome. Lin Ma had said China wanted more than jade and nephrite boxes from Khotan—it wanted Khotan. He was unhappy about that.

When it was known that Musan would definitely continue his education in Rome, the Khotanese gentleman had twenty cases, each with twenty magnificent rings, for him as a gift. These he wanted Musan to take to Rome to give as presents. A gift with which to begin what Lin Ma insisted should always be his parallel career. Trading. Deleig nodded his head in gratitude and to show he understood. He promised that whatever else he did, he would never neglect trading.

Then Lin Ma said, "Go to Grandfather: two hundred Parthian gold pieces for my gift to you."

The grandfather was outraged.

For an enjoyable hour Musan sat on a cushion as the grandfather and Lin Ma cajoled, shouted, extolled, threatened, drank each other's health, left the room, returned to the room and started again. The eventual price: one hundred and forty one.

As a parting gift—one for which his grandfather did not have to pay—Lin Ma also gave Musan a small sandalwood box containing a smaller jade box that contained a smaller still silver box which in turn held the final item, an egg of solid gold. The egg matched the two on the bracelet Musan wore. Those eggs, and the bracelet, were a gift from his grandfather, acknowledging Musan's skill in Latin and Greek. This third egg was for his Khotanese Chinese.

Musan treasured his Lin Ma memories. Most particularly the final one.

At that last meeting, for Musan had known it probably would be such, the teenage boy had formally presented Lin Ma with a highly decorated Parthian sword.

"This sword, Eminent Lin Ma, was the personal ceremonial weapon of our famed Parthian King of Kings, Cyrus the Great."

The Khotanese gave a squeaky little chuckle. He slapped his knee with delight. The pleasure on the Khotanese gentleman's face was the true treasure Musan treasured.

FIVE

Leaning on the wall of the escarpment three hundred feet above the River Euphrates' eastern bank, fourteen-year-old Musan Deleig was determined to engrave on his memory the scene below. His eighty-five-year-old grandfather, mounted on his favorite but elderly white Arabian stallion, was in full uniform, with insignia and decorated breast-shield, as the Commanding General of the Royal Parthian Army (long since retired).

The general was flanked by two senior officers, as aides. The general guided his horse and guards down a slight slope onto the ferry landing just below the wall. Separately, six lancers guided their horses toward a second ferry. Musan's signal.

He jumped up onto the wall and from there onto the back of his horse to race down the slope into the bustling market area of Dura-Europos. He navigated a tight turn at the end of the lane and headed to the River Gate. Outside the gate, his young horse, excited by the burst of speed, almost crashed into the two rear lancers, but steadied and stepped aboard the ferry after them with stately steps. Musan felt quite stately himself.

For the first time he was wearing what he always thought of as his "Parthian hunting outfit." He, his mother and the tailors had created it, and he would wear variations on it the rest of his life. It was quite unlike the normal Parthian outerwear of robes: a tooled and embossed leather jacket and cotton leggings that stretched from under his jacket down into his tooled and embossed leather calf-length boots. His leather-topped cap had a slight bill and catches at the rear from which to hang a neck-cloth when necessary in the desert sun.

Musan was unexpectedly in Dura-Europos. It wasn't the usual winter working stint, but July, the second hottest month of the summer, when temperatures could exceed 110 degrees. He might need that neck-cloth.

One advantage of the Dura-Europos escarpment was that it enabled the citizens—and military—to watch, day in, day out, the maneuverings of the extensive Roman army camped on the western bank of the river, where the ferry-rafts were now headed. His grandfather later told Musan that as the party was ferried across, "the ferryman was trembling more than the water's surface at the prospect of coming face-to-face with Romans."

A contingent of Roman soldiers, who, obviously, could see this party headed toward them, was lined up behind a centurion. The Dura-Europos arrivals on their chargers stepped ashore. The Romans undoubtedly noticed that the scabbards at the side of the grandfather and his two senior aides were empty, and that the lancers had their lances pointed down, not up.

Those signals were sufficient. Neither side moved except for a Roman soldier who turned and ran to the rear accumulation of buildings. Then the centurion approached.

The grandfather said, in carefully rehearsed—with Musan—polished Latin, "I am General Deleig of Deleig of the Royal Parthian Army. I wish to speak to your commander."

The centurion saluted this most senior Parthian officer and sent an aide to summon the commander. The Parthian horses were shifting their feet slightly. The heat was considerable despite the early morning, and it was as if the horses could sniff the general unease. With two aides, the Roman commander, a smartly attired man, bareheaded to signify an approach in peace, walked briskly toward the Parthian group and stated, "I am the Centurion Quintus Linius, commander of the Legio Sexta Ferrata. Your reputation has preceded you, General Deleig of Deleig, please state your intentions."

The Legio Sexta Ferrata were the famed Iron Clads under Julius Caesar. Iron in that broiling heat, Musan thought. Unconscionable. No wonder the leathern-armored Parthians had been more than their match at Carrhae.

"You have children?" the grandfather asked.

"Indeed, and I have grandchildren."

"You appear too young, sir, but it is a concern about a grandson that has brought me into Roman territory. May we talk in the shade?"

"Please dismount, sir, as my guest, enjoy our Roman hospitality." At that point Linius turned toward Musan.

"This gentleman," the Roman said, "is, I presume, the grandson? Come join us, young man." He turned to the centurion, gave orders that that Parthian officers and men be given refreshments in the shade, and the horses cared for.

Musan alighted and approached the commander. He bowed his head in a homage greeting and said, "Thank you, sir. Musan Deleig at your service."

He knew the commander thought, because of his height, he was older than he actually was. He was now six-foot-two. Determined not to leave the Roman confused, Musan continued, "Despite my height, sir, I am fourteen. My height is displeasing to my father because I am now taller than he is. He considers the fact irresponsible on my part."

The commander chuckled and said, "Your Latin is superb, Musan Deleig, your height impressive. I am pleased to meet you."

The Roman and General Deleig walked up the slight slope toward higher ground, Musan a few steps behind them. It led into an oasis where the surrounding palms provided shade for a modest building, behind which were the fort and barracks. From the escarpment, these crude buildings were plainly visible. Circled around the fort, almost to the Euphrates' edge, were the locals' houses, shacks and market tents, a shanty town.

There were two soldiers at the entrance to the main building. The centurion gave orders in a Latin too fast for Deleig of Deleig to catch, but Musan knew he'd said, "Juice, fruit and nuts."

Commander Linius gestured the Parthian general into the building and through it into a densely palm-shaded atrium with a swimming pool, ornamental ponds, low tables and cushions.

Fruit juices, nuts, dates and some form of bread Musan did not recognize were quickly brought to a table. The centurion gestured to the general to remove his helmet and breastplate. He said, "Please accept my hospitality. Visitors are not rare here. They are non-existent. Musan, make yourself comfortable alongside me."

General Deleig handed his breastplate and helmet to a waiting soldier and, as he said later to Musan, "creaked my way down to the cushions, hoping my bones wouldn't make too much of a cracking sound when it was time to rise again."

The general explained that he wanted his grandson not just to experience a Roman education, but hoped he could be accepted formally in Rome. He would not send him if it meant he would just arrive and have to make his own way. He wanted him to be welcomed as a friendly visitor present for the best education Rome could afford, perhaps as the temporary ward of a high Roman family. Cost was not an issue. He mentioned Musan's fluency in three languages and familiarity with world affairs.

The grandfather explained that he and the boy's father, also a general, wanted Musan exposed to the libraries of Rome, collections not duplicated in the eastern Mediterranean since the destruction of the Alexandrian library. How, the grandfather said he wanted to know, could he, or should he, proceed with this request? His own thought was to ask for safe conduct in order to discuss the project with the Roman Legate in Syria. The Legate had the security of the entire region under his control, and the legions to ensure it, and was undoubtedly a man of high repute in Rome.

Quintus Linius looked at the general and asked, quite pointedly, "Can I trust you, sir? Can I say something in confidence knowing it will not be repeated?"

"Indeed, sir," the grandfather said. Musan lowered his raised eyebrows and tried to appear mature. He sat up straight.

"The Legate has a particular dislike of Parthians. I cannot say more on that topic. I can say that in Caesarea Maritima, Judea, the governor there, the Prefect Annius Rufus, has none of those ... animosities, perhaps ... toward particular peoples. From here Caesarea Maritima is an onerous journey—you would need to skirt Damascus to make it—but I suggest you avoid the Legate and approach the Prefect in this matter."

Deleig of Deleig said he realized how difficult it had been for the commander to say what he had and he honored him for his candor. The grandfather later would cite the instance to Musan on more than one occasion as to how a man must deal with conflicting loyalties and kindnesses by resorting to conscience. Musan's private opinion was that his enjoyable but irascible grandfather treated his own conscience as an occasional, perhaps rare, visitor.

The grandfather told the commander that if the Prefect agreed to grant an audience, the desert crossing would be made. Linius said he would contact Prefect Annius Rufus on the general's behalf and safe passage would be "guaranteed, if the Prefect will see you both," a request he felt the Prefect would grant.

The commander further recommended the travelers wait until the very close of September when the journeying would be more bearable. He would assign four of his own men, seasoned desert soldiers, to accompany them and to guarantee safe passage once they were in Roman territory.

Musan was overwhelmed by Linius' generosity. Quickly Musan reached for a cup of juice to hide the fact his eyes had teared up. His own feelings of conflict were tremendous because he now realized the gravity of what he was being assigned to do—to spy on a country that could produce people such as Linius.

The three chatted for an hour more, Musan occasionally peppering the commander with a burst of questions. As time came to leave, General Deleig of Deleig extended the hospitality of Dura-Europos to the Roman commander and his officers at a time of the commander's choosing. The offer was accepted. Deleig of Deleig said a messenger would be sent.

The visit unwound, the visitors re-boarded the two ferries and the oarsmen, headed for the Dura-Europos landing upriver, had to vigorously battle the current to get across.

Slowly, over the next few weeks, messages went back and forth across the Euphrates, with the result that the governor of Judea, Prefect Annius Rufus, would receive General Deleig of Deleig, and grandson.

Musan, whatever his doubts about his grandfather's integrity, could not deny that for a man in his mid-eighties to insist he would make the grueling desert journey bordered on the heroic, and the foolish. There was no easy route. In order to avoid Damascus, it was decided to journey some three hundred miles across desert and scrub to Jericho.

For a month, while the trip was organized, bad dreams and anxieties plagued Musan. The main one: Would Grandfather die en route? Others were: Was the entire escapade a trap? Had the Romans agreed in order to have an important hostage? Was his grandfather immoral at base? Would he himself be sent to Rome only to be seized and never heard from again? Then he would wake up, or go for an extra-long run and an extended exercise period, and the anxieties would evaporate.

The only comment his grandfather made was, "I wonder if I can find a wadi-man. They've just about disappeared you know, Musan. With all this Roman road-building only the trade caravans cross the desert, and they've got their routes."

"What is a wadi-man, Grandfather?"

"I'll tell you if I find one," was the only answer he would get.

His grandfather sent for Myrmid, his personal general factotum, close friend, problem-solver and, most reliably, journey-planner. Myrmid supervised the family members' desert journeys to the family oasis in El Qassassin.

Then one day the grandfather sent for Musan. "Come Royal Highness. Myrmid found a wadi-man," was the servant's message. Musan hurried along the corridors into his grandfather's wing of the palace.

He was there when Myrmid—"he of the bushy eyebrows," as Musan always thought of him—arrived at the grandfather's quarters. Myrmid walked in without announcement, saying, as if he'd been talking to an audience in the actually empty corridors, "... Then for the desert crossing we'll need a twenty-six-strong group, including the four Roman soldiers. Simply can't count less than that. Pack men, servants, water carriers—that's it. I've ordered the camels—need those larger desert-breeds. Harder to handle, raw, savage, but tough, tough, tough."

"Much of the journey is uncharted because sand shifts cover known routes," he continued, addressing the ceiling. "Deviations or delays mean water shortages—might be a problem. Traveling light is the only way to manage the route, thirty to forty miles a day on average, depending on the terrain. That is why my route makes sense—water hole to water hole, small settlements to oases. If the water source has disappeared in any area, we continue on. In any abandoned oasis, the wadi-man will find water—if any remains. We will collect him at Qasr Zebde—he has already left here to get there before us."

In an after-thought, Myrmid said, "Musan, you will have two water skins. Do not attempt to fasten or unfasten them. Let the servants do it. Except to drink from them, never handle them. Undoing them is a skill, and you wouldn't want to drop one, believe me. People's lives depend on it."

Myrmid, a bulky, muscled, determined man, sat down with a thump on a divan. The pause gave Musan time to formulate his question, but Myrmid forestalled him, saying, "So, what does a wadi-man do? He finds water."

Myrmid took the wine cup and drank in one swallow. The servant refilled it.

"The wadi-man is a water-diviner. His symbol is the red silk slippers he puts on minutes before divining. The silk sensitizes his feet before he explores for water with the soles of his feet."

"Myrmid? Which language does the wadi-man speak?"

"Surprisingly, Greek, as well as his native tongue, which I don't recognize but you probably will. I couldn't even understand his language's name."

"The wadi-man's name?" Musan asked.

"He does not offer a name. He is simply the 'wadi-man.' Maybe to share his name with strangers would be to share his soul." He held his wine cup out for the servant to refill. The servant understood his role when Myrmid was present.

"What's it like trying to ride a desert-bred camel, Myrmid?"

"Difficult, highly uncomfortable. It will take you two days to manage to stay on, two more to convince the foul beast you are its master, and a week to ease the discomfort in your backside. Speaking of backsides, that's what all camels' breaths smell like, but desert-breds, arrrgh! Nothing prepares you for them. Avoid getting too close to its head, a bite worse than its breath. Its teeth won't cut your fingers off, they will simple crush them."

He paused. "Three weeks maximum in each direction, two weeks if we are extremely fortunate. Unpredictability, shifting terrain, weather—specifically sandstorms. Four Roman desert soldiers—they'll be great handling the water-bearer camels." Myrmid sat back, closed his eyes and began to snore.

September, second week, and they moved slowly out of Dura bearing southwest. What annoyed Musan was that Myrmid's prediction came true—Myrmid's caution about the desert-breds scarcely scratched the surface of how unruly the beasts were. Musan was thrown off his camel three times the first day, once the second, but by the third the camel—reluctantly and only temporarily, Musan suspected—was yielding to his directions.

By blistering day, draped under very thick black woolen Bedouin desert robes and indistinguishable from nomads, they plodded through everything except sandstorms. Bedouins had learned over generations how to remain relatively cool in blistering heat. The thick black wool robe was draped so the interior was loose enough it acted like a funnel, allowing the hot air inside to escape at the neck. So there was a constant funneling of air up from the opening around the legs. Hot air, yes, but mobile air, and therefore, offering a modicum of cooling. The wearer otherwise was dressed solely in a white cotton shift, a *thobe*.

The moment dusk came, if there were stars or moon, there was a break for water and an accelerated two or three hours of rapid travel before halting for the night. There were the cold, clear dark nights that only deserts can provide, the ideal setting for storytelling around the nightly fires. The black of night can be a truism and a fact.

There was something in Musan, as one who had been pressured to learn everything, that reveled in the unknowingness the blackness represented. These were nights, too, when he and his grandfather sat together, a short distance from the others, as the elderly man told of his battles, both military and in the Royal Palace. He wove together many of the strands of what Musan had heard Hatra and learned at Dura-Europos. He talked about power and why he had guided, even forced, Musan's education in the direction it had gone.

Musan did not have to follow his lead, his grandfather told him, but that if he understood power and knew how to keep out of its shadows by always standing at its side, life in its entirety would be an education. Whatever you do, he told his grandson, "Do it in such a manner that you could see yourself as if you were on the stage of the theatre at Dura-Europos watching the plays of Aristophanes or Terence, and yourself as one of the players. And find someone to write to in order to keep a record."

Ovid, the grandfather said, warned against thinking "the great" wish to make friends with those beneath them. To counter falling into that error in Rome, hear what Ovid counseled: One could seek a placid life *and* serve the great *provided* one avoided their friendship. *Vive sine invidia, mollesque inglorius annos Exige, amicitias et tibi junge pares:* "Live free from envy, and without a wish for glory, desire only placid years, and live in friendship with your equals."

"But Grandfather," said Musan. "I am a prince. I am of the great. I don't have these concerns."

The grandfather was dumbfounded.

"These were magnificent times, these desert conversations," Musan wrote to his mother a decade or so later from Caesarea Maritima. "Grandfather wished me to know my 'equals.' He'd be surprised to learn they were the top rank of Rome. How comforting for me that so many of those equals proved to be fine women, Lady Lydia, Claudia and skillful chief cooks of villa kitchens. As well as fine men, of course, but that's to be expected.

"Desert conversations, too, with the Romans. Ah, we were not friend and foe, but fellow travelers crossing a cruel place, a cold place that becomes hot, searingly so, during the day when each grain of sand that penetrates the folds of the robes is like a miniature hot coal burrowing into the pores of the skin. What we loved was the night, what we survived was the day. That is desert life."

Musan knew what would remain clearest in his memory was the joy of doing all this with his grandfather who, despite great physical trials due to his age, proved indefatigable, good humored—and imaginative in the crisis. The crisis came several days after the wadi-man was collected at Qasr Zebde, along with his camel, a scrawny thing as emaciated as the wadi-man himself.

This day, they were about two hours from stopping and setting up camp. Myrmid—after confirming with astronomer Musan—predicted a moonlit night. He wanted the exhausted travelers to have a six-hour rest, then travel until midday the next day. Suddenly a ravine opened in the sand.

Musan heard the cry come from the rear, turned and watched the land collapsing as the gap widened. Two camels were disappearing into it, despite a soldier's desperate and courageous attempt to prevent one from slipping over the brink. But the beast with its load was too heavy, and as the camel slid down into the huge hole, the soldier was dragged from his mount and went down with it.

The two camels were shrieking and baying. One carried water, the other, Roman armor. The soldier had broken his fall by landing on one of them. He had rolled off and was lying at the bottom, soaking wet from broken water-skins, the water pooling in one corner of the hole, then rapidly draining away.

The grandfather, as the senior officer, had immediately taken charge. Soldiers were lowered down to rescue the injured soldier, and servants to butcher the camels for meat. The wadi-man demanded to be lowered, too, and Musan asked to go down to help. As he was being lowered, Musan looked up. High above their heads, as if a summoning bell had been rung, vultures, six or seven, already circled.

Musan looked at the walls and wondered if there would be another cave-in. He saw the wadi-man watching him, understanding, and the wadi-man shook his head to signal "no," no danger.

The fallen Roman soldier was not unconscious. It appeared he had broken, or dislocated, his left shoulder. They made a rope harness that relied on his right shoulder and had him carefully hauled to the top.

The wadi-man went to an unoccupied stretch of the hole and from around his neck, by pulling on a string, brought out a pair of red silk slippers. He stood like a stork on one foot, slipped one slipper on, then repeated the process for the other foot. He stood very tall, absolutely erect, a straight line heel to head. He glided one foot forward on the rough sand. Brought it back and repeated the process with the other.

He then removed the slippers, put their string around his neck and dropped them back down the front of his shift. Stepping forward slowly, the wadi-man rubbed his right foot in a circle in the sand. Stepped forward another pace and made another circle. He continued this until he was about a foot from the great wall of sand that faced him at that end of the hole.

Agilely he turned around, walked to where the camels were still being butchered, though not much was left on the bones, and retrieved a Roman shield. Back at the sand wall, using one of the pointed ends of the square shield as a chisel, he jabbed at the wall. A huge chunk of sand broke off.

He called in Greek for Musan's grandfather. Deleig of Deleig peered over the edge. The wadi-man said he needed the general to order two Roman soldiers to work for him. The general did that, much to the soldiers' dismay, for they were about to be hauled up.

Musan told the wadi-man he spoke Greek and acted as interpreter as the wadi-man asked the soldiers to use shields to clear away part of the sand wall where he had started. One soldier wore a short sword he'd brought down in case it was needed for killing camels; the other used the corner of a shield.

Once the soldiers had cleared an area of about three square feet, the wadi-man stopped them. He borrowed the sword and carefully scraped a small section of the wall until he revealed stonework.

He had Musan tell the soldiers to remove sufficient bricks to make a two-by-two-foot opening low down in the wall. It was not work willingly undertaken, but they continued on until they could ease one brick out. Through Musan, the wadi-man cautioned them against hurrying in case they brought down the entire brickwork.

The wadi-man put his ear to the space vacated by the brick. "Water," he told Musan. "Have someone carefully bring down empty water skins. Tell the soldiers to continue to make the hole."

Musan did so, and the soldiers went to work willingly. They knew the value of water in the desert—and much had been lost. Two large kitchen scoops were sent down.

The wadi-man said to Musan, "Once the skins are filled, everyone should bathe. There's sufficient water. This was a cistern in a building buried a hundred or hundreds of years ago by the sands. I shall go in first and handle the ladles out so the skins can be filled."

Musan called up to his grandfather what the wadi-man had said and suggested men come down no more than two at a time in case the sand walls collapsed. With that, the wadi-man dropped his clothes, placed his red silk slippers carefully on top of them and climbed through the hole.

Filling the skins took more than an hour. As the wadi-man exited the hole, Musan, his clothes folded neatly on the sand, went in. The water was cold, refreshing, cleansing—and totally unexpected. Perhaps that was the thrill of it. But Musan was fearful of the enclosed space and soon exited. He dressed and was hauled up as replacement bathers came down.

In all, they spent almost two hours at the cave-in. Although the stench from the butchered camels was appalling, everyone felt clean and refreshed. Knowing they had a new supply of water generated a great air of optimism. The wadi-man was repeatedly congratulated.

For almost another week the expedition plodded on, or for brief spells, trotted on. There were no more adventures apart from a sandstorm, quite brief, while they rested in a caravanserai, a sheltered area where desert travelers could take refuge. Then they came out of the desert into Judea and into Jericho.

The Winter Palace, the pools, the beguiling climate—Jericho had Musan enthralled. He had thought Dura-Europos magnificent. Now, by comparison to Jericho, it was a village. Nothing had prepared him for this.

Six days later they were at Caesarea Maritima, greeted warmly by the waiting Prefect Annius Rufus. After Rufus' welcome, they were supplied with refreshments and shown to their quarters to give them the opportunity to bathe.

The Prefect was not only voluble, but entertaining and witty. Obviously well educated and learned, he permitted his jocularity to overlay all. Later, when a tired Rufus momentarily closed his eyes, Musan looked at the closed eyes and nodding face of this kind and generous guardian, who had taken him into his family in an attempt to keep him safe in Rome during his education. He estimated the man's age at eighty, certainly approaching his grandfather's age.

The relaxed, long, thin face, with its deeply etched creases, was a character study, the huge sagging eyebrows that hung over Rufus' eyes gave the Prefect, even when awake, the appearance of an aging and friendly hunting dog. It was a face—as in a hunting dog—that masked a firmness of conviction and an ability to act quickly. Firm, yet most kindly.

Musan's weeks in the desert, conversing for hours on end with the Roman soldiers, had brought him to a high degree of fluency in Latin and in Roman patois. He could keep pace with Rufus' asides and Roman wit. When necessary, usually when Rufus was telling an amusing tale with words only a local to Rome would use, Musan acted as constant interpreter for his grandfather. Otherwise, Deleig of Deleig, too, was more fluent than when the expedition had set off.

The other thing about Prefect Annius Rufus, as the general and Musan quickly learned, was that when he was talking, he never knew when to stop. Nonetheless, he was entertaining and within his monologues, highly informative.

Rufus was short and stout and made fun of himself as Prefect. "This command," he said, over-solemnly, "is for young men on the way up, not old men on the way down, but I asked for it. I'd tired of Rome. They do say that anyone tired of Rome is tired of life, but that is only the nonsense parroted by people who have not seen the world, as I have.

"Rome is magnificent. Rome is everything it believes itself to be. It is the city that makes us Romans—we are what the city is. We take our personal stature from Rome. If other Romans say we are important, that we are famed jurists, brilliant soldiers, commanding politicians, then we are. If Romans do not say that about us, even though we may be those things, we are not those things. The world, however, remains bigger than the city even when that city is the best, the premier city, of the world."

Musan enjoyed Rufus' insights into Rome and Romans as the man talked to his grandfather, but apart from the moment of introduction, Rufus had never directly addressed Musan. He spoke as if addressing the Parthians as a single entity. That changed mid-afternoon. He asked to speak to Musan alone. The grandfather was agreeable, and Musan joined the Prefect for a stroll on the grand promenade, the avenue from the Prefect's palace onto Caesarea Maritima's harbor.

Certainly its man-made harbor had him realize that technologically Rome seemed like a distant planet, far from Parthian reality. If this was a province, he thought, what could Rome itself be like?

There was no one else on the promenade, but the harbor over the way was a scene of activity unlike anything the young visiting Parthian had ever witnessed, or imagined. He had never seen a harbor, or ships, only river-craft.

The Prefect was all business. He first asked if Musan wanted to be educated in Rome, or was it simply something the family wanted for him. Musan said he did, because it appeared he had already utilized all the available educational resources that Dura-Europos and the Royal Palace at Hatra could offer. Musan continued that judging from Jericho and Caesarea Maritima's grandeur, in design and construction, there must be an abundance of knowledge to equal the magnificence of the architecture and commerce. Musan's words, like the Prefect's, were rolling out without pause for breath.

An hour later, after they had walked out into the Mediterranean along one of the two wide stone harbor walls jutting out into the sea, Rufus told Musan he was intrigued by his grasp of languages, dismayed by his ignorance of law, assured from the conversation he had a natural gift for rhetorical training, offended by his lack of musical education, horrified by his ignorance of Roman history, applauding of his grasp of geography, distraught by the fact he had neither fished nor sailed, highly impressed by his manners and composure, and delighted by his storehouse of epic sagas, poetry and mystical tales and fables.

He had Musan recite two fables as they walked back along the harbor's outer wall and down the promenade. Once they'd returned to the palace, Musan hoped his feeling of mental exhaustion was not showing, for indeed he had enjoyed myself. But there was to be no respite.

They did not go to the quarters to be occupied by the grandfather and himself, but to a different wing of the palace. There he was introduced to two young men roughly his own age, possibly six months younger, Rufus' grandsons.

"This is Remus and that's Romulus," Rufus said.

He pointed first to a slim, dark-haired boy and then to an obvious brother, yet a duplicate in miniature of his grandfather, short and tubby.

"Twins. It would have been disrespectful to Rome's founders," he told Musan, "for their father to name them in the same order as Romulus and Remus." Fortunately, Musan knew sufficient Roman history to realize the significance of the names and the fact the boys were twins.

"This is Musan Deleig and he's spending the next several days with you. He is fourteen. He cannot sail, you must teach him. He is an expert reciter of tales. Ask him to tell you about the monkey with the flying carpet. No, better yet, young Musan, recite it now."

Remus and Romulus looked at him, amazed by his height at age fourteen, their age, though they were short. They half grinned an acknowledgment of welcome and quickly looked away so they were not gazing at him. They knew their grandfather had put the boy on the spot, and Musan suspected from their air of commiseration it was something he enjoyed doing to them.

Musan had to stand there and recite one of the lengthy stories of the mythical flying carpet and the adventures of the monkey who commanded it. Though he really only knew it in Aramaic, he had rapidly translated it into Latin for the Prefect as they'd walked along the promenade and harbor. He'd presumed, Musan hoped, that his translation pauses—as he had sought the correct word in the Latin for something obscure even in Aramaic—were understood by Rufus as pauses for dramatic effect.

Now, a second time through, he was very comfortable, though inordinately weary of talking. Having told one tale, he was obliged by the twins to tell another. At the end of that one, the Prefect cut Musan off and said, "You will live with my grandsons until you depart with your grandfather."

And that was that. Innocent as he was, Musan never suspected that the Prefect had planted him on Remus and Romulus so they could provide him with insights into Musan's character that Rufus could never obtain from a series of interviews. It was no surprise a man that crafty had been appointed Prefect of Judea.

What endeared Musan to the twins is that the tan of his Parthian skin and his Eastern origins disturbed them not one wit. Except in the ordinary way of conversation about origins, the issues of race and Carrhae never arose.

The immediate upshot of being thrown together was that after talking half the night, and after they had given Musan his first sailing lesson the next day, they were a threesome of colleagues who might one day be friends. Musan learned they were orphans, their parents killed in one of Rome's notorious fires.

His presence in their lives in those early days gradually appeared to improve their ability to deal more impartially with each other, for they lessened their endless bickering between themselves. Probably it was just having a third person their own age present.

They dined each evening with the Prefect and his wife, Musan's grandfather and always other palace officials. After several days, late one morning, Musan was summoned from the twins' quarters without them to meet with the Prefect and his grandfather.

Apparently, though he never learned it for certain, because he never asked, the twins had reported favorably on what manner of person he was. The Prefect assured Musan that when the Rufus family returned to Rome, less than a year hence, Musan would travel with the twins, in his entourage, as a member of his household.

Little did Musan realize at the time the multiple benefits this would confer on him, not least of which, that he'd be somewhat sheltered from Rome's ingrained bigotry toward non-Romans in general, Easterners as a category, and Parthians in particular. Rufus was candid when he explained this Roman bigotry was quite prevalent among Rome's military and higher social echelon.

Musan suspected that Prefect Rufus regarded his presence as a calming and providential influence on his grandsons and was pleased with him as a person. Rufus said he was a close friend of the family of Octavia Minor, late sister to the late Emperor Augustus. He would arrange that Musan could study with a tutor at the fine library at Porticus Octaviae, which the Emperor had built in his sister's memory.

The grandfather was called in. Annius Rufus said Musan would receive a letter as to when to return from Parthia to Caesarea Maritima, probably in August the following year. He would be there for a month or six weeks before sailing to Rome.

Musan was to return to Caesarea Maritima at that time, with a mature guard, a second adviser, if thought necessary, and two Parthian servants, and he would have two personal slaves assigned to him in Rome. His education after the first year of settling in would follow the Roman model.

The first year, the Prefect explained, he would need to adjust to living in the city—the city of the Empire, Rufus stressed. His studies in the library would be sufficient activity until he felt settled. After a year in Rome, Musan would be sent back to Parthia to his family. The twins would likely accompany him for the experience of travel and of a different culture, a quid pro quo, Rufus grinned. The grandfather was elated.

Musan could scarcely believe his good fortune. He was so grateful he could scarcely get the words out. He left his hassock, boldly went to the Prefect, took his hand, knelt and kissed it. He didn't know what else to do. Deleig of Deleig was beaming at the spontaneity of Musan's action.

Later, as they left Rufus' quarters, his grandfather explained that Musan would have only a month at Dura-Europos that winter and the rest of the time would be in Hatra with the family. Grandfather said he would accompany Musan back to Caesarea Maritima to deposit him there for his journey to Rome.

Because they were accompanied by a squad of Roman soldiers, Prefect Annius Rufus arranged for them to travel back to Parthia by the far less perilous *cursus publicus*, the Roman Empire's courier system of horse-drawn carriages manned by soldiers. Emperor Augustus had established the *cursus publicus* network for speeding information around the Empire, originally relying on slaves on foot or on horse. Consequently, Musan and his grandfather's return to the Roman side of the River Euphrates, opposite Dura-Europos, was accomplished in considerable style, compared to the outward desert journey, and took only seven days.

Almost a year later, after his farewells to the family, Musan again crossed the Euphrates. This time taking the *cursus publicus* to Caesarea Maritima. He was accompanied by Myrmid, but not his grandfather. Myrmid, from this point on, would be his full-time chief aide and adviser, meaning guard and defender, in Rome. His grandfather had insisted.

When the *cursus publicus* stopped at Damascus to change horses, two Roman senators got on. The Legate, the military commander of the entire region, was there to see them off. Neither he nor the senators deigned to address a Parthian. Musan realized the senators' disdain was a taste of the cool reception he was likely to receive in Rome.

SIX

Seven weeks later, Musan and the Rufus twins, with family and retainers, were aboard a *quinquereme* headed for Rome's port, Ostia. He had never been on a huge ship, nor in the constantly damp atmosphere of a vessel at sea. Its rolling progress reminded him of the waves seen on many a desert surface. Nor had he anticipated he would have to recite an entertaining saga to the many travelers after each evening meal. Nor that once his store was exhausted, he would have to start again.

One afternoon, as they were standing on deck, idling, Remus and Romulus asked him to describe the battle of Carrhae, the brutal defeat of Rome by the Parthians sixty-eight years earlier. But from the Parthian perspective.

"Find me a piece of chalk. We'll sit against the bow, and I can draw on the deck." Romulus quickly hopped up, ran below and returned with a lump of chalk. On the deck Musan knelt and scratched a "U" shape. Then he drew a line under it that slanted down from right to left.

"My full name is Musan Shaheen Deleig. 'Shaheen' is the Farsi word for 'falcon.' That U is the southern end of Caspian Sea. The line below it is the Kopet Dag mountain range, the northern limit of what, three centuries ago, would begin to grow into the Parthian Empire. Not until the piedmont does the range offer the promise of fruit trees and berry bushes. Lower still farmers try vines and grains and other crops. The lowest elevation is scrub and rocky desert, flint-sharp shards, sand and razor-edged gravel. This was an era when Parthia was less a country than a region.

"This was Greek territory, though not a particular jewel in the Hellenic crown. The Hellenic culture had tended over the centuries, out of trickle-down inevitability, to apply the thinnest of veneers to Parthia's turbulent, though scarcely ruling class. 'Class' in this instance denotes the slight change in social status from being of the local tribe to ruling it.

"Meanwhile, some 1,500 miles away, on the northern side of the Mediterranean, was Rome. It was already a well-organized and possibly already over-populated walled city-state. Even so, three centuries ago, mind you, Rome hardly recommended itself as a future empire either. Its expansionary vision was limited for another century yet. When not reeling from the sackings and sieges of marauders, Romans conquered nearby territory—mainly forest folk—with commendable determination. That done, the Romans would return to safety inside their walls.

"The lives of the populace were governed by a developing system of laws, regulation, religion and ritual. These developments might appear to prepare the Romans for their later military and cultural dominance, but it was a matter no Roman Republican of those centuries speculated on. There was a certain provincial self-satisfaction to Rome's residents. Wealth was in the hands of the large-scale farmers who sheltered in the city at night. It took a minority of ambitious strivers to stir Rome to its expansionist aims."

Deleig explained how, a little more than two centuries earlier, Parthia began its expansion—thanks to others. Earlier, the region was part of Cyrus the Great's Persian swath. Then the expanding Seleucids brought Hellenistic influence westward along the Mediterranean coast, conquering Babylonia and Mesopotamia.

"This is where it sounds confusing, so let's just say the mix of Seleucid and Parni invaders—and the invaded—all the way back to Cyrus the Great became the foundation of modern Parthia. Seleucid kings went to war using the region's Syrian elephants, behemoths larger than either their Indian or African cousins. It was said that a century later, Hannibal's favorite elephant, the enormous 'Surus,' was of the same stock.

"But it was not elephants that stirred the Parthian-Parni-Seleucid-Persian fortunes. The future was based on the Parthians' horsemanship and archery. Over time, the region developed an extremely lethal light cavalry of superb horse-mounted archers of enviable skill. The Parthians' devastating assault was known far and wide as the 'Parthian shot.' It was the 'Parthian shot' that defeated the previously highly successful General Crassus at Carrhae.

"How? Imagine you were a falcon circling high over that battle, what would you have seen? Theatre. High drama. Action spread across dozens of square miles. The centerpiece? The crushing defeat of a 40,000-strong armor-clad Roman army poised for battle in an open square.

"The Parthian action? A dramatic cycle of repetition played out to the near-silent music of the wastelands' winds underscored by the percussion of chargers' hooves in their thousands. Eleven-thousand Parthian warriors, superb athletes all, surged toward that enemy. Two ranks of horse-borne archers were spaced with such precision that an archer in the outer line had a clear field between two archers to his right.

"With eight seconds only between arrows, an archer might have as many as three arrows in the air by the time the first one hit. Even when the Roman soldiers locked shields together as an armored protection, arrows got through the cracks.

"This was a merciless fusillade from the powerful compound-wood bows—the metal-tipped arrows could pierce armor. As the mounted archers swung away, then came the parting 'Parthian shot.' Each rider turned fully around in the saddle so that his knees were tail-ward. Riding backward, each archer continued to loose his contribution to the unending storm of arrows.

"Now a different, thunderous confrontation: the charge of the cataphracts—the thousands of heavily armored men mounted on 'war horses.' These were thick-bodied, muscular beasts, bred for endurance rather than speed—endurance was essential given the enormous weight the horses carried, their own chain metal skirts in addition to their armored riders. As the cataphracts charged from the front, the archers swept around to attack at the sides. The Roman soldiers could not simultaneously shield themselves from the armored warriors to their front and the airborne arrows at their sides."

The twins were fascinated; Musan, a master storyteller, held them spellbound.

"The beasts were good for a series of sustained charges in a kill-or-be-killed attempt to subdue an enemy barely holding fast under the constancy of the light cavalry's archery bombardment. The deadly finality of the Parthian cataphract came from his exceptionally long and thick lance. It could be driven through two men at one time—though if just one was mortally pierced, cataphract honor, however gruesome, was satisfied. And on the cycle went, archers re-arming, cataphracts charging, more 'Parthian shots' until the enemy yielded.

"Carrhae's carnage: Crassus defeated, the Legionary Eagles lost to the enemy, 20,000 Roman dead, 10,000 fled and 10,000 prisoners sold as slaves to the Chinese."

"Slaves?" said an astounded Romulus. "No one ever told us Romans were sold as slaves."

But Musan did not veer from his story.

"Yet Carrhae is why I am here, a guest of your grandfather, Prefect Annius Rufus. My grandfather, General Deleig of Deleig, was a younger officer at Carrhae. As only a young and foolish young man would, he galloped into the fray and seized a Legionary Eagle, the golden *aquilae*, the regimental honor. Then he kept going. He seized two more. This was a tremendous disgrace for the regiments, and Rome."

The two boys, crestfallen, were as interested as ever.

"Years later, with *Pax Romana* bringing unprecedented prosperity to the Mediterranean region, it was now General Deleig of Deleig who convinced my other grandfather, King Phraates IV, to return the three regimental honors to Rome. And it was my grandfather who presented them to the Roman Legate at Damascus for transmission to Emperor Augustus. It is because my grandfather's is an honorable name in Roman military circles that I am here. I'm still technically the enemy; yet here I am en route to Rome with you, my friends."

The main blessing of the trip, Musan found, was that if he stayed up half the night, above deck, curled up on the deck under a blanket and oilskin, the solitude in the bow was as calming, as refreshing, as the desert. The difference, apart from the rolling motion and the sound of the sea, was the moisture. He had this solitude, too, for his exercises.

The *quinqueremes,* with their five rows of oarsmen, were built to repel pirates—or enemies—with their battering ram prow, but nothing unplanned occurred on the voyage.

After twelve days at sea, the *quinquereme* docked at Ostia, Rome's port—a record voyage time Musan was told. The Roman passengers on the *quinquereme* had been friendly enough—a contrast to the coldness of the two Roman senators at Damascus—but possibly because he had entertained them. They had all continued to Rome by boat up the River Tiber and then in a fleet of carriages specially commissioned for the final leg of the journey.

Watching the landscape as the carriage made its way to the Palatine Hill, Musan was transfixed. He gazed across the expanse of buildings atop the hill. A huge palace, no, two palaces. Those two closer buildings could be shrines. That impressive portico. Something colossal under construction close to the western edge. The brute architectural power of it all confronted him. Parthia was no match for this. This was the moment the boy Musan turned into the young man Deleig.

The carriage, a four-horse-drawn contraption with steel-rimmed wooden wheels, had four luxuriously comfortable bench seats occupied by the elderly Rufus and his wife, his two grandsons, two attendants, Deleig and Myrmid. Three of the luggage pieces atop this carriage were Deleig's. Two very small, very heavy chests contained gold coins. A larger wooden container held nothing but precious gems.

When they arrived at Rufus' villa, all was chaos, an outburst of greetings from kith and clan, friends and servants. Rufus eased his wife awake. Her twin grandsons assisted her out of the carriage and into the villa to her quarters. Meanwhile, Rufus supervised the unloading and distribution of luggage.

Deleig was to live in a villa within sight of where they stood. The two slaves provided by Rufus had made the villa ready. Deleig's two servants, with the rest of his belongings, would shortly be delivered there in the carriages that followed.

Rufus signaled Deleig to separate himself from the greeting crowd and join him. Alongside Rufus was a quite short, not quite stout, smiling woman. This, Deleig knew, was the Lady Lydia who would escort him this evening to Emperor Tiberius' family gathering. As Deleig walked toward them, the Roman woman, dark haired and square faced, said in a deep and commanding voice of some volume, "Do they not make any small Parthians, my prince?"

"They do indeed, Madame," Deleig replied, "but they sent me to frighten the Romans into thinking we were all this tall."

"Tall, dark, handsome and golden-tongued. You'll have to be watched, my prince. And are all Parthians as self-assured as you?" she asked, as he drew closer.

"No, Madame, I'm an oddity even by Parthian standards. I'm shy."

In an easy movement he knelt in front of her, touched his forehead to the ground and gracefully stood again. "Your servant,

Lady Lydia." She knew she was impressed, indeed almost overwhelmed by this daring young man. She was usually in command of any situation. He had out-maneuvered her. She couldn't recall a previous experience.

"An oddity in Parthia?" she said. "Well, you're certainly an oddity by Roman standards. We shall meet here an hour before sunset." She had a sly glint in her eye that transformed itself into a smile as she turned away.

She turned back and said, "My prince, you will have very few friends in Rome—everyone else is an enemy. Stay close to your friends." Deleig was taken aback, disdain he had expected, but not actual danger. Rufus gave him a nod that suggested Lydia would be one of the friends.

Myrmid appeared. As they walked over to Deleig's villa, Deleig told him he thought he had just been warned to be on his guard.

"Musan," Myrmid replied, "I've been on my guard, our guard, since we stepped ashore. We, I, don't know *anything* about Rome, or about Romans."

"Quintus Linius, the Roman commander I met last year at Dura-Europos, was a decent and straightforward man—it's easy to be thinking one person portrays them all. Easy, and a mistake, perhaps?"

Myrmid thought for a moment. "That commander's like those Romans we traveled with across the desert. But that also was different—we were all desert colleagues. Here? In Rome? Stay alert. Do you want me to come with you to the imperial palace?"

"No thank you, I don't think I'll be at risk there—apart from some sneering looks. I've only just realized how often I'll be among strangers now. I'll give you my impressions when I return."

The villa had been rented for a year for Deleig. The two members of his retinue, Myrmid and S'veyda, would arrange their own quarters. S'veyda was a last gift from Lin Ma. He was to be Deleig's confidante and the man in charge of building Deleig's trading empire.

Once he'd arrived, S'veyda would worry about the vagaries of being a Rome-based Silk Road trader while Deleig was busy with his studies. The sole injunction was to follow Lin Ma's injunctions: "stick to sea routes" and "stay with one product: extremely precious stones—gems are portable."

Building a family fortune was the lesser of his grandfather's reasons for sending Deleig to Rome, but while the grandfather imagined the boy's education was a ploy to gain acceptance among the Roman power elite—in order to report to Parthia on Rome's plans for the region—Deleig was determined to focus on his education to the exclusion of all else. He was quite aware that was why *he* had agreed to come to Rome.

A half-hour later, his vigorous exercise routine and a mile run at speed concluded, Deleig bathed and, refreshed from fruit, nuts and juice, dressed in fresh finery similar to the hunting outfit he'd traveled in.

Deleig was escorted to Emperor Tiberius' palace to meet once more with Lady Lydia. He saw her standing alone at one end of the imperial palace steps. He dismissed the servant and walked to her. He again knelt, touching his forehead to the ground as salutation.

"I cannot say you appear refreshed, my prince, when in fact you haven't appeared to be anything other. A word about this huge gathering before we enter. All of Caesar Augustus' family—the esteemed Emperor was my uncle—and the families, therefore, of his adopted heir, Emperor Tiberius, plus Tiberius' friends and related enemies, are here. As are the Julians, all those with connections to Julius Caesar's family.

"Imagine, you can meet Marc Antony and Cleopatra's children. And grandchildren. Octavia, Emperor Augustus' wife, raised Marc Antony and Cleopatra's children after their deaths at Roman hands, as you may well know. Perhaps you'll meet Emperor Tiberius himself. No, second thoughts, do not do that, you a Parthian on your first day in Rome. Too soon. A gaffe at a Tiberius' family gathering might be regarded as an impertinence. What would *you* like me to arrange?"

"I mentioned I was an oddity, Lady Lydia. I would like to be introduced to someone who, equally, would be regarded by most here as an oddity. If that's possible."

Lydia was standing two steps higher up the flight of steps than Deleig and close to his face. She gazed in a hard manner into his eyes and was satisfied with what she saw, that he was serious.

"By the gods, I can already tell I'll never understand you, my prince, but you have a fascinating turn of mind. Yes, I have an oddity, as you call it. We shall walk straight through the crowd in the aula. I shall nod to people. I will call out your name.

"Everyone will be staring at you—you'll have to get accustomed to that. Many won't like you—Parthians are still the enemy despite the *Pax Romana*—but that does not mean you are in danger from *them.* At least, not *all* of them. Beyond here, meaning in Rome at large, you may well be in danger. What weighed on you that you'd risk that in Rome? Rufus said education. Is it enough?"

"It is for me, Lady Lydia. Rome is for me what Greece is or has been for Rome, a different world, and a world well worth understanding, with a history well worth learning, and learning well worth acquiring."

"That's a mouthful, young man. So be it. Hold my hand, nod, smile, do not speak. If any comment is required, I shall provide it."

Deleig hid what he could only presume was glee, a most unsuitable response. Hours only in Rome and he was about to walk through the center of its power base. Somewhere in this vast gathering space was the Roman Emperor. Imagine!

The hubbub started to quiet at the sight of Prince Musan Deleig. The lessening noise caused others to turn and see the reason. He accepted that he had to steel himself inside for any eventuality while being his affable best—the very tall Parthian accompanying the very short Roman with the booming voice through the crowd of generations of imperial family in the imperial palace.

The booming voice did call the crowd to attention. Within moments, it seemed to Deleig, the hundreds of people in the grand aula were staring at him.

"Meet our Parthian prince, His Royal Highness Musan Deleig, grandson of a king, a visitor come for a Roman education," said Lady Lydia. "The oldest among us recall when it was King Herod's two sons, Agrippa and Antipas, who made a similar journey for an education. Prince Musan is a ward of the returned and retiring Prefect Annius Rufus, and contrary to all appearances, he is fifteen years old. Ladies, be warned; Gentlemen, beware. Thank you. Off we go."

A smattering of people applauded; then the applause grew louder. Deleig stopped, bowed to left and right and took a step to catch up with Lady Lydia, who was charging her way across the room. The sound of her voice had made him relax. He could handle whatever came next.

Lady Lydia stopped part way along the entrance hall to someone's quarters and signaled an attendant. He came, bowed and stood before her.

"Sammid, tell your master I am sending him a prince from Parthia, and ask your master to receive him."

"Yes, Lady Lydia," the attendant said. He turned, trotted down a corridor leading off the entrance hall at the left and was back within two minutes. "He said yes, Lady." She nodded as the attendant went and stood by the wall from where she'd first summoned him.

"Follow Sammid, my prince. I regret I cannot be privy to what will be a quite remarkable encounter. I shall return to the aula and enjoy myself. The envy of all because I have attracted the attention of a man younger than myself. Leave here once you've met your oddity and join me."

Deleig smiled and gave a slight bow. He followed the attendant along the corridor.

Just before showing him in, Sammid hesitated. Dropping his voice, he said, "Your Highness, you are in danger from some of the Praetorian Guard in the palace. I dare not say more."

Deleig was startled; he had not expected to encounter trouble on his first evening in Rome. He would have to take evasive action—but what?

Putting that aside for the moment, Deleig entered a spacious living and working area. A young man looking no odder than any other male Roman he'd seen sat on a long divan. He lifted his head as Deleig entered.

The man had a slightly triangular narrow face, the Roman nose and chin the face warranted, hair that needed attention, sharp, indeed penetrating, eyes. The sort of eyes, Deleig suspected, that could be switched cold in an instant. Yet rarely were.

The man's unruly hair had waves, rather than curls. Otherwise, there were no distinguishing features interfering with a placid face alive with those intelligent eyes.

He looked at Deleig, unimpressed, and asked, "Parthian? Have you come to spy on us?"

"Of course, sir. That's what peace is for."

"Honesty is a rare quality in Romans. I'd presumed it non-existent in Parthians, or Persians, if that's what you prefer to be called. Or Parni-Seleucid-Hellenistic-Persian might be closer. Do you know who I am?"

"No, sir. Obviously, you know history."

"It's useful. People do not like me. My mother avoids me. My aging grandmother, Livia, writes me bullying little notes. I'm about to divorce my wife of two years, another bullying and nagging woman who is of no political value to me as my wife. Wants me dead. Given a free hand, she'd willingly kill me herself. What is your name?"

"Musan Deleig, sir. My father doesn't like me because I am the taller, though there may be other reasons. My older brother ignores me. My mother and younger sister love me, and I have a grandfather who dotes on me. There, sir, is my intimate family accounting."

"Are you married, Musan Deleig? At that length of yours you would certainly overwhelm any female body I've ever seen. Were she below you she'd be nose deep in your chest."

"No, sir," said Deleig, "I'm not married. I am only fifteen."

"There's a surprise. A boy I thought was a man, though I suspect more man than boy. Sit down, do. I'm Claudius. Why did Lady Lydia deposit you in my chambers? Are you her latest acquisition, her Eastern totem? She is fickle. So commanding. They should give her a regiment to play with on the German border. I said I am Claudius—does that mean anything to you? Fifteen, you say. Have you known women?"

"One. Once. The only gift my father ever gave me was the week I was leaving the Hatra palace for Rome. I was asleep on my cushions and a young woman entered my quarters and slipped under the covers with me. She said my father had sent her. I said, 'My grandfather, surely.' She said, 'No, sir, your father.' I thought it typical of him, my father that is, he could think only of passions, bodily functions, and never the mind or emotions. And I apologize, your name means nothing to me."

"One woman. It's a start. Why are you seeing me, not knowing who I am?"

"I'm here to study. My Roman guardian is Annius Rufus—"

"A fine man. Rufus and I are good friends—"

"And he had Lady Lydia bring me to the family gathering. She asked me whom I wanted to meet—she mentioned the Emperor and Cleopatra's children. I said as I considered myself an oddity, even in Parthia, I would like to meet a Roman whom Romans considered an oddity. She brought me to you, sir. Are you an oddity?"

"Hnnnnn," Claudius muttered through clenched teeth.

"I had not realized how great an oddity I would be here. I arrived only today at Ostia, from Dura-Europos by way of six weeks in Rufus' household in Caesarea Maritima."

"Literally? This morning?"

"Yes, sir."

"Claudius, not sir, and I'll call you Deleig. In which case you need me to say this: you are in danger. Not from anyone in the aula. They might hate you for being a Parthian but would enjoy your company for the same reason. Others would hate you and try to harm you—because of Carrhae. Romans have long memories. You know of Carrhae?"

"I do."

"I thought you might. Parthia's triumph. Rome's shame. Most Romans cannot talk in these terms, even in this household. Historians, however, cannot lie. Or at least ought not to. Oddity you ask: I have been despised, hated, mocked, bullied, disregarded. I was raised being told I was nothing more than a stupid cripple. 'The idiot' is another. I have been left out of the normal honors of my class by my immediate relatives. I am highly educated, Livy—you might know the name?"

"In difficult and desperate cases, boldest counsels are best."

"Close, very good. You are a scholar. Thank Jupiter. I am otherwise surrounded by tent pegs. Livy saved my mind; history—writing it—has saved my life. Or given me one. I am not yet sure. This is Rome, you see. Where the certain never happens and the incidental is the norm. My historical scholarly work frightens people because of its frankness. My prospects are dismal. I am a keen and seldom erring judge of men and a foil for women who push me around as if I had no will of my own—and where women are concerned that is a fair assessment."

Claudius continued, "My assessment of you, Deleig—apart from possibly highly educated for you age? Assessment deferred. Lady Lydia would not have brought you if she thought you lacking. She called you 'prince.' Are you a prince?"

"My mother is the daughter of King Phraates IV's first wife," said Deleig. "I can only thank Ahura Mazda I am not related to my royal maternal grandfather's second wife."

"Ah, a crack in the façade. Who is Ahura Mazda, and what's wrong with the second wife?"

No answer came. Deleig blinked. It had been a long day. He was beginning to feel overwhelmed by the powerful arena he had stepped into—and by the possible danger he faced from the Praetorian Guard. Claudius thought that he was wilting under the barrage of questions.

"My apologies, my apologies, Deleig. Permit me to send you back to the aula to reconnect with Lady Lydia."

Deleig smiled—he had an idea. "Thank you, sir, but could your servant rather take me first to the palace kitchens?"

"The kitchens? The kitchens? Quite honestly, Deleig, I'm not sure where the palace kitchens are! Sammid does, I'm sure. Why kitchens?"

Improvising, Deleig said, "To inquire about what range of food is available for someone who is accustomed to Eastern food."

"Ahh, of course. Sammid ...," Claudius called. The attendant appeared. "Please take Prince Musan to the kitchen and attend to his needs. Then escort him to the aula. Deleig, I am nine years your senior. My education, brilliant as I said, Livy. I know everyone and will suggest tutors if you wish. Second thought. Will you come tomorrow morning to see me? Break the fast with me. I promise I will be informative. Questions to a minimum."

"I shall come, Claudius. And thank you for the invitation. By which time I hope I'll have learned more about who you are. Honored to be regarded in this way. Thank you."

He stood and nodded his head to Claudius, who remained seated and nodded back. The attendant led the way out, but Claudius changed his mind, was up from his sofa and walked rapidly—though with a slight limp—to join Deleig and Sammid.

"Beware the women, fear the haters—you'll meet many, won't be able to avoid them. The women will want you as a trophy. Don't grant them that. The haters will want you dead or expelled from Rome. Don't allow that either. Are you wealthy, Deleig?"

"Extremely."

"That's useful. Because I had a novel thought, so rare these days. Buy the Janiculum, the unoccupied part of it. It is a hill outside the walls of Rome, edges the Vatican swamps. We shall talk tomorrow."

Claudius stopped. Deleig and Sammid continued on. Their descent took them first onto a broad open expanse surrounded by doors and several corridors. Sammid said senior officials had their offices there.

Their second descent down steps left no doubt that this was home to the kitchens—not so much the smell of food, but the noise from clanking pots and pans surmounted by calls, loud shouts, at least two people singing different songs, and a level of chatter that would drown out any attempt at normal conversation.

Sammid led Deleig into a vast pillared crypt-like area. A double arching set of work spaces, each with blazing ovens, dozens of cooks supervising, and at least a score of lesser cooks, pot-boys, carriers-and-fetchers, slaves—all busy. Each master cook appeared to have her own pair of pot-boys on hand to cool her by wafting a huge fan on the end of a pole.

Sammid indicated Deleig was to follow him into the more distant work area. Under a row of small open windows above a long worktable, a solitary person—"head cook," mouthed Sammid—had her head down over a slate. Propped up on the lengthy table, against the wall, was slate after slate showing the cook's instructions for the food dishes to be prepared, and in which order. Another cook came and removed a slate on the far left and returned with it to her workbench.

Sammid bowed to Deleig and indicated a far opening where he'd be waiting. Deleig nodded and walked to the right end of the head cook's table. The head cook did not know Deleig was there. He did not announce himself. He picked up a piece of chalk and drew a symbol on a blank gray slate. She watched him out of the corner of her eye while continuing to write out the menu. She then retrieved Deleig's slate and chalk in hand still, drew a symbol on it. She looked at it, looked at him and raised her eyebrows.

His symbol was a line drawing of a two-headed regal bird. It announced two things: that he was an astrologer and of Persian ranking stock.

She drew an eye on the slate and a ram's head, mere scratches of the chalk. She slid the slate back to Deleig. She designated her greater skill at soothsaying and as a psychic. The ram's head was her astrological sign. Deleig scratched his Gemini astrological sign and slid the slate back.

The cook turned and called to another cook nearby, who came and listened to the head cook's instructions in her ear. She nodded and took over the head cook's place at the long table. Immediately the new cook was writing on a slate.

The head cook faced Deleig, beckoned with her right hand he was to follow, turned and led him to a small door that took them out into the light of a late spring evening. Deleig had forgotten it was still daylight after he'd descended down the two long flights of dark, barely illuminated stairs to enter the flare-illuminated kitchen.

"You're a Parthian, sir. Your Latin is superior to mine I'll be bound. Parthian. That's taking a risk in Rome. You need my help and you offer what?"

"Two Persian sooths you do not know, and these." Deleig

opened his hand. There were two gold *aureus* in his palm, undoubtedly more money than the cook saw in ten years.

The cook made no attempt to take the money. The "sooths," she wanted to know. He told her, then repeated them. She nodded, accepting both their novelty and utility.

"What, sir, do you want from me?"

"Gossip, particularly about me. For the next five to ten years. You will receive a gold piece at the start of each year. It may not always be myself who comes to collect the gossip. Right now, I need a potion and a pair of gloves."

He described the potion. The cook nodded, as she now held out a hand to accept the gold coins. She said the largest gloves available, oven mitts, would be tight on hands with fingers as long and huge as his. He acknowledged that. He asked if she would sprinkle some of the potion on the back of the leather fingers of the right-hand oven leather. She nodded a yes.

Deleig turned, showed her the half-belt at the rear of his jacket and said she was to slide the right-hand oven mitt under it, potion-side facing out. He asked for several fruits, juiced. She nodded that she understood and went back inside.

SEVEN

Twenty minutes later she returned. She handed Deleig the left mitt and tucked the other into the jacket belt at the rear, as he'd asked. The fruits she had for him in a corked jug inside a cloth bag. A small, separate bag inside it held the potion, she said.

They conversed for a few more minutes. The cook warned him to be careful. Parthians would have few friends in Rome—or her kitchen. She had not accepted him because he was Parthian, she said. She had accepted him because he was, like her, a soothsayer. Then she left and returned to her work.

Deleig waited for a moment before going back inside. He thought about his situation. He had attended this gathering without Myrmid, his guard. It had not occurred to either of them that he might be in danger at an event in the imperial palace.

Deleig went in through the kitchen door, determined to test whether he was or was not safe, given Sammid's warning. He paid no attention to any of the dozens of people in motion, firing ovens and cooking. He headed to the doorway where Sammid said he would be waiting, but he was not there. This put Deleig on his guard.

He started up the stairs. Just as he came level to the floor of officials' offices, he saw three Praetorian guards by the opposite set of stairs. They were obviously waiting for someone. Two stood at the bottom of the stairs while the third, a commanding figure, was on the first landing. He spotted Deleig as he emerged from the stairwell and shouted an order to the others. As they started toward Deleig, he suddenly looked up to the top of the stairs, beyond the third guard, and called out in a delighted voice, "Claudius!"

In the split second the three men deflected their attention to the top of the stairs—to find no one there—Deleig dropped his bag and took a great dancer's leap forward, a huge bouncing stride. He landed on his right foot and spun with his left leg outstretched, kicking the nearest guard, at a high velocity, under the ear with the point of his leather boot. Deleig heard a bone break. He winced.

As the guard fell to the floor, Deleig switched to his left foot in a second Whirling Dervish spin, smashing his right boot squarely in the second man's solar plexus. As the man doubled over, Deleig chopped his neck with side of his right hand. Again he heard a bone break. Once more, he winced. This wasn't what he wanted. He turned back for his bag and then headed over to the stairs.

"I'm next, I suppose," said the third guard. "My name is Sejanus."

Deleig ignored the overture as he started up the stairs. "Step aside."

Sejanus, uncertain, but not showing any of the fear he may—or may not—have felt, moved to one side on the landing.

Deleig, as he walked past, whipped the glove from the back of his jacket and slapped the glove across Sejanus' face.

He said, "You will be seriously ill tonight. I shall come to your quarters tomorrow."

Sejanus felt something itching his face and looked terrified. Deleig continued up the stairs and returned to Claudius' quarters. Sammid was waiting in the corridor as before.

"You left?"

"I followed your instructions, sir. The pot-boy from the kitchen said you would make your own way back."

Deleig realized that even coming to Claudius' quarters with Lady Lydia he had been followed. He would constantly have to exercise greater caution than he had imagined. He thanked Sammid for his warning about the guards and asked to be shown in.

"Back already?" said Claudius. "Sammid said you were returning to the aula on your own."

"He was misinformed. When I returned to where I'd left Sammid, he wasn't there. I mounted the stairs and ran into trouble."

Deleig provided Claudius with a shortened version of what happened and asked, "Who is Sejanus?"

Claudius was not about to be deflected.

"You may have killed two men?"

"I may have."

"You have signaled your own death," said Claudius, a tinge of anxiety to his voice.

"Possibly. That will depend on my meeting with Sejanus tomorrow, in his quarters."

"How do you know he will see you?"

"I have no doubt. I've left him somewhat incapacitated, and he cannot recover without my assistance. But I would prefer to say no more at present. Who is this man Sejanus?"

"His father, Seius Strabo, is extremely important. He commands Emperor Tiberius' household troops, the Praetorian Guard. The son, who accosted you, is Lucius Aelius Sejanus, a vicious, power-hungry bully and manipulator who next month will serve under his father. He will assume command of the Praetorian Guard once his father retires. Tiberius does not know he'll have the proverbial tiger by the tail."

"Will you tell the Emperor?" Deleig asked.

"The Emperor and I are not on easy speaking terms, though that may improve over the next few years. Let me know the outcome of tomorrow, and I shall use the event to keep Sejanus and others away from you—as best I may. An improvement that may be brought about … Never mind. How were you able to maim or kill two of Sejanus' bullies? An astonishing feat."

"With astonishing feet," Deleig said, stamping his boots on floor in a sharp rat-tat-a-tat.

"Two years ago, when I was thirteen, my height became conspicuous, gait erratic. My mother hired two Egyptian male dancers from a touring dancing group that entertained at the Hatra palace. She ordered them to teach me how not to be clumsy, how to care for my long legs and dangling arms, and how to move gracefully given my height—and at that point, combat my natural awkwardness. Not only that, she daily—for the first couple of months—supervised the three hours as I ran, danced and exercised.

"Once she was satisfied the dancers understood her instructions, she told them to teach me how to defend myself, given that my height made me an easy target for bullying and my boyish attractiveness made me vulnerable in others ways. The latter I did not understand until the dancers explained. So, for the remaining four months, I did my daily exercises—and still do—and ran for an hour, which I also still do, and learned how to defend myself. Which I just did. All this from two tall male dancers who had oft-times had to defend themselves. There you have it, and I've taken too much of your time."

"You are an elusive creature, Musan Deleig. Don't go yet. I was born with a limp, and I've been branded idiot and fool. Could, would, dancers help me?"

"Undoubtedly."

Claudius said, "Here is my revised thought. Come as early as you can tomorrow morning, I will supply a good mount. We'll ride out beyond the walls for you to inspect the Janiculum hill. For your own safety's sake, you and your people will need to see the enemy approaching. I shall talk to Lady Lydia and Annius Rufus, and to two others I trust completely, to ensure your safety as best we can until your Janiculum residence is completed. I presume you know what you'd want in a villa?"

"I do now, sir. Thank you, Claudius. I have a guard, Myrmid. He is battle hardened and was my grandfather's aide de camp. He is not with me because, innocently or carelessly, I did not expect an attack in the imperial palace. Till morning."

Early the following day, Deleig exercised for over an hour. Then he made his way to Sejanus' quarters in the imperial palace. The Parthian carried the jug of liquid. It was the fruit plant squeezings he'd been given in the kitchen the previous evening.

Admitted to Sejanus' inner sanctum, where the future Praetorian commander lay in some distress, Deleig said, "The two of us will never be friends. There is no reason we should be enemies. I will cure you of what I've inflicted on you. All night it has emptied your bowels and stomach. Drink two beakers of what is in this jug. A couple of hours from now, finish what remains of the liquid—you'll never know you were ill. Drink up."

A servant brought the ailing soldier a beaker, filled it for him and stood by while Sejanus drank it. Sejanus then swung his legs off the divan and sat up, still pale faced.

"A caution ...," Deleig said, speaking slowly. "If you ever move against me again, and don't succeed, you will be dead. If you ever move against me, and do succeed, you will be dead. A permanent truce? Like the Roman-Parthian Peace Line?"

Sejanus nodded.

"As a Roman officer?" He had no intention of saying gentleman. Sejanus again nodded.

"Why, in this time of peace, do you hate me so?"

Sejanus burped and held out the beaker to his servant for a refill. He drank that and replied, "I hate you for the reason all Romans hate you. Carrhae."

"But the battle of Carrhae was sixty-eight years ago. You lost because Crassus was vain, a once-brilliant then stupid, ill-prepared and arrogant field commander who misunderstood terrain and had forgotten both strategy and tactics. It was Rome's fault you lost."

"Precisely," said Sejanus, his voice notably strengthening as the juices took effect. "We know that. It was Rome's fault we lost. That's why we hate you."

Deleig was on the threshold of Claudius' quarters before Claudius was awake. Claudius' attendant, Sammid, asked Deleig not to enter the quarters, but wait while he sent for someone from the stables. Sammid suggested Deleig take care of seeing the horses prepared for their journey to the Janiculum, thus giving Claudius time to rise and bathe. Then they could break the fast together.

Deleig did as bid and enjoyed being in the stables again. He had decided against bringing his own Arabians until he was settled. Claudius was urging him to build outside the city walls. So he would. Stables, too.

Almost two hours later, Claudius and Deleig approached the initial slopes of the Janiculum. To the west, the swamps *Vaticanus*, to the east, woodland and open, drier stretches.

The top of the eastern part of the hill, served by its own primitive winding road, boasted shrines and some neglected burial mounds, but not much else. The higher reaches of the western side, undeveloped, looked promising. They rode up past smithies, bakeries, small manufactories and three smaller villas, all on the lowest slopes.

About halfway up, they left the horses tethered to walk a narrow, overgrown winding path, several hundred feet through thicket and bramble to the western top.

Deleig had brought sheets of papyrus and a charcoal stick. On the first, with Claudius' help, he drew an aerial view. The second soon bore a sketch of the planned road to be carved out of the hill, his independent and private access. Then he sketched the approximate location for his home, with its extensive roof garden covering the entire property. Daily water wagons would be essential.

"An enormous cage of song birds, here," he said, pointing to his roof garden, "and a balustrade here to lean on and to look at city, grateful I'll be, apparently, to reside at some remove from it."

"You probably don't know yet how glad," Claudius said.

Deleig showed Claudius how he'd wanted the house partially set into the hill at its eastern end, with the south and west open. Three huge water cisterns well above the height of the roof garden, not merely to power the springs and streams across the roof's water garden, but for household use.

There was a third use for those cisterns, but Deleig decided it would not be appropriate at present to mention it to Claudius—he didn't know him *that* well. Deleig saw that if he carved the road carefully, on the final, somewhat tight turn coming up, he would deliberately narrow the road. The road would be walled at that point on up to the villa.

"How do I arrange to own this, to get the work done, Claudius?" he asked, as they started back down the difficult path through brush and gorse. Claudius, fit despite the limp, was the next item on Deleig's Claudian agenda. He would have those dancers—or similar ones—located this week.

Claudius was a fund of knowledge for Deleig, but not the original source. It was knowledge Claudius passed on from his attendant, Sammid, until after three days, Deleig persuaded Claudius to allow his servant to sit in their presence.

At that point, the planning went swiftly. Deleig showed Sammid the scaled model Janiculum he'd created from clay and exquisitely carved thin sandalwood. It had a carefully laid out provisional design of the roof garden, with the house underneath.

Sammid was amusing, as well as informed.

"Bring the contractor here, into the palace. He'll be terrified," said Sammid. "And he'll listen. He may still attempt to rob you, but not if you ask for the costs as the construction goes ahead."

It did not quite work out that way. The contractor who came was not cowed by the imperial palace. He did not give his name. He said he was known as "the villa builder." Everyone knew him by that. Deleig thought him arrogant, but apparently with something to be arrogant about, for he appeared extremely competent.

The builder said he'd consider the job for three days following receipt of Deleig's scale model and plans. He returned to report he'd climbed the hill three times and now knew the topography intimately, and what was under—earth or rock—at key places.

The cisterns would have to be blocked and cemented. The cement doors, if ever opened, would have to be replaced. The house presented no difficulty, and the roof was an interesting challenge. He wanted this much money, half in advance, take it or leave it. He would finish seven months from the day he started.

Deleig and Claudius listened to the contractor slightly wide-eyed. Impressed at his grasp of his business—villa-building. When the contractor had finished, at the table on Claudius' balcony, Deleig counted out the fee in gold *aureus*, added twenty percent more and said, "Six months."

The contractor pushed the additional twenty percent back and said, "Seven." The deal was struck.

The only other figures Deleig had from the contractor were that eighty-four people would be building the house and cisterns, starting the moment the provisional road was cleared, a task that would be accomplished in eighteen sixteen-hour days by a sixty-strong road-building crew. Deleig was to stay away until the complete roadbed was laid. After that, he could visit daily, if he cared to.

The next day, S'veyda, his trading chief bequeathed to him by Lin Ma, arrived. On meeting him, Deleig would forever think of him as S'veyda of the Furrowed Brow. He was a charming person, immediately likeable. A short and wiry man who was usually smiling, but when not, his face in repose was a furrowed anxiety. When not speaking, he gave the impression he was pondering the eternal verities. Deleig, amused, realized he now had Furrowed Brow S'veyda and Bushy Eyebrowed Myrmid. He wondered what their nickname was for him.

Myrmid had been exploring Rome's Suburra, a mixed neighborhood. On its perimeter were Rome's middle-class houses, with a selection of higher-class stone or brick villas. Julius Caesar was born and raised in the district.

Closer to the center the Suburra became crowded with six-story wooden tenements—fire traps, the incendiary point for many of Rome's frequent fires. On the street level, the tenements had arched areas, occupied by taverns, workshops, garment centers and the city's best craftsmen—not least in jewelry and gold, the reason for Deleig and S'veyda's interest. Suburra's center was also a training ground for the city's pickpockets and the home of its extensive red light district.

Deleig's interests were both practical and slightly fearful. During his initial stay in Caesarea Maritima with Prefect Annius Rufus, he and his grandfather had visited Herod Antipas, Tetrarch of Galilee and Perea. Herod Antipas had also been educated in Rome.

In an aside to Musan, he had told the boy that at some point he should visit the House of the Blue Hyacinth in the Suburra. It was not a brothel, Antipas had said to the blushing fourteen-year-old, but a place where one bought for a lifetime a young woman companion who would always remain in the shadows. Yet the commitment was for her lifetime support, even if he tired of her. All the blushing boy had said was "thank you."

Now, not much more than a year later, Deleig, who genuinely felt far more mature, felt his confidence slipping away as the surroundings compounded Antipas' words and escalated his embarrassment in recalling the conversation. Antipas had described the building, but pushing their way through the often shoulder-to-shoulder crowds, Deleig caught no sight of it. Not that he intended to visit.

Discreet earlier inquiries by Myrmid produced a certain Maggot as the official leader of the informal but healthily unified jewelry and gold trade, organized to ensure prices could not be suppressed by buyers.

Maggot had welcomed Deleig mistakenly as an important buyer. His premises were well guarded, inside and out. The "buyer" mistake lasted only until Deleig laid before the jeweler a small, superbly lacquered silk-lined box that contained a ruby, a topaz and an emerald. Maggot was invited to examine them. The jeweler could not contain his amazement at the quality. He betrayed himself with his quick intake of breath. He sent for an assistant and had him examine them, too.

No one spoke. Deleig placed a second box on the table: a diamond, a pearl and a tourmaline. And a third: an opal, an amethyst and a sample of white jade.

"I cannot lie to you, and I cannot pretend," Maggot said. "These are the finest examples ever to enter the Suburra, either in a jeweler's bag or around someone's neck. Superb. Why are you here?"

Myrmid stood outside with one of the guards while Deleig and S'veyda spent the next hour with Maggot and a second hour meeting with a dozen jewelers brought to the next-door tavern, a meeting over which Maggot presided and guided the questions.

During the sessions, Deleig met the best gemstone carvers, for when he wanted specialized rings made, and made provisional deals with the jewelry cooperative, such as it was. S'veyda, they understood, was in charge on Deleig's side.

One jeweler asked if S'veyda's vessels from India and the East could also bring precious woods, silks and carvings. An additional line of business was provisionally agreed to. Deleig realized what and who Lin Ma had sacrificed by giving him S'veyda.

All S'veyda said, when Deleig later mentioned it, was, "You are his son." If S'veyda was envious of that fact, he did not show it.

Days later, when Deleig told Prefect Annius Rufus of Sejanus' attack, he was horrified, but acknowledged the man was indeed venomous. He didn't quite understand how Deleig had arranged some form of truce with Sejanus, but as mentor and guardian—and substitute grandfather—he had his own agenda for the boy. The elderly Prefect's plan was that a Parthian highly educated in recent Roman history might carve a protective niche within his social circle. Distinguished scholars and librarians, Rufus reasoned, could well be a partial buffer against Sejanus.

Rufus hired a tutor, Delcas, who was at first uncertain how to deal with this young man more widely experienced than most fifteen-year-olds he taught. This was a Parthian with a totally different view of the world than his own. He said as much to Deleig, but immediately solved the problem by assigning the boy four Roman biographical studies: Julius Caesar, Octavian—but not in his Augustan period—Agrippa and Maecenas.

Delcas declared, in his tutor voice, "Julius Caesar will give you the Republic teetering toward Empire. Octavian will give you Parthia and open the triumphal gateway to Empire. Agrippa will bring you back to Rome, and Maecenas will unveil the city for you."

Lady Lydia had important connections and eased Deleig's access to the excellent library at the Porticus Octaviae. With the help of the librarians there, he began his research.

Later, he undertook one-on-one interviews. Delcas, Rufus and in one instance, Emperor Tiberius, who had learned of the project, enabled Deleig to meet elderly Romans who'd served under Julius Caesar, as well as others who had known Octavian, Agrippa and Maecenas, who had not long been dead.

Emperor Tiberius had twice in one day asked to speak to Deleig. The jurist Massurius Sabinus, the Emperor's friend, had interviewed Deleig to determine whether to take him on as a law student and had told the Emperor the young man was worth assisting. The first time Deleig was called into the Emperor's presence was to be asked if Parthia was planning an attack. Deleig had said no, that indeed the reverse was true.

Tiberius sent the boy away, but recalled him later. He said he would like to see what Deleig finally wrote before it was made public, and to tell his tutor as much. Deleig said it would be done.

The Emperor, who had a droll, though not original sense of humor, asked Deleig—as had Lady Lydia—if all Parthians were as tall. Deleig gave the same answer as previously, that he had been sent to frighten Romans into thinking so.

"All I actually do, Your Eminence, is rather stand out at gatherings."

Tiberius appeared to be making him something of a pet, for he said he would call him "my Parthian prisoner." That familiarity would stand Deleig in good stead later, as would his guidance under Massurius Sabinus, a Tiberius favorite.

Within two years, Deleig produced four volumes jocularly referred to as "the Parthian's Quartet." They were written in the words of those who had known the recent giants of Roman history, augmented by Deleig's research.

Whether any of this helped keep Sejanus at bay, Deleig could not tell.

EIGHT

Blazing with enthusiasm, powered by youthful energy, Deleig pursued his studies and research with a zest absent from his Dura-Europos days. He was pursuing men who'd known Julius Caesar, possibly the most famous person in history since Alexander the Great.

Myrmid, in an oft-repeated caution, would tell him, "Don't become a trinket on the bangles of these Roman women, and don't become a Roman for the sake of the learning. Remain Musan Deleig."

He also drummed into the now sixteen-year-old he should return home for a visit earlier than twelve months. Deleig certainly paid attention to that counsel. He had not sent any reports to his grandfather and the "governors" because he had realized that the Parthian Empire could not now compete with the strength of the Roman Empire. He needed to tell the royal officials in person to put aside their claims to Armenia, to the north of Parthia, or they would end up in a war with Rome they could not win.

Before the six-month mark, therefore, he, Myrmid and the twins, Remus and Romulus, set off for Hatra. Deleig's two Parthian servants, who wanted to return permanently, were with them. Deleig agreed they'd never adjust to Rome, nor learn the language.

At the Euphrates' western edge, as close as the *cursus publicus* would get to Parthia, the party hired a ferry to take them across the river to Dura-Europos, where they stayed with Deleig's grandparents before riding to Hatra.

As Remus told his grandparents later, "The royal treatment, servants bowing their heads to the ground each time we approached, meeting every demand, was becoming a way of life." Added Romulus, "We had to leave just as we were getting to like it."

Deleig's meeting with the royal officials was not a success. They chose not to believe his report. So, he formally resigned as the Parthia Empire's spy in Rome, not that he had been undertaking any espionage on its behalf so focused was he on his studies.

Back in Rome, Deleig returned to his previous pace, but now his Janiculum villa was almost finished. He rode up to see it, up the brand new paved road carved into its side. More cautious than previously, he had Myrmid travel to the Janiculum's summit by its rough eastern-side path. He wanted Myrmid, with his Parthian bow-and-arrow, quietly secreted on high—in case of what, Deleig didn't know. At least he was heeding Myrmid's warnings.

The contractor welcomed Deleig somewhat sulkily, "It's about time you came."

Deleig, as someone paying on time and paying well—and just returned from Hatra where his place in noble society had refurbished his sense of rank—was in no mood for arrogance from a contractor, no matter how skilled.

"Are you this arrogant with all your clients, or is this insolent tone reserved for me?" Deleig asked.

Four nearby workers stopped what they were doing to see how this would play out. They knew their boss was short-tempered even if Deleig did not.

The contractor's head jerked up toward Deleig as he slid from his horse.

"Young pup, who do you think you are, an Easterner with money, to speak like that to your elders?"

"Elder but not better, and watch your tone. I've come to pay the rest of the bill. One more word and I'll kick you and your men off my property and get someone else to finish the villa."

Deleig, watchful, from the corner of his eye saw the worker nearest him close his fist and take a step forward. Oh not again, Deleig thought, spun, kicked the worker unconscious with a blow to the side of his head. He swung further and kicked the contractor's feet from under him and placed his boot across the man's throat.

One worker raised his shovel high, one hand at the handle, the other halfway up the shaft. He screamed as an arrow fastened that hand to the shaft. The two remaining workers on the scene turned and saw Myrmid near the middle cistern, his bow ready. Perhaps they'd heard of Parthian marksmanship because they remained rooted to where they were as their colleague urged them to pull the arrow from his hand.

"I'll let you up," said Deleig, easing his boot off the contractor's throat. "You will leave my property. Here's your payment in full. You will be known forever as 'the villa builder who didn't finish the Janiculum villa,' and this will be known as the unfinished villa."

Deleig dropped a small leather sack of gold coins on the man's chest, walked over to the screaming man and broke Myrmid's arrow as the easiest way to pull the man's hand free.

"Get out, all of you. Are there any more inside?"

"Four," said one worker.

"Get them and be gone." To the contractor he said, "You've ruined yourself. Send a cart tomorrow to collect whatever tools and materials are still here."

The contractor, shocked at what had transpired in only minutes, was speechless. Dumbfounded, he nodded and motioned to his men. All nine of them set off down the road.

Deleig did not feel jubilant. That had not gone well. He swung back up on his horse. He now, potentially, had the entire artisan class of Rome as an enemy. That would have to be repaired before it festered.

He signaled to Myrmid. Myrmid swung up behind him and the two of them returned to the city, passing the contracting crew on the way down.

At the villa, Deleig called for wine and food. Because Deleig's two Parthian servants had returned home, unable to adjust to living in Rome, Myrmid had hired an Egyptian couple, man and wife. They were still learning to cope with the villa, aware that soon enough they would be working at the Janiculum residence—provided Deleig approved of them. The idea of living outside the city suited them; consequently they were striving hard to please this prince and improve their Aramaic.

Myrmid and Deleig conversed freely in front of them. Both servants had been warned that if they ever repeated a single word of what they heard in the household, they would not only be dismissed, they would be seriously punished.

Therefore, Deleig was quite comfortable saying to Myrmid, as the servants served the wine and placed platters of food on small tables nearby, "Myrmid, would you find out where this contractor lives? I need to see him. This situation cannot be allowed to fester."

Just then, Myrmid saw one of the servants signal him as needed elsewhere. He nodded to Deleig and left the room. A moment later, he returned.

"No need to find out where the contractor lives, he's standing outside asking to see you."

Deleig told a servant, "Bring the man in, and bring an additional wine cup and platter, please."

Myrmid looked at Deleig with a curious expression, as if to ask, now what's he planning? Deleig merely smiled. They could hear much exchange of words in the corridor leading to the room, but silence when the footsteps drew near. The servant appeared with the contractor.

The man had freshly bathed, was dressed in his best tunic, his unruly hair plastered, his red-rimmed eyes scanning the room with uncertainty. His face had lost its color—he was anxious. Hesitantly, he stepped a little way into the room and made a slight bow.

He said nothing, waiting, apparently, for permission to speak. Deleig had never seen a confident man so thoroughly drained of personality.

As the servants entered behind the contractor with a platter and wine cup, Deleig said to the new arrival, "Sit down there," he pointed to a divan opposite him and Myrmid, "and join us."

"I cannot, Your Highness," said the man, who looked at the platter as if it were the final meal for a condemned man.

"You must," said Deleig. "Otherwise we cannot eat. It would not be polite. Please join us."

Embarrassed and awkward, socially out of his depth, he sat down. A servant moved a small table closer to him and filled his wine cup. It took quite some courage, Deleig thought, as the man raised his cup.

"To your continued good health, Your Excellency, and you, sir," the man added, including Myrmid.

They reciprocated with a slight gesture of their wine cups, as Deleig said, "And yours. Now tell me what happened this morning, once you've told me your name—if I've heard it, I've forgotten it."

"Brutus Netta, Your Highness," he replied, searching for some appropriate appellation for a man he'd recently learned was a Parthian prince—from his own wife. The man went silent. He appeared to be gathering his thoughts.

"I had written to you—actually my wife had done the writing—three times inviting you to visit your villa. My wife had each time prepared a table, she's an excellent cook and I had fine wine. My uncle has an excellent vineyard, Gauaranum."

"Excellent indeed," said Deleig, appreciatively. "You've just been served some."

"I noticed, sir. Not once did you arrive, Your Highness. My wife was saddened, lest you think her food was inferior to your standards and that was why you had not come."

Brutus was sweating a little, nervous, but holding himself together without taking another sip of wine. So, said Deleig to himself, he was concerned for his wife's feelings.

"But how did that deteriorate into what occurred this morning, something that could have led to me being very seriously injured and you being seriously prosecuted, if not executed?" The latter was not quite an exaggeration and in any case, had the required effect of maintaining the gravity of the incident. "You were rude, arrogant, when I arrived this morning. I was there to pay you. Until two days ago I was not in this country—I was home in Parthia. I knew nothing of the invitations. I was gone for seven weeks."

The builder was now more shocked than crestfallen. He stood.

"Sir, Your Excellency, I am deeply, regrettably, sorry. I am here to return your last payment and to offer to finish your villa at my expense. Most of all, if you will not permit me to finish it, I would at least—it matters deeply, to me, and my wife—beg you to accept my apology."

Deleig leaned back into his divan and fed a couple of nuts into his mouth with two fingers. He said, after he chewed them, "Please do sit down. I am sorry your wife was unnecessarily upset. That is most grievous. Amends must be made. How is your worker's hand?"

"It will heal. One bone is broken in it, he was fortunate. Painful. We had to carry him home, Excellency." Brutus the contractor looked at Myrmid and said, "That was a true marksman's shot, sir. I hadn't realized what the phrase 'Parthian shot' actually meant until I thought about it later."

Myrmid, still stone-faced, nodded acknowledgment.

Deleig continued, "I recall you told me when first we met you built a large house for your family and your parents and grandmother on the outskirts of the Suburra."

"Yes, Excellency," his voice taking on a slightly more hopeful note.

"And there is a little land?"

"A quarter hectare, slightly more, sir."

"Would you ask your wife if she would accept an apology from Myrmid and me for thrice missing a chance to enjoy her cooking, and would she graciously, for a fourth time, cook and cater and invite us again to dine, to an outdoor gathering of your entire family. Children?"

"Three sir, fourteen, twelve, ten. Boy, girl, girl."

"They would be present also?"

"Yes, if you wished, Excellency, my wife would be pleased—and my father and I would be honored."

"In that case we shall be honored to attend. We hope all your extended family will be there. And I would be grateful if you would keep the final payment and complete the work on the villa."

"Honored, Your Excellency."

"Fine, now sit back, have a sip of wine, some of our Parthian food, and tell me how—architecturally—you managed to slightly cantilever the leading edge of the balcony with the balustrade over the western wall of the villa."

"Metal girders, Your Excellency," said Brutus the contractor, after he'd sipped his wine. He then held Deleig and Myrmid's attention for twenty minutes as he described some of the difficulties overcome in mastering the site.

It was a delighted and slightly dazed Brutus who later left for home. Once he was gone Myrmid gave Deleig a pitying look.

"Was all that really required? Have you no spine?"

"Myrmid, how often do you see your wife and family?"

"Once a year or fifteen months."

"That man sees his wife daily. He is obviously fond of her—you saw his face. He was hurt she felt hurt. She was what, aggrieved, angry? Left raw, that could ruin a family. He cares, Myrmid, he cares about his wife. If she is honored, he can handle the rest."

"I don't understand you, at times, Musan. His men, perhaps he himself, were going to seriously injure you, perhaps kill you!"

"True enough. But they didn't. Thanks to you. Now they won't, nor will anyone in the artisan class of Rome if Brutus hears about it first. I did not say what I said to protect us, but that's the effect, Myrmid. Make no mistake."

Myrmid opened his eyes wide in appreciation and nodded in agreement. Deleig was nothing if not astute.

"Brutus the Builder's stature in his Roman stratum is undoubtedly high. He makes a great deal of money building these unimaginably expensive palaces and villas. 'The villa builder' is secure among his own, and admired. That will continue, a reputation that for a fleeting moment almost disintegrated."

"You're quite right, Musan," Myrmid said, "but someone deserved to be punished."

"One was, severely, and rightly, and all of them were. For many hours today they thought—still think until Brutus returns home—they had permanently lost their livelihood. Tonight I am to dine with Lady Lydia, but within three days or so the two of us will be dining al fresco with Brutus and his extended family in the Suburra. Which do you think will be the more enjoyable entertainment?" Deleig was smiling.

Myrmid asked, quite seriously, "Do you need protection tonight?"

"No, Sejanus is biding his time. He won't plan anything serious for a while. Though it will come, but not in the palace. Go ahead now and buy that building on the Janiculum you want for the guards you intend to hire and train. Eighteen did you say?"

"Yes, but I've increased it to twenty-four."

"Fine."

"Walk me over to the palace tonight, though. To the kitchen door. I need to stay current."

Myrmid nodded, closed his eyes and laid his head back on the divan. Within minutes he was snoring. His bushy eyebrows a single thick black line across his forehead.

Three days later, Myrmid watched Deleig in his element. They were at Brutus the contractor's. His wife had not only filled two tables on the grass with food end-to-end, but had invited the entire extended family—and that included about a dozen children under twelve.

Deleig was doing conjuring tricks, baffling them with rings around his sleeves, a dove under his hat—now flown away over Rome looking for a companion—and clever ways to magically distribute small coins from behind children's ears. Myrmid had seen him in an entertaining mood since he was a boy of six—he hadn't changed much when it came to creating fun.

From his large chair away from the crowd, Myrmid knew what was coming next. A tale from the Monkey with the Flying Carpet series. A promise of a second one—if they were good—before he left for the evening, or before they went to bed.

Done with the children, Deleig would circulate, talking to the women, pulling beautiful silks from his sleeves and dazzling them with flashing eyes. He was an entertainer all right—it was his release. Within, he was driven to succeed.

Myrmid accepted his own limitations as a philosopher—his job was strong man. Yet he saw Deleig struggling to be something, or someone, to satisfy voices from the past. Whereas, left to himself, the man could live in the desert and commune with the isolation, and never feel lonely. Simultaneously an innocent and a savant.

Myrmid signaled for another wine. It was of exceptionally good quality.

NINE

Musan Deleig stood at the western balustrade of the flourishing garden atop his Janiculum Hill villa, scanning the city. He'd recently returned from a visit to Parthia, where he had turned twenty-seven. He had said goodbye to a mother with graying hair and a sister with three children.

His hands rested lightly on the stone parapet. What was he, he asked himself: a chirping talking point for Roman women; an accepted, indeed admired, military historian; a man of wealth beyond the dreams of avarice; in the aggregate, a nothing.

Worse, a bored nothing.

Rome's one-time solid buildings were by now so familiar they were simply extensive rectangles with no flowing lines. Roman men, at the level he circulated, were self-centered careerists uncertain how to pursue further stature, given Emperor Tiberius had moved permanently to Capri, and his former pro-consul, Sejanus, was running the Empire in his absence. And controlling the city.

He gazed because he was trying to avoid thinking depressing thoughts. He preferred to allow his eyes to follow the shadows of two clouds crossing the city. Neither cloud contained rain. Tomorrow it might be different, for this was the extreme tail end of winter, the changeable time.

Like two black footprints, the two clouds, white atop cast shadows below that stepped from one building's roof to the next, coursing over the roofs, curving over the domes, and sliding down the building's side and up the side of the next one.

He stood turned away from the city and surveyed his extensive roof garden. It was, as always, a means of finding tranquility. The garden induced nostalgia, for the garden setting was entirely Eastern in concept and execution, even down to the entire roof also serving as a cistern for the precious rainwater. Beyond nostalgia, it was beautiful in and of itself.

Solemnly, Deleig turned back to continue to look at the city which was also the Empire, an empire in which he took great pride, an empire that he had already served with some minor distinction as a historian and writer.

As he'd told his mother and sister during his recent visit, two things he knew for certain: that he loved Rome and that he would shrivel up and die if he had to spend his entire life on the northern side of the Mediterranean Sea. Desert night, dry cold, the fire, stars, moon, he found essential "in order to breathe mentally."

Then he walked back to his writing table and sat down in his wooden armchair.

Deleig slid a sheet of papyrus from under a carved stone weight, selected a pen, dipped it in the stone inkwell, and was about to write when his servant appeared with a letter on a tray.

My Dearest Musan,

You are returned and I haven't seen you. I haven't seen you for such a long time I've forgotten what you look like.

You must come tonight. Someone you must meet—in order to help me, and possibly yourself. Seven, in the grand aula.

Lydia

That letter suggested it was to be a fairly intimate dinner—three or four dozen people. Small for an imperial palace gathering. That evening, as he arrived, Lady Lydia came bounding toward him. Where, at her age, did she get the energy?

"Musan, I have been asking for you everywhere. Thank heavens you are back. That villa on the Janiculum is magnificent, your roof garden spectacular, but it is not convenient when I need you. There is something you must do for me."

"Anything, Lady Lydia, anything," he said, not realizing—how could anyone—what would result. The effusive Lydia had stood squarely in front of Deleig as if to prevent him from moving until she'd said what she wished to say.

"Our nephew, Pontius Pilatus—I know you know him, or of him—will be the next Prefect of Judea. Isn't that marvelous of Emperor Tiberius? Pilatus wants to be fluent in Aramaic by the time he arrives in Judea, and I said you were just the man to teach him. I am correct, aren't I? Pontius is headed to Capri tomorrow to meet Tiberius."

"I would be honored to teach the Prefect," Deleig told her. "When will it be possible to discuss this with him?" He asked that less than innocently. Could this be worked into an opening to return to the eastern side of the Mediterranean, and close to the desert? "When might he take up his appointment?"

"Five or six months from now," Lydia replied, "but ask Pilatus yourself. I'll get him alone in a few minutes. He's of the equestrian class, grandson of one of Rome's more famous builders—his grandfather engineered—or was it designed—the harbor at Caesarea Maritima. Pontius is back only temporarily from Gaul and the German frontier wars. We intend to hold a welcoming banquet for our returning hero and his wife, Claudia Procula, when they come from Gaul to take up their appointment. They'll live here, of course. I understand all her servants are Greek-speaking—only Greek is spoken in the household for the benefit of the boy. They have a young son."

Deleig said, "I've met her, Lydia, not him. She was here perhaps three years ago with the child."

He recalled that evening as if it were yesterday. Lydia had said to him, "I must say, Prince Musan, when surrounded by the multitudes, everyone seeking a word in my ear, and me looking for an exit, you do provide a gateway to sanity. I've someone I want you to meet."

Lydia had gestured in the direction she arrived from. A young woman was emerging from the dense pack of the crowd into the lesser congestion with a small boy in tow. The woman, his mother, was lithe, energetic, slightly taller than average—and absolutely beautiful. Her black hair she wore loosened slightly, a contrast to most of the other more tightly coiffed women in the aula.

The hairstyle of the day was generally of three types: the hair woven in a double-braid laid across the head close to the forehead, or cropped fairly short with sufficient to be pulled back into a bun decorated with jewels. The third style, where the woman had particularly wavy or curly hair, was to have it cropped fairly short, but still long enough for the curls or waves to be obvious. Claudia, by contrast, had her long black hair caught up from the rear in a manner Deleig found difficult to describe—except that the effect was alluring.

Lydia had said, "Loose hair, loose woman does not apply to Claudia." It was a caution, but he was captivated, and Lydia had witnessed it. "She's quite stylish—she's my cousin within this extended Augustan clan. I'm related to her that way, and through Pontius. Currently he's assigned to Gaul. Fighting. He's good at that."

Lydia had seen his mooning expression and added, "She has morals to match her height."

Deleig knew that Lydia was warning him away. From his earliest days in Rome, Deleig had been enamored of a certain type of Roman woman of the superior class. If widowed they were sometimes independent in their means, as well as their manner. As a rule, these noblewomen, as he thought of them, were slender, seemingly as independent in their learning as their means, intelligent, disciplined and self-assured. He had not experienced that combination of qualities in Parthian women. Yet as a Parthian, it was unlikely he could ever aspire to having a Roman noblewoman for his wife.

At that meeting, he had asked Claudia what the boy's name was.

"Formio. He is five."

"Formosus, surely?"

"It's a pet name. His legal name is Cletus. Formio *sounds* so much better on the tongue than Pontius Cletus Formosus, an old man's name."

She had dark eyes.

"There's an ambivalence to my own name," Deleig had said easily, for he felt comfortable with her. "The only 'Musan' I can trace in my antecedents is a woman, the Parthian Queen Musa." He laughed.

The five-year-old boy was looking up, up, up, so Deleig half knelt to be closer to his face. Deleig asked, "Do I look dark and strange to you amid your Roman friends, young Formio?"

"No, sir, you look very fine indeed. A warrior from the desert, my mother said."

Had she indeed? She had noticed him earlier then. Lydia had stepped away to greet someone, and Deleig was well aware it would not do for him, a single man, to linger long, un-chaperoned, with the young wife of a prominent general.

He had said, "It has been a pleasure to meet you, Madame. You have stolen my heart." He had blushed—he hadn't known he was about to say that. "I am sorry, I am young and foolish, and fairly new to Rome. May I return you to Lydia?"

She had said, half laughing, "Foolish, I doubt, though young? I'd say we are of a like age, or perhaps you have several years on me, sir."

As a diversion to cover his embarrassment, Deleig had asked the boy, "Want to be as tall as me?" He told Formio to hold his arms straight and stiff by his sides, with his hands flexed up at the wrist. Deleig put his hands underneath the boy's and raised him up to his own eye level and then higher to see over his head—all the while Formio kept erect, pushing down on Deleig's hands. It was as if he were levitating. Formio let out a delighted yell.

Dozens of guests in the bustling aula turned to locate the noise. Smiles broke out as they spotted a child peering at them high above their heads. They returned to their talk as Deleig lowered the boy to the floor and turned him toward his departing mother.

"Off you go, Formio," he had said. "I hope we shall meet again."

Now, to Lydia, Deleig said he would commit himself to teaching Pontius with the proviso Pilatus found him congenial—no Carrhae bitterness to deal with.

Lydia said, "Pontius doesn't think in those terms, backward that is. Without wishing to totally ruin your impression of him, there are times when he barely thinks ahead, either."

Four days later the Prefect-to-be arrived from Capri, his appointment to Judea confirmed. He and Deleig met, and Deleig invited the Pilatus family to his villa. Formio, fascinated by the birds and the creatures in the waterways and pools, was in his element.

Looking at Pilatus, Deleig felt he was gazing at the quintessential soldier, not least the quintessential Roman military general of the imagination. The man was of average height and Deleig guessed, now in his early forties. He had a distinguished, not quite gaunt, appearance. His brown eyes were set in a narrow face with a high forehead; an eagle beak of a nose presided over a wide smiling mouth spoiled by very thin lips.

Deleig knew from Claudius this man was a general who lacked what all generals coveted, a really huge battle from which they could emerge victorious—their name linked to it forever in Roman circles, an arch of honor constructed. He had served on several frontiers. One with distinction—though not with sufficient distinction to satisfy his ambitions.

Battling the German tribes on the Gaul frontier had served other ambitious Romans well. Caesar reveled in subduing them. Drusus—Emperor Augustus' stepson—was successful, too, as he waged war along the Elbe and Rhine frontier. When Drusus was killed, Tiberius took his place and succeeded Augustus as Emperor. Pilatus had only relatively briefly succeeded Tiberius in Gaul.

Now, however, Pilatus was condemned to become the essential peacekeeper—the warrior chained to a provincial backwater, Judea.

Conversely, Pilatus was impressed that as a young man Deleig had first-hand knowledge of Judea, had met the Tetrarch, Herod Antipas, and had been to Jericho and Jerusalem. Pilatus knew—probably from Lady Lydia—of Deleig's connection to the late Annius Rufus and of his brief time in Caesarea Maritima.

In turn, Deleig was impressed Pilatus insisted on an intense and rigorous regime for their language instruction and that he intended to achieve a genuine fluency. They decided on a tutorial schedule. That settled, the discussion turned to Deleig's life to-date—and developed into a discussion of Roman law, for both had studied it deeply. Pilatus again was impressed, he said—this time because he realized Deleig in fact possessed a deeper knowledge of Roman jurisprudence than his own.

The following day Pilatus with two guards rode back to Deleig's Janiculum villa for an introduction to Aramaic, but they never actually broached the topic. Rather, they found, as they talked, though slightly wary, they were comfortable with one another. A trust based, Deleig suspected, on Pilatus' acceptance that Deleig—want him or not—was more or less a part of the extended imperial family mix. Deleig, buoyed by that awareness, had decided on a gamble—a gamble on his future.

"Given that I already know something of Judea," he said, trying to sound the innocent, "why not have me travel to the province ahead of you, renew acquaintances and expand my knowledge of—the place, the people and those in power. I could surreptitiously determine the major currents, dangerous trends and the more dangerous people. I would go as a trader, practice as an astrologer, whatever the occasion demands. But I assure you I could gather information for you that no other could achieve. It would be a form of protection for you."

Pilatus asked, "You would then return to Judea with me, wouldn't you?"

Joy of joy, Deleig, who hadn't realized he was an opportunist, had never anticipated this—working for Rome close to the desert. Yet opportunist he was because Pilatus' entreaty was part question, part plea. He decided to press his advantage and nodded agreement.

"In which case," Pilatus continued, "I think your initial idea needs some consolidation. You are familiar, in principle, with spying—how could you not be, this is Rome."

Again, Deleig nodded.

"I shall have an official spy network, the military, of course. Would you consider spying on the spies who spy on me? Those who might hinder my work in Judea, or sully my reputation back in Rome. My private head of espionage? The current Prefect in Judea, Gratus, will offer me his spy network, naturally. But only so that his legionary allies in Judea can report to him once he's back in Rome. In Roman political circles, Musan, information is a form of currency," said Pilatus, somewhat pompously. "Gratus' offer can now be declined with thanks."

Deleig had taken several deep breaths. Now inwardly calm, a rapidly beating heart quieted, he was able to say, in an even tone, "May I expand on that excellent thought? If I am to be the one who keeps a constant watch on the watchers, and the shifting, ebbing and flowing of power and threats to your rule, it would be important that people not immediately know it. Yet it would be important, for me, in effect, to spend some of my time by your side. My suggestion is, if you and she are agreeable, that perhaps I be seen as engaged as your wife's personal astrologer.

"I'm aware that in Rome astrologers are periodically subject to severe punishment—though most Romans consult them. In the eastern Mediterranean, they are commonplace. As such, I would be generally discounted, at least at first, until it became obvious what I was up to—that early misunderstanding on the part of the locals would be to both my advantage and yours."

The expression on Pilatus' face was confirmation enough. His raised eyebrows and his approving eyes said it all. What amused Pilatus, and little did, was the fact that in Rome astrologers, like Jews and philosophers, sometimes fell into disfavor. They'd be banned from the city during a purge triggered by some unsavory incident. Harsh penalties could be meted out.

He mentioned this to Deleig, who said, "And yet, the contradictions. At the highest level of the Roman structure, the *augurs* of the priestly caste are charged with knowing God's intentions and demands; the *pullari* read the future from the behavior of sacred chickens. Those dumbest of birds. *Pullari*. Honored until they get it wrong."

Pilatus laughed.

Deleig continued, "And yet the astrologers never quite disappear, do they? Even banned, they are at the fringes of the Circus Maximus performances, or around the borders of the Field of Mars during military maneuvers and sporting trials. Heavens, Pilatus, soothsayers and astrologers are as much a fixture as prostitutes—though considerably more expensive: a rare instance of future promise outweighing immediate gratification."

The Prefect's laughter was full-throated and genuine. Deleig was never to know it, but it was that brief sortie into Rome's contradictions, that single snatch of conversation, that tipped Pilatus toward Deleig as someone he needed, someone with soldier talk—straightforward, with a twist of humor. Pilatus regretted he was not himself capable of humor.

Pilatus, however, switched topics and moved in for a kill—in case a killing was required.

"You have no designs on my wife, I hope. She is more your age than mine."

What a childish statement to make, but how perceptive, thought a worried Deleig. Did it show in his face? Lydia had noticed.

"Sir," said Deleig, "would you like to reconsider that question? It is insulting. To the lady, and myself."

Pilatus accepted he had misspoken and apologized. Deleig had been alerted to steer clear of entanglements just as he was hoping entanglements were a possibility. Deleig wondered about the age gap, possibly two decades between her and Pilatus—didn't she feel she was married to an old man? But he would discover the following evening, listening to her and watching her interactions with her husband, that not only did Claudia appear to be in love with her husband, but their relationship appeared companionable.

Now, Pilatus was saying "... When I tell my wife about this, there is little doubt she will enjoy the astrologer subterfuge—she might even ask you about astrology. Do you know anything about it?"

"Oh yes," Deleig said. "And soothsaying and conjuring. I don't believe in any of it, but as entertainments I don't mind them."

"Talented indeed," said Pilatus, nodded to his two guards to retrieve their mounts and left to return to the city.

Moodily, Deleig, from his balustrade, watched Pilatus and his two guards canter toward the Tiber. O Ahura Mazda, he said, how could you allow me such a dilemma?

Thinking back to his conversation with Pilatus, Deleig wondered if the association would make him more or less suspect, the unwelcome Parthian. He guessed, accurately, that he'd soon find out. He did—Pilatus was having him watched.

Deleig knew he was mistrusted or hated by some in Rome. One prominent Roman, Tullius, took against him and had started to lobby in the Senate and Forum to have Deleig removed from Rome's service before he even began. Tullius saw Deleig as an enemy spy.

Deleig decided to send a shot across Tullius' bow. He gave his operatives a question to ask in the villa kitchens across the city, a question that could never be traced back to him. A first-class untraceable rumor starts as a question, and hangs there. It is the question—"Is it true that …?"—that turns into the eventual statement. Was it true that Tullius had said at a banquet that Emperor Tiberius might as well stay in Capri forever and leave the ruling of Rome to the Senate? That was a whiff of Republicanism.

Innocent servants visiting the kitchen heard it as part of the gossip as they told of their own day. Some servants carried it back with them, and those few who were close to their masters or mistresses repeated the by-that-time embroidered rumor, as always happens, as a statement.

Sooner or later the information was circulating around the palace, in the Senate and as common gossip in the Forum. Rumors float on wind. This one floated across the waters to Capri.

Tullius was lucky to escape with his life. The indictment was multi-layered, Tullius' denials vociferous. He forfeited two of his estates and that was the end of it, as far at Capri was concerned. Deleig wrote to Tullius, commiserating with his rapid downfall. Tullius then knew what had happened. Tullius' circles would be much more circumspect where Deleig's reputation was concerned.

Three weeks later, after Aramaic tutelage every other day, Deleig handed Pilatus over to two other Aramaic speakers for conversation practice. Deleig was leaving for Parthia, he had informed the Prefect, and would return to Rome through Judea as he wanted to renew an old acquaintance.

TEN

Vasas' compound in Jerusalem was everything he needed in a hiding place, Deleig thought. And he'd made a promising start in setting up his personal spy network—in advance of moving to Judea as part of Pilatus' retinue.

His meeting with the high-stakes gambler, Talca the Saka, had boded well. Talca seemed to have an intelligence equal to his own. Now to ascertain his loyalty. Complete, unquestioned loyalty was vital in a second-in-command, a second-in-command about whom Rome would know nothing.

Deleig had taken an exploratory trip outside Vasas' compound, up the alley into the market square and back, simply to orient himself. He banged on the wooden door for readmission, crossed the courtyard and ascended the stone stairs. Vasas was not yet at the table by the edge of this most pleasant roof garden. Deleig sat there and stared over the edge of the wall. The world below the rooftop was totally clogged with humanity and its beasts.

After a while, Vasas joined him. Deleig spent a pleasant half-hour chatting. He drank a little wine, talked and leaned against the parapet, chin on elbows, gazing down, hoping to spot Talca. Then he saw Morden with Talca three steps behind. Morden whistled. The wooden gate opened quickly and then re-bolted and barred.

Morden guided Talca toward the flight of stone steps to the roof garden. Deleig and Vasas stood, waiting. Talca was introduced formally to Deleig as His Royal Highness Prince Musan Deleig of Parthia, and to Vasas as his host for the afternoon.

Obliged to sit down, Talca accepted the situation and was not uncomfortable in Deleig's company, nodding thanks for wine, certain it would be of good quality. He studied the prince for a moment, knowing on the basis of their exchange through the curtain that he was a knowledgeable and straightforward man to deal with. As his own life might be on the line, he felt he could deal with him almost as an equal.

Talca rhetorically asked Deleig, "How will we know, sir, that none of the men we hire as spies will betray us to the people they're spying on? My answer is we don't—and I am bound to say that and ask other questions."

"Ask away, Talca," said Deleig.

"How will you know which of the servants in the Caesarea Maritima palace and compound are spying on you?"

Vasas gave a tight-lipped grin. He was enjoying this.

"Talca, I leave soon and will return in four months. In that time reflect on this: you tell me, not me tell you, how to detect who among the staff in the Roman compound is a spy for High Priest Caiaphas down in Jerusalem. He is most likely to have people reporting to him on the Roman Prefect's activities. Who else is spying on Prefect Pilatus—the Tetrarch, Herod Antipas? Then, how do you, or we, determine among the half-legion of Roman soldiers in Judea who is loyal to the new Prefect—as distinct from those loyal to the previous Prefect?"

Talca listened intently, absorbing it all, as Deleig concluded, "Finally, who is reporting to whom in Rome, and who to the Emperor in Capri?"

Talca said, "Rooting out Caiaphas' people in the Roman compound isn't spying, sir, that's preventive."

"Correct," said Deleig. "Not espionage but counter-espionage. But now step to the other side—who and how do you recruit people as spies who are loyal to you? Loyal to you personally and me as a matter of course—and necessity. I'm the paymaster.

"How do you do that inside Caiaphas' circle of senior priests in the Temple? And among the scribes, the Temple's legal scholars? How do we get inside the official judicial council, the Sanhedrin? And what about the Pharisees, those synagogue leaders who are fixated on the Law and keep a tight rein on their liturgy and ritual? It is in these groups that the potential for being betrayed is greatest. How do we know any contact we have inside these groups—even if they are on the payroll—won't betray us?

"Then, groupings of Zealots, messiahs, high-profile healers, magical sorts and rabble-rousers—how are they penetrated?"

"Zealots we cannot infiltrate, or annihilate," Talca said. "Messianic upstarts are easy: place people in the throng of followers with instructions to ingratiate themselves toward the center. The same is true for the crowd around healers. Rabble-rousers just have to be suppressed."

"Correct," said Deleig. "Then, Talca, how do you, I, we keep track of all the information that confronts us?"

Vasas looked at Talca. "You can't memorize it all, can you?"

Talca said nothing for quite a while. Then he smiled, a broad smile. He stood up and said to Deleig, "May I take your hand, sir, for a moment."

Deleig held out his hand. Talca grasped his arm, so Deleig grasped his.

"Congratulations, sir," said Talca and sat back down. "Now I know why you hunted for someone like me. Then hired me!"

His eyes were bright with amusement, and he locked them on Deleig's. Deleig, equally delighted, said, "Good."

Vasas wonderingly looked first at one, then the other. He felt he was missing something. Then he said to Talca, "I think I just realized what happened, yet I'm not certain."

But Talca said to Vasas, "Not until you looked at me, sir, and asked your question, did you make everything fall into place."

Deleig said, "We'll explain to Vasas—that way he will know whether he is correct or not. I wanted a gambler—that is, a highly successful gambler who plays to exercise the skill as much as to win the money. A gambler has to be able to read his opponents while reading the gaming board. Their faces, their demeanor, their reactions, their strategies. All the while, planning his own ever-changing gaming strategy and adapting his tactics accordingly—tracking dice-play-by-dice-play, every board move, non-move or potential move, to advance his purpose."

"And not let his demeanor or reactions be detected," continued Talca. "All the while, absorbing, monitoring and making decisions on everyone else's dice-play-by-dice-play and subsequent moves."

"Who better as a spy?" said Deleig.

Vasas laughed, slapped his knee and said, "I knew it was something like that. I just couldn't have put it into words."

Addressing Deleig, Talca said, "But we've not answered the question yet about keeping track of the information. And, Your Highness Prince—"

"Stop a moment, Talca."

Talca was quiet.

"As long as you never forget our relationship, you are to call me Musan, and call Vasas whatever he chooses?"

Vasas said, "Vasas."

"Now continue."

"You have not told me how you'll recruit your most important listeners and informers."

"True enough, Talca. I probably won't," Deleig said. No one must know of his planned soothsaying expeditions—his access through kitchens. His starting point would be the chief cook at the Caesarea Maritima palace.

"To answer Vasas' question," Deleig said. "Every one of our employees must be literate. Must write a daily report in Aramaic no matter how uneventful."

"Yes, I see," said Talca.

"You will be in charge of gathering all these reports in one place—coordinating them. We must develop categories and appoint a head of each category; he will selects his team from the spies. Someone, or several, must daily read every piece of information from every other category—and fit that into a coordinated report. Interlocking directorates is the only way we can know what is happening everywhere, all the time."

"Talca, think on these things for four months. Find yourself accommodation in Caesarea Maritima and keep yours in Jerusalem. Morden will be your paymaster for expenses on my behalf. I have given you sufficient pay for a year or so. You will know when I have returned—there'll be a ceremonial change of command in Caesarea Maritima as Prefect Pontius Pilatus takes command. Deliver a note to the palace the day after to say you are standing at the gate there."

Talca understood he was being dismissed. He thanked his host, bowed to Deleig and left. Vasas said he hadn't enjoyed himself so much in years. Later that same day, Deleig left—bound for Rome.

ELEVEN

Weeks later, as he relaxed in his own rooftop garden, seated at his stone table, writing, Deleig decided on something out of character. He looked at the word he'd written: "Reception." Yes, he would have a reception for Pilatus six weeks hence, both honoring the Prefect's appointment and signaling their departure for Judea four weeks later.

Deleig had been surprised by Pilatus' dedication to learning Aramaic. He was approaching a degree of fluency and would soon be able to conduct official business in the language. The Prefect-to-be was well aware that in Judea, Greek was still the language of the upper classes and official classes, and that in their everyday conversation many Judeans flowed between Aramaic and Greek.

Deleig looked at the word "Reception" on the papyrus on his table. Claudius was the answer. He'd ride over and ask Claudius whom he should invite. Should he invite Sejanus? He and Myrmid saddled up and rode down the hill to the city.

An hour later Claudius answered the Sejanus question directly. "Emperor Tiberius has decamped permanently to Capri. He's growing rhubarb and experimenting with a crop of new plants and a crop, it is said, of new young men. Not simultaneously. The latter may be Sejanus-planted malicious gossip. The man is without morals or decency himself. However, Sejanus is the power in Rome, polishing his image as future Emperor. For a Prefect's official send-off you'd have to invite Sejanus, unless you deliberately want to snub him. Not an action I'd recommend. So who else?"

"I'm certainly hoping you and Aelia will attend—"

"We shall if invited—"

"You're invited. The twins and Lady Lydia. I'll have a carriage for her and a sedan chair to take her up to the rooftop garden—"

"Makes sense—"

"Massurius Sabinus—must have my most important tutor and his wife. My first tutor, Delcas. Pilatus, his wife and son—I'll ask them for four or six names. Brutus, who built the villa, deserves to be introduced. I'm thinking of having his wife, Prosperina, cater—good solid Roman workers' fare. Eighteen or twenty people—"

"Suburra cooking—I'll send up plenty of my best Falernian ... given the Suburra is just below the Carinae, where most of the senatorial class live, it might be wisdom to include two or three favored senators and spouses. You need suggestions?"

"Thank you, I'll suggest three names and you react to those," said Deleig. "Early afternoon to mid-evening, I thought."

"Daylight hours. Most people will blanch a little at your mountain road; so let them know in your invitation about the hill climb. Looks like you're set. What next?" Claudius asked.

"Want to ride with me to the edge of the Suburra to see Prosperina, Brutus the contractor's wife?"

"Love to. Give me twenty minutes to organize the stables for a mount. Sammid!"

They were slow to leave, standing talking to others headed in and out of the palace. They were not at the Suburra's edge, and Brutus' domicile, until well over an hour later. It was that sort of lazy, sunny day and they were making the most of being unhurried.

Prosperina, at a neighbor's, was sent for and was so taken by surprise she arrived blinking wildly at her two visitors. They were invited into the spacious main room and declined food and drink as Deleig explained his purpose. Prosperina admitted she'd never catered for anyone but the family, but liked the idea very much.

Deleig asked her to work out all the details and send a note to Myrmid. Deleig did a conjuring thing with his hand and pulled from his sleeve a silk scarf. He said, "There is something inside to cover all costs. Please do not look until we've left." They took their leave and returned to Claudius' area of the palace. There was a gold *aureus* in the silk scarf, enough for a dozen banquets.

The planning went smoothly until four days before the reception. Prosperina's nephew was in the Praetorian Guard. It was an important and prestigious post for a young Roman selected from the army ranks. He had no desire to jeopardize it. But he had been told he was one of two dozen guards who, wearing their ordinary clothes, were to stealthily attack a villa on the Janiculum Hill and wreck the inside and roof garden, disguising it as the work of robbers. He knew it was the place to which his aunt was traveling daily as she prepared to cater a reception.

Brutus rode to the villa to give Deleig the news, asking for complete anonymity for his nephew—which Deleig assured him was guaranteed. After thanking him for the information, Deleig told Brutus to tell his nephew that on that night, as the guards approached the curve in the road with a low wall at its right edge, he must be on the opposite side, close to the rock face. And if he heard water, to get behind a rock or to a higher level than the road.

The night came. Blackness. No moon. Sejanus had selected the night with care. Deleig knew his own two dozen guards, under Myrmid's command, were strategically stationed all over the Janiculum. The attackers would come by road, but his guards were strategically placed all around to hill to prevent surprises. Deleig himself would sound the alarm. He hoped.

It was an hour after midnight. He was at the rear of the villa. Earlier he'd been able to detect faint lights in the city, but the night was ominously murky; everything felt clammy. From the balustrade he was looking at the top of the light mist that blanketed the Tiber—though he could see neither Rome nor the Tiber. He simply knew both were there.

He was apprehensive. He hadn't felt like this since the night he thought Fefeel was about to throw him off the Dura palace roof into the river. Not remembering, as sleepy as he was, that the Euphrates was a quarter mile from the palace.

This night, as he made his way down the exterior stairs to the rough and rocky surface of the hill, he smiled at the reminiscence. His mood lightened. He looked again up into the mist layer above him and felt immediately wrapped in a blanket of vulnerability. Deleig wasn't cold, but he gave an involuntary shiver. The action jerked him out of his despond. He didn't want anyone dead, but it would happen. He'd get through this. Confidence returned. What had just gone wrong with him? He didn't know. It was over. It was a matter of waiting. He was good at that. He allowed himself a slight smile.

Though he knew he could not be seen, he stooped as he made his way through brush, gorse and small bushes to the slight promontory on the hill above the curve at the top of the road. It was a lookout. He could lay flat above and opposite the curve in the waist-high wall. The wall itself ran from the villa's courtyard around the tightly sweeping bend and stopped abruptly just below the promontory on which Deleig lay. Where the wall ended, the cliff-edge was exposed the rest of the way down the Janiculum.

Peering into mist-shrouded darkness was tiring to the eyes. His ears picked up a slushing sound, like wood being dragged over gravel. The soldiers were approaching and deliberately not marching in step. Deleig could now detect a long darker smudge making its way through blackness up the Janiculum. He blinked. A voice nearby whispered, "Guard here, sir. Men have long since crossed the Tiber for the Janiculum."

Myrmid's system was working. That meant it would always work. Deleig decided that once he left for Judea, he'd ask S'veyda to reside permanently in the villa until his return. S'veyda would do that—it would be useful for entertaining the Silk Road and Roman traders he dealt with. He, too, would have the guards.

The next signal would not be a guard's voice, but the sound of a small tree crashing down. It had already been loosened at the roots. All on watch knew where the tree was. It would be tipped over the moment the Praetorian guards were within a dozen yards of the start of the wall on the curve. All ears would then be attuned for Deleig's voice.

The crunch of the falling tree as it brushed against bushes and growth was muted by the mist. Discernible, though, to those listening for it. Deleig was now at the very edge of the promontory. He leaned over and could see darker shapes within the darkness. The first couple of lines of guards—seemingly four men across—were passing below him. Six rows of soldiers walked by, and as the last row passed, Deleig shouted, "Now! Now!"

The cry was picked up by his own guards so it would reach Myrmid and two others with sledgehammers on the roof of the lowest cistern. They pounded the segmented concrete door holding back the water. Cracks spread and the first spouting rush of water did the rest—a six-foot-high wall of water cascaded out of the cistern. The wave-like roar of the water seemed unearthly, out of place, a noise that shattered the calm imposed by the mist. There was a tumbling sound of concrete chunks sliding down the road.

More hammering and the tidal wave was backed by a second deluge as the three men smashed the second cistern's frontal slab to create a six-foot-high wave that gushed down the slope of the courtyard that led into the roadway.

This tidal wave caught the first two or three lines of Sejanus' guards, who screamed and cried a water-borne cacophony as they were knocked off their feet, smashed into the low walls or jettisoned over the side of the hill. Two men were carried at speed even lower down the road.

Deleig issued no further orders. His silence meant everyone was to gather in the courtyard. What no one had anticipated was a Praetorian guard carrying an injured comrade up the roadway to the villa for attention. Deleig ordered the injured to be attended to and any bodies on the hillside brought up to the roadway. Barely fifteen minutes later it was obvious more than half the attackers had been killed by being jettisoned off the hill onto the rocks. Deleig felt sick but unrepentant.

Two days later, on a warm, sunny afternoon, the first of the three carriages Deleig had hired to carry his guests from the city to his home made its way slowly up the incline. It bore Lady Lydia, Remus and Romulus. There was a sedan chair waiting to carry the elderly Lydia to the roof garden. Deleig walked alongside it in order to point out and describe his roof garden's wonders. He was frankly impressed each time he stepped into it, the gardeners' craft at its best. He gave Lydia seeds to throw to the peacocks.

The eastern side of the garden was given over to tables of food and drink, with divans and wicker chairs in abundance. Invariably, however, visitors were drawn to the balustrade so they could look out across to the city.

Claudius arrived on horseback, dismounted as a servant took his mount and bounded up the steps. The dancing lessons were beginning to take effect.

Twenty minutes later, Deleig was back down in the courtyard waiting as Sejanus arrived on a fine Arabian. As an attendant took the reins, Sejanus slid off his mount and greeted Deleig, "The cistern was clever. You'd thought out your defenses before you built your villa."

Before replying, Deleig studied Aelius Sejanus. He'd never previously appraised the man. What was he? Early fifties, medium height, broad-shouldered, confident but no swagger. Not a large head, but broad of brow, moving to a slightly triangular formation toward his chin. Large nose, full lips, rounded chin. Appealing to women? Likely, given the advantage of an officer's uniform.

Deleig said, without emotion, "My hill was your Carrhae. You lost half your men. Killed them. You planned like Crassus—

underestimated your Parthian prey. But why do you persist in this enemy nonsense? Over ten years ago you were determined to injure me, perhaps kill me. Two nights ago, you attempted to wreck my home and ruin my reception. And lost more men. You lost what—thirteen men to add to the original two? You are a quiet laughing stock in the city. In all this time, Sejanus, I have never spoken a word against you, nor done anything to impede your aims or rule. Why, Sejanus? Why this? Why now? After so many years?"

"I'm not sure. To punish you before you left for the pain you inflicted?—"

"You intended to kill me—"

"No, just break an arrogant arm or leg—"

"So how many Praetorian arms and legs did I break?—"

"I still think the cistern idea borders on the brilliant, and that inoffensive defensive short stretch of wall ... a weapon well-planned, I admire that—"

"I have no interest in your admiration, only your reasoning—you should be required to wear a muzzle. You're either rabid or mad—"

"You obviously love your Janiculum hideout. I thought it would be good to hit you in your hole, so to speak, to punish you a little before you left for Judea. I may not see you again—"

"Definitely not. I'll be in Judea for six or seven years, apart from mandatory visits to Rome, and you'll be dead within five—"

"Before I become Emperor?—"

"Before, Sejanus, Emperor Tiberius dies—"

"He made you a Roman citizen I hear—"

"The greatest honor in my life—"

"Special pleading on your behalf, Deleig, by Lady Lydia and Massurius Sabinus, I gather—"

"Quite likely, I was not party nor privy to it—"

"I understand you have some excellent busts here of Julius Caesar, Augustus, Agrippa and others. I would like to see them—"

"You may not. You were invited, Sejanus, without my realizing you would use the invitation as an opportunity to attack me—"

"You are wrong to cross me, Deleig, I am very powerful. With Tiberius in Capri, I rule Rome—"

"And quite well, I gather. I know you are powerful. I am not afraid of you now, and was not a decade ago. You wear your ambition like a toga for all to see. And all see it—"

"And you are not ambitious?—"

"Aelius, please. Ambitious—nursemaid to a Prefect in a provincial backwater? Really. I'd be grateful if you'd remount and leave."

Musan Deleig flicked a finger for the attendant to walk Sejanus' mount back to him. Deleig really did admire Sejanus' poise, but it would be a shame to admit it as it would please the man enormously. He had not realized Claudius was standing watching the exchange. Their eyes met. Claudius nodded.

Aelius Sejanus mounted, looked at Deleig, smiled slightly, swung his horse around and left.

For the next two hours, Deleig played delighted host. He introduced his guests to his balcony-length aviary of finches and the various fish and mammals in his pools and streams. He explained why certain plants were chosen for the pergolas and described how his writing desk moved around with the seasons—lifted by four strong men. And told funny stories about adventures in Parthia as a boy.

The grand room in which they were now standing contained frescoes and a selection of busts, statuary and other minor displays along three walls. The frescoes depicted his family and family life in Parthia. One showed the boy Deleig with his grandfather and father battling a sandstorm. A second depicted the chaos of a desert expedition party surprised by a desert sinkhole. There was a particularly fanciful rendering of the family oasis at El Qassassin. The fine, extended fresco of Rome's cityscape was already out-of-date—one or two features of the ever-evolving city had changed.

The busts and statues, in marble and cast bronze, were of those he admired, or had known and liked. The most prominent were of Julius Caesar, Octavian and the late Annius Rufus. The two Parthians he most admired, his mother and paternal grandfather, were memorialized in the frescoes.

The fourth wall had only two busts. One, on a plinth opposite the interior staircase to the roof, was of Marcus Vipsanius Agrippa, a tidy man with a tidy mind—Deleig's assessment of Octavian's companion in battle and triumphs. Deleig admired Agrippa for his maps. The second, in the corner, was Maecenas, a man of great wealth who knew what money was for, and of great skill, for Emperor Augustus appointed him to administer the complex city of Rome, and tumultuous Italy itself.

"Agrippa," said Deleig, "tidied up the known world, reduced it to something one could look at and examine. He was acting on

Augustus' instructions—mapping surveys throughout the Empire in those regions where none had been carried out. This remarkable person then combined those with existing surveys to produce the famed circular map engraved on marble at the Porticus Vipsania near the Via Flaminia.

"I admire Maecenas for his skill as an administrator of something smaller than the Empire, smaller and in some ways more complex: the city-state that is the Rome on the Tiber, and Italy."

To his surprise, that remark brought Deleig a smattering of applause. Others felt as he did.

"Regarding Agrippa, among his many maps—and I have copies of most of them, executed on papyrus, parchment, wood and marble—I particularly treasure his engraved-on-wood schematic of the Empire's system of 50,000 miles of roads. Those roads and this schematic—it's twenty-two feet long—give credence to the Roman's self-flattering phrase, 'all roads lead to Rome.' "

In his early writing and talks, Deleig never mentioned the fact that Rome's initial impetus for its military highway-laying came from witnessing the utility of Parthia's own extensive—though not as well constructed—road system.

He invited his guests to dine. As late afternoon set in, Deleig introduced the builder, Brutus, and his wife, Prosperina, the caterer. Prosperina's tables of refreshments had brought praise, and Lydia now had a means of contacting her as she had taken a fancy to Suburra-style catering and intended to use it herself. Prosperina was delighted.

To conclude, Deleig brought Pontius to the fore and made a short speech regarding their future together. They toasted Pontius, wishing health to his family and success to his prefectureship. Deleig's friends had enjoyed themselves. He ordered their carriages. A most successful event.

Pilatus, Claudia and Formio did not leave immediately with the others. Pilatus had asked for a more detailed explanation of Deleig's collection—with the emphasis on Augustus' impact on future emperors.

While Deleig obliged, Claudia was happily spending time with Prosperina, recalling foods from her own childhood summers in Tuscany. Formio, meanwhile, was satisfied simply trailing around behind Deleig, listening.

As they eventually headed for their carriage, Deleig said to the little family, "Thank you for coming, it was a pleasant occasion. It'll be many a year before we gather here again." He turned to Formio and added, "And you'll probably be a man and no longer a boy."

The boy, eyes appealingly glistening, replied, "I won't mind that if you are my friend."

"Don't be presumptuous," Pilatus told his son. "The prince is an important, high-ranking person with a busy life."

The boy, chastened, dropped his head down.

Pilatus turned to Deleig, "The farewell reception was a kindness, Musan. Thank you. Thoroughly enjoyable."

Deleig bowed to Claudia. As Pilatus climbed into the carriage following his wife, Deleig tapped Formio on the shoulder and, as the boy turned, gave him a wink to signal all was well.

TWELVE

It was late in the afternoon of Deleig's first full day in the province as spymaster. He had spacious quarters, and in the section he'd designated as his official meeting place and work station, he was seated and had picked up a pen.

My dear friend Vasas,

Three weeks ago I left Rome with a general. Two days ago I arrived in Judea with a pompous hyena that shouted, brayed and barked. The rapid rise from equestrian to royalty began with his first step aboard the quinquereme *in Ostia for, unfortunately, he was the highest ranker aboard.*

The arrival in Caesarea Maritima, late morning on a glorious day, allowed the departing Prefect, Valerius Gratus, to order the ship into a fast turnaround so he could depart quickly for Rome. A military fanfare had been summoned there for Gratus' farewell rather than Pilatus' arrival, but Pilatus assumed he was worthy of a military fanfare fit for an emperor, accepting all the bowing and scraping half a legion in full regalia can manage at short notice while Gratus' goods were being loaded onto the vessel not five hundred yards away.

What am I learning about my newly trodden place? Temple senior priests tend to keep the role within their aristocratic family. It is not an exaggeration to say the High Priest is both the leader of Judean society and the leader of the religion, as practiced in the Temple. When the current High Priest, Caiaphas, succeeded his father-in-law, Annas, it cost Caiaphas a considerable amount of money to acquire his prestigious appointment, money paid to the Prefect, the departing Gratus. I was not surprised to learn, therefore, that Prefect Gratus changed the High Priest three times and was going home wealthy.

Please quickly come to visit me in Caesarea Maritima for a week, or more if you've the time. Return the same messenger with a note saying when I can expect you. If you know where Talca is, please bring him with you, but not into the Prefect's palace. Leave him at the door in Myrmid's hands.

I need your counsel. I need my sack with gold and silver coins you know about. I need someone to talk to.

After twenty-one days of travel, I am sickened. Not sea-sick, but from watching Pilatus' public image of himself accelerate from general to monarch— from noble serving soldier to prancing make-believe king of all he surveys.

And we haven't been here two days.

Meanwhile, as his opinion of himself has advanced my *assessment of his personality has deteriorated—he has gone from frog to tadpole. He isn't even in the job yet and he is already totally out of his depth.*

O Tiberius, what woes you have inflicted on Judea, and your servant Deleig!

So, Vasas, come because—because while I know I have a task worthy of my service to Rome, under a master unworthy of serving, I am myself feeling hollow. Whatever I had seen myself worthy of becoming, perhaps as Pilatus once saw himself worthy of becoming, I have lost sight of.

My daily routine will develop; I love the climate, the dust, the dry air. I shall accomplish my tasks, but none of that will answer who and what am I. What am I at my core? Have I even got a core? Twenty-seven years old and less secure than when I was fifteen. Why?

I don't expect you to answer these. But you'll take me by the shoulders and shake me until I point me in a worthier direction than I can detect through the miasma, the clouded situation of being a member of an occupying force in a country that wants to be left alone. Understandably so.

Come, and show me what I'm not seeing. And if you can't tell me what I'm not seeing, come anyway for the joy of seeing you.

Ever your friend,
Musan

From that moment on Deleig wasted no time on self-pity—Talca was already at the palace's outer gate. He had sent in a note to Myrmid who, quick to respond, was pleased to meet Talca in order to establish who was in command: Myrmid. Myrmid told Talca that until the deception could not continue—or was not worth continuing—it would appear that Deleig's role was merely that of astrologer to the Prefect's wife. That he, Myrmid, was Pilatus' personal espionage master.

Talca, Myrmid happily understood—not that Myrmid ever revealed anything approaching happiness—was a quick study and someone he would enjoy working with. He sent a note into Deleig and said he and Talca would be at the inn outside the city gate.

Deleig had the messenger take him there. The meeting of the two men had apparently been cordial. Deleig was immediately at ease when he saw Myrmid was not hostile to Talca—it had been a primary worry.

The first step, all three agreed, would be to rid the Caesarea Maritima palace complex of High Priest Caiaphas' spies—and those of Prefect Gratus, meaning Rome's. Those spies could, of course, be one body serving two masters: Rome and Temple, Sejanus and Caiaphas. That would have to be ascertained promptly.

Without saying how this would be done, Deleig told Myrmid and Talca they would meet at the inn same time tomorrow and he'd outline the next steps. He returned to the palace to respond to Pilatus' invitation to join the family for their evening meal. Any excuse to spend time with the beautiful Claudia Procula.

First, however, the palace kitchen. Deleig returned to his quarters, took two small pieces of papyrus and drew on them. His kitchen soothsayer calling card. Let's see, he said to himself, if what Fefeel said holds true for Judea.

Deleig had brought his two Egyptian servants with him, and to ease them into the Judean world, he had engaged, as their aide, a multilingual Samaritan teenager familiar with the palace layout and the city. Deleig had the teenager take him to the kitchen by the outside door and leave him there, facing it. Deleig pointed him to a tree about fifteen yards away and told him to wait there.

It was a small kitchen of fifteen workers and not easy, when he first stepped in, to determine who was the chief cook. His presence was ignored—no one would have the temerity to approach this obviously very senior person. Finally, he saw who was giving the orders and walked over to her. She was tall, younger than he'd expected—he'd assumed soothsaying and age went together.

He handed her the piece of papyrus with the two-headed symbol on it. She turned the sheet over, dipped an asparagus spear point in what looked like gravy and drew a crude ram's head. Deleig presented her with his second piece of papyrus, the concluding symbol for Gemini.

He said, "Here is what I offer. Two sooths you will not know, and two gold *aureus*. May we step outside?"

She headed straight for the door. They talked outside for almost ten minutes.

The cook was deeply impressed with the quality of this man's knowledge. She understood what he wanted, accepted a payment of two *aureus* a year and asked how she would contact him. He pointed to the Samaritan teenager. She nodded to the boy, and he nodded back.

Rather than returning by the outside door, Deleig told the Samaritan to show him the interior route from the kitchen to his quarters so that he knew the palace's layout. Deleig then dismissed him. He was tempted to give the boy a *denarius* but knew that would be a poor move, ruining the master-servant relationship.

What to do next? Where else did a spymaster start?

At the next day's meeting, Deleig, Myrmid and Talca devised the system for hiring spies. They decided which centers of information mattered to them. Their list was: Tetrarch Herod Antipas in Tiberias, High Priest Caiaphas in Jerusalem, the Roman legionary headquarters in both Caesarea Maritima and Jerusalem. Put two operatives in Jericho simply as listeners. What about someone in Rome's eastern Mediterranean headquarters, the Legate's palace in Damascus? Talca said to trust him to do it. Myrmid nodded; Deleig agreed.

A roving circuit of listeners? Talca said he could utilize gamblers without them knowing it. That would keep him absent from Caesarea Maritima one week a month. First step, however long it took, was to clear the palace and compound of spies—while finding out whom they worked for.

Two days later Vasas arrived. No announcement. The first inkling Deleig had was a soldier at the entrance to his quarters saying he had a guest from Jerusalem.

"You called, I came," Vasas chortled.

"Welcome to my humble abode," said Deleig, with mock gravity. "I'm thinking of adding to it—space is so tight."

Vasas simply stood there, expectant, beaming and pleased to have arrived. Deleig's delight exceeded boyish enthusiasm; loneliness had enveloped him without his realizing it. Plus, everything he'd left with Vasas was now on the threshold in two small trunks ready to be carried to his quarters.

"Food, drink, relax? What would you prefer?"

"Musan, that was a long ride—bathe, a meal, a long walk and a good talk. In that order, I think."

"To my quarters so they know where to put these trunks. Have some fruit juice, and I'll show you to your accommodation—come when you're ready to dine. Then a tour of my favorite walking and talking point: the harbor. You've never seen it?"

"A year or so ago, returning from seeing my plantations in Egypt, we arrived in the dark, flares flaring."

The two friends walked through the palace to Deleig's quarters. After barely five minutes, they moved onto Vasas' quarters. It was at least an hour later when they walked to the palace promenade through an entrance on the north side of the complex.

"Espionage," Musan said to Vasas, "is a damnable trade."

With his right forefinger, he scratched at his hair just above his ear. The itch satisfied, he continued, "And I have no wish to return to work."

"Tell me enough about it that I know what you're talking about, but not enough to bore me."

"I course along the wide industrious boulevard of this southern breakwater at great speed, though not at a run. I take refuge in the din and the activity. Here, if anyone noticed a Roman official's lack of gravitas in my remarkably adroit pirouettes, as I practice staying limber, I am unconcerned. The harbor's daytime activity, Vasas, clears my head almost as surely as the peace of the desert at night clears it. And I am prattering on, dear friend, because I'm confused. That is, I'm adrift."

Vasas enjoyed the bustle on this broad thoroughfare with its lanes of vehicles in both directions. Ships were anchored near warehouses at wharfs on each side of the boulevard, many poking their prows practically inside the buildings.

He turned to his friend and said, "I like it out here, Musan, and can see why you do, too. But I don't fully understand—or even partially understand—your problem. Give it to me in separate pieces, the professional and the personal. Whom are you spying on?"

"Apart from Pilatus, you mean," Deleig said, with a laugh. "Caiaphas, you know who he is. Herod Antipas—or at least trying to. Listening in to the military espionage network to learn what it's saying about Pilatus, so I can counteract it. The main focus always is to locate in advance those who will make trouble for Rome in Judea. Just look at all this, Vasas." He waved his arms.

After a while, what Deleig found soothing, Vasas did not: the noise from the charivari of the constant passage of loaded carts; of raucous stevedores, cursing and shouting, trying to make themselves heard above the din of iron-rimmed wheels; snorting draft horses and camels; bellowing, slow-moving yoked oxen and clip-clopping donkeys. Deleig put his arm through Vasas' and walked him into the traffic. "Look," he said.

Men with the reins on the harnessed draught beasts ignored the two of them. They were too busy watching vehicles around them trying to push their way into line to pay attention to pedestrians.

"The breakwater's width is necessary to handle the huge volume of incoming and departing supplies and material," said Deleig, as he guided them between the two streams of traffic, dodging around carts that suddenly emerged from warehouses to force their way into the line.

The road only deteriorated quickly into a disorganized jumble whenever dozens of carts began fighting for headway or a place in line at once. But then order was restored and the afternoon traffic moved smoothly once more.

Acting as a guide to "his" harbor, Deleig began to calm down. He explained the fair-weather anchorage side of the breakwater, said humorous things about the gangways from the ships down to the jetties, comparing them to ant hills—long lines of workers moving up and down, loading and unloading. Booms swung netted cargoes down to the stonework in front of the warehouses. Deleig looked up between two prows at the cloudless sky.

"Spying has its drawbacks," said Deleig, still in a good-humored frame of mind. "Socially, certainly. Introduced to people, it will feel a little ludicrous at times to ask how they are when in fact one is well aware not only of how they are, but who they really are, what they are actually doing, and where they have been doing it."

He laughed at his nonsense.

At the end of the southern breakwater, the massive stonework took a dogleg turn at an east-pointing mole five hundred feet long. At the point where it would have touched the northern breakwater—much shorter than the southern one due to the curvature of the mainland—there was a sixty-foot-wide harbor entrance. Massive beacon towers flanked the entrance.

"These are what you saw at your night-time anchorage from Egypt. Now you see them in daylight: belching flames twenty and thirty feet into the air, angry beacons at the gate of Hell. To harbor-bound mariners in driving rain, mist, fog, or the blackness of an overcast night, the lights of Heaven."

Deleig and Vasas wandered among the stevedores and carters beholden for a living to the work and income represented by the multi-oared Roman Navy military *quinqueremes*, the passenger and commercial vessels, possibly a hundred ships in a slow week.

Vasas said that from his perspective, though Emperor Augustus had been dead now for more than a decade, his *Pax Romana* had ushered in an unprecedented period of peace for the region. The Euphrates' Peace Line with Parthia held. Peace had brought not only tranquility to both sides, but immeasurable prosperity.

"*Pax Romana* has created a Mediterranean collection of extremely high-stake gamblers," Vasas said. "Not Talca's sort, but men gambling their worth and their future on agriculture particularly, knowing nothing about it except its profits. Nothing about weather, locusts, drops in demand. Consequently, this staging area, the material supply base for maintaining the fruits of Rome's wars of conquest in the Mediterranean East, is even busier as a commercial port."

"And while you deal in bankruptcies and money transference," Deleig said, "I have my Zealots, messiahs, healers and rabble-rousers."

"Tell me about the Zealots," said Vasas.

"To me, messiahs are Zealots in training. Or, if not, messiahs could quickly turn into rabble-rousing troublemakers, troublemakers almost as bad as the Zealots. The Zealots, may I remind you, are the enemies of Rome. Stated purpose: expel the Romans from Judea—by force of arms. They're closely tied to Jerusalem's Second Temple, to Caiaphas, High Priest Caiaphas, whose outer-garment is usually a striped robe, a striped hyena."

"Have you interviewed, or indeed met Caiaphas yet?"

"No."

"Then you must do so immediately," said Vasas. "Tell him he has a week to withdraw his spies from Caesarea Maritima or you will do it for him. Then keep your word. How would you do that?"

"Stealthily. Stealth frightens people; it tends to subdue them for the longer term. A bold frontal attack, rarely."

Impressed, by Vasas, Deleig said, "You may be better than me at this. You really have a feel for it, Vasas."

"Ah, it's not much different from doing business, Musan. Then there's the other thing, the personal. At a guess, given your age, same as mine, you need either a wife, a woman friend, or a concubine."

"What—or rather who—I want," Deleig said, "is the Prefect's wife, Claudia Procula. Not for reasons of lust, though that lurks, but because I am in love with her."

"You are more likely in lust with a lovely, endearing Roman woman and hope it is love—to cover your baser feelings. Pining for her, if there's no reciprocity, could turn Judea into a decade of torture for you. Has she given any indications?"

"To the contrary, Vasas. She makes it obvious she has no interest. Not that we've discussed it. But one knows. Plus, she obviously loves her husband, but she's my age, not his."

"Lust."

"You think that's it?"

"Lust. Look elsewhere. I think you are a remarkably mature person who has not hit a rough spot since you were twelve. You're spoiled, Musan. Wealth, access to the highest powers in the world, trusted by many, liked by most—with one good, solid enemy in Sejanus to maintain a healthy balance—an intriguing challenge ahead as a spymaster, and all I hear is a twenty-seven-year-old bemoaning a fate most Romans would sacrifice everything for. My advice: stop thinking about yourself and start thinking about the job. Primarily the job of reining in your lord and master here before he lands you both in Emperor Tiberius' bad graces. Now, this incredible harbor you brought me here to see has been worth the effort. You can return with me to your quarters and take me to meet your master and lady-friend-in-your-dreams. But first a beaker of water and a cup of wine. About turn and let's go home!"

Deleig laughed. "Yes, sir!" he said, but not chastened. "Two things to say—not in my defense, dear Vasas, but so you might understand me better. First about where I am, and second about what I'm doing.

"If the harbor is impressive, the city, the palace and official buildings of this provincial capital are superb. The palaces King Herod constructed serve Pilatus—as they had his predecessor prefects—as their residences and military headquarters. The walled city encompasses not only the commercial and residential quarters, but also the enormous public buildings the populace by its thousands can enjoy. The amphitheatre, the hippodrome, the theatre and particularly the marble temple honoring Emperor Augustus were constructed on a colossal scale. Behind and beyond the city walls, a lesser 'town' survives on the pickings from the city. Caesarea Maritima has all the strengths, opportunities, crime, sins and degradations of a major seaport.

"I occasionally wander in both the official city and its impromptu town. More routinely, I prefer the harbor to the official city. I visit the town because that's where my domestic life is centered, close to the Zoroastrian temple I'll attend."

Deleig sighed. "Espionage was not the career I'd intended. In retrospect I see myself as a lifelong legal scholar, a historian of power, politics and religions—a linguist, and a compiler of books on military tactics, astrology, Parthian tales and superstitions. It was a simple human failing, a momentary flush of nostalgia for my love of the Parthian desert of my childhood that has brought me as a servant of the Roman Empire to Judea. I've traded Rome's monuments honoring itself, for King Herod's monument honoring Emperor Augustus—this same Caesarea Maritima. I've traded study, history, law and commerce for the potentially law-breaking troublemakers of an occupied land."

Looking slightly abashed, Deleig said, "I'm actually excellent in my accidental calling. My capacity for hard work and my—and others' around me—imaginative means of keeping track of the moods and methods of the various factions in Judea will impress and satisfy the Prefect, my on-and-off friend, Pilatus." He curled his upper lip and once again semi-pirouetted to face the other way for their return to the palace.

They strode toward the palace promenade.

"I suppose," Deleig said, "that espionage as a pursuit has some merit. It intermittently tests one's intelligence and constantly sharpens one's wits. It is not a job for the cynical; cynics are terrible judges of character. Nor is it work for the totally committed loyalist. Loyalists typically lack depth of understanding. It requires, if not a duplicity of mind—that would suggest deceit—then perhaps an ethical agility, an acceptance that, finally, there are no ultimate loyalties for an honest man. Except one: to his innermost beliefs. My innermost belief is set, my Zoroastrianism, my belief in Ahura Mazda."

Vasas was staring at him. "You really are a believer, aren't you? Why did you let me bully you? Though I was honest in what I said, and you know I love you as a friend."

"Because I needed it, Vasas. I needed someone to see me from the outside, and you have done wonders for me. Our friendship is deeper than ever."

"You are very strange, Musan Deleig."

"I'm afraid you are correct, Vasas. And you are very straight forward, and every word, every single word you've said, struck home. I thank you for it. Who else could have done it? As for lust, I can wait for Claudia. Now let's plan an excellent evening."

Two months later, Myrmid, as facsimile spymaster, visited High Priest Caiaphas and informed him he should remove his spies in the Caesarea Maritima compound, or Myrmid would. Caiaphas denied their presence, said he had never even thought of such a thing. It took a further half-year to thwart the High Priest.

Deleig worked quietly with the soothsayer in the Caesarea Maritima palace kitchen. She said there were several palace servants and one Roman soldier on outside payrolls. She explored further. During a visit to Jerusalem, she talked quietly with the chief cook in Caiaphas' palace. She said there was no likelihood the Jerusalem cook would become a conduit for information for Deleig—it was a one-time favor for a fellow cook.

Without doubt, she said, the Caiaphas spies were four servants: two middle-grade functionaries and two house-servants. All four were separately followed on their individual occasional journeys south to Caiaphas in Jerusalem. The fifth spy, the Roman soldier, reported from inside Caesarea Maritima, but to Sejanus.

Pilatus, informed of this, wanted to ride immediately to Jerusalem, seize the High Priest, treat him ignominiously, appoint his own High Priest and execute the spies. Where Caiaphas was concerned, Deleig urged restraint; he would arrange things otherwise.

From Caiaphas' cook Deleig had a detailed map of the palace's layout, and Myrmid and Talca knew who was passing information to the High Priest. Together, they sketched out an audacious gambit—Deleig's first Judean counter-espionage foray.

The complete operation took two nights, with six of Talca's operatives pressed into service as guards. The first night, all five of the High Priest's spies were rounded up—three were women. At dawn, the four servants were transported in secret to Jerusalem. That night, Myrmid and Talca's men quietly subdued the seven sleepy guards allegedly on duty in Caiaphas' palace. Then, the four miscreants were bound and gagged, and stealthily carried into the High Priest's main reception area to be gently deposited on the floor. Laid alongside them in a neat line, also bound and gagged, were Caiaphas' seven guards. Deleig's crew departed.

"Far better," Deleig had told Pilatus, "to have the High Priest in a constant state of uncertainty about what you might do than to actually do anything. He knows you know. That's unnerving. The Roman is in the basement here, bound."

The soldier was handed over to the centurion commander and with Pilatus' authority, executed and buried in an unmarked grave. Deleig blanched at the thought. The soldier's treasonous behavior was kept from the Roman gossipers.

The Prefect included the Caiaphas details in his report to

Emperor Tiberius as an example of how he could govern Judea without violence and upheaval. The story of the bundling of the Temple spies made the rounds in Rome to Pilatus' credit at a time when he was beginning to need credit. It also made the rounds in Jerusalem and made a laughing stock of Caiaphas.

THIRTEEN

Bounding at his usual brisk pace along the harbor three years later, Deleig mused on his mother's caution to her children, "Troubles come in twos, grief travels alone." Deleig decided his grief was lovesickness for Claudia; the troubles came when Talca caught up with him on the causeway.

Vasas, through a contact from south of Jerusalem, had received word of a possible Zealot uprising. The urgent message stated a Zealot cell had been infiltrated by one of Vasas' operatives. That cell and two others within easy distance were planning an uprising. All this was about a half-day's ride southwest of Jerusalem. What surprised Deleig was that Vasas referred to one of his own "operatives." Deleig didn't even know Vasas had operatives.

Myrmid, aware of this at the same time as Deleig, had already organized horses and supporting guards and servants for a rapid trip south. Deleig made the news known to Pilatus, who congratulated Deleig. He commented that his military network had discovered nothing.

Pilatus would send in the troops the moment Deleig gave the word. Deleig asked to be allowed to attempt to resolve the problem his own way. The Prefect was about to insist, but Deleig reminded him how he'd stopped the High Priest from spying on Pilatus and his household in their first year in Judea. With Deleig fashioning a snare to emasculate the Zealots' plans, Pilatus reluctantly agreed that Deleig could apply his formula for incapacitating the Zealots. If it didn't work, he'd lead in his troops.

Vasas was asked to order his operatives to immediately acquire the names and locations of every male family member related to the lead Zealot. The list must extend to second cousins, cross the generations and include in-laws. Similar material was needed on the other two suspected cell leaders, apparently brothers.

After an overnight with Vasas in Jerusalem, Deleig rode south to the small town under surveillance. Myrmid and Talca were already there. The place itself was unremarkable, a modest commercial center serving the farming community. It had a sizeable inn for north-south travelers and two substantial wells in the public square.

At the inn, Deleig paid for rooms for four nights for Myrmid, Talca, himself and three guards. He told the husband-and-wife owners they could keep the money if the rooms were only used for two nights. He asked them about the area. They said it was rather odd that another "Northerner," meaning someone north of Jerusalem, had asked similar questions the day before. Obviously Talca's man at work.

Opposite the inn, which bordered the market square, was a quiet spot of trees and benches. Deleig seated himself under a tree. Opposite him were several stone benches also shaded by trees. Deleig was on the bench that best positioned him as a judge.

Myrmid and Talca had offered to accompany him, rather than witness everything from the opposite side of the road. He said no and encouraged them to watch—indeed witness—the proceedings from a bench against the inn wall. The innkeeper and his wife, at Deleig's insistence, also sat outside the inn as witnesses. The couple was assured nothing would happen to them; he just wanted them to hear what was said. The couple thought better than to protest.

As he waited, Deleig studied the operatives' reports on the men's families in the two scrolls he'd been given on arrival. He'd wondered how he might handle this. He'd thought about his standard interrogation technique, from behind a silk curtain in a room somewhere. That was important, after all, if he wanted to maintain his cover. Yet, in this case—and this far south—he thought he might risk personal exposure to conduct his quasi-interrogation in public. Further, he realized he no longer cared if his cover was penetrated because he had already decided his term in Judea would not last forever, whether Pilatus was recalled or not.

He reasoned that in this town everyone watching would know why these men were being questioned. That benefitted Deleig, for it added a weight the three men had to bear. The innkeeping couple was the capstone. Of course, the public might also be wondering why there wasn't half a legion present, while suspecting it might not be geographically far off if required.

The revolutionaries were brought to Deleig, unbound, by several of Talca's operatives. Deleig had given orders they not be mistreated. The three looked little different, one to the next. Hard-working farm owners or workers present in their work clothes, dragged here from their fields. Dirty faces, sweat-stained clothes, no attempt at bravado. One, probably the leader, walked a pace ahead of the other two.

Deleig had placed the two scrolls beside him. Now he retrieved one and opened it. He looked at the leader, said nothing and looked back at the scroll. He kept reading for five minutes, occasionally looking up at the man.

Cold-eyed, top lip curled to reveal his fox-like teeth, Deleig was a terrifying prospect as a judge. He re-rolled the scroll and replaced it. He went through the same process with the second scroll and the other two men, concentrating on it, then staring at them, sometimes disdainfully, sometimes sadly, before returning to the scroll.

Finally, he rolled the second scroll and placed that on the bench. He stood up. His height added to the ferocity he exuded. He concentrated his eyes solely on the ringleader.

"Look at me!" he yelled. The innkeeping couple jumped a little. The man himself shuddered, startled. Then, he resigned himself to a fate he'd already imagined and probably accepted.

"You were brought here un-bound and treated decently. No threats have been made. Now I make them. I intend to release you," Deleig said.

All three men were blinking, unthinkingly surprised and caught totally off guard.

"If any of the three of you makes one move toward an act of rebellion against lawful authority, here is what I will do. Not what I simply intend to do. Not what I might do. But what I will actually carry out. Systematically and completely. I will have your sons killed."

He concentrated now solely on the leader. "You have three. Then I shall have your father and grandfather killed. I shall have your four brothers and their sons killed. Then your one grandson by your oldest daughter. Your two brothers-in-law and your father-in-law will be killed, but keep this in mind all the time I am speaking: you will not be killed. You will witness this. You will be kept alive. Even when your many cousins, their fathers and sons and grandsons are dead, you will live. And that," Deleig's voice thundered as he looked at the other two, "applies equally to your sons, you with the one, and you with the three. Your entire male family members. Nor will you two die."

He lowered his voice. It was chilling as he said, slowly, "One move against authority. I shall hear. And I shall wreak such death throughout your families the lessons will become part of Judea's history. Go!"

Frozen by the horror of the threat, no man moved. "Go!" bellowed Deleig.

The startled men glanced at him, at each other; they turned, looking around, wondering if it was a trap. Realizing it wasn't, they ran—constantly turning to see if they were being followed.

Deleig politely thanked the now-unnerved innkeeper and his wife for their presence and bid them return home. He walked from the shaded benches into the sun's glare on the rough road and into the inn where Myrmid was waiting, a scroll in hand. Before handing it to Deleig he said, "Why the innkeeper?"

"Who better, with his wife, to spread the news of what was said?"

"Ah," said Myrmid, handing him the scroll. "From Vasas. Prefect Pontius Pilatus yesterday had the Legion standards taken into the Temple, where they are now on display. The Judeans are in an uproar at the sacrilege. The Temple functionaries kept the matter quiet for many hours so that a delegation of the conservative sect, the Sadducees—also representing the Sanhedrin, for some of its members are among them—could depart for Damascus to complain to the Legate. They wanted to be beyond Caesarea Maritima before Prefect Pilatus learned there was a delegation to Syria. The High Priest is organizing a delegation intending to leave for Rome within five days or so to seek an audience with the Emperor, either in the city or if necessary Capri."

"Trouble comes in twos," Deleig said. "That's the second one. Mother would be pleased. So, Myrmid, as fast as we can to Caesarea Maritima. I must see Pilatus and then leave immediately for Rome. Send your best messenger to Pilatus and tell him to hold any *quinquereme* due to sail until I reach there. Tell him further to delay any dispatch to Rome from the governor of Syria until after I've sailed.

"Write that out, and I'll stick my seal on it. The first news the Emperor hears of this must come from me, not the Judeans. We're leaving immediately for Caesarea Maritima but your messenger can ride through the night, changing horses at each station, and give us an extra half-day. I have to depart for Rome at least two days ahead of the High Priest's delegation."

Thirteen hours and one change of horses later, Deleig was in Caesarea Maritima, hot, filthy, tired and seething. He went straight to his quarters and bathed. Then he slept for an hour. En route to the military wing of the palace he stopped briefly at Pilatus' family quarters and told Claudia and Formio of his departure.

"The outward voyage could take three weeks—even more if the weather's really foul. Sailing westward at this time of year means strong headwinds. We'll probably be hopping port to port around the Mediterranean. You know that. A *quinquereme* with its five banks of oars is good for port-hopping—and ramming pirates. But its sails are puny for the open sea, rowing against the wind. Returning I'll look for something light, with plenty of sail. If we catch a good wind in our sails, the journey could only be ten or eleven days."

Claudia asked if she could give him a list of things she would like done in Rome and brought back from the city. Deleig said to hurry, a ship was being held for him. She went to her quarters to write out the list.

As Deleig approached Pilatus' command center, he wasn't thinking of Pilatus but of himself. This one had to be carried off with consummate dignity. He walked in, nodded to the secretaries and aides and entered Pilatus' main operations salon.

The Prefect was alone. He looked neither defiant nor apologetic; rather, he looked as if he were awaiting with interest what Deleig might say. Deleig spoke first.

"Never mind why, Pontius. I'm leaving for Rome. If I get to Emperor Tiberius before the news and the delegations do—as I assume the Damascus delegation will also travel to Rome with the Syrian governor's blessing—he hates you enough—if I'm there first, I'll squash this incident flat."

Deleig wrinkled his lips and before Pilatus could speak, added, "It is the last time I shall save you from yourself. This is costing me more in favors expended, friends cajoled and the risks that stem from misleading an Emperor, however mildly misleading him, than it is worth. Say nothing, please. We shall talk when I return with news of what I have or have not been able to accomplish."

With that, Deleig turned on his heel and left. On his ride to the harbor, Deleig smiled—this journey to Rome suited him very well. He would ask his dear friend Lady Lydia to arrange matters in the months ahead to have him brought back to Rome for a project to be undertaken at the Emperor's pleasure. Perhaps writing a series of comparisons between Roman law and the law in Rome's provinces, and the law in those countries it faced across borders. One on Judean law would be most useful to any future governor, and he could certainly do one on Parthia.

Twenty-two days later, in Rome, he stepped from the carriage at Lady Lydia's villa and in great dancerly strides, took the broad steps three at a time. He stopped two steps before the top. He knelt down to bring himself closer to the elderly Lady Lydia's height.

His grin wide, yet his lips barely parted so white showed but not the fox-like bite, his eyes shining, he held out his arms and she walked carefully toward him, smacked him lightly on the head with the fan in her left hand. She said, "To your feet, my giant prince, you're too young for me." He remained where he was, reached out and kissed her on the forehead.

She huffed and puffed. She said as she turned carefully away to take careful steps back into her villa, "I suspect you'd better come in. You'll want the gossip."

Three days later, on Capri, the Emperor Tiberius, his balding head increasing his turtle-like appearance, cordially welcomed his Parthian friend. He immediately recalled how he had been prevailed upon to make Deleig a Roman citizen *in anticipation* of his service to Rome, whereas the normal procedure was citizenship after service.

"Annius Rufus loved you like a third grandson, a fine man. With Lydia on one side of him and your tutor and your lawyer friend on the other, all pleading your case, how could I refuse? See, I still wear the magnificent signet ring you gave me."

He bent his hand forward so Deleig could examine again the finely etched symbol of Tiberius' regimental commands cut into the deep blue gemstone.

They sat to dispense with the business at hand. Tiberius listened keenly as Deleig told how he'd put down the Zealot uprising, while Pilatus, *mistakenly*, had planted his legion standards *inside* the Temple rather than around its walls as a reminder of Rome's strength—a reminder aimed at the Temple aristocracy and would-be troublemakers.

Tiberius looked at Deleig, head tilted down, eyes twinkling as he looked up to suggest he doubted the accuracy of this report.

Deleig smiled and nodded in agreement. "It is likely, sir, that the

Emperor will soon be receiving pleas to meet with Judean delegations—sooner rather than later. They could be ignored. The standards have been withdrawn and placed outside the Temple courtyard walls, *as intended*," Deleig stressed, smiling—both of them were aware there was scarcely a shred of truth to the account—"and the careless soldiers punished for their stupidity, of course."

"Of course," echoed Tiberius.

He was silent for almost a minute, gazing toward a wall filled with regimental insignias. Then he looked at Deleig and said, "I should have made you Prefect and Pontius your counselor, Musan. In any event, your talents are wasted. When this is done, return to Rome; there are histories to write. Enough of this. Come and see my gardens—my rhubarb is magnificent this year."

Three days later, back in Rome from Capri before once more leaving for the Ostia harbor and a fast vessel to Judea, Deleig asked Lydia if there was a way, when the time came, that she could have Sejanus, the Praetorian Prefect who acted for the Emperor, send an order to Pilatus requesting Deleig's immediate return from Judea. Lydia looked at him pityingly, as if he were a simpleton. It was her way of saying, of course she could.

Then she added something Deleig had not expected, "Sejanus' days are numbered. By the time you reach Judea, he will be no more."

"Truly? What's happening?"

Lydia would add nothing beyond, "I'll write." Then she blurted out the question that had been hovering on her lips ever since he'd returned, "Have you kept your hands off Claudia?"

"Not from choice, alas," he said. "She will not come into my arms. Not on any terms. She wants to. She knows I would ask her to divorce Pontius. Her scrupulosity dismays me, though I understand it."

"My poor lovesick Parthian," said Lydia, sympathetically.

Fourteen days later Deleig was on the Caesarea Maritima harbor walking toward Rome's headquarters in Judea, to meet not only with Myrmid and Talca, but also Formio, Pilatus—and Claudia. Everything she'd wanted from Rome was unloaded and en route to the palace.

Claudia had left a note for him, simply saying, "I'd like to see you while Pontius is absent." Pilatus had been summoned to Damascus by the Legate, the commander who had three legions to Pilatus' half-legion, to discuss the complaints from Judeans.

Claudia wanted to see him. Deleig dropped the bag he was carrying and raced off, his long legs at speed streaking him forward into the palace and along the corridors to Claudia's quarters.

He entered and saw a servant. "Lady Claudia?" The startled servant pointed to another chamber, and Deleig ran to Claudia's bathing pool.

On hearing his approach, she called, "Musan, you shouldn't be here." Yet she wanted to be seen and waited until he entered to emerge from the far side of the pool, her back to him, knowing he gazed on her nakedness. She signaled a servant to hand her a robe, took it but did not throw it around her. Instead she half turned, her face flushed, toward Deleig. She shook her head and departed.

He turned. He forced himself to take one step toward retracing the way he'd come. In the corridor, as Deleig emerged, Myrmid was there. Solid, stolid Myrmid took a step toward him and clasped him close in his huge arms.

"You love her because she is a virtuous woman. Her virtuous approach to life is the strong element shining through her beauty. And because she is a virtuous woman, you may not love her."

Deleig was partly shaken out of the shock and despond increasingly engulfing him. Myrmid, all along, had understood. This stoic, almost taciturn man was a philosopher of the heart. He had the words, which Deleig did not. He gave a huge sob and drummed his hands against Myrmid's back.

"Thank you, my very good and very dear friend."

Myrmid released him.

FOURTEEN

Myrmid gave him news of the messiah called the Baptizer by the people because he had baptized thousands in the River Jordan. The man, known also as John the Baptist, had called Herod Antipas a fornicator for stealing and marrying his brother's wife. Outraged, Antipas had had him arrested and, though fearful of having the man on the premises, had put him in the dungeons in his palace.

"*Anything*," said Deleig, stressing the word, "to do with the Herodians seems to come up smelling of the cesspit. Didn't he steal his brother's wife—and snared the wife's daughter into the bargain?"

"The version I accept, and there are several, is that after he divorced his first wife, his half-brother Agrippa—that's Herod II—was tiring of his wife, Herodias. You know, Musan," said Myrmid, who almost never joked but seemed to be trying to tell one, "given their father's fondness for tossing wives out of windows and killing his sons, wife-stealing seems innocent by comparison. There are tongue-waggers, we've no proof of course, who said that it's vice versa: Herodias' daughter, Salome, she's after him."

"And that's all there is to it, one jailed messiah?" asked Deleig.

"No, Musan, far from it. A new messiah, a follower of the Baptizer, a man called Jesus—or Yoshua in the Hebrew—has picked up the preaching and baptizing and is vastly popular as a healer. Talca's people confirm the same thing. This Jesus has an appeal not previously witnessed by the older folks around here. His preaching breaks new ground. There's a note for you from Talca."

"Agitating against Rome?" Deleig asked.

"Not heard him myself, Musan. I'm not sure what Talca's discovered or is recommending. Why not bathe, relax? We can have a meal together, and wait for him."

"Myrmid, I've not stopped since I left here. Cooped up on a ship when I needed to be working here in Judea—Rome, Capri, another vessel back here, travel and no rest—and far less exercise than I'm used to. I need half an hour or an hour out on the harbor. Meet me back here."

Myrmid nodded. Deleig turned, took a couple of lengthy strides and broke into a run. He raced along the deserted palace promenade toward the harbor, blinking and trying to clear his head. He suddenly didn't want to deal with all this.

As he reached the start of the harbor trafficway on the southern wall he slowed. The first large warehouse was just ahead, dense traffic rattling past it. The sun hit the side of the building, and there was an unoccupied bench.

Deleig went over to it and sat down. He closed his eyes, leaned his head against the wood-plank siding and tried to banish all thought for a while. Even of Claudia—no, especially of Claudia.

Along with the noise, and despite the fact he was at the sea's edge, the air smelled, nay tasted, dry—as least in comparison to Rome. That feel he sniffed, the slightly different smell, I'm home, he thought, almost.

After relaxing for ten minutes, he pulled from his pocket the message from Talca that Myrmid had handed him.

Talca's note said Jesus the Nazarene was currently in Capernaum, but headed toward the lakeside towns of Galilee, the Decapolis region, the "Greek" cities. Talca strongly recommended Deleig ride out to Galilee to hear him, to match the preacher's words with the reaction of the crowd. Then they could discuss in person the possibly vital need to increase their monitoring on the two Judean religious factions, the Pharisees and the Temple priests. These two factions were on the fringes of the Nazarene's activities, hostile to him and his followers. Their reactions would be crucial to an understanding of the extent to which the two factions, which normally shunned each other, were prepared to cooperate.

Talca suggested Deleig and Myrmid meet up with him at Capernaum, on the northern edge of Lake Galilee. It was a suggestion that pleased—Deleig knew the travel was relatively easy.

Deleig headed a working team. The flow of reports could continue to wherever he was. Myrmid was the complete organizer, and Talca was quite brilliant in the way Talca was brilliant. Deleig needed another as good—Rome, S'veyda. S'veyda could delegate his top aides to superintend the Deleig family trading company's sea trade. I need S'veyda here, he thought. Might it trigger a clash of strong personalities? He'd have to see.

Deleig ran his usual route and headed back. An hour later, a messenger arrived from the port. A just-docked vessel, obviously faster than the ship that had carried Deleig because it had arrived so soon after his, had brought the letter. It bore Lady Lydia's seal. He flicked off the seal with his thumb and opened the sheet.

My esteemed Prince Musan,
Sejanus was ordered executed by the Senate. The execution was immediate. Breathe easily, although I doubt that's a possibility if shoulder-to-shoulder with Pilatus in his merry monarch mood.
Come back soon, my dear, dear friend,
Lydia

Lydia was correct—"shoulder-to-shoulder" with Pilatus was no easy situation. Deleig knew relations between himself and the Prefect were permanently strained. Pilatus equally was well aware this was the fourth time Musan had saved his hide with Rome—though it was the first time he had actually had to travel to Rome to do it. How much longer would Deleig remain, and how much longer Pilatus might last without him?

The looming Parthian had certainly made Pilatus' time as Prefect easier for him than he'd deserved. Pilatus knew himself well enough to know he was an ingrate, but that only disturbed him when it resulted in his feeling threatened.

The next afternoon, an invitation arrived from Pilatus to come for the evening meal. He had returned from Damascus. Deleig replied he'd be pleased to accept as there was a fresh problem to deal with. He'd tell Pilatus about it that evening.

"A crisis?" asked Pilatus when Deleig arrived at his quarters.

"You heard about a messiah, the Baptizer, attracting thousands to his gatherings, preachings and baptizings at the Jordan?"

"No, my military intelligence people tell me nothing."

"So you don't know the Tetrarch, Herod Antipas, has arrested the man and imprisoned him in his Tiberias dungeons?"

"No."

"You should send your military intelligence people back to

Rome, demoted. Well, there's a new messiah immediately sprung up to take the Baptizer's place, one Yoshua, or Jesus, the Nazarene, even more popular—"

At that moment Claudia and Formio entered to join them for the meal. Deleig stopped talking and greeted both of them. Claudia smiled warmly—no more than that, "Greetings, Musan."

"I was just telling Pontius about a crisis I must attend to."

"You're not staying to eat?" asked an alarmed Formio.

"Oh I am, Formio, yes. But forgive me and let me complete this with your father. I'm not certain yet, Pontius, whether I'll directly approach the Tetrarch—"

"You know him, don't you?" asked Pilatus.

"I've met him previously, yes, but I am certainly intending to leave tomorrow for several days to ride out to hear this new messiah, this Jesus man, and determine how threatening he is.

"Pontius, I'd be interested and willing to take Formio with us tomorrow—it's risk free—if you and Claudia feel it would be good. He could use the company of men, new vistas and a slightly more rugged and unpredictable life for a few days. Broaden his experience, build him up somewhat physically."

"Excellent idea," Pilatus said. "Should have thought of it myself. Don't make a nuisance of yourself, boy. Prince Musan is kind to do this."

"I won't, sir."

The evening continued, Pilatus on tenterhooks the whole time because he and Deleig had not discussed Rome. He more or less finally dismissed his wife and son so he could say, "I am truly grateful to you, Musan. I know you've saved my reputation and my post here. I realize my shortcomings, but I just flare up. What did the Emperor say?"

"Nothing."

"Nothing?"

"Nothing specific. I suggested a plan of action regarding the Judeans and he accepted. By the way, Sejanus has been executed—by the Senate."

"By Jove, if they're prepared to execute Sejanus, no one is safe. Who is the new Praetorian commander? Who is in charge of Rome?"

"I've no word on a new commander, nor on Rome's governance. The Senate has a freer hand than ever. My guess, knowing who is in charge, they'll appoint a new Praetorian Guard commander and then back to business as usual."

Pilatus nodded his agreement.

The evening was still young; details for the journey were still coming in from Talca—he was arranging mounts. Myrmid's planning, equally crisp in approach and clear in execution, recommended the group leave at dawn, cooler for the *cursus publicus* horses. Overnight in Capernaum.

Northern Galilee was not an area of the country that Deleig knew. He was aware Capernaum was one of the newer Judean cities. It had grown from a village in the previous century as trading around Galilee grew. The region was prime agricultural land as well as abundant in fish.

It was a watering hole for traders on the Silk Road, a center for replenishing supplies, not least because of its specialties: dried fish and dried fruit. The city's role as a hub for trade routes was such that Capernaum also served as a customs post and a base for Rome's tax collectors.

The following day, departing while it was still dark, the Caesarea Maritima party made good time. Shortly after noon, Talca, waiting at the Capernaum changing station, greeted the arrivals, surprised to see the Prefect's son was one of them.

"My Lord Deleig," Talca said, smiling and extended his arm in greeting as the ostler led the *cursus publicus* mounts away, "one of the residents, a centurion in command there, has offered you the freedom of his second villa. It is not a half-mile from here, an easy walk after that long ride. There are refreshments ready. It is possible to bathe if you wish."

The tall Deleig wrapped a long arm around his friend's shoulders in an embrace. He signaled to Formio, who had collected his bag, to join them. Deleig and Talca watched the boy approach. He was a couple of inches above Talca, with dark curly hair and an innocent but not bewildered air to him.

The boy's face was large, almost round, with large curious dark eyes set wide apart below a wide forehead—curious as if trying to take in every detail of his new surroundings. There was a slight hesitancy as he neared Talca and Deleig, as if uncertain whether to greet the frowning Talca—who was, after all, an employee—or wait to be greeted. His seeming dilemma was resolved by Deleig.

"Formio, I'm sure you've met the honorable Talca previously, at least in passing. Talca, his Excellency, Formio, the Prefect's son, as you know."

"Your Excellency," said Talca, bowing his head.

"Honorable Talca," replied Formio, "I do know you by sight. Prince Musan treats you as an equal, I notice, even though …" The boy faltered. "Perhaps I am speaking out of turn?" he asked Deleig.

"No, continue with the thought," Deleig said.

"Well, I was going to say, honorable Talca, that you address the prince as 'your lordship,' and he calls you 'Talca' and wraps his arm around your shoulders. Therefore, I wondered if, when men travel in close quarters like this, they tend to not use honorifics, for Myrmid simply called me by my name all the way here, therefore you might, too. Though not in the palace, for Myrmid does not."

Talca, inclining his head in agreement, said, "A sensible arrangement, sir."

"Then perhaps we may all be on first name terms," suggested Formio, not sounding quite as bold as he apparently hoped. "Except you, Prince Musan, sir," he added, with a nod to Deleig.

Deleig enjoyed the exchange and felt a slightly paternal glow at Formio's attempt at a mature manner. Talca and Myrmid both nodded in agreement.

"Talca, Formio must accompany us for the time being. Let the others remain here. Where's the Nazarene now?"

"Within a half-day's ride, headed toward the Kheresa area. Did Myrmid receive all my messages, sir?"

"He did if the 'early start' was the last one. Now, food, wine and water, Talca, in reverse order. I've a thirst a drunk would envy."

Two hours later, Deleig had bathed and eaten. He had extolled the virtues of the freshly landed fish, sent for and rewarded the kitchen staff and praised the wine selection, duly rewarding the major domo. Now he sat, lightly clothed, legs extended on his divan, and gazed idly at the Sea of Galilee spread before and below him.

The villa was on a high bluff. Talca and Formio had positioned their divans at an angle, their backs toward the sea, so they could face Deleig as they talked. Deleig was curious that their host was nowhere to be seen.

"He did not want to impose on your honor by being present. He knew you were from the Prefect's household and had imperial connections, and I think that rather terrified him. He has a larger villa away from the seashore in the town itself."

Deleig thought a moment.

"We must walk over to thank him if opportunity offers a time."

Deleig looked at Formio and said, "I am going to talk frankly to you. When I was fourteen years old, same age as you, my grandfather and father—and their high-ranking military and official friends—trusted me entirely. There was no information, no secret, hidden from me. I was being groomed to be important. I have never broken that trust. The conversation Talca and I will now have—and other conversations you will hear—will reveal matters to you that are highly official, consequently of great importance, therefore secret. I am not going to insult you by asking if I can trust you. I know I can."

The boy's eyes grew large. He stared without blinking, as if preparing to be astounded by what might be revealed.

"Do you know what a spy is, Formio?"

Formio blinked, nodded, but didn't speak for a moment. "... A person who gathers information others do not want revealed. A discoverer of secrets."

Deleig said, "I am not your mother's astrologer. I am your father's spymaster, his head of espionage. His chief counselor."

As if in relief, Formio burst out laughing.

"That's so clever," Formio said, laughing still. "I knew you weren't her astrologer, and you spent so much time with my father I thought you were his astrologer instead, but he didn't want to admit it. What a marvelous disguise, a ruse—a trick."

"Consequently," said Deleig, not changing his tone, "Talca and I shall at times—indeed Myrmid and I, too—discuss secret matters. Information gathered on your father's behalf. Why am I revealing this? Indeed, why have I brought you along on this journey? You are almost at the age I was the first time I visited Caesarea Maritima. I knew nothing of the world, except through the words of others, and except for the desert. I do not want you isolated from your natural place—Rome. At some point you'll be there and know the city intimately. My concern is you not grow up ignorant of your immediate surroundings.

"Again, I stress, I am always working, always dealing in information and responding to new developments. I cannot hide that and do not wish to simply because you are present. You are not being treated as a boy, but as a young man. And yes, mine is a clever cover, because I also am an astrologer."

He smiled. Formio smiled back. He obviously felt much older than he had a few moments earlier. No longer just a boy, or not quite.

To Talca, Deleig said, "Now you can tell me all. Don't worry that it may repeat what was in your messages. Formio will benefit from whatever you say. Formio, you are not to interrupt or ask questions. You may listen, that is all."

"I understand, sir," Formio said.

Talca sat up, swung his legs over the side of the divan, rested his elbows on his knees and his chin in his hands. And thought. Brow furrowed. Then he brightened.

"John the Baptizer," he said, "was a preacher who emerged from the desert five months ago to baptize at first scores and then hundreds of people in the Jordan. He called for repentance from wickedness. More significantly, however, this John spoke of the coming of a savior, a Messiah—a man from Yahweh, that is, God. He was heralding a new messiah, but said he was not that man.

"Apparently, one of those John baptized, but I've no confirmation, was this Nazarene, Jesus. This new man, Jesus, had begun preaching in a manner that had impressed not only John, but all those who heard him. Among those who heard about him are the Pharisees and the Temple priests. They want this man's head. They're already thirsting for it. It's something in what he's saying, but it's too obscure for me."

"Talca, I'm seriously considering sending to Rome for S'veyda, my chief assistant there," said Deleig. "I intend, because of the trust level, to have him join us if—and I do say if—this Jesus is a bit too oblique for minds like ours to penetrate the intent behind the words. Let S'veyda listen; he has the temperament and the manner."

Talca nodded agreement and said to remember that the Baptizer had not specifically identified the Nazarene as the Messiah, but he had broadly hinted such a man was already among them.

"Think, my lord. The Baptizer is confined in the dungeons in Herod Antipas' palace in Tiberias, not that far away. I'm sure Antipas would permit your honor to interview this Baptizer. Actually, I am not sure, but he might."

He looked at Deleig, his friend and master. Talca enjoyed his company, though he rarely had time to relax with him. As a rule when they met, it was strictly business.

He added, "We ought to meet like this more often, my lord. It has much to recommend it."

He knew Deleig would answer in his own time, in his own way. Talca said no more, swung his legs back onto the divan and found a satisfyingly recumbent position while awaiting his master's further questions.

Finally Deleig responded. "I was a boy Formio's age when I first met Herod Antipas. I didn't like him then and have avoided him since. He and his half-brother, Herod II, are unpleasant and, I suspect, desperate men. Men I gauge to be mediocrities. Beware the mediocre; they are more dangerous than fools. Tell me more about the Nazarene's appeal, but don't sit up. Relax."

"What is astounding, sir," said Talca, sitting up, "is that the Jesus character has been attracting crowds that grow almost exponentially. He is a phenomenon throughout all of Judea and even into Syria. It isn't just that the multitudes follow him in their thousands, it's that the people come from everywhere, from Tyre and Sidon and Damascus, from the Decapolis, and obviously all around Galilee—but hundreds from Jericho and Jerusalem and far, far south. Obviously his ability as a healer is part of it. People will go anywhere, do anything, for a cure."

"What did he *say* that got you so alert to him?" asked Deleig.

"He told the crowd, 'The time has come. The Kingdom of God is close at hand. Repent.' "

"What did the crowd think that meant?"

"I'd guess many of them thought—no, hoped—he was talking about throwing off the Roman yoke. That it was the Judean kingdom whose time had come—come back."

"What would the others think?"

"Well, that wasn't all he said. He said, 'Repent, and believe the Good News.' They thought he was talking about God. To them the word 'repent' meant to change one's life around by looking at the world in a new, more wholesome way. But that isn't necessarily a political concept; these followers are very ordinary Judeans—and others. I don't see many educated among them, except for the Temple priests and scribes—and of course, the Pharisees. Yet these men are there for a different purpose, I'll wager. This 'Good News' is what I want you to hear him talk about. My men say this is his current theme."

Deleig asked, "What is 'Good News'?"

" 'Good News' for the poor, he says, sir. As I see it, he himself is the 'Good News'—he's curing hundreds of diseases, including madness. Well, perhaps dozens of ailments, not hundreds—but by the hundred. You'll have decipher it for yourself. What I hear may not be what you hear."

Deleig nodded at that—it contained wisdom. He said, "You contend that what is different from the other messiahs and crowd raisers we've followed is his singular effect on that crowd, his listeners. That, and the fact you've heard nothing that might be a threat to Rome. Yet two major Judean religious factions are regularly in the crowd. Please explain that, now. Why are they there?"

Talca swung his feet to the floor. He always appeared disconcerted when required to speculate when he felt he didn't quite understand the facts. By comparison, reporting what was said was simple.

"I have no need to tell you, my lord, that the Pharisees and the Temple priests and their scribes are not allies—a degree of animosity, no, perhaps 'hostility' is more accurate, exists between them."

Deleig said nothing, though he was well aware of the antipathy between the synagogue Judeans and the Temple Judeans.

Talca was continuing. "The Pharisees believe in the most strict and literal observance, and constantly refine their regulations. The Pharisees are synagogue, not Temple, adherents. The Temple leans to a slightly less literal approach to the Tanakh, the complete Hebrew Bible, and takes something of a lead from its senior priests. What keeps these two groups apart, I don't know."

Myrmid joined them and with one hand dragged a large divan into the group. He asked Deleig, "Why do you think the Senate executed Sejanus?"

"Why? Power mad. Wanted to take over from Tiberius, King of Capri."

Myrmid thought for a moment. Then he asked, "Who might succeed Sejanus?"

"That's what Pilatus asked. I've no idea. I said I thought the Senate might go mad with the sudden freedom. There was no one groomed because Sejanus didn't want a threat from below, and because he was relatively young. You know what Tiberius said—I didn't know he had a sense of humor—he said he should have sent me as Prefect of Judea and Pilatus as my assistant. We both had a good laugh at that."

Deleig suddenly blushed. He was looking at Formio—he had just maligned his father.

"My apologies, Formio, for criticizing your father in front of you. I forgot, though I was simply reporting the Emperor's words."

Formio said, "Prince Musan, sir, I suspect the Emperor was correct."

"You don't know about my earlier meeting with the Tetrarch, do you, Myrmid?" He was now well aware he was speaking in front of a fourteen-year-old boy, but decided adult talk was one purpose of bringing him along. He was living in a silken cocoon.

"This all happened when I was fourteen, Formio." He turned back to Myrmid. "As Antipas had been educated in Rome—along with his half-brother, Agrippa, now Herod II—Prefect Annius Rufus sent a servant with a letter to ask if the Tetrarch would receive the Parthians—that's my grandfather and me—because the boy, me, was headed to Rome for further education. Herod Antipas sent word back with the Prefect's messenger that he would be pleased to welcome us. He'd be in Jerusalem, however, not Tiberias, and we must travel there. With two of Rufus' guards as escort, we went to Jerusalem, where Antipas briefly saw Grandfather alone. Then he had me sent in, alone."

Deleig said that Antipas had struck him as a nervous man, almost jumpy, given to occasional jerky movements as he quickly acknowledged his presence, without a formal welcome. Antipas had insisted they immediately go up to the roof of the palace so that he could show Deleig the city of Jerusalem. There, in the dark, the Tetrarch had seemed quite at ease. He'd asked nothing about his education, nothing about why he wanted to go to Rome, but said only he must, while there, go early to the Suburra and the House of the Blue Hyacinth.

"Not a brothel," Antipas had said, "and something more than a house of assignation. Young women, thirteen to seventeen. You select one with the understanding you'll care for her for life—there's a written contract. These young women are educated in what they must do, will always be obedient, but must always be cared for, even after the signatory's death."

Deleig said he had been horrified, embarrassed. He knew he was blushing to the point of his face exploding with embarrassment—and delighted it was dark and there were no lamps so Antipas could see it.

Myrmid said, "You know, Musan, you are something of a prude."

Deleig looked at him, slightly nodding his head several times. "You're correct; at heart I probably am," he said. "Though with an exception, perhaps." Both men knew he was speaking of Claudia.

Myrmid said, "That does not alter my statement."

Deleig continued, "Antipas suddenly shifted topic. 'Parthians. Magi. Magic. Believe in superstition, boy? Spells, potions, sooths?'"

Deleig did not mention that he had been relieved by the Tetrarch's change of topic.

"I told him, 'I know everything about them. I can cast horoscopes. I was trained by the palace astrologer in Dura-Europos.'

" 'Cast horoscopes?' Antipas said. 'Excellent. Excellent. Find my hand, hold it and cast my horoscope.' "

Deleig said he had reached out in the dark and his fingers touched the Tetrarch's. He had turned Antipas' hand palm upward, as he'd seen Fefeel do so many times. He had rested Antipas' hand on his own left palm and placed his own right hand on top.

"What should I say?" Deleig asked rhetorically. "I hadn't the slightest idea. I was silent while wracking my brains, hoping it seemed as I was calling up mumbo-jumbo. Then I created a distant prediction. I told Antipas, 'You will, in old age, travel once more to Rome. In old age, you will, for a time reside there.' "

" 'Excellent, boy. Excellent,' Antipas said. 'I thought there was something special about you. Follow me, return below. Time you left with your grandfather.' That was it."

Myrmid was quite surprised at Deleig's candor—he was usually more closed mouthed. Talca made to speak. Deleig held up his hand, "Delay one moment, Talca, while I finish a tale for Myrmid. Antipas did not offer hospitality for the night. Grandfather and I were indeed shown the door, almost literally, and our guards had to be called from the palace guards' quarters to join us. The guards knew of an inn of high reputation outside the city wall. Horses were called for. We mounted and left the city. Antipas had not remained to say farewell."

Deleig stretched his hand above his head and waved it over the back of the divan, signaling the servant to bring wine for them.

"Talca, what word?"

"You've been deprived of assessing the Baptizer because he was arrested so quickly. I really do think you should approach the Tetrarch. And we need to hear this Jesus in case he's next for the dungeon. He's the phenomenon, this Nazarene—from an insignificant town up here north of the lake. I am told he is so well versed in the Scriptures, he seems to have the entire Torah memorized and can rapidly pick out the precise reference he wants."

"Thank you, Talca," Deleig said as he accepted a cup of wine from the servant. He took a sip and closed his eyes. He tried to think of nothing for a while and when that didn't work, decided that tomorrow, all would be resolved.

One of his working theories, he thought, was that what cannot be anticipated cannot be avoided. Only repaired if bad, welcomed if good. He liked the playwright Terence's line—a gift from his constantly quoting paternal grandfather—"When we cannot act as we wish, we must act as we can."

So, he told himself, that which could be anticipated simply needed a plan—and considering a variety of likely outcomes from a single premise on the spur of the moment might be one of his skills. Those close to him regarded him a brilliant planner; he thought of himself as slightly better than adequate. Any respite from the confined demanding world of Pilatus' palace was welcome.

He'd been fourteen, a shy boy from Hatra, four hundred miles distant to the East, when he'd first seen Judea. It had been a liberating experience. He'd achieved the threshold of young adulthood on that journey. Deleig thought of the Prefect's son close by. He was fond of the lad, a boy much neglected by his father, a boy who spent his days sequestered in the palace complex much as Deleig himself had been sequestered during his winters with his grandparents in the palace at Dura-Europos.

Still, it was a gamble bringing him, if he said anything.

Formio was a precociously intelligent boy who thought too much, relaxed too little and played not at all. He was smart enough to know he was neglected by his father. Deleig had advised Claudia to arrange for Roman tutors and language instructors.

The justification Deleig offered Pilatus for taking the boy out of his environment—exposed to the company of men, letting him experience the Judea of the people and the messiahs—would force him out of his personal shell. Deleig mused that his own interest in messiahs actually might have less to do with his job of helping the Prefect keep the peace than with his own interest in people's beliefs.

He could enjoy a Judea where religion was a major source of unity—and some disunity—and there was a venerable body of teaching and practice. Trying to understand the Judean factions had become a hobby as well as a pursuit. Studying their laws was an avocation. Spying on everyone he felt was worth spying on was simply his profession.

Galilee was a region only slightly less volatile than Jerusalem, a city always fearful of a Zealot uprising. Similarly, anything could happen anywhere. And did. Far too often.

FIFTEEN

The early morning sun provided light but not yet much heat. Even so, a hawk circled, catching the thermal from a patch of land warmed by weak rays. Songbirds with competing choruses had been welcoming the dawn for more than an hour. Their music currently drowned out by a leathern-hoofed drumbeat as the men, and one boy, cantered out of Capernaum.

Within the half-hour they rounded the curve of Lake Galilee. As the road turned south, it gradually moved away from the lake closer to the slopes of the hill country on the party's left. Morning clouds, slow moving, almost stationary, still nestled around some of the hills. The hills were an introduction to the mountain range far beyond. This was a well-tended and highly productive agricultural region. To the riding party the vista was a feast for the eyes.

"Gorgeous, isn't it?" Deleig called out.

"Too green," returned Myrmid.

"Too early," shouted Talca.

"Too noisy," called Formio. "I can't enjoy the beauty for all the shouting!"

That brought a round of laughter. He'll be all right, thought Deleig. Deleig's horse needed no guidance. It was cantering behind Myrmid's on the scrub and grass alongside the road, a softer surface than the hard, durable Roman road, one of the abundant inter-connecting Roman roads the Empire's provinces, including Judea, boasted.

To anyone watching, the group would have appeared a splendid sight: Talca and Deleig, Myrmid and Formio, plus four guards and three servants. Colorfully clad men led the jaunt. Deleig, as was his custom, wore a Parthian hunting outfit: a highly embroidered thigh-length maroon leather jacket, white leggings, fine tan leather ankle boots and an embroidered cap. Talca wore something vaguely similar, but the dominant color was green. He had no cap.

Myrmid could have passed for a soldier on home leave in his rough and ready riding clothes. Formio, uncertain what to wear, and too shy to ask, had left Caesarea Maritima in a loose green tunic, with a red and tan leather jacket and tan leather kilt-like skirt. The four guards wore their uniforms, the servants a motley of robes and capes of varying color, cut and cloth.

The ride passed pleasantly as the men, riding in twos, shifted configurations to have different people with whom to converse. Talking and calling while cantering could be harsh on the vocal chords after a while.

After a couple of hours, Myrmid sighted a stream, and each man watered his horse. At the roadside, they drank, nibbled on yoghurt cakes flecked with seeds and herbs, chatted and relaxed.

Deleig walked up a steep slope and climbed on to a rocky promontory. He saw the shadowy suggestion of a hill distinguished by two high mounds. Talca's man had reported the previous evening that this was their destination, a place called the Mount. Twin Mounts might be more accurate, thought Deleig.

An hour of idling and they resumed their ride. At least another hour later, and within a half-mile of the site, Deleig could see a dense mass of people milling in a dip in the land just down from what he thought were twin mounds, but were not. A single mound and possibly a dark cloud suggesting a second. The land of the mount was concave at the base and created a natural amphitheatre.

Had these people been there all night? Had they come by boat? Were they all from a nearby town? The horsemen soon reached the edge of the crowd. Deleig signaled the men to halt.

As he dismounted, he said, "Talca and I will join the throng on this side. Myrmid, you go down the center so we're not together. Formio, you go with Myrmid if you want to hear the man. Myrmid, when you see me leaving, you leave, too."

Myrmid gave a nod of understanding and gestured with his hand to Formio. The two headed toward the edge of the crowd at its center rear, several hundred feet away. Deleig eased his way into the crowd where they had dismounted, Talca alongside.

Happily, Deleig was familiar with the ordinary Judean populace. The families he'd met when he had first entered Judea from the desert were imprinted as part of the Pilatus' story. He found he was comfortable with those he met on the Caesarea Maritima breakwater, the men he hired to build his Zoroastrian temple and the women he knew from during his sorties into the kitchens.

Consequently, he had some understanding of the population's views and discontentment. Even while ensuring that the three Zealots would never again try to overthrow the Romans—at least while he was working for Pilatus and Rome—Deleig sympathized with their reasons for wanting to. Were he living in an occupied Parthia, or a Rome dominated Parthia, he'd feel the same. He firmly believed that one day Parthia would be little more than a Rome-controlled entity.

As he and Talca continued to ease forward in the crowd, he towered, as usual, above these people, noting their nods and gestures as they responded to the speaker's words. People in well-traveled clothes. They gave off a mild stench. Judea offered little by way of public baths. Deleig mused—perhaps the Sea of Galilee could serve that purpose.

He liked these particular people immediately, he decided. Why? Possibly because they weren't looking at him, even as he headed past them. He was not on display; there was another attraction.

Normally, people did stare at him. There was a part of him that hated being a six-foot-four Eastern oddity with his height and physical and sartorial distinguishing characteristics. He had no privacy in public. Strolling along the harbor helped, but in reality only the desert kept him sane.

Two things, totally unanticipated, occupied him as he made his way deeper into the crowd. Despite his considerable distance from the speaker, he could clearly hear the man's words. "Blessed are the poor in spirit ..." The clarity was uncanny, inexplicable. Even the hill's natural amphitheatre assistance could not account for the projection.

Those words, he wondered, are these the poor in spirit? "Blessed are those who mourn ..." He kept looking down to his left and right at the faces of the people listening. From their expressions, he detected mourners among them.

The second phenomenon was equally eerie. It was as if the crowd were a single organism. Of its own volition it seemed to part ahead of him and Talca, pulsating the two of them onward toward the front, despite the multitude being quite densely packed together.

The momentum was such he could not have remained in place even had he chosen to do so. "Blessed are the meek, they shall inherit the earth." Are these the meek, and what does he mean? Deleig wondered. All they'll inherit is death. Deleig estimated the crowd at possibly 3,000 or 4,000, but accepted crowd numbers were not one of his skills.

However many people, it was almost five minutes before he arrived close enough to the front to see the speaker's face. As he moved forward, he saw the multitude's front line formed an arc that touched each side of the amphitheatre hill, stretching without a break from one end to the other. It curved in front of the speaker more or less equidistant from him at all points. There was almost a precision to it, Deleig saw, as if there was common agreement on what was a respectful distance from the man.

Now the tall Parthian was in the seventh or eighth row from the front. It was not surprising Jesus caught sight of him. Their eyes did not meet, but the flicker of the unexpected in Jesus' eyes caused some in the crowd to look up at Deleig for themselves. "Blessed are those who hunger ... Blessed are the merciful ..."

If Jesus was not expecting an elegant giant, Deleig had not anticipated the Nazarene. He had thought the man might be small and wiry, like Talca, and radical-looking. He was not a bedraggled person, a ragged person with wide dark-eyes, red-rimmed with passion and lack of sleep, a haunted man with a weathered face and straggling black hair that needed washing and grooming. None of that.

The Nazarene's hair was as much brown as black, perhaps because of the sun. His face was darkened from the constant outdoors, but not greatly weathered or lined. The eyes were indeed dark, but rested and smiling, and his beard had been trimmed within the past two weeks for it was almost neat. The man's mouth was wide, with full lips. His nose had a curve, midpoint. A merry kindliness governed his expression, not from personal comfort, deduced Deleig, more from his fondness, or was it caring, for those listening to him.

He said, "Blessed are the pure of heart, for they shall see God."

He was the average Judean male height, five-foot-six. This was a Nazarene with a fed and comfortable air about him; a man who enjoyed a good meal.

"Blessed are the peacemakers ..."

Deleig turned and looked back into the crowd. The people were intent, but not mesmerized. They were listening, ears cocked for the most part, hearing something that meant something to them, something new, perhaps, something reassuring.

It seemed to Deleig as if the Nazarene was a man winning people through the lively impetus of his passionate belief. They were responding, judging from their expressions of interest and comfortable curiosity, to things they had not considered but, on consideration, found gratifying. But what things? What did it all add up to?

He found himself fascinated by the word "meek." As the Nazarene used it, in the Aramaic, did he mean they were in thrall to something, to someone? Trapped or deceived by someone—perhaps the "brood of vipers," the Pharisees, priests and scribes?

Or meek as in patiently waiting, confidently so? The Nazarene did not appear from the content to be talking of the "meek" as servile. Obedient to something, perhaps. But what? What were they obedient to? Would their belief make them stand firm against their Roman occupiers and lead to a major uprising?

No, Deleig decided, this man was well educated. It was the Greek usage, "gentle," as the Nazarene himself apparently was.

Perhaps Deleig would never know. He'd better find out what the Pharisees were doing that antagonized this man. That would be instructive, as Talca had suggested.

Had the Pharisees and Temple priests turned the previous belief viperish and stung the people with it? Deleig ended that line of reasoning. He allowed himself a little smile. He was pleased with himself for knowing when he didn't know.

Other thoughts occurred. He himself was a man raised in power; he was steeped in power because he was schooled in power. These days he exercised power, the power of life and death if called on. Yet he was faced by a man with a power so tremendous—at least that was what he sensed—he dared to use it only for the benefit of others.

Does that make sense? Deleig asked himself. Why I am thinking such things? Am I oscillating between this man's words and Zoroaster's words?

He forced himself into a different line of thought: he was present at this spot for another reason, based on his espionage responsibilities. Was this man talking in code?

Deleig felt a tapping against his leg. He looked down. It was a young boy.

"I can't see, sir."

Deleig looked at the men in the immediate vicinity, but none appeared to express a proprietary interest in the child. So Deleig bent down, lifted up the boy and set him into the crook of his arm.

Young though he may be, Deleig thought humorously, this child certainly isn't meek. The boy, who appeared to be about six, was travel dirty but not filthy or neglected.

The boy said, "My brother can't see, either, sir."

This young man will go far in life, thought Deleig, smiling at the audacity. He looked down and saw a smaller boy gazing up, smiling broadly. Talca, watching all this, lifted up the second boy.

Deleig returned to concentrating on the Nazarene's words. "... They persecuted the prophets before you."

Now the Jesus man had his elbows tucked to his sides, his hands cupped, palms upward. He had changed his delivery from declamation to presentation. It was, Deleig thought, as if this messiah now had a gift to give, an offering to make.

"You are the salt of the earth," Jesus told the people, opening his hands as if offering them salt and then widening his arms to embrace them all. An audible buzz traveled backward in a wave toward the rear of the vast gathering. In reaction to the words the people seemed to stand a little taller, as if to listen even more intently, as if in acknowledgment the Nazarene was about to explain something fresh.

This upstart messiah's skill appeared to be that he made each listener feel the speaker was talking to him or her alone, thought Deleig. This Jesus also, like Zoroaster, implied the contest between good and evil was to be fought internally, in the soul—and also in the open with public words.

In his spymaster mode Deleig acknowledged he had heard nothing yet to suggest the Nazarene was a threat to Roman authority.

"But if the salt should lose its taste, with what can it be salted?" The Nazarene brushed his hands as if dusting the salt from them.

Heads were nodding, what indeed.

"It's good for nothing but to be thrown outside and be trampled underfoot."

Murmurs, agreement and more vigorous head-nodding. Deleig thought about it. What was the "salt"?

"You are the light of the world."

A gasp. Of awe? Of surprise? Of gratitude? Deleig couldn't tell. The crowd leaned forward a little, to catch what would come next. Deleig turned, the boy on his arm uncomplaining, to gaze on the people looking past him to the speaker, barely noticing him despite his height and prominence so fixed were they on the man.

As the words "Let your light shine before men ..." were being absorbed, Deleig saw tears welling up in people's eyes. "... That they'll see your good works and glorify your father in Heaven ..." These were tears of understanding and, possibly, joy. Deleig gathered that although the words had not touched him in the same way, something was happening.

Now the crowd was shouting "Halleluyah" and "Heal me, Lord," and calls Deleig did not recognize.

He half turned toward the crowd, detected figures moving toward him. These, he suspected, were the boys' parents. To Talca he whispered, "*Denarii.*"

To the boy he was holding he said, "What is your name?"

"Eli, sir." Talca passed Deleig some copper coins and two *denarii*.

"Well, Eli," Deleig said, as he lowered the boy, "give this to your parents, but keep the others to share between yourself and your brother. Be a good son to your parents."

"Yes, sir. Oh! Thank you, your majesty," he said when he saw the money in his hand.

Talca followed suit with coins so the two boys were united. The parents approached anxiously, not an easy approach given the density of the crowd, and hesitantly, given the stature and obvious importance of Deleig.

The Parthian eased the two boys toward them and nodded to the father, who half bowed respectfully in return. Then Deleig turned his attention again to the front.

Jesus had paused. Deleig said to Talca, "A moment more, then we shall leave. I do not want to be caught up in this crowd if it starts to shift."

Jesus said, "Don't think I came to overturn the Torah or the prophets: I came not to destroy, but fulfill ..."

Deleig was delighted with himself. That's what the "salt" is, he told himself. Not the message, not the words and injunctions of the Hebrew bible, but the manner in which it is implemented by these everyday people. Quite pacifistic, Deleig decided.

He narrowed his eyes to gaze again at this Nazarene. As a preacher and teacher, the man surely was a modern Zoroaster.

Deleig turned, tapped Talca on his shoulder and indicated they should exit to the side, across the crowd and skirt back to where they'd left the guards and servants. The crowd parted for them as if soft earth before a plow. It was almost fifteen minutes before they were back at their horses.

Deleig said, "Thank you, Talca. I appreciate what it was you were trying to tell me about this man and his followers. This is not a cracked-pot messiah leaking nonsense or sedition. There is something more." At the same time Deleig wanted to be on guard against being unwittingly lulled or lured by someone else's message.

He'd felt a strong pull on hearing this man's commanding words—that, he knew, was due to the preacher's skill and the crowd's reaction. He wasn't sure what the sum total of what he'd heard amounted to. It was so fresh that people who knew the Torah were entranced. And yes, people are inclined to hear what they want to hear.

Some *might* be convinced he was talking revolt. Yet *why* was the Nazarene doing all this? He hadn't focused on God. He had not told the people what to do so much as what to be. Undoubtedly a further clue would be in the behavior of the Pharisees and Temple priests. He'd increase surveillance on them. Talca was good at that.

Formio and Myrmid arrived back.

"What did you think of the man, Formio?"

"I had no concept of the man," the boy said. "I couldn't actually see him. My Aramaic is, as you know it to be, good but not excellent. From what I could understand, I was entranced. I am going to concentrate on my Aramaic so I can hear him again. Will you take me, please, if you go to hear him, Prince Musan, sir?"

"Yes, I shall," said Deleig, "if your father permits it." To Talca he said, "What do we know about the men around Jesus?"

"There seem to be four or five principals he relies on, most of them former fishermen, my lord, but I'm not close enough to them yet to answer the question."

"When S'veyda gets here, I want him with this crowd all the time. S'veyda will look into the principals' backgrounds for us, see how this Nazarene recruited them, and why."

With a laugh, Deleig added, "Let us learn what his guiding principles are for selecting *his* deputies, eh? Assign someone to stay with this crowd, no, not the crowd, the preacher, until S'veyda's here. Must have good notes of what he is saying—you've people you can rely on absolutely for that, I'm sure."

"Yes sir, everything is under control," Talca said. Deleig had no reason to doubt it.

SIXTEEN

The ride from the Mount back to Capernaum was uneventful; conversationally it was also quieter. Apart from one exchange with Talca, each calling to the other as they trotted along, Deleig was lost in thought, his expression impassive as he tried to decipher what he'd heard. Even the exchange with Talca was quite brief.

"Talca," he called out, "be sure to note every time he refers to the Law. If the Law is the fulcrum of the seesaw, is he at one end, the Pharisees and Temple priests at the other? Or is he one point of a triangle: Nazarene, Pharisees, Temple? That's what it seems from what you've told me, and what the reports are saying. I must admit to be confused."

"I will, yes, my lord," called Talca, replying in a loud way to be heard above the noise of wind and hoofs. "I will give you a report."

Deleig nodded. He was satisfied. He must hear this man, Jesus, again. Almost immediately.

He needed to know what a Judean, a preacher, would hear when he listened to these words. That was it; he needed advice, guidance. He knew the words, but he was missing the nuance, the implication.

Deleig leaned over, tapped Formio's shoulder and indicated he would return. He urged his horse forward until he was alongside Talca. Myrmid immediately dropped back. Deleig shouted to Talca that once they reached Capernaum, Talca needed to locate a preacher.

He wanted a preacher who would accompany him to wherever was necessary the next time he listened to Jesus. He hoped it would be the next day. That way the preacher could explain to him the significance to the Judeans of what Jesus was actually saying.

Deleig needed someone who knew what was behind the words. Talca said he understood. Deleig dropped back, and Myrmid resumed his lead place.

That evening, Talca went to find a preacher, while Myrmid was at the changing station organizing everything for the next morning. Deleig spent an hour going through reports delivered to Myrmid and Talca from their operatives.

Deleig and Formio were together inside the centurion's seaside villa finishing a meal. It was nightfall. A servant lit a series of two-wick and four-wick lamps around the room, and offered to lower a many-wicked hanging lamp, but Deleig said just to bring the existing lamps to their side of the room.

They sat opposite each other across the narrow width of a rough dining table. It had been scrubbed often. The veins of the wood stood out slightly where the softer wood had been scrubbed away. Idly, Deleig ran the nail of his right forefinger along one of the veins, and back again. He could tell he was relaxed. It was rare he found time for such simple-minded nonsense. He could also tell the boy was determined to ask him something, but was struggling for words. He'll find them.

"Prince Musan, sir," said Formio, pulling Deleig out of his dreaming. The boy's brow was creased, his eyes betrayed his uncertainty. "May I ask you a question? It will probably come out the wrong way."

Formio was seated upright on his bench, his arms tight to his side, his hands lightly resting on the table as if facing a tutor—or his stern father.

"Of course you may, Formio."

The words tumbled out of the boy's mouth, anxiety in every phrase.

"How can a Parthian, once the enemy, work for Rome, and why did you leave Parthia, and what is Parthia like and is it an empire as powerful as Rome, and will there be another war and we'll be actual enemies again? Oh, and how did the Parthians defeat Crassus at Carrhae?"

He caught his breath. The velocity of his delivery slowed as he continued, "What was it like growing up as a prince, and would you mind telling me what your name means, and why did you come to Rome?"

The boy was sweating. Whether from embarrassment, or from the exertion of pulling all his concerns together—Deleig wasn't sure. He smiled, reached across the table and tapped Formio on his left hand.

"There are no questions you cannot ask me. Whether I can or will always answer them is a different matter. I know you want to know about Parthia. But I can't do all that in one evening. I will tell you it can be brutally hot, the air is always dry, there are occasional floods during the rainy season; otherwise it is sand, and wind, and heat. There are finely built monuments, temples and official residences from earlier times, decorative work of the highest order some thousand and more years old. Perhaps before Talca returns I can tell you about the Parthian Empire, and Crassus' defeat and the loss of the Legionary Eagles. If Talca comes in, we'll have to stop, and you'll have to remember where I left off."

Formio smiled and said, "I'll remember."

"Bring me my wax tablet and stylus from over there," Deleig said, pointing to a side table, the centurion's work desk that Deleig had claimed as his own. Deleig traveled with various forms of writing materials. He liked the Roman variety, not least the ready availability of sheets of papyrus. In Hatra, he'd written and drawn on vellum and other finely tanned animal skins. He found papyrus with an ink quill an easy medium.

Formio quickly hopped up from his bench as Deleig said, "And sit opposite me again. I'll begin to sketch in the Parthian Empire." The boy placed the tablet and stylus in front of Deleig and went to sit at the opposite side.

Deleig drew a "U" shape on the tablet and then a ragged line under the U that sloped down from right to left. He turned it around and pushed it toward Formio.

He said, "My name is Musan Shaheen Deleig. If we reach that point, I shall explain 'Musan' to you. What matters for the moment is that 'Shaheen' is the Parthian word for 'falcon,' the Turkic and Arab word, too. That 'U' is the Caspian Sea. The line below it is the Kopet Dag mountain range, the northern limit of what, two and three centuries ago, would begin to grow into the Parthian Empire."

He laughingly told Formio, "In an era when Parthia was less a country than a region, local tribes, impoverished rather than not, galloped around the steppes and, to occupy the time, fought one another for supremacy."

The boy's obvious fascination kept Deleig going.

"This was Greek territory, though not a particular diadem in the Hellenic crown. The Hellenistic culture had applied only the thinnest of veneers to Parthia's turbulent though scarcely ruling class. 'Class' in this instance denotes the slight change in social status from being of the local tribe to ruling it.

"Meanwhile, nearly a thousand miles away, on the northern side of the Mediterranean, the well-organized and possibly already overpopulated walled city-state of Rome—three centuries ago, mind you—hardly recommended itself as a future empire either. Its expansionary vision was limited.

"When not reeling from the Gauls' sackings and sieges, Romans conquered nearby territory—mainly forest folk—with commendable determination. That done, the Romans returned to safety inside their walls. The lives of the populace were governed by a developing system of laws, regulation, religion and ritual. These developments might appear to prepare the Romans for their later military and cultural dominance, but it was a matter no Roman republican of those centuries speculated on."

Deleig looked at Formio to gauge whether he was absorbing it all. He was.

He said there was a certain provincial self-satisfaction to Rome's residents even then. Wealth was in the hands of the large-scale farmers who sheltered within the city walls at night. "It took a minority of ambitious strivers to stir Rome to its expansionist aims."

Deleig explained how, a little more than two centuries earlier, Parthia began its expansion—thanks to others. Earlier the region was part of Cyrus the Great's Persian swath. A mix of invaders and invaded—Persian, Greek, Seleucid, Parni, Parthian—was the amalgam that coalesced into modern Parthia.

"Seleucid kings went to war using the region's 'Syrian' elephants, behemoths far larger than their Indian cousins, Formio. It was said that a century later, Hannibal's favorite elephant, the enormous 'Surus,' was of the same stock. But it was not elephants that stirred the fortunes. The future was based on the Parthians' horsemanship and archery."

He told how over time the region developed an extremely lethal cavalry of horse-mounted archers of enviable skill, a devastating assault was known far and wide as the "Parthian shot." The archers could swing around on their horses, continuing to shoot their arrows, and ride in their line past the boys on camels who snatched their enormous but now empty quivers and slotted in filled ones.

"This was the 'Parthian shot' that defeated Crassus. First Crassus, then the battle?"

Formio nodded.

Deleig slouched back in his chair and smiled. He found another raised vein in the wood and ran his fingernail along it as Formio watched. He was pulling the account together.

"Marcus Licinius Crassus—a man you wouldn't want to know. Rome's richest man and all his money gained the same way. Every battle he won gave him the opportunity to extort money from the populace, and he was as good at that as he was at winning battles. It was why he was good at winning battles." Deleig was still smiling, and Formio was now smiling, too.

"Men grow old, Formio, and make mistakes. Women grow old too, but become wiser with age. Perhaps it is retribution for all the indignities men inflict on them while they might. Julius Caesar came back wealthy from his battling in Spain, but that was after Crassus had paid off his earlier indebtedness, which was considerable.

"Sooo, Crassus used his wealth generously for the populace, distributing vast amounts of free grain. And among his friends spent his gold freely, yet still possessed thousands of talents—and could well have been the wealthiest man in the world ever. You know the Greek King Midas myth?"

Formio nodded several times.

"Crassus' greed in age was not for more gold, more talents, but for a battle honor so huge it would raise his stature as a general higher than that of his greatest rival, Gnaeus Pompey. That need for stature consumed Crassus as Midas' greed had consumed him. The myth is Midas prayed for gold and it was granted as a 'golden touch'. Everything he touched turned to gold. He died of starvation.

"As I mentioned, as men age they make mistakes, and Crassus, now entering his eighties, made a huge mistake. Whether he prayed for a victory I know not. What he decided, however—and he could afford to wage any war he wanted—was the 'triumph' rewarded superior warriors."

Then, just as he had told the Rufus twins a decade earlier, Deleig recounted the story of Carrhae. As he finished, a shocked Formio said, "That's horrible."

"War is horrible, Formio. I don't like it, but I know its intricacies of movement well enough. Crassus was killed. There were plenty of myths as to how he died. One was that to punish him for his constant greed, molten gold was poured down his living throat. I doubt that—it takes a great deal of heat to melt gold, and the battlefield isn't a likely place."

Deleig knew he would not lose this audience of one, but wondered how many times in his life he would have to tell this same tale. He continued, "The Parthians seized three golden *aquilae*, the Legionary Eagles, the regimental honors. The young officer who accomplished that was my paternal grandfather, Deleig of Deleig. He was also the one who persuaded my maternal grandfather, King Phraates IV, to return the Legionary Eagles to Rome—as a gesture to Rome once the *Pax Romana* became an actuality. General Deleig of Deleig was the one who presented them to the Roman Legate in Damascus for forwarding to Rome. Carrhae is how my father's family rose to prominence in the Parthian scheme of things. So high was his military reputation, with the Romans even, he was able to have me educated in Rome."

He was about to continue that through such warfare, Parthia had extended its reach through Babylonia as major cities became Parthian. But Deleig realized he'd said enough and just added that the Empire ended on the Syrian-Judean border, just below the Roman-held Armenian line—much to Rome's annoyance. Parthian rule extended south and west, down the chain of Arab cities to the southwestern edge of Arabia, down almost to the Straits of Hormuz.

At that point Talca returned to the villa, collecting water from a side table as he entered the room. He greeted Deleig and Formio and sat down at the table. He saw the wax tablet but made no comment.

He had located a preacher, Yosef ben Shimon. But Preacher Yosef had begged off accompanying Deleig anywhere. He had said, however, his brother, Yaakov ben Shimon, a religious scholar of some repute, would be available the next day. Deleig would do better consulting him. Talca had agreed.

Preacher Yosef had also said it would be more seemly if Deleig came to the synagogue. If he or his brother went to a Roman official's Capernaum villa, it could be misinterpreted.

Deleig asked Talca to have Myrmid join them in the morning. They'd go to the synagogue together. A messenger was sent to inform Preacher Yosef of this and to ask him to tell his brother it would involve a journey to the Decapolis area. Within a half-hour the messenger returned. Preacher Yosef said his brother, the scholar, would accompany them if the Romans supplied the transport. Talca excused himself, saying he would go to Myrmid and tell him the latest developments.

"Where were we?" Deleig asked Formio as Talca left.

"Blood and gore and war—and the Straits of Hormuz," said Formio. He slid the wax tablet closer to Deleig. Deleig was again idling, his fingernail running along the vein of wood that fascinated his forefinger. He stopped and picked up his stylus. Deleig kept the tablet facing the boy so Formio could follow as he sketched in a rough and shaky attenuated and tilted "Y."

"Mesopotamia is called 'the land between two waters'. The River Tigris meets the River Euphrates to form a 'Y' shape, and Mesopotamia is between the two prongs. This dot up here is Hatra, where I was born and raised, and down along the Euphrates is Dura-Europos, here, where I was educated during the winters under my grandfather's keen eye."

Deleig explained that while Parthia would become an empire, it was barely one in the Roman organizational sense. Not particularly centralized, it was a collection of kingdoms, such that Cyrus the Great had been correct to described himself as "king of kings." Deleig said, "Parthians are Zoroastrians. They believe in the one God, Ahura Mazda, not like Romans with a pantheon of gods."

Formio said, "I don't know anything about religion. Or politics, or what my father really does. I have no family, no relations. There are no children my age in the palace. My tutors—those you brought in for me—test my rhetoric and my Aramaic and Greek. I don't know how well I'm doing. My tutors never leave the palace with me, never, ever take me anywhere. I know only I'm the Prefect's son.

"Are people afraid to talk to me or be seen with me because of it? You're the only one—apart from my mother, of course—who knows I exist. I have never had a conversation with my father, beyond his asking if I need anything and me replying, 'No, thank you, sir, I have everything.'

"For me to be here, for you to say, 'ask questions,' for Talca and Myrmid to address me—not as a peer, I know that—but as a, what, I don't know, but as one of them, is remarkable. If I were a year younger, I'd probably cry with relief. At this age, I'm just relieved. Confused, too. I don't know how to act or—"

"Formio," interrupted Deleig, "quite simply, you are among friends. Even if they are much older than you. Where were we?"

"You'd mentioned God and Zoro ..."

"Zoroaster. He was a widely traveled preacher, an interpreter of Ahura Mazda, who created Mazda's words in poetic form. A preacher much like this Nazarene we heard. Except Zoroaster dealt in sensitive poetry. Much poetry is retrospective. It looks back to a person, a moment, a love, an era, a glimpse of beauty—lost."

"I'd like to read some plays and the poetry from other lands," Formio said.

"Ahura Mazda's preacher, Zoroaster, must have been a remarkable man," Deleig said, "for he was certainly an impressive poet. His metrical brilliance was such that the stanzas of his works—known collectively as Gathas—could be rearranged like dominoes."

Deleig could tell Formio didn't quite understand but decided to keep going. "By rearranging the stanzas but keeping the words the same, he could oblige his listener to look inward, outward, up or down, but always toward God—Ahura Mazda. Zoroaster poetically sings of these expectations and the means to achieve them. Personal interior moral conduct is the key that unlocks the desire and ability to achieve goodness of thought. Poetic songs, along with the fire and water rites, provide Zoroastrians with symbols that represent those attributes."

He told Formio that the Parthians and Romans were not pitted one against the other for religion's sake. It was territorial acquisition. Parthia in its own region had been successful and would have held Syria after defeating Crassus had it not been for a forceful Idumaean, Herod the Great.

Herod employed less conventional fighting methods than Rome's, including luring Parthian forces away from the flat plains—flat plains were where the Parthians had the advantage—to much rougher ground that required more close-contact fighting.

"An uncouth savage, and good fighter, Herod the Great did push the Parthians out of Syria and back behind the River Euphrates. The victory altered Herod's life," Deleig said. "As a reward, Marc Anthony installed him as Rome's King of Judea, a decision confirmed by the Roman Senate. Herod was still on hand for any Parthian incursions into neighboring Syria.

"To celebrate his defeat of the Parthians, Herod built Herodium. After Herod died came Herod Archelaus, ethnarc of Judea, Samaria and Idumaea. Twenty-five years ago Rome took control of the Judean province, ended the idea of a king and reduced the Herodian influence to Herod Antipas and Herod II: Antipas as Tetrarch of Galilee and Herod II as Tetrarch of Judea. That's enough history for tonight."

"You didn't describe *Pax Romana*," Formio insisted.

"In the years following Julius Caesar's assassination, the Republic metamorphosed politically into Imperial Rome. Octavian, later Emperor Augustus, more skilled in battle and negotiation than Crassus, was also alert to the limitations of Empire.

"He declared the front between Parthia and Rome at the Euphrates the 'Peace Line' between the empires. Augustus' prolonged *Pax Romana* in the region is what brings you and me together as friends. It also allows Rome to turn its attention, or at least its expansion, away from the Euphrates and the East, to look northward toward the outermost boundaries of Gaul, to the threshold of Germania. And that's where your father was before his promotion to Prefect of Judea."

Deleig felt it would be unworthy of him to suggest it was anything other than a promotion.

"That's very informative, and interesting," said Formio, stifling a yawn. "But what about you. Where do you fit into all this?"

Deleig placed his stylus on the table and flapped his hands like bird wings. His fingers were stiff. Formio, somewhat sleepy-eyed by this time, looked expectantly.

"You'll enjoy this. My paternal grandfather and my father deposed my uncle King Phraates V, and that's how I got my name, Musan. These periodic ousting of our kings always much amused military Rome. We didn't keep kings we didn't want—"

"But what about your name, Prince Musan?"

"Another time. Head for your room and sleep; otherwise you'll keep me talking all night."

Formio, alert now, thought for a moment. Then he said, "What if we talk until Talca returns?"

"No. Go."

Deleig smiled, partly commiserated with what Formio was doing, seeking company. He commiserated because he kept going back to his own feelings of isolation at Dura-Europos when his grandfather was otherwise occupied. He hadn't realized how neglected the boy felt, nor, until then, how neglected he himself had been.

SEVENTEEN

The following morning Deleig left with Talca and Myrmid to meet the preachers at the synagogue. They were there, smiling. Deleig said he would never have assumed they were brothers.

Preacher Yosef was a short cylindrical figure, white bearded, curly haired, round-faced, with small, merry eyes. Preacher Yaakov was tall, broad, with a sizeable stomach. He was balding with long black hair and a matching beard. A more serious mien.

"You are an Aramaic-speaking Roman?" Preacher Yosef asked.

"A Roman citizen, Parthian by birth and a Zoroastrian by belief. I am interested in belief ... religions. I have studied Hebrew."

Preacher Yaakov looked surprised. "Where did you study Hebrew?"

Deleig told of the Judean community in Rome's Porta Capena. Both brothers were amazed there was such a community in the city, but Deleig could not tell them why it was there.

Preacher Yosef said, "May I ask, sir, your function in Judea?"

"You may ask," Musan replied, "but I doubt you'll receive a satisfactory answer."

"That is a satisfactory answer."

Yosef gestured they should leave the synagogue, and he gently led the five of them toward a modest building next door, obviously his home. He gestured they should enter, but Talca indicated he and Myrmid would remain outside.

The house was actually a pleasant structure with an atrium. The two preachers and Deleig selected benches. A woman in dark clothing appeared with fruit juices and nuts, which she placed alongside Preacher Yosef—likely her husband, Musan decided. The woman hurriedly departed, as if eager to remove herself from any possible contagion from Roman presence.

The preachers seemed fascinated. Both men said they had heard of the Nazarene, but neither had gone to listen to him. He was, they said, a Pharisee preacher like themselves.

Preacher Yaakov said, "So, explain, sir, your concerns regarding the Nazarene, this Yoshua, the man your servant referred to as Jesus. As we mentioned, Yosef and I have not heard him, only of him and his cures. There has been his like before in terms of healers. I went to the Jordan when the Baptizer was there. He was unusual. Original. We hadn't seen or heard his like among the would-be prophets and messiahs in our time. I understand the Nazarene is the Baptizer's follower, if so, he is as likely to be arrested by Herod Antipas."

He looked around as if expecting to be asked questions.

"The Baptizer was remarkably—pleasingly—outspoken about the Tetrarch's moral and, should I say, 'administrative' excesses, as a ruler. Am I speaking in confidence, sir, or am I liable to arrest?"

The question surprised Deleig. It was evident on his face.

Preacher Yaakov realized he had misjudged the situation, for he immediately said, "My apologies, I understand. As a ruler the Tetrarch is erratic, arbitrary and inclined to cruelty—the characteristics of imposed rulers, and far too many selected rulers. As an aside, that was. Herod Antipas is a haunted man—"

"Haunted and superstitious, and reliant on horoscopes," interrupted Deleig. "I once cast his horoscope for him, but please let that slide away as another aside—"

Somewhat startled, Yaakov said, "So, there is trouble ahead for your Nazarene if he, too, criticizes the Tetrarch. Now you want me to travel with you. I am willing, quite interested, in doing so."

Deleig said, "I know what this Jesus man says, and I have some notes. But I don't know what he means by what he says. That is, I tend to hear something behind his words. I cannot explain quite what I hear to myself, let alone to you. I seem to hear more than he is saying."

"He's an excellent preacher then."

"I watched the crowd's faces. There were several thousand people, by my estimation. Yet all could hear him. More than that, however, I sensed—it was no more than that—that what they were hearing was not necessarily what I was hearing."

"In which case a superior preacher. Now I am really interested. What has he said?"

"Well, as I said, when we arrived he was talking about people as 'blesseds.' "

Deleig gave examples: "Blessed are those who mourn ... Blessed are the meek ... the peacemakers ... the merciful ... those who hunger ..."

"How learned a Zoroastrian are you?" Preacher Yaakov asked.

The question surprised Deleig, but he answered, simply, "I have both studied and memorized Zoroaster's poetry and his writings on Ahura Mazda. I attend the temples."

The preacher continued pressing him, "You are familiar with the metrical intricacies of his poetry?"

"That the stanzas can be moved around and re-arranged to provide a different message on a different topic with a differing final point. Yes."

"Well," said Preacher Yaakov, "all preachers are faced with the same ... test. How to keep saying the same thing differently about a finite number of variations on the human condition. Dare I begin the list ... love, honesty, fidelity and on? But it *is* limited. What is demanded of us on this topic or that? What we do about it? Yes?"

Deleig nodded that he understood.

"Yes," said the preacher. "Your Preacher Jesus appears—I am not certain, I have only your few words, and your presentiments—your Preacher Jesus appears to be describing how God sees the masses as individuals—individuals, not in a group."

"He did not focus on God," said Deleig, who realized the preacher was not addressing his question.

"He is letting the individual see himself in the setting. Whether I am right or wrong, I shall be pleased to listen to him. The 'blessed are the meek' is from Psalm 39. What else?"

Deleig said, "The Pharisees—a 'brood of vipers.' "

"Ah! Genesis. The viper is the devil. He is calling them, calling me, a son of evil. That I must certainly hear. The context is key," said Preacher Yaakov. "That I must hear. Then I shall tell you what I think. But why are you disturbed?"

Deleig was slow to answer. Finally he said, "I am afraid he may go too far and force either the Pharisees or the Temple priests to retaliate violently against him. I see that. He wants that—according to my interpretation. My first worry is keeping public trouble in Jerusalem to a minimum, and my second worry is why?"

"Why indeed? When do you want me to be ready?"

"I shall send a messenger to you in the morning once I have intelligence on where he is. We shall go by boat if he is close to the shore. Otherwise on horseback. His location will determine the time of our leaving."

"I have never ridden a horse," said the preacher.

"Would you be comfortable riding behind me on my horse?"

"Yes."

Deleig thanked both preachers. They walked with him to where Talca and Myrmid now waited.

As it turned out, there was no need to ride out to hear Jesus. The watcher reported Jesus had returned, by boat, to Capernaum. Obviously hoping to escape the mob, he had come ashore to the west of the city quite early and entered the home of a friend. Talca's contacts said he did intend to preach in the area but for the present the Nazarene was resting in a friend's home.

Deleig was again impressed with how efficiently Talca's men functioned. He sent a messenger to Preacher Yaakov. He doubted the Nazarene's presence would be secret for very long. In that Deleig was soon proved correct.

When he, Formio, Preacher Yaakov, Talca and Myrmid reached the house Jesus had entered, it was already surrounded by hundreds of people. Deleig remained fifty yards away from the edge of the crowd. Something had altered since he had last heard the Nazarene. In the countryside of the Decapolis, the crowd had been patient, attentive, respectful. This crowd was frenzied. There was agitation, murmuring. People with sick relatives deliberately jostled against others in an attempt to force their way closer to the surrounded house.

There were sick people everywhere. Relatives carried them on their backs, or two supported an ailing person by his or her arms. The all-pervading sound was of supplication, with perhaps a tinge of suppressed anger at receiving no response.

Deleig sensed a group such as this could be provoked into fury by troublemakers. There were pushy relatives and friends, a minority, who shouted rather than called, who demanded Jesus come out and cure the sick. These were not respectful requests to a preacher and healer. That these were stop-at-nothing demands quickly became evident.

Several men climbed onto the house roof. They systematically dismantled a portion of roof while others maneuvered a sick man on a pallet up to them. From there he was lowered down into the house where, Deleig presumed, Jesus was teaching.

Deleig was simultaneously horrified by the men's aggressiveness and fascinated by their determination. He did not push through the crowd. In fact, he was about to suggest they return to the villa to await information from Talca's Jesus-watchers when the crowd began to quiet down, hushed, wary.

Heads were turned in Deleig's direction, but he realized no one was looking at him. He turned around. "That's our host," Talca whispered, indicating a centurion who was approaching. Many in the crowd around the house quietly began to ease away, uncertain what to expect.

No one wanted Roman force unleashed. People who had been besieging the house were briskly walking down alleyways on either side of it, heading for either their homes or their boats.

Deleig's group remained where it was. As the centurion kept his steady pace toward the house, he turned slightly and nodded to the easily recognizable Deleig.

Preacher Yaakov whispered to Deleig, "We know this man. He built our synagogue for us. Our people do well under his rule."

Deleig said nothing. He watched the centurion. Those from the crowd who had not fled also watched with interest, realizing they were not being threatened. The centurion had come alone.

Word of the centurion's approach had obviously reached those inside the house because the door opened. Jesus stepped out into the tiny courtyard. He looked careworn, or perhaps disappointed in the crowd's behavior.

"Sir," Jesus said.

The centurion looked at Jesus, saying, "Preacher, my faithful servant is a good man and a loyal friend. Now desperately ill. I fear he is nearing death."

Jesus said, "I will come to him."

"There is no need, sir, for you to enter under my roof," said the centurion. "If you say the word, my servant will be cured."

Jesus opened his arms; his exultation erased the creases of care, the lines of disappointment. His arms were now at their fullest extent as he turned this way and that to address the crowd. Arms still wide, his pleasing voice, magnified joyously by diaphragm and chest, in a cadence of almost hymn-like glorious notes, filled the area. He crooned, "Hear what I have heard, O people. Not in Israel have I found such faith. Listen to me, O people. Not in Israel have

I found such faith."

Jesus nodded slowly to the centurion. The soldier understood his servant was healed. A servant sent quickly to his villa soon confirmed it to the crowd.

Deleig was extremely impressed. He touched Preacher Yaakov's arm. "Jesus can work these miracles? What does that say about him?"

"Beyond that he is a miracle worker? We shall have to listen more, to learn. I'll take my leave. Send for me if you want me."

But it was not that day. Jesus had returned to the house. Within a short while it was common knowledge he had left through the rear and gone quickly down to the seashore. He had stepped into a boat and was being taken out to sea.

Deleig said, "Talca, let us thank our centurion host for his hospitality. At the same time, I can learn from him whether a miracle did truly occur."

The centurion was flattered to receive so august a guest, though Deleig was trying hard to downplay his importance in Rome. The centurion's servant was healed, and the party spent almost an hour in comfortable company. They discussed Judea, messiahs—and obliquely—issues in Rome. The centurion was extremely impressed with Deleig's knowledgeable authority—and place in the highest Roman circles—and had not yet learned of Sejanus' execution.

Jesus did return, later. Talca's watchers reported he dined in Capernaum at a tax collector's home; other guests included prostitutes. But the Nazarene was gone again—he had left by boat mid-evening. A storm had blown up, and no one was quite certain where the boat had headed during the squall.

"He's in the hands of first-class sailors," Talca said. "Remember, many of his intimates are fishermen."

According to those on shore, the boat had taken up full sail and headed into the fury of wind and rain as if making for Tiberias, on the western shore of the Sea of Galilee.

During the night, however, an astute employee of Talca, a watcher familiar with the whims of Galilee's squalls, had traveled by boat along the lakeshore. By mid-morning the watcher was at the villa Deleig was using to announce Jesus was in Gennesaret, a mere five miles from Capernaum.

The messiah had arrived early, cured many sick and then entered a house. Its door had remained closed. Another watcher had been posted. Deleig, pleased by the man's astuteness in following the squall along the coast, thanked him and had Talca reward him.

"Are all your men like that? So bright and dedicated?" asked Deleig.

"All your men are, my lord."

EIGHTEEN

As they rode back on the *cursus publicus* to Caesarea Maritima from Capernaum, Deleig and Formio were engaged in a minor battle of wills. Formio several times tried to engage Deleig in conversation. Deleig wanted the time alone—to think.

"Not now, Formio."

Traveling leisurely in a carriage, eyes closed, almost in danger of nodding off, suited cogitation. Deleig was reviewing what he knew about the Nazarene. He'd been wrong to assume one could make something of Jesus' message simply by analyzing it on the spot.

The well-informed Judean, a preacher, an authority on Jesus' religion, couldn't or wouldn't explain or speculate on the meaning behind the words. Preacher Yaakov had played the words against his own preferences, including apparently, a preference for refusing to commit himself. The surprise was, to Deleig, that Talca had been sharper.

Talca lacked Yaakov's knowledge, yet had keener insights. When they'd stopped for a break, Talca argued that to gauge the Nazarene's impact meant understanding how the people reacted. As simple as that: did they believe him?

His friend had a knack for incisive, insightful interpretation. It was always Talca's notes he relied on. It was Talca who'd initially insisted Jesus was an intriguing character. He was correct, and Deleig was enjoying being intrigued. It was a break from the boredom of routine espionage—a routine interspersed with Pilatus' eruptions.

He allowed his mind to wander further. Then he had it. Those who most clearly understood the Nazarene's words weren't people like Yaakov, or the scribes and Pharisees, or observers like himself.

It took the stranger—the uninformed, the uneducated, the sick, the outcast or the desperate—to most clearly hear what he was saying. Deleig allowed himself to be pleased, yet felt slightly embarrassed doing it.

It had taken him the hours since leaving Capernaum to reach that conclusion. He rebuked himself: how slow he was. He signaled Formio. "Formio, come and see me this evening. After you've dined with your parents. I might forget because I shall be going through my reports. Come to my quarters and tell Myrmid you're expected." The now ecstatically pleased young man nodded.

The first duty of a returned espionage chief is to report to his superior. Pilatus was notified of the party's return even as it was still approaching. The Prefect sent a servant to tell Claudia their son was coming, and they both walked rapidly to the palace's grand entrance to greet him.

Pilatus immediately said he had chosen Deleig's Capernaum excursion to raid the Roman treasury in Judea of funds earmarked for an aqueduct, but he wanted the money for something else. When Deleig asked what, Pilatus replied he was using it to complete his Tiberium.

To Deleig the building was a theatre that was nothing less than a temple to the Emperor, a grand gathering space. The Tiberium, Deleig surmised, also served another purpose. Pilatus, denied honors in Gaul, did not want to die unnoticed and unknown. An exterior part of the Tiberium's southern wall—though the building was not yet completed—was an inscribed marble slab stating who had built it in Emperor Tiberius' honor.

"The money was there," Pilatus barked. "I used it. That ends this discussion."

Deleig simply said, "Pontius, your son was excellent company. His behavior as one of the team was exemplary. He earned the respect of all."

The Prefect beckoned Formio forward. Uneasily and briefly, the father rubbed his son's head, saying, "Glad to hear that, very pleased. Well done, boy. Very pleased. Do you need anything?"

"No, thank you, sir. I have everything."

"Good. Good."

To Deleig Pilatus said, "Anything notable?"

"Herodias wants the Baptizer dead. Antipas is resisting. He's afraid of the Baptizer—and there's always the chance his death could cause a riot among the followers."

Pilatus nodded, "We'll confer later. Good trip?"

"Most productive. This evening, before dinner?"

"Good. Good," said Pilatus. He turned and left.

Deleig stretched his arms in the air. He must go for a run and do his exercises. Formio, who had greeted his mother, was helping—or hindering—Myrmid in selecting which pack went to which servant to be carried to which quarters. Deleig took the few steps necessary to be able to address Claudia in private.

"Greetings, Claudia. It is always a pleasure to see you again. I never realized that Formio was so isolated, that he has no friends his own age. Perhaps we can do something. There must be other Roman boys in the city: sons of freedmen even, those looking after commercial interests? I'm sorry I hadn't realized it, but then I don't see much of either of you to discuss these things. You never seem to want your future told by your personal astrologer."

"I know my future," she said with a wry smile. "No, that's not true. Rather, what I know of my future does not allow for the hopes a horoscope might express—Musan."

Her remark was pointed. She understood how he felt about her. Deleig's heart leapt and sank. She maintained her social distance.

"As for poor Formio," she continued, "I've never thought to look outside the palace, Musan. It never occurred to me." Her expression suggested she felt remiss.

Deleig said, "Talca and I know a couple of people in the *argentarii* district. I'll inquire into their family status. They may be bankers but that doesn't disqualify them from having decent, well-mannered and educated sons. Give me a few days."

"Of course, thank you," she said. The accompanying smile hurt him more than it gratified. He wanted her smile for himself. All of her for himself.

In their early years in Judea, Deleig had been treated as a member of Pilatus' family. These days he rarely saw them socially in their quarters. The intermittent tension and arguments between Pilatus and himself had created the social distance. Invitations to dine in *familia* became rare, then finally ceased.

Later, in his quarters, rested and bathed, Deleig was back at the reports.

Formio arrived. He had changed into a fresh tunic, his curls no longer rat's tails after the long trip.

"Prince Musan, sir, my father asks if you would dine with us this evening within the hour."

Deleig swung around on his seat to face Formio and answered, more stiffly than he'd intended, "I am honored, please tell him so."

Deleig was at his desk. As he had been poring through the day's reports, he'd been thinking about the boy, uncertain about continuing to take him into his full confidence. By default, Formio would hear more and more things he wasn't supposed to know. Would he tell his father?

His father would be outraged the boy was privy to so much. To Deleig, however, who had never been shielded from the highest machinations of state and throne, trust was the only issue, not youth.

Poor Formio, thought Deleig, if I asked him, "How do I know you won't betray me?" he'd possibly burst into tears.

To break the awkward silence, Deleig said, "Formio, sit down."

The boy dropped down and squatted on the floor. Deleig asked, "What do you want from me? My professional life is crowded with detail. I cannot be your tutor. I will try to be your guide. I shall find ways and time to answer your questions. I will continue with the story of my life in coming to Rome, as and when I can." He paused.

Formio breathed in deeply, looked directly at Deleig and said, "This is very bold of me, sir. Will you be my friend, Prince Musan, sir?"

"Formio, I am your friend, but I cannot be your boyhood best friend. I can deal with the mature side of you, the boy who is becoming the young man, but I have little time for the young man-to-be who is still a boy. Do you understand?"

"Yes, sir."

"I know you would like companions of your own age. That, I think I can arrange. And I apologize I'd never thought of it previously."

Formio's eyes glistened.

"I am willingly to include you at times in what I am doing. Yet I must stress again: the proviso is everything you hear is heard in complete confidence, and I do mean *complete*. Do you also understand?"

"Yes, sir, I shalln't tell Father or Mother."

That was more direct than Deleig had wanted to hear, but very much what he wanted to know. The most he could do was nod. He continued, "How adventurous are you, Formio? You know that annually I either go on a desert expedition, or I go home to Parthia to see my family. Would you like to come on a desert expedition—are you adventurous enough to travel to Parthia on a camel, weeks on end? That would give us the most time to talk."

"Oh sir, to visit your palace ... to meet your family ... a dream come true."

"In that case, my next expedition will be to my family's oasis at El Qassassin, then on to Hatra. One way or another I shall convince your father. Don't you *dare* say a word about this." The boy nodded. Deleig said, "That's settled then. Off you go."

"May I first ask you a question, Prince Musan, sir?" said Formio. "It has nothing to do with what you are saying but with what we did these few days past."

"Of course."

"Well, sir, listening to the conversations you had with Talca in my presence, and in your other comments, it seems to me—how can I say this?—that your interest in the Nazarene is greater than an espionage chief's practical, professional interest. It is as if you are fascinated by him. I hope I'm not being impertinent?"

"A highly intelligent observation. I am fascinated. At one level I have to examine the man's remarks in a most detached manner—as coolly as I do any messiah, Zealot or troublemaker. My question is: Is this man a potential threat to your father's governorship of the Judeans? What are the consequences for the Empire? With Jesus, however, I have a dual interest. What is he saying that threatens the peace? And Judea's is never an easy peace. That's my work, making those assessments and advising accordingly—"

"And having your spies bring you that information," Formio said, rather pleased with himself.

"Yes, that's so. But I listen to the Nazarene out of personal interest. Like my interest in the stars, I am fascinated by the idea of God. Does that answer you?"

"Yes, Prince Musan, sir, thank you. But I heard you talking to Talca. You want notes when Jesus refers to the Law. Aren't you a lawyer, sir?"

"More a legal scholar than a jurist. I want to know where and why Jesus' view of the Law offends the Pharisees and the Temple priests. Now, off you go."

The dinner passed pleasantly. Pilatus told Formio it was his moment—his parents wanted his impressions of Galilee: what he had seen and what he thought about what he had seen. Formio glowed at suddenly becoming the center of attention. Haltingly at first, he described the countryside and the people.

But by the time the narrative reached Capernaum, with the Mount still to come, his parents were flagging from the surfeit of detail. Finally, his father suggested he save the second half of the trip for another night and pleasantly dismissed his son. Claudia left as well.

As Deleig was taking his leave, Pilatus said, "Musan, never seen the boy so animated. Journey brought him out. Good. Should have thought of it myself."

They bid each other good night.

Two weeks passed. Talca had remained constantly on the move with those around Jesus. His reports to Deleig came daily, sometimes twice daily. There was an urgency to those of the past two days. Talca's record of the Nazarene's words was comprehensive, his asides about what he thought they meant, extremely useful. He simultaneously painted a remarkable picture of the Nazarene and his intimates as a group on a mission.

Shortly, however, S'veyda would arrive to relieve Talca of the major burden of watching Jesus and his intimates. S'veyda was expected on a vessel arriving that evening from Rome. Talca was delighted.

It was that time of year, as everyone on the coast knew, when bitter winds and rain could end the day even when daytime temperatures could soar. It was still bitter now, outside, late evening, as Deleig arrived on the palace promenade at the point before it reached the harbor road. There was a gibbous moon, myriad stars, with the harbor beacon and other lighted pylons cutting into the darkness. He regularly used the darkness here as his place to think. Or to not think.

Filled with joy, Deleig could detect the well-cloaked S'veyda approaching the promenade and raced toward him. They greeted one another with an embrace. Deleig, accustomed to the miseries of the voyage, hurried S'veyda to the warmth and comforts of the Prefect's palace.

They dined together. S'veyda had said he would bathe before he retired for the night. That actually suited Deleig, for Talca also was arriving that evening. Deleig hoped the two men would be comfortable with each other.

Seated relaxing on divans, wine to hand, Deleig asked, "Were you able to learn anything for me about Vasas and about his business associate, Marianus, who is a member of the Sanhedrin?"

"Indeed, my lord—"

"S'veyda, I am Musan to you—"

"You are 'my lord' to me as long as I am in your employ, my lord."

"Very well."

"The Vasas-Marianus relationship is not what you were told. Marianus is the moneylender and owns the international bullion and coin exchange. Vasas operates it. It certainly is not his."

"Oooh," oohed Deleig, surprised, "I am glad I asked."

"You are skilled in your—if not calling, my lord, your current occupation—you knew to ask."

"Thank you, and I thank the Heavens, S'veyda, you are so well connected and talented. That said, I'm responsible for knowing who is who in Judea; so I had to check out even my friend. If he needed to bolster his standing, that is his concern, he is still my friend."

"A lovely, human and kindly answer, my lord. Our friend, and my master, Lin Ma, has died. An amazing man. I did not write it. I wanted to tell you in person—as the only two who know him, we can share our grief for a most unusual human being."

Deleig felt the stab of loss. He was silent for several seconds and asked, "When and how?"

"Two months ago, my lord. In the desert while traveling down the Persian Gulf, in bed, at night, in his caravan. Good and generous. I had to tell you in person."

Deleig could see his friend was shaken, reached and held his hand, and then let it go.

"Half of his possessions go to you—he saw you as a son, you know—and half to me. I have set two associates whom I'd trust with my life to operate the trade route as did Lin Ma. We can make larger decisions later. He was buried in the desert, no marker. He wanted nothing like that."

A voice, Talca's, addressing one of Deleig's servants in the corridor, announced his arrival. Deleig quickly said to S'veyda, "That's Talca approaching, whom I've mentioned in letters." S'veyda nodded.

Talca entered and said, "Good evening, Your Highness." He walked over to S'veyda, "Talca, at your service, sir."

"S'veyda, at yours, Talca. I've heard much about you, all of it impressive."

"We have formed a duo of plaudit exchanges—His Highness Deleig praises you highly. I am little more than a raggedy-arsed Saka plucked from ignominy—"

"And I was raised in the desert. We haven't much between us by way of birth, have we?"

Deleig, enjoying the exchange, said, "Why didn't I know these drawbacks before I hired a pair of misfits such as yourselves? Woe is me." They all chuckled, and Deleig bid them sit down.

Talca was immediately all business and said he was worried for the Nazarene's safety. Jesus wanted to avoid Jerusalem, but knew he must not for that was where his teaching was having its greatest impact. He was en route there once more with his followers.

"The Nazarene had already told his disciples that his 'enemies' wanted him dead, and by 'enemies' he meant High Priest Caiaphas and the Temple priests, with the Pharisees as pleased onlookers. Jesus said Judea stones its prophets, and he expected little else. However, the Nazarene has a mission and a vision. There was much he still wanted to say, and he would choose where he said it. He is a fine person, S'veyda, sir, and you will enjoy listening to him and watching him, while adjusting to constant long hikes and asking yourself, 'Where did he just go?'"

"This is all very useful, Talca, sir. Please continue," S'veyda said.

"There's danger from abduction on the road. The likely outcome of being abducted—a quick stoning to death to be rid of him. There's even more danger from the Nazarene suddenly being seized by a Temple-inspired mob. Goaded by Caiaphas' anger if Jesus criticizes yet again the Temple priests' deliberate disregard of, and the Pharisees misuse of, the Law."

S'veyda nodded to acknowledge he understood as Deleig scrutinized the interactions between the two men to see if there were any traces of underlying hostility. He was delighted to detect, rather, a willingness toward friendship.

Deleig said, "The consequences of a stoning: Pilatus would turn Jerusalem in particular and Judea overall into a blood-bath to create a more repressive armed camp than it is now. That's because, while the Sanhedrin retains the right to condemn to death for blasphemy and other transgressions, a death sentence can be carried out only if the Roman governor gives his approval. To spontaneously stone the Nazarene after seizing him would be a contemptuous affront against Roman authority, precisely the type of affront Pilatus longs for to justify a brutal military reaction."

Talca said Jesus and his intimates had five general precepts governing the messiah's movements: speed, support from increasingly large numbers of followers, avoiding Judea by traveling through Samaria, suddenly appearing in Jerusalem and teaching on the Temple steps, and then disappearing.

"Abduction there would be considered an outrage. At the moment it is probably the safest spot for the Nazarene in all Judea."

Keeping to these precepts, the Jesus assembly, as Talca now sometimes referred to the Nazarene and his immediate circle, could leave a place quickly. Just be gone, he said. Out the back door and away by boat or donkey or on foot, or any combination of the three. By avoiding main routes, they reached the next place before the authorities were aware of it.

One of Deleig's servants appeared to say that "His Young Highness," Formio, was in the corridor. Deleig looked at the other two. They nodded. "Please send him in."

Formio came in and was introduced to S'veyda and invited to sit down. Deleig knew he no longer had to tell Formio not to interrupt.

Talca explained to S'veyda that by preaching near the towns, if Jesus acquired a large following—from an initial few hundred to a few thousand—it was safe to slowly progress to the next place as a great throng. The slow pace gave the rest of Jesus' intimates and close followers time to strategize and catch up on the latest information.

If his appearance did not attract a great crowd, the Nazarene once more slipped away. At a moment of Jesus' choosing, he would then appear once more in Jerusalem, though he was currently headed to Jericho and Bethany. He would make an appearance at the Temple but then disappear to Galilee.

More lightly, Deleig commented he could readily understand Jesus' decision to go to Jericho at any time of year: even if snow fell elsewhere in Judea, the Jericho valley remained warm, fruitful and pleasant.

"King Herod's Winter Palace had been built there for a reason, Talca," said Deleig in a light vein, for he realized he'd be traveling again. "Herod didn't like Judean winters either. Again, what happens after Jerusalem?"

"They intend to return to Galilee for a while. They're relatively safe there—because the Temple is unpopular. I don't think Jesus will take to the road much—certainly not Jerusalem—until closer to Passover."

A sudden gust of bitter wind made its way along the palace corridors. "Must be the gale that was threatening and they have doors open," Talca said. "I don't like Judean winters either, nor Roman winters for that matter. I didn't like Saka winters either."

Deleig said, "Here's what I intend. We'll leave immediately for Jerusalem. But that does not include you, Talca. You will remain here, in my quarters, and take responsibility for the entire network. Send messengers to Vasas' house. When we arrive in Jerusalem, S'veyda will head off to Jericho to join Jesus' throng, once it arrives. When Jesus leaves Jerusalem, I, too, will head for Jericho and the desert. I intend to take Formio to Hatra by way of El Qassassin. We can be safely gone for six weeks, Talca?"

"Yes, by my best estimate. Your reports will follow you."

"I'll show Formio the Winter Palace. Then my desert sojourn. Come with me to Pilatus, Formio. Oh, Talca, we need to find a couple of companions for Formio. Boys from good families around his age. What about the *argentarii*—surely some of those financiers have their families here? Studious boys who could study with him twice a week and then do whatever boys his age now do."

"Do you particularly want Romans? I know of some Greek families."

"Better yet, his Greek's good—it's the language his mother and her servants speak. Claudia says she has Greek-speaking servants even in Rome—that way they can't gossip with the palace household staff. Please arrange an introduction for some suitable companions for Formio, and their parents, when we return. Pilatus, Claudia and Formio can meet with the families here, informally—if Pilatus is capable of doing anything informally. But Greeks, I do like that. Thank you.

"There's one other thing, Talca. Could you bring in four or six copyists to rapidly copy all your notes to me? We're going to spend two nights in Jericho. I don't want to lose the originals. I'd be grateful if you could get them done and to me before we leave. In Jericho I want Formio to read them all. In part to give him something to do so he won't keep pestering me. In case of dire emergency only, send a message or messages *cursus publicus* to Dura-Europos and hope the commander sends them across to the palace."

Talca laughed and said that could be done.

Deleig sent for Myrmid and sent Formio back to the family quarters. He then sent his servant to ask if Pilatus was available. He was, so with Myrmid and Talca, Deleig went to the Prefect's work quarters. There Pilatus was compiling a report for Emperor Tiberius with his secretary taking down the notes. It was work the

Prefect found laborious, and he stopped immediately Deleig appeared with his aides, whom he introduced. Pilatus didn't seem to notice.

Deleig explained what was happening. The Nazarene was back in Galilee—he wasn't yet, but Pilatus did not need to know that, Deleig decided. And he wanted to make time. Deleig outlined how the Nazarene was traveling to ensure his own safety. Pilatus remarked that the man would have made a good military leader. Talca was invited to provide his observations.

"I'll head for Jericho. Then onward to my annual desert sojourn. Talca will be left in charge here. Given our recent conversation, when you suggested travel would broaden Formio's mind—could I take him along? Full complement of guards, there'd be no danger. There by camel, back *cursus publicus* via Damascus. Four weeks at minimum, six weeks maximum."

"Of course, of course. Good plan. Excellent for the boy. I'm grateful. When?"

"A week tomorrow."

"Tell his mother. Him, too, of course. Just as you're leaving." Pilatus nodded to his secretary to be ready for more dictation.

Deleig shepherded Myrmid and Talca out of Pilatus' family quarters where one salon served as an office. While they waited in an anteroom, Deleig explained to Claudia and Formio the plans for Jericho and the desert, and the possibility of some Greek friends on his return. Claudia was pleased. Formio was ecstatic.

"Dawn, a week tomorrow," said Deleig, winking conspiratorially at Formio.

"I'll be up all night waiting," replied Formio, in the same spirit.

NINETEEN

It was pre-dawn. A promise of day but, within the cavernous entrance to the Caesarea Maritima complex, a cold darkness enveloped people and place. The blackness was broken in the theatres of light cast by the mounted torches as servants quietly acted out their last-minute parts.

Everyone wore heavy cloaks against the morning chill and dampness. Equally, all waited for the signal from Myrmid. He was outside, gauging when dawn light would reveal the Via Maris.

The party was mounted. Off to Jerusalem to hear the Nazarene who then, by way of Jericho, would return to Galilee.

Claudia and Pilatus had said their farewells to Formio. They stood by an ornamental fountain, originally a well-head, waiting to wave him off. Only the gurgling of water deep in the well, and the snuffling and shifting of the horses, broke the pre-departure silence.

Talca had dispatched messengers to Jerusalem the previous evening. That meant Deleig, on arrival at Jerusalem, would know whether Jesus had reached the city, and his location in it if he wasn't already teaching at the Temple. S'veyda had decided to leave earlier to join Jesus' entourage once it arrived in Jerusalem.

Talca had warned Myrmid and Deleig the city would be more crowded than usual. It was the Feast of the Tabernacles, a seven-day festival, one of the three that brought pilgrims to Jerusalem. Deleig had inquired further and had learned it commemorated the Judeans' own desert journey, their years in the wilderness after their slavery in Egypt had ended. "Great venue for gamblers," said Talca, with a laugh. "Always one of my favorites."

Myrmid arrived from the promenade, his horse at a brisk trot. He circled around the pack, silently checking each animal and rider, the entourage of six Roman guards and eight servants with previous desert expedition experience. Outside in the darkness were four more servants, each with a string of six horses. The eighty miles would be hard on the horses, but Deleig intended to make it with only one stop. What was uppermost in his mind was whether the Nazarene would dare again to venture into Jerusalem. If so, what might happen next?

Myrmid nodded respectfully to Pilatus and Claudia in the flickering torchlight. He guided his horse through the pack until he was at the head of the column. It was still far more night than day in the gloom beyond the entrance. Myrmid's eye was on the uppermost part of a tower, waiting for the dawn light to turn the black stone into its honey-colored daytime self.

There!

Myrmid's right hand was raised and swiftly lowered.

No words were spoken; the party moved off. Formio gave a final wave to his parents and they waved back.

"Formio," said Deleig, the horses still at a walk as they reached the barely visible Via Maris for the ride to Jerusalem, "ride close to me for an hour. It will mean shouting, but I want to tell you about Dura-Europos so you'll understand about Vasas, my friend in Jerusalem."

To Myrmid, he called, "Myrmid! Hold it to a trot-canter-trot for the first hour until there's a good light."

Under average conditions the journey normally would require at least fourteen hours of riding, not including time for the change of mounts at the halfway rest stop. Deleig had told Myrmid he wanted to make it in twelve hours, including the stop. They were riding Arabian horses, excellent for speed and endurance, but that pace would be hard to maintain. Hard, but possible.

A fairly easy first hour would give man and beast time to condition themselves for the intended faster pace.

"Yes, my lord," Myrmid replied.

They did not speak to each other again until the rest stop and mount change. Normally Roman travelers would have made this trip at a slower pace and without taking their own string of spare horses. But the quality of the mounts available at the rest stop was uncertain. At least with their own Arabian steeds, the quality was assured. Nonetheless, the spare horses would already have covered some forty miles before they were mounted up for the second half. The first batch of ridden horses would remain at the stop and collected by servants later for a more leisurely return to Caesarea Maritima. The same would be true for those left at Jericho when the party switched to camels.

At the easy pace of a trot, Deleig told Formio about his world in the palace at Hatra, his first meeting in Dura-Europos with Vasas and the things they got up to. Fortunately, Deleig called to Formio, he himself had a facility for languages that matched his incapacity to understand mathematics and engineering, Vasas' special ability.

He told of his many playmates in Hatra, but not in Dura-Europos, none at all, except for Vasas, similarly the grandson of a general. They became inseparable. Years later, said Deleig, when he needed a person and a place in Jerusalem, Vasas and his residential compound served.

In Hatra, Deleig continued, his daily lessons concentrated on Greek, Arabic and Latin. His grandfather enjoyed a game he played in Latin with the boy, tossing phrases, sayings and law maxims back and forth to one another. Who lasted longest was the winner.

Musan's more exotic language education, Khotanese Chinese, he said, was built up by Silk Road traders his grandfather invited to enjoy the palace's hospitality. They were from Khotanese China's outpost in the Saka region. A man such as Lin Ma.

What Deleig gained from Lin Ma, he said, was more than conversational Khotanese Chinese; it was insight into how the commercial world functioned. And Buddhism.

"He'd regale me with incredible tales of the risks he took—as he traveled with a small army to protect the diamonds, silks and carvings that were his trade goods."

"I'm envious," said Formio. "I'd like a Lin Ma."

There was a hubbub in the line of riders behind him. Deleig turned around to see what it was, but Myrmid had already wheeled his horse around and was galloping to the rear. The riders stopped on the road.

Myrmid rode back to Deleig, a horseman, a stranger, following. Myrmid said, "A messenger, my lord, from our man up north."

"Bring him forward," Deleig said. As the man rode up, Deleig said, "Forgive my remarks but despite your fine steed, you are a little old for lengthy rides. Your master must trust you to a considerable degree."

The worn, gray-haired and apparently somewhat bent rider replied, "He does, my lord. With a report not committed to writing, which is why I was sent. John the Baptist has been beheaded."

"Thank you. Is there more?"

"My master said there are Jesus stories too numerous to note circulating wildly and widely throughout Judea. John's death, my master said, was the price of anger and lust: Herodias' anger and the Tetrarch's lust. He added with some humor that Salome was never known as a *modest* dancer, but he did not explain the significance of the remark."

"Who is your master?"

"I'm sorry sir, I am not permitted to say. He sent an old man so that if you kill me for not telling, it won't be a great loss."

Yes, a man with a sense of humor, confirmed Deleig, who nodded. He said to Myrmid, "I know you'll see to his needs."

To the man he said, "Thank you." The messenger made a courteous bow.

Myrmid gestured to the man to follow him to a servant. The horses shifted and snorted, but the line remained as it was.

To return himself to the present, Deleig looked at Formio and said, "Where were we?"

"Lin Ma. What was one thing he said that really impressed you?" called Formio.

"About the warlord in Tibet attempting to subdue a village. The monks came to the warlord's camp outside the village. One by one. They set themselves on fire. One in the morning, one midday, one in the evening. After the fifth monk had immolated himself, the warlord withdrew."

"Aargh!" groaned Formio. "That's dreadful. I'm glad Romans don't do that."

"Yes they have," said Deleig, as Myrmid returned to head the column and indicated they could continue.

Amused, Deleig watched as Formio shook his head in wonder. Then the riders were signaled to start up. Deleig called to Formio, "My voice is going. That's it until we stop."

However, by the time they stopped to drink, eat and change horses, Deleig was too tired to recall more events from his life. Formio was too weary to press him.

Formio asked Myrmid how long it would take to reach the city. Myrmid lowered his eyebrows to the point that they almost blocked his eyes and said about as long as they'd taken to reach here. Formio groaned again. Myrmid laughed and asked him if he did not like Jerusalem. The boy said while he been there several times, no one had ever told him what all the buildings were.

"You know some of them though, from your previous visits. One for certain, 'the four towers.'"

"You're right, Myrmid," Formio replied with a laugh. "The Fortress Antonia."

"Which, as you know my lord, King Herod named for the famed Marc Antony," Myrmid said.

"Who married Cleopatra and both of them were killed by Julius Caesar," Formio answered, proudly.

"If you say so, my lord," Myrmid laughed, bowing his head. "I know there's a Psephinus Tower, but I don't know who Psephinus was. Thinking about that, which I never have, I find I don't mind that I don't know."

Formio laughed, partly in amazement. He'd never previously heard Myrmid joke.

The column was under way at a good pace. The light was fading fast, and Myrmid pressed the horses from a canter into a light gallop and, where the setting sun still hit the road, a gallop. They were racing the sun, and scarcely any light remained as the weary men and horses slowed on the road that led to the Fortress Antonia and turned in toward the guards' gate.

Myrmid slid from his horse and, riderless, let it walk the final few paces. As the guard commander came into the courtyard, Myrmid bent and stretched, giving moans of contentment mixed with discomfort.

Deleig, always an unmistakable figure, swung off his horse. Formio followed suit. The commander approached gesturing toward two nondescript men standing at the entrance to the guardhouse.

"This man is waiting for you, my lord," the commander said, saluting Deleig and acknowledging Myrmid with a courtly nod.

Deleig acknowledged the commander. Myrmid, his eyebrows raised to their uppermost in an anticipatory demand for information, approached the man. Deleig followed him.

A clear voice said, "I am Oller, your majesty, S'veyda's assistant." He spoke softly to Myrmid, as if afraid to address Deleig. "My lords, I have much to tell. High Priest Caiaphas has men everywhere watching out for the Nazarene. They cannot find him. He has not been sighted. It is dark now; he will not appear this evening. But he is here, or near here. I am certain. At some point in the morning, he will be at the Temple steps. My watchers are better than Caiaphas' men. He will simply emerge from the crowd. The Temple police never find him unless he wishes to be found. He is most adept at disguising his presence. I know his own people do not yet know for certain if he is coming."

The man stopped talking so abruptly it was as if he felt he spoken out of turn.

"Excellent, Oller," said Myrmid. "Remain at the fortress while we bathe and eat. Someone will come for you in the servants' quarters."

The commander said, "One of my men could take this man to be fed."

Myrmid replied, "It's all right, commander, thank you, our servants will look after him as they know their way around."

Other soldiers appeared from the gloom, greeted their soldier colleagues in Deleig's guard and took charge of the horses. Formio, quite as weary as the other riders—most of whom were rubbing their buttocks to restore circulation and ease the pain—had come alongside Deleig.

He was stretching his arms high above his head, bouncing up and down on his toes, throwing back his shoulders and moaning, in a self-mocking way, "Woe is me. I don't want to do that again."

With that, Deleig draped an arm across Formio's shoulders, saying, "Lead on, young man, you know the way to your father's quarters. We'll use them in his absence."

They walked along the familiar corridors through the Praetorium, the governor's official residence within the fortress complex. "Formio," he said, "if Jesus is making his way here undetected, he'd certainly have made an excellent spy. Everyone seeks, and no one finds. Once I've rested I'm going for a long run."

At the Temple early the following morning, the Nazarene showed he had indeed confounded the police. He emerged from a crowd that didn't even know he was among them and went up the Temple steps. By the time Deleig and Formio arrived there, he was telling those closest to him, essentially the Temple priests, "... When a man's doctrine is his own, he is hoping to get honor for himself, but when he is working for the honor of the one who sent him, then he is sincere and by no means an imposter. Did not Moses give you the Law? And yet not one of you keeps the Law?"

Turning toward the larger assemblage, he said, "Why do they want to kill me?"

Voices from the crowd told him he was crazy, that no one wanted to kill him, though Deleig noticed that none of the priests supported that assertion. Jesus had challenged the priests by curing a man on the Sabbath. That had given Caiaphas yet another excuse to press for the Nazarene's death.

Deleig noticed that none of Jesus' intimates had appeared with him. Perhaps, fearing arrest, he did not want them implicated.

The messiah continued that the priests and Pharisees should stop judging on the basis of what they thought they saw. He said to look to the Law to see what was right and just.

It was obvious he was expecting them to attempt to arrest him. That some Pharisees and priests wanted to was obvious from their facial expressions and mutterings to one another.

Deleig was fascinated. It's theatre, he thought. Very dangerous theatre. The Nazarene walked away from the priests and drew closer to the crowd. The gathering had grown considerably since word had spread that he had arrived.

Formio tugged on Deleig's sleeve, and when Deleig bent toward him, the boy said, "Jesus is fearless, isn't he?"

"Fearless and calculating," whispered Deleig. "Watch what happens next. He's using his popularity with the crowds to further offend the priests. The crowd's presence is a measure of protection. The Temple police will be afraid to arrest him because they don't know how the crowd will react."

Meanwhile, Jesus had started to tell the crowd he would leave them shortly and they would not be able to find him. Given that he was often disappearing from them, even when in their midst, but returning nonetheless, they were confused. Confused but trusting, for many in the crowd shouted out words of affirmation. The Temple police did not move against him, and then it was too late. Suddenly Jesus stepped into the crowd and was gone. That was very well done, Deleig thought.

As Jesus was disappearing into the crowd, Myrmid and Oller joined them. Oller said, "Unlikely he'll return today, my lord. Tomorrow's the final day of the feast; he'll be sure to have the last word then. That's his style here, goading the authorities before the crowd. And a very dangerous and unwise strategy it is, too."

"S'veyda's opinion, also?" said Deleig.

"Yes. My lord. S'veyda has the best understanding of the man among any I've heard. When you hear my words, you really hear his."

Myrmid told Deleig they might as well leave. Then they could finalize desert expedition plans if he wished. He knew they'd delay their intended departure in the morning if Jesus was likely to return. Myrmid asked if they'd better stay another twenty-four hours, but Deleig said no, they could make Jericho in the afternoon if the Nazarene was gone by the noon hour.

"You don't think they'll arrest him tomorrow, Myrmid?"

"No, Musan, I agree with Oller," Myrmid said, consternation bouncing his eyebrows up and down. "They daren't do it in public. Crowds are fickle and turn into mobs in an instant. Trouble is, even if you've *agents* steering them, you don't know which way they'll turn. I see no sign of Temple priests being able to infiltrate and influence this crowd—it's mainly visitors, not the more malleable Jerusalem population."

Deleig's eyes were a little wide with wonder, so he blinked. He'd never heard such a comprehensive summary from Myrmid. He said, "You're the planner, Myrmid. We should come here tomorrow, slightly earlier. I agree with Oller—and S'veyda—the Nazarene will leave here once the safety of the crowd's numbers begins to evaporate. But I want to hear what he'll say to them tomorrow."

With that decision made, Oller left them, and the other three cut across the courtyards to the Fortress Antonia entrance inside the city walls.

Deleig needed to see Vasas and hear Marianus, the Sanhedrin member who was Vasas' friend and sometime business associate. Deleig asked Myrmid if a message could be sent to Vasas to arrange a meeting that night—preferably within the next two hours.

"I'll go myself, Musan, and await an answer from Marianus. That'll save wasting time."

"Thank you," Deleig said, as they walked to his quarters. "Formio, I know you want more stories, but the fact is these are important times and I have urgent business. My business is always urgent. That's why I take off to the desert. To get away from it all.

"Here's what I promise you. Tomorrow we go to Jericho and will be there at least one overnight, perhaps two, before we leave for the desert. Each evening I'll tell you part of my story. Then, in the desert, at those times when we camp, when we're not around the fire conversing as part of the group, I'll continue with the story. More than that I cannot promise and, indeed, cannot give."

"You are always so generous to me, Prince Musan, sir. Thank you. I'm sorry I have been behaving like a child."

"Not that, I think. Just a highly inquisitive, normal young man. It is not so long ago that I cannot remember myself at your age. Now leave me, please. I have a report to write to your father before I go out."

Deleig wrote the note to Vasas, asking if he would like to join the desert exploration, and if he would invite Marianus to meet at his home that evening, though it was already late. Deleig nodded his thanks to Myrmid, who headed off with it. Deleig then began his report to Pilatus regarding the day's events. He wrote a shorter version, but more speculative one to S'veyda.

He decided to take as a gift for Marianus the magnificent finger-ring of Alexander the Great. He knew Marianus would appreciate it. When he'd purchased it, Deleig intended it as a token for Emperor Tiberius the next time he saw him. However, true to the dictum of Lin Ma, Deleig knew he could always get another Alexander the Great ring crafted for Tiberius by the jeweler in Damascus who had made him the first one. He smiled to himself—he did have a trader's instincts after all.

Despite the late hour, Deleig guessed that Marianus, a member of the Sanhedrin council as well the Sadducee sect, would attend. Deleig suspected that he was chief of espionage to Caiaphas, his nephew. Brilliant, likeable, as well as a seemingly bumbling alcoholic, Marianus was voluble and liable to speak freely about Caiaphas and Temple matters. His business relationship with Vasas struck Deleig as odd, but he would never think to ask Vasas about it.

The High Priest was a Roman satrap, beholden and subservient to the Tetrarch, who was a surrogate for the Roman occupiers when necessary. The High Priest could not even wear his ceremonial robes without the permission of the fortress's commander because the commander had them under lock and key.

Caiaphas was vulnerable on that count—he had responsibility without full authority, even though, by his appointment, he was the pre-eminent religious and political Jewish authority, the leader of its aristocracy. Deleig found he could not think about Caiaphas without also considering Herod Antipas. Where did Antipas' sentiments rest where the Nazarene was concerned? Indeed, were Caiaphas and Antipas aligned?

Deleig arrived at Vasas' compound ahead of Marianus. His boyhood friend was enthusiastic about undertaking a desert adventure. They discussed it seated in the great room. Vasas loved to play the nobleman, which, Deleig acknowledged, he was. It counts for nothing, thought Deleig, except personal bearing in the new lives we've chosen for ourselves.

For the first time, Deleig felt obliged to explain more fully why he was doing what he did, though he wasn't quite certain himself. Possibly, by telling Vasas, he'd have a clearer idea.

"Vasas, I have never properly explained why, as a Parthian, I am in Rome's service."

His friend waved his hand at Deleig to stop him. He was a tall, handsome man, slightly overweight, who immediately commanded respect and encouraged confidences.

"Musan, you do not know what I am about most of the time. I do not intend to tell you and do not wish to know of your quieter affairs. We are friends. Activities outside our friendship have no bearing on that. Whatever you might ask for, I'd grant you if it is in my power. You would do the same for me. Nothing else is relevant. Given what we both do—if I'm not mistaken, there is sufficient activity and noise in the atrium to indicate the arrival of the ebullient—and extremely useful—Marianus."

Within seconds the rotund and rubicund presence of Marianus was upon them, beaming and voluble.

"Vasas, Vasas, to take wine with you is to not face wine again for a week, except that I am inclined to force myself to face it again the following day, but the pleasure, sheer pleasure I say, Vasas, of an invitation to your home is sufficient to provide a thirst an entire army might envy." All this while placing both hands on Vasas' shoulders and kissing his cheeks. A servant arrived with wine.

Marianus continued, "And you, Musan, with a generosity that exceeds all bounds, included with the invitation a finger-ring beyond price, which I have with me but am not wearing—not because I feel myself unworthy in the one sense but because I am fearful of losing something so unique, and as we are such close and dear friends, I know you will not be offended if I decline to accept on the grounds that I would not be able to sleep for fear of its loss or theft ..."

While reaching a hand into his robe and drawing from it the lambskin ring-purse, he stood on tiptoe. Deleig bent forward to be kissed on each cheek as the purse was pressed into his hand. Deleig smiled inwardly. At least he wouldn't have to trouble the Damascus jeweler to make another for Tiberius.

Marianus babbled on, "The crowds, where do they come from? I cannot remember a festival so crowded ...," sip, sip.

Five minutes with Marianus was wearying. An evening exhausting. However, the value of his random and unrestrained conversation—not conversation, a wine-driven monologue—was twofold, for a single word or phrase could direct Marianus' outpourings in the direction the listener wanted it to go. Deleig knew an element of this was that he was being played, but he still managed to extract useful information from the wine-soaked tongue.

Marianus talked as if he never realized the import of the information he willingly imparted. Or did he? It was the habit of Deleig and Vasas to let him continue with his stream of relevancies and irrelevancies until it seemed appropriate to offer some direction. Deleig expected to have to utter a phrase to prompt Marianus into discussing Jesus.

That proved unnecessary because, apparently, it was such a current and vital topic within the Temple community of priests, Sadducees and Sanhedrin members. Given that when not conducting his business affairs, Marianus was frequently at the home of his brother-in-law Annas, who was also Caiaphas' father-in-law and a former High Priest, Marianus was particularly well informed.

"Their latest obsession," said Marianus between sips of wine, "excellent wine, Vasas, excellent ...," sip, sip, "is dreaming up ways to trap this Nazarene nuisance, a nuisance because he is making even the Pharisees and scribes—with all the knowledge they have at hand—look like biblical naifs in front of the people ...," sip, sip, "in fact, the Nazarene—at least as they see it—takes a particular delight in taunting them and mocking them for not understanding the Law which, for most of them, is the only thing they do understand. They wouldn't last a moment trying to survive in commerce, I can tell you. It's their farms and our generosity that keeps the whole thing operating ...," sip, sip, "but the Nazarene outwits them.

"As I understand it, he has a great gift for knowing when they're about to seize him and disappears. Some of the simple folks say he can disappear at will, like an Eastern genii, begging your forgiveness, gentlemen, I meant Eastern in the kindliest way, but that's nonsense ...," sip, sip.

"What we do know is that even though the police did not touch him yesterday, they'll be there tomorrow. Annas keeps telling Caiaphas, 'not yet, not yet,' and not under any circumstances in public ...," sip, sip, "and of course they try to get some of their people close to the Nazarene or his people, but either their nerve fails, or those around the Nazarene suspect them and they're kept at a distance—not, I may say, that the Nazarene seems to care.

"And that's the other thing …," sip, sip, "Annas says, 'Don't go looking for him, he'll come to you, he can't resist, he has to make his mark in Jerusalem if he's to make it at all …' and of course it's true because he does keep coming back to Jerusalem for the feast days …," sip, sip, "he can be sure of a crowd—thank you, Vasas, just a little more, it is late, and I can't stay long, man to meet down at the Gulf of Aqabar in three days time and need to travel at a leisurely pace given my age …," sip, sip, "beautiful quality this. So they'll certainly catch the Nazarene in the city during one of these feasts. My only contribution has been to say, 'Why don't you take him at night, instead of thinking of doing it in the daylight?' But who listens to me?"

Eventually Marianus stopped. He bid good night and aided by a servant, departed at the same slow speed he arrived, sprinkling good cheer and kind words on his host and Deleig and the two servants alike. Marianus disported himself like a kindly gardener absent-mindedly watering flowers, sprinkling his pleasantries on those whose presence has pleased him.

The Sadducee gone, Deleig and Vasas, too exhausted to speak, smiled knowingly at each other as they sank silently into their divans. They both liked Marianus. Being wearied afterward was simply the price they paid for his company.

TWENTY

Deleig slept deeply, if briefly. Images and questions had chased one another around his mind all night. His body had awakened to give his mind a rest from the flight of white birds that swooped and wheeled around or through his dream questions.

He idly scratched in the hair above his right ear. The sound and irritation combined to force him awake. It was not long after dawn. He could tell from the light—thin light, like leftover moonlight.

He rolled grumpily off his cushions. Batting away sleep with fluttering eyelids, as if obliging the eyelids to send a continuous stream of intermittent wake-up signals to his brain, he groggily walked across the cold tiles to the balcony. He dipped his right index finger into his morning bowl of washing water, set on the balustrade. Home or away, it was his habit to look at the morning as the chill water on his face jolted him into the day.

Ten minutes later, dressed, his ablutions completed, a servant summoned, instructed and sent on his way, Deleig was at his desk in the Praetorium, the governor's official residence within the fortress complex. His servant would return with tea, hot and welcomed, the beverage he was introduced to by his Khotanese trader friend, Lin Ma. Deleig had continued the habit in Rome, much to the surprise of his hosts, for whom the breakfast beverage was always watered wine. With his tea and the round Roman bread he'd developed a taste for, the day was under way. He had letters to write, reports to act on.

Myrmid arrived at Deleig's quarters with Formio. The three of them made their way out of the fortress to the Temple. As they stepped into the vastness that was a series of courtyards and open spaces, Deleig was struck again by King Herod's sense of scale. Everything the king built, he told himself as he surveyed the scene as if for the first time, was more vast than even the grandest designs in Rome. Obviously the availability of land made the difference. And yet it didn't, did it?

Caesarea Maritima was created in the sea, Herodium was built atop a man-made mountain, and Temple Mount was an artificial construction. Deleig shook his head. Herod seemed to build on what wasn't there to begin with. A little like espionage, he thought. He gave a little laugh. Myrmid and Formio looked at him, but he chose not to elaborate and offered only a smile as recompense.

Their destination was the Temple steps where the crowds would likely gather to listen to Jesus speak. Despite Deleig's little laugh, the trio's mood lapsed into solemnity, a touch of foreboding, perhaps, thought Deleig.

S'veyda's deputy, Oller, arrived to announce the Nazarene was en route. The Temple priests and Pharisees must have received a similar message, for they were grouped together, unlikely allies, silently waiting. To one side about two dozen Temple police stood, shifting on their feet, gazing around idly, as their chief conferred with Caiaphas.

Oller handed notes to Deleig of everything that had been compiled to date. They concerned Jesus' previous Jerusalem visits. Deleig was again impressed with S'veyda's ability, like Talca's, to stay on top of events while organizing written communications.

"There will be more of these, Formio," he said, handing them to the boy. "They are from Jesus' visit last Passover. Read them while we are staying in Jericho so that I can have them returned to Oller. Be careful as there are no duplicates of them."

"Thank you, sir," Formio said, flushed with pride at being treated more like an equal than a boy. "That is very thoughtful and generous of you."

Deleig was impressed by the change the trip was bringing to Formio. He was ceasing to be the "little boy" and was starting to act his age, or slightly older than it.

"Take good notes of your own today, Formio," Deleig said. "Memorize what you can't write down, and commit it to papyrus once we're back at the Praetorium."

As a pleased Formio nodded agreement, Jesus appeared. The crowd pushed in around the four of them. The mass of people propelled Formio ahead of it, Myrmid remaining close for protection. Formio was now nearer to the Nazarene than Deleig, who stood behind a bench, Jesus not thirty feet away. By allowing others to crowd ahead of him, Deleig was hoping he'd be less prominent, that Jesus would not notice him in particular.

He was surprised to see that the priests and Pharisees had retreated somewhat, though still within earshot, while the Temple police had moved in closer. Was this the day?

Deleig studied the Nazarene, who had not yet spoken. The light of friendship in Jesus' eyes must have been obvious to the people within Deleig's orbit. They seemed relaxed, even pleased they were present. The man had an infectious manner. The Nazarene was, as Deleig had last seen him, alert, self-possessed, not disheveled. Apart from the obvious dust of his sandals and clothing that none could escape on the roads.

Then Jesus spoke poetically, evenly, clearly, without strain, from deep down in his body.

"As I told you, 'You will look for me and will not find me.' But I will not leave you without."

Raising the pitch of his voice, and allowing it to reflect his compassion, he appealed loudly, "The man who is thirsty, he can come to me. Come and drink. This is the breast the Scriptures speak of. From his breast shall flow the fountains of living water."

There was approval in the crowd at this. Deleig, while listening to what was being said around him, was watching the priests and the police. The police had moved within a few feet of Jesus. He paid them no attention. They made no attempt to arrest him, nor was he intimidated. People in the crowd spontaneously formed small discussions groups, turning to those next to them to ask what *they* thought the preacher meant.

From close by, Deleig heard approving references to the quality of the Nazarene's knowledge and authority, and to his being the Messiah. One man asked, "How could the Messiah come from Galilee?"

It was a remark similar to one Deleig had read in S'veyda's notes. Deleig looked around when one man said, "They're going to arrest him," to see who had spoken. It was an observation by a pilgrim, not a person with a personal understanding of the drama being played out before them.

In fact, no arrest was made. The police chief signaled his men, and they turned and walked unhurriedly back to the High Priest.

Jesus, who probably heard them leave, walked down the steps into the crowd and as if performing a magic trick, simply disappeared.

There would be no arrests this day.

Deleig, selfishly, was relieved; he wanted his desert expedition. Myrmid and Formio rejoined Deleig. He whispered to Myrmid so none in the dispersing crowd would hear, "Ask Vasas to find out what happened, and let me know where Oller says Jesus has gone. And, will he be back tomorrow?"

Myrmid nodded and held his left arm high in the air. Within a minute Oller was present. The Temple area was rapidly emptying. Myrmid gave his instructions. The three returned to the fortress.

Less than an hour later, Oller reported Jesus had followed his general practice when in Jerusalem. He had sought solitude in the quiet shades of the Mount of Olives. As best as Oller could determine, the Nazarene intended to quickly return to either the Decapolis or Galilee, but certainly move rapidly up the "far side" of the Jordan to decrease the chance of the priests' agents snatching him away from the safety of the crowds.

Deleig was satisfied it was safe to travel to Hatra. Myrmid had planned ahead and somehow sent a signal they were departing, for the horses were being brought around even as the trio reached the guards' gate. They'd be gone shortly after the noon hour. They'd be in Jericho in good time to take advantage of the warm afternoon to swim in the swimming pools of the palace.

A half-hour later, Deleig—who'd had Myrmid take a circuitous route—reveled in watching Formio's amazement as, from the lip of the Wadi Qelt, the boy looked down at the spread of palaces, pools and gardens. The Winter Palace, far below, was cosseted and protected from winds by the high desert escarpment, the viewing point Deleig had insisted on.

The Winter Palace, though actually a complex of many palatial buildings, was so far below sea level it escaped even a hint of winter. The oasis of Qelt, more than a thousand feet below sea level, had first attracted the Hasmonean kings early in the previous century.

"Impressive?" asked Deleig.

"Why isn't this the capital, Prince Musan, sir? This is paradise! The people look like ants. It's a busy place."

"A palace needs a lot of ants. Wait until you've slid your body into one of those warm water swimming pools, young Formio. Then imagine that during your next Caesarea Maritima winter. That's paradise. You've never been here because your father prefers the invigorating northern chills to the south's heated caresses. Enjoy these two days, because the desert's hot caresses burn, not soothe, and its chills can make teeth chatter and arm and leg joints stiff. Fine Myrmid, to the pool!"

Less than an hour later, the trio was lolling on the wide underwater steps of one of the swimming pools. Servants bustled around placing drinks at the poolside for the new arrivals and picking up leaves blowing down from trees caught in the light breeze. Formio was staring down at the shimmering distortions of the underwater mosaics.

"I know you cannot swim," said Deleig. "But hold your breath and put your head underwater with your eyes open. Then you'll see the mosaics."

The boy did as bid and pulled his head back out.

"I could spend the rest of my life here, sir. Then I'd learn to swim and see all the mosaics down there. Did you know that Jesus walked on water—that's what S'veyda told me."

"No. By the way, S'veyda's reports are being delivered here, may already be here, for you to read during the next two days. If you find the part about Jesus walking on water, show it to me."

"All his reports? That's fascinating. Myrmid said I'm going to have Oller's, too."

Deleig glanced over at Myrmid, in the water on the lowest step, only his head above the waterline, his back against the pool wall, eyes closed. He didn't open them, but gave the slightest nod to confirm he'd told Formio.

Deleig said to Formio, "Then you'll know as much about the Nazarene as I do, perhaps more. I didn't know he'd walked on water."

"Prince Musan, sir, could we stay here and not leave for the desert until I've finished reading everything from S'veyda and Oller? Then I'd have many things to talk to you about. Perhaps what Jesus was saying at the Mount will be clearer."

"Myrmid, how long will it take Formio to read Oller's reports?"

"Depends how fast he reads," replied the taciturn aide without opening his eyes.

"Faster than you but not as fast as me."

"Half a day."

"And a full day to read S'veyda's reports, at least. Can we leave for the desert two mornings from now without disturbing your arrangements, Myrmid?"

"Yes. It will give me time to find yet another wadi-man. We were lucky last time."

"What's a wadi-man, Myrmid?" Formio asked.

"I'll tell you if I find one," he said, happy to echo General Deleig of Deleig.

Formio and Deleig finally accepted that Myrmid simply wanted to be left alone.

After they'd dined, Deleig was once again at a table going through reports. Formio, at right angles to him at the table's end, was doing the same. He looked up and said to Deleig, "Prince Musan, sir, I wish you were my father."

He looked down and resumed reading before Deleig could think of anything to say. They continued on, silently.

TWENTY-ONE

"The whole Rome enterprise was a dream," said Deleig as they wandered through the Winter Palace. "I was given tutors for the first seven months and studied in the library at Porticus Octaviae, which Emperor Augustus had built in his sister's memory. After I'd been in Rome for half a year, I returned home for a visit. The twins came with me—"

"Your life is so exciting, Prince Musan. Mine's so dull."

"The desert will change that."

"Do you have a wife and children in Parthia, like Myrmid does?"

"No. I have no wife, no children."

"Don't you want some, sir? You're a very kind person, if you'll forgive me for saying so, Prince Musan, sir. That's why I wish you were my father. Could you not find a wife?"

Deleig said nothing, but with just the slightest of smiles in his eyes, pointed his finger at Formio's face. He said, "Walk quietly and think about what the reports you've been reading are telling you. And then tell me as we cross over this bridge on the way back. For now, silence."

Damn the boy. What a question.

By very early the next morning Myrmid had located a wadi-man, but came to Deleig's quarters in far greater haste than that warranted. Deleig had dressed listening to the dawn chorus. Now he stood at his balcony. He turned.

"Musan, the Nazarene has a huge following just a few miles north of Jericho. S'veyda sent word. I've ordered horses. S'veyda said they'll disperse quickly because the Jesus group knows Jerusalem will soon learn where he is."

"Get Formio, Myrmid, I'll be down there," said Deleig, already crossing the room, tapping Myrmid a thanks on his shoulder and hurrying off along the corridors to descend to the palace entrance.

The early morning gallop had the three of them out of breath. They dismounted on the road where a crowd had gathered, although the Nazarene was not yet there. Deleig led Formio into the mass of humanity, while Myrmid went to leave the horses with Deleig's two servants, who had followed at a distance.

Easing through the many hundreds gathered, perhaps even a thousand, Deleig wondered how they knew to be at this spot at such an hour. Had they followed Jesus from Jerusalem? Had he spent the night in Bethpage? Were the High Priest's men already among them?

The crowd did not have long to wait until a huge agglomeration of men and women, all shapes, sizes, dress, demeanor and states of physical condition, started slowly coming into view up a slope in the road, following behind the Nazarene. As the two crowds merged, Jesus found a place to stand and speak.

Again, the carrying quality of his poetic strains astonished Deleig. The Nazarene was calling to the people about the scribes and the Pharisees who "look to one another for approval and are not concerned with the approval that comes from the one God …"

Formio tugged on Deleig's cloak and as Deleig leaned his head down, said, "Jesus is paraphrasing for a different crowd what he's said before. In Jerusalem." Deleig nodded several times, appreciating the information.

"… I tell you solemnly, whoever listens to my words, and believes in the One who sent me, has eternal life … for the Father who is the source of life has made the Son the source of life, and because he is the Son of Man, appointed him supreme judge."

He sticks so closely to the Law and the legal model, Deleig told himself. The Nazarene continued to speak, Deleig paying close attention. "… I can do nothing by myself; I can only judge as I am told to judge, and my judging is just because my aim is to do not my own will but the will of Him who sent me."

Deleig lightly shook Formio's shoulder. "Go up to the front, I don't want get closer. Listen, but most of all, look. Gauge the man as you hear his words. Memorize them. Take aim at that cypress tree as you walk to the front; then you'll walk in a straight line. If I need to come for you, I'll find you easily. If the crowd disperses, remain at the front, watching. Do not come for me, or to me."

"Yes, sir," said Formio. He eased his way further ahead. Deleig was able to follow his progress from the ripple he created in the crowd, the ripple of an eel swimming just under the surface of water.

The Nazarene's topic was still scribes and Pharisees who study the Scriptures believing that in them there is eternal life. "... Yet these same Scriptures testify to me, but they refuse to come to me for life."

Deleig watched as Jesus stretched his arms as wide as they could go, embracing the crowd with, "You! You! You know what God is offering through me." He watched as Formio stopped just short of the front of the crowd, turned around and identified where Deleig was standing. They nodded to one another.

Rather than continue on, Formio began easing his way back toward Deleig. When he reached Deleig, the Parthian bent down.

Formio whispered, "I saw S'veyda and he gestured me away. He is with two men. If you see, look left, to where there are donkeys on that slight rise ... a stubby tree that's lost branches in a storm." Formio was standing on tiptoe but couldn't see over the crowd. "S'veyda is at that tree, but you have to be closer to the front to see him. He must have seen you and noticed me coming forward."

"I see it, and where he might be. We shall leave."

Deleig turned and looked to the rear. He could see over the crowd to where Myrmid had been joined by the servants with the horses and led the way back.

Within the hour, they again were lost in preparations for the desert expedition. They were done before midday, their clothes and needs taken to wherever the pack camels were stationed. Formio had wanted to accompany Myrmid to watch the loading, but with a lowering of his eyebrows Myrmid indicated otherwise.

To soften the blow, he added that Formio would please Deleig enormously were he to finish reading all S'veyda's reports before they left Jericho. Myrmid had much work to complete this day. He wanted to depart in the morning, the moment dawn broke. He did not need an inquisitive boy pestering him for information.

S'veyda by messenger told Deleig that Caiaphas, poorly disguised, had been in the crowd. He felt Deleig would not have wanted to be identified, especially in the company of the Prefect's son, taking such an interest in purely Judean matters.

For six dedicated hours Formio plowed on. He let out a whoop when he finished reading the complete batch of scrolls and miscellaneous single-page accounts.

Deleig was bewildered. That was unusual for him. Worse, he knew the reason he was disconcerted, and it was trifling. A still-young boy wanted his life story, and as a result he felt trapped, or wrong-footed—or something he couldn't quite find the word for. Deleig had been surprised to discover that the more he revealed to Formio, the more he enjoyed talking about it. Yet he was saying too much, revealing too much.

He was at an ornate desk old enough to have served the Hasmonean kings when they wintered in Jericho. Its carving and decoration had survived in fair condition. Deleig was running his finger along the carefully carved trajectory of an arrow on the backboard. The arrow was destined for a large stag. But for a century or more, both arrow and stag had been frozen in place. The stag's eye was focused on the approaching arrow.

The artist had carved alarm into its bare-toothed expression. Deleig looked at the archer. He appeared alarmed, too, as if, at heart, he didn't want to kill this magnificent animal.

Deleig could sympathize with both. He didn't like killing or killers. Surely, though, he could handle Formio. He swung around on his stool to face him.

The lad was ten feet away, his legs tucked under him as he nestled into the corner of an outsized, stuffed fabric divan. He was lost in his reading. The carelessness of youth—he was untidily stacking the scrolls he'd finished reading on the floor instead of in the containers they were kept in. It looked as though some of them might have rolled out of order as he put them down. Yet he was not entirely careless, Deleig decided.

The boy had four wax tablets. He would stop reading, select a tablet, make a note, replace the tablet and continue reading. The scrolls were S'veyda's and his operatives' accounts of Jesus' travels and acts and preaching.

The salon they were in was shaded by awnings over the balcony. Deleig glanced toward the open balcony and closed his eyes against the sun's glare. What to tell the boy? Images floated around in Deleig's mind, each vying for primacy in the telling.

He could hear echoes of phrases from his past—all were connected to his grandfather, the man who had dominated his early life. He'd loved the man, but his grandfather had been truly fixated on seeing him educated, constantly pushing Musan to learn everything the old man wished he had learned, languages especially.

Formio looked up and asked, "Where is Gentile, sir?"

"It isn't a place, it's a category of people. It is what Judeans call anyone who doesn't follow their religion."

"What's the difference, sir?"

"Primarily, I believe, because Judeans are circumcised and Gentiles aren't."

"We Romans aren't circumcised, are we? Why do they do it?"

Deleig was amused that Formio considered him a Roman.

"No, nor are Greeks. It's primarily a health precaution. Or was, originally. Unlike Rome with its public baths, desert lands rarely offer places for regular bathing. As with many rituals, adopted for one reason, they get loaded up with religious significance. I suspect that's what happened."

Formio gave an embarrassed laugh, "I thought Gentile was a place somewhere near China."

"Formio, what do you want to be, to do, and where? What profession do you want to follow?"

It was the boy's turn to be bewildered.

"I don't know, sir. I haven't thought about it. I know where I want to be though, in Rome or anywhere except Judea. I can't imagine why I had to come. Mother doesn't like it either. As for a profession, Prince Musan, sir, I haven't given it a thought."

"Then you know my situation in the scorching hot summer when I was fourteen. It was Dura-Europos; previously I had only been there in winter. Now I knew why. It was a week of 120-degree temperatures. On horseback I was alongside my grandfather. He was in full dress uniform, his six-man ceremonial guard with him—though he was long retired as supreme general.

"We boarded two rafts—riders on each—upriver from Dura, to sail to the Roman encampment on the opposite side of the Peace Line. We were on the raft before my grandfather told me we were taking the first step to see if I could continue my education in Rome. I was scared to death—I thought he was going to leave me in the Roman legion encampment that very day, but I didn't dare say anything."

"What did you want to do, yourself, sir?"

"In Dura all I wanted to do was go home. I always longed for winter to end so that I could leave and return to Hatra, play in the gardens, watch the birds, draw, talk to my mother, and occasionally my father and my older brother—who didn't bother with me very much. I had never given any thought to life beyond that, despite everything I was being forced to learn."

Deleig left his chair and went over to the other end of the large divan Formio nearly occupied with scrolls and tablets and sprawled against its corner. He related in brief his Dura-Europos odyssey. He described the city of Dura, built, and in some parts being rebuilt, on an escarpment three hundred feet above the River Euphrates' eastern bank. It was not a crossroads city, but a regional capital, prosperous and crowded.

Its prosperity showed in the white and ochre plaster that covered the entire city wall, he said, a wall built, as practically everything in Dura was, of mud bricks. The Roman encampment on the opposite bank was clearly visible from the higher city walls.

"That's my story for the moment. What about yours? What are you discovering about Jesus? Indeed, what are all these tablets for?"

"Well, sir, Jesus the Nazarene isn't one story. There is so much going on all the time where Jesus is concerned that I'm dividing it into four sections: his travels, they seem very important. He wants particular people to hear him. For instance, he never goes south of Jerusalem. Next, there are his cures. That's why people come to him—I'm sorry, sir, that is an opinion, not a fact. I believe that's why people come to him—initially.

"Then there's what he says, his teaching. That's what makes other people come to him, out of curiosity, possibly, but after he's cured them, or they've witnessed cures, it's what makes them stay with the crowd. Finally, his battling with the Pharisees above all, and then with the scribes—who are part of the Temple, sir."

"Well done, Formio, I'm very impressed. Do you want to go into detail on one of them? Now?"

"No, sir, I want to save that for the desert. I want to lie on my back and look at the stars as you did as a boy, and talk to you the way you did with your grandfather. And that's when I'll tell you."

Formio paused. "But didn't Myrmid tell us we travel by night? When do we lie on our backs?"

"We'll travel by day until we get to the desert—mountains to cross," said Deleig, "And we don't want to do that in the dark. Once we reach the wastes, the daytime temperature will soar beyond anything you've experienced in Caesarea Maritima. That's when we begin traveling by night and taking our night break. By my estimation, the first twenty-four hours after you've shifted from daytime waking to nighttime waking, you'll be too sleepy to rest on your back looking at stars. You'll be asleep. By the second night, perhaps. By the third night, certainly. Myrmid will have rehearsed everyone in setting up and striking camp. Even if you see something you can do, stay out of the way."

"Yes, sir. Will we share the same tent?"

"Many of us will be sharing three tents. But I will want your roll next to mine where Myrmid can see us both and then go on to worry about other things."

Later, looking back on the journey, Deleig realized Formio's incisive and insightful assessments of Jesus, culled from the mass of reports he'd read, coincided with the major watering holes. At Qasr Zebde the boy explained his understanding of the impact of Jesus' cures and miracles. At Ar Rutbah it was the Nazarene's travels. At Tubal, the content of his teaching. At the Deleig family oasis at El Qassassin, Jesus' verbal dueling with the Pharisees and scribes. The lazy overnight at the lake at Al-Fallu was a meandering discussion between them as Formio strove to grasp the concept of God, as if anyone really can.

When they'd crossed the mountains for Qasr Zebde, Deleig's thoughts had been that he was providing Formio with an opportunity to grow up, to gain some self-confidence. Deleig had not expected to be a prime beneficiary, for the boy was making a community out of the caravan. His rapid development came from his easy, unselfconscious manner with his traveling companions. Soldiers, servants, all spoke to him willingly and answered his constant questions at length. The wadi-man was only the prime example.

Formio had a persistent streak in him. Deleig had experienced it. Now it was the wadi-man's turn as Formio continually pressed him about the nomadic life.

"What are you and the wadi-man conspiring about?" Deleig asked Formio. "You've become firm friends. Are you going to be a water diviner?" They both laughed.

"He has told me about the nomadic code, Prince Musan, sir, and it's like John the Baptizer and Jesus. He grew up in a desert in a different country long ago and far away. He said, if we are stopped in the desert by nomads—you know this already, don't you, because you know the desert?" Vasas and Myrmid had joined them and listened quietly.

"If a nomad comes out of the bush and asks for water, you must give him half of all the water you have, that way each of you has some. The nomads actually could not take half your water—they carry only what they need and the amount, apparently, is modest. Otherwise, everything, and it isn't much, of what they have is one of each—except they wear two sandals of course. John the Baptizer and Jesus both talked about taking only what you need. S'veyda's notes have it all. The Baptizer and the Nazarene both came out of the desert and had found some of their values in the nomadic code, hadn't they?"

"If you say so, Formio, that's quite possible. You are proving extremely astute." Vasas applauded; Myrmid nodded to the boy.

Formio glowed with appreciation.

"The wadi-man said he was from a tribe of nomadic herders. Nomads are followers of the rainfall. It is essential for their herds. A noble people, the man said, for they have their code and their livelihood. It demands people share what they have with those in need. He told me that if nomads stopped this caravan train—appearing out of the brush, always unexpectedly—they'll ask for water if they're without. But not if they do not need it. Equally, nomads expect to be asked for half of their water—by a person in need. So, a nomad such as himself carries nothing else because he has what he needs—his robe, his slippers that are his livelihood, his water and the promise of food."

Formio said the wadi-man had told him the women had the harder choices. When the child was born, the herd stopped for thirty days. The woman remained in her hut, food passed in, waste passed out. At the end of thirty days, the mother must decide whether the infant was strong enough for the nomadic life. If not, she must stop feeding it. During a drought, if she had twins, she must feed only one.

Formio, as he recounted the conversation to Deleig, said he was horrified by the harshness of the nomads' world. Yet he could understand that a nomadic band simply did not have the capacity to support the sickly or infirm.

Almost fifty years later, when Musan read an account of Jesus' life written by Marcus, he recalled the wadi-man. The Baptizer in his camel-skin was probably as poorly clothed as the wadi-man. Jesus told his disciples to take nothing—not a spare tunic, and no food or money. Jesus had indeed learned that from the nomads when he was in the desert.

The wadi-man encounter was only one of the elements that enlivened and intrigued Formio. Vasas made his contribution—he was a beautiful singer. And Formio revealed Deleig's secret—so he had to tell all the Monkey and the Flying Carpet stories one night at a time, and repeat them.

Deleig saw the boy was brimming over with new experience and newfound knowledge. He had no complaints about the hardships.

The monotony of desert travel set in.

"Tell me about Jesus," said Deleig one night. He was expecting, prepared for, half an hour or more of statements and questions. Not at all. Formio surprised him, catching him totally off-guard.

"I decided the only way to truly understand what is under way is to look at everything from Jesus' point of view—or at least his cures and miracles, his travels, his teachings and his battles with the Pharisees and the scribes. All this I got from the commentary and reporting from S'veyda, Oller and their operatives. What, Prince Musan, sir, was Jesus' initial challenge?"

Deleig mentally stepped back from the question long enough to place himself in the Nazarene's position when John was baptizing. He said to Formio, "He needed followers. He needed an audience."

"Yes," said Formio, "and the way to attract that audience, the way to get the crowds coming to him, rather than him going to them, was to be known for curing people. The people would walk for hours, for days, to be cured—or even to see cures accomplished. Jesus was an attraction as well as a healer. But he was something far more—a teacher. But you can't teach if there's no one present. That's why he had crowds following him—at least that's part of it.

"The thing is, he complained that people were coming to him to be cured and not for his message, but I don't think he fully believed that. Think about his miracles not related to curing people. He did those. I'm thinking of the report that he fed thousands of people. They'd already heard what he had to say. He had cured no one that day. He fed them because he cared for the people, because he understood their immediate needs. He spoke of man not living by bread alone, but he understood bread, too, was necessary. I sense, however, he also fed them because they were prepared to listen—not there merely to be entertained by the spectacle of a cure. I'm speculating Prince Musan, sir. But it's not fanciful."

Deleig was taken by surprise by the range of Formio's interpretation.

"No, Formio, not fanciful. You never cease to amaze me. May I now impress you with my knowledge of the sky?" Deleig asked.

A moment or two later he raised himself up on one elbow, but Formio was already fast asleep. Deleig lay back and slept, too. The servants would waken them.

TWENTY-TWO

The next night, they'd chatted on, wandering over myriad topics. Then Deleig said, "We've strayed from the topic. Back to the Nazarene."

"I think you are correct," said Formio. "What Jesus wants his listeners to do is to believe. To accept that his words are from God. Beyond that, because he knows he is going to die, he wants lots of followers—as many as possible of them—believing in him so that his words will carry on once he has gone. From S'veyda's reports I've learned a little of what Jesus has been saying to his immediate followers. He is expecting them not to *continue* his work, but to *be* his work. To *be* as he is, *doing* as he has done. But S'veyda says that one of the men closest to Jesus, Judas Iscariot, says most of the immediate circle don't really understand, or can't accept, Jesus' explanation that he must die."

Days later their next stop was the Deleig family oasis at El Qassassin. From Caesarea Maritima, Myrmid had sent word to Hatra that the oasis was to be staffed pending Deleig's arrival. Vasas greeted the members of Musan's family present. Then he took his leave and set off with one guide to spend as much time as possible at his own family near Dura-Europos.

The oasis was bustling with activity around the small lake with its low buildings sheltered by stands of tall palm trees. The palace servants came up to Deleig and prostrated themselves before him. They shifted to their knees and touched their heads to the sand. Deleig watched Formio's amazement with some amusement.

They repeated the same before Formio. Deleig extended his hand, palm upward, as a signal to rise. As the palace servants withdrew, Formio whispered to Deleig, "I suddenly see what it means to be a prince, sir. Do I have to do that when I meet your senior family members?"

"If you'd like to," said Deleig, with a chuckle. "My family will show you what to do." And he left it at that.

The only time at the El Qassassin oasis they discussed the Nazarene's world was standing in the lake, neck deep on Formio, just over waist deep on Deleig. They debated the reasons behind Jesus' hostility to the Pharisees. Formio was filled with examples, gave them and asked Deleig to summarize what it all meant.

"With the Pharisees and the other learned men, it is a competition—a contest in front of the crowd, a contest the learned men are pushing," said Deleig. "The Nazarene has little interest in debating them. He simply strips down their arguments—he lays their grasping ways and detail-laden lives bare in front of the people. To me he seems to be exceptionally successful at it. Little wonder they want to kill him."

"What will you do about that, Prince Musan, sir?"

"Me?" said Deleig, surprised. "Why should I do anything?"

"But you intend to, don't you, sir?"

Deleig dove into deeper water and let the question hang.

At Al-Fallu, two nights after El Qassassin, seated at a palm-shaded table by the side of the lake, picking at dates and nuts in a bowl, Formio asked Deleig what praying meant, and why would one pray—whatever it was—to a God like Ahura Mazda, whom Deleig had never seen or heard.

"Isn't this," asked Formio, "just something drummed into the child, that the child accepts because the parent said so? So it is out of tradition, not belief, a sort of loyalty bound up in family affection?"

Formio flicked a date aloft in an attempt to see if he could catch it in his mouth. Deleig snatched it out of the air and popped it into his mouth.

He said, "How we believe, pray, worship is very individual. You saw my servants make an obeisance kneeling at the oasis. That is the way I pray to Ahura Mazda. But it is personal. The ritual at the temple is a worshipping that follows a routine, but I just pray my way until I feel filled, or empty perhaps. It is hard to describe. Then I join in the ritual with everyone else. Sometimes the filled or empty moment never comes."

"As for God, Formio, do you really think it is family and inheritance and tradition—that *that* is what is captivating those in the crowd who are actually listening to the Nazarene? No. Nor is it just the power of Jesus' words, but the power behind them. Those who feel they accept them, that they believe, know these words are from somewhere they don't know. Hard to comprehend, isn't it?

"Isn't there something the people are hearing that reaches inside them—to places that are personal, intimate? The why and how in how they respond to life, to love, to others—and to God, a God that they have never heard, or reached into, before? I don't know how other people respond, or what they think. Only how I respond and think."

Formio said, "I can't envision these things."

"It doesn't matter. If you believe, you believe. If you don't, you don't. Just don't be concerned. Did you think, resting on your back and looking at the stars, 'I wonder where they came from? Where everything came from?'"

Formio was silent for a while. Resigned, he said, "It's the same answer, isn't it, to my question about God. You believe in God, Prince Musan, sir. But I still can't see why."

"My grandfather, and you know how close I was to him, wasn't a believer. He attended the temple and went through the forms because it was expected, but he thought it was nonsense. I go to the temple. I hear the words in the chants and the music, and I willingly, out of my own will, place myself in the possible presence of Ahura Mazda who helps me lead a decent life. I suppose he is like an extra father I've never seen.

"I loved and love my now absent, strange, distant grandfather, long gone—and I love Ahura Mazda. Yet these are different loves. I love my mother most of all in a particular way as much, perhaps, as I do Ahura Mazda. You can say I inherited my love for my father and my grandfather, and it was reinforced by proximity and affection. But the love for Ahura Mazda springs from within, like the love of a man for a woman.

"Formio, I'd love to marry a woman I loved. If I had children, I'd want a son such as you. But to return to the topic. Jesus is saying his Father loves you, even though you don't feel that love. Belief in something will come to you or it won't, and you'll still be the same decent person either way. More than that I simply do not know."

Forty-eight hours of on-and-off hard riding later, the party arrived near Hatra. A servant was sent ahead to the palace to announce their approach. All those in the desert party stopped, washed and dressed in their finest. The moment they were seen riding at a fast pace toward the palace, the gate was thrown open. Deleig held up his hand, and as their lead camels stopped, he and Formio expertly slid to the ground. A pack of people—who in age and size ranged from elderly to infant, from tall and elegant to small and chubby—enveloped the newcomers.

Deleig and Formio were surrounded. At one level small children wrapped their arms around their legs, indiscriminately calling both of them, "Musan." Any intended formality was blown to the winds as Musan's mother wrapped her arms around Musan while Deleig's sister, Megga, wrapped hers around Formio.

As she let go, more children seemed to be at their legs, more women grasping and hugging them in welcome. Voices were saying, "Hasn't he grown?" and "How handsome these young men are," and other compliments lost to the noise of the children.

Musan bent down, picked up a child. He didn't know whose she was. He wondered how many his brother and sister now had between them. Then he saw two married female cousins. Some of the children were theirs. Carefully Musan threw the small girl into the air a little—not inches from his hands. She squealed in delight.

Watching, then instinctively copying, Formio did the same, and they each had a succession of children squealing in delight—until mothers reclaimed milling offspring so the arrivals could be greeted by the men of the household. Musan's father, brother, brother-in-law and husbands of the two cousins hurried forward lest there be another wave of children.

Formio was blinking furiously. "I've never held a child before," he said. Then he and Deleig were swamped under a welcome from the men almost as effusive as the women's had been.

Within twenty-four hours, Formio was thrown into a family far less staid than anything he'd known. He was the delight of the mothers and children alike. Having never been around young children, he reveled in it. Over the next three days, everyone settled in, and the children settled down.

On the fourth day, Deleig and his entire family—with Formio—went to the Zoroastrian temple. Deleig explained, as they walked to the temple, that fire and clean water were not what Zoroastrians *believed in*, as some sort of gods, but were symbols of their belief, key elements of the ritual. Extemporizing, he said, as the fire in the home was the gathering place for the family, so the fire in the temple brought the Zoroastrian family to the larger campfire. He emphasized that Ahura Mazda was God, a single, solitary God, who expected people to be clean of heart, clean of mind and body. The water and the fire both represented, also, a cleansing.

When Formio asked him what that meant, Deleig explained the concept of personal purification as ridding oneself of past failings, committing to better conduct and making sacrifices as a pledge to that commitment.

"Does that seem very strange to you?" Deleig asked.

"I like the concept," said Formio, "but who gets sacrificed?" He said this lightly, and Deleig knew he wasn't serious.

"I can make sure you are if you're not careful," Deleig laughed. "Offerings can be thrown into the fire, perhaps even valuable objects that in some manner symbolize what it is that needs purifying. Or, facsimiles of valuable articles are made, in wood or mud, and they are consumed by the flames. The actual object is sold, and the money is always used to provide food for the poor. You may have to be patient, the ritual is quite lengthy."

They had arrived at the temple. Formio was entranced. What impressed him most was not the ritual, exciting though it was: songs, laments, chants, exhortations from leaders, bells ringing, water poured, great fires in urns rising ever higher into the vaulting as leaders and acolytes went through the rites.

What conveyed the depth of the belief to Formio was Deleig's behavior. Kneeling, his body folded down so his head could have touched the floor, he remained that way for extended periods. Then he'd be up on his feet to join in the recitations of poetry and song in a language Formio could enjoy only for its cadences. Yet in those extended periods when others in the temple lounged on carpets, Deleig returned to his former, silently folded position.

While Myrmid was making a fast journey to see his family, Darius, Deleig's brother, took Formio to Dura-Europos. That left Deleig for a time alone with his former "governors" and parents. His lectures and seminars left the officials in no doubt that they had created a brilliant young man. His information was invaluable. The discussions on how they might apply some of it quite challenging. Without knowing about his Rome-based trading empire, they knew he had founded an overland trading empire, now run by Darius, and were interested when he explained how they should combine resources to create their own empire, by buying into existing companies, running vessels and overland routes.

On the second day, when he switched to politics, he began with asides about Rome. His former mentors found these hilarious.

"A classic example," he said. "You'll know the expression, *vanitas vanitatum, omnia vanitas: vanity of vanities, all is vanity*. This is the Roman usage—it is the Hebrew rendered through the Greek into Latin. But in the Hebrew it is far more cutting. Are you still masters of your Hebrew, gentlemen?" he asked, mischievously, as most had never heard the language.

"*Hevel havalim, hakol havel: utter futility, all is futility*. How like the Romans not to consider anything in their lives futile. Such arrogance. Such infants. I don't sneer at them, I accept they were sucking on the hind-tit of a she-wolf when Parthia was a great empire. Away from their mechanics, and law, and fighting and rhetoric, the infantile segment of their personality still remains, on the hind-tit. *Hakol havel*."

He enjoyed their laughter and took pleasure in momentarily showing off. He launched into the Romans as conquerors. "The difference between the Roman and Parthian empires? Ovid said that Romans as conquerors believe they dictate their laws to a willing people. Parthians, by contrast, believe the conquered should be ruled from horseback." He laughingly described to them how the Romans relied on birds to determine their future moves, hostage to the *augurs*, a priestly caste, and their *auspices*.

Several days later Deleig and Formio, plus Myrmid and Vasas returned from seeing their own families, rafted across the Euphrates to the riverbank opposite Dura-Europos. They entered the Roman encampment and waited for two more days for the *cursus publicus* that would return them to Caesarea Maritima.

TWENTY-THREE

Six weeks had passed. Deleig's mounting anxiety over what might await him on his return from the desert had collapsed into sheer relief when they arrived at Caesarea Maritima. Pilatus has been true to his word.

There had been no fresh outrages against the Judeans. The Prefect's energies had been spent supervising the now nearly completed Tiberium. That evening S'veyda had arrived in the dark after a long absence. He'd been accompanying the people around Jesus, for while the Nazarene had avoided Jerusalem, he had not slowed his teaching activity.

Musan insisted his friend take a nap. He had ridden half the night and all day. Now they were together on the huge breakwater, away from the palace and passing ears. Bobbing yellow dots, oil lamps on anchored vessels, added novelty to the otherwise quiet and pleasant scene.

"You're rested?" Musan asked. "I am, my lord," S'veyda said.

A blast of wind had them quickly turn their backs on the sea. It was early spring, but despite the offsetting influence of the sea, the winds could still contain a remnant of winter's bite. The days were warmer, but not yet the nights. Yet it was spring: the same wind's tang seemed to have collected evidence of it—the delicate aroma of budding plants—as the wind had blown along the coast.

"It doesn't apply to anything," S'veyda said, "but I do wonder why the Judeans would worship in a Temple built by a man who'd murdered so many of their preachers. The wider Judean populace, I suspect you would agree, sir, hates both King Herod's memory and his successors. What do you think?"

"I think it best you never address a crowd in Jerusalem on these topics," Deleig said.

S'veyda burst out laughing and replied, "It depends who is in the crowd, sir. The Pharisees would probably applaud. There's the great anomaly—isn't it, sir?—Pharisees united with the Temple priests, whom they particularly despise, on the necessity of depriving Judea of the presence of Jesus of Nazareth."

They pulled their cloaks more tightly around them as the wind picked up. Deleig indicated they should return to the palace. He smiled, his friend was both explaining his views and recapitulating events, apparently to straighten out the facts in his own mind.

"So Jesus is what his supporters—the Twelve, the main ones—say he is: kindly, a miracle worker, learned, driven in a sense of service to the poor, devoted to God," said S'veyda. "His followers believe he is the Messiah. He is also talking more and more often about his death."

S'veyda paused and then, to Deleig's mind, bravely continued, "And, sir, I must believe them. For in truth, when he is debating the Pharisees, he always knows more than they do. Yet more than that, his assurance in his God is complete, but wholly constructive. It is as if he is taking directions from God—that sounds silly coming from a grown man, meaning me. But I can't seem to find other words to describe what I mean."

He lapsed into silence. After a few minutes Deleig asked whether their continued view that Jesus was apolitical and no threat to Rome remained accurate. Further, had the past six weeks confirmed that the priests and Pharisees would combine to kill him, despite Rome's presence?

Deleig said, "I'm beginning to suspect, S'veyda, that his enemies want to bring him down using his own words. But I have no idea what those words could be. Or how they'd proceed from there. I have no firm plan—neither strategy nor tactic. Yet. But I have a next step in mind. I shall mention it when ready."

S'veyda agreed it remained wrong to classify Jesus and his movement as revolutionaries. That implied armed insurrection. "He does not propose, nor will he, an uprising. What he has done," said S'veyda, as he animatedly bounced around in the shadows—the moonlight catching his excited face—"is to alter what is meant by the term 'messiah.' As I interpret it, in the past, what was expected in a messiah was a king and general, like David. The messiah would unite the Israelites, drive out the Romans and other foreigners and bring back those dispersed by the ancient diaspora. I'm not certain whether you agree with this interpretation or not, but to me Jesus has inserted into, or perhaps, better, superimposed on the concept of a 'messiah' an over-riding religious connotation: messenger from God, foremost.

"The way the Nazarene has it, the messiah is directly from God and has a religious purpose, not an earthly purpose, except to spread his 'Good News'—which I still do not completely understand. So, he greatly complicates the issue: he is preaching a religious revolutionary message—as the Pharisees and Temple priests assess it—with no immediate revolution in sight. He and his inner circle call God 'Father.' Isn't that odd? They're Judeans; I didn't think they did that.

"So, no, there is no rebellion. That leaves only the Zealots, who after what you did to them last time, skulk, lick their wounds and hesitate to rebuild their networks in case you are watching." S'veyda said with a rare chuckle, "They promise revolution now, or at least as soon as possible."

There was a long pause. Deleig thought S'veyda was finished, but he had not. "Jesus is so convinced he is going to Jerusalem to die, he has named his successor, Simon Peter. He is the broad-shouldered Galilean fisherman. You know who he is, the married man of powerful opinions, totally in Jesus' confidence.

"The second man I would single out is Judas Iscariot. I would categorize him as one of the most intelligent of Jesus' 'Twelve,' as they're referred to. He is the most anxious. In conversation with him, for we have developed an easy familiarity, he is the most far-sighted, the one convinced that Jesus is determined on creating confrontation—not physical but, I suggest, religious—that cannot fail to rile Caiaphas and his priests. Judas has several concerns. One is that he believes the Nazarene is going to get them all killed. And if so, to what purpose?

"Just before I left to ride here, Jesus told the Twelve he was going to Jerusalem to die. So, Judas asked me, if all the followers are dead, what has everything amounted to? This Judas is troubled precisely because he is far-sighted, and far-sighted not just selfishly, but also on behalf of his friends and their families. He himself is unmarried.

"His repeated refrain when we meet is that they do not deserve death just because they believe in everlasting life—rather a nice turn of phrase, sir, don't you think? Judas said he believes deeply in the essence and value of Jesus' miracles—but not his strategy. He asks, is the annihilation of all who blindly follow Jesus worth the benefit of the memory of a few miracles, if that's all that remains after the Nazarene's death?"

As they left the promenade for the palace approach, S'veyda continued, "Judas is most disturbed—seems particularly dismayed—by the fact that the other apostles, as he calls them, hear what Jesus is saying but don't understand the significance of it."

Deleig interjected, "You mean that Judas believes Jesus' death will ensure his followers are killed?"

"His intimates, certainly. Judas says, 'We've all heard him say the priests and scribes will put him to death. And not just once. It is as if the others, while they *hear* it, they don't understand he *means* it.' Judas contends they think it is some sort of parable he will explain later. 'They can't countenance the truth,' Judas says, 'that Jesus is headed for death. Yet his closest allies are deaf.'"

"Where is the Jesus character headed to now?" asked Deleig.

"Off to Jerusalem by way of Jericho, for the Passover."

S'veyda fell silent as they moved slowly toward the gateway of the massive hulk that was the palace at night. They were inside nearing Deleig's quarters when Deleig said, almost to himself, "Judas is my next step."

S'veyda said nothing.

Deleig was obviously arranging and re-arranging the pieces in his head to gauge where they might point. Deleig had been agonizing over whether to involve himself, unofficially, in resolving Jesus' deepening plight. Could he, he wondered, steer events in a direction that met Jesus' needs for a final confrontation with the Temple priests and Pharisees, that would answer Iscariot's worries and not result in anyone's death? Perhaps not even the Nazarene's?

Deleig would alert Vasas to sound out Marianus. He needed to know the Temple gossip, more particularly, what Caiaphas and his family and closest associates were planning. Vasas could arrange a meeting for the three of them. What he most needed, Deleig decided, was more first-hand information. He would go with S'veyda to Jericho to talk to Judas Iscariot himself.

"I will talk to Judas Iscariot, S'veyda," said Deleig, "once we get to Jericho. You see him ahead of me. Talk to him again. Ask him what he thinks should be done. Ask him what he himself will do if Jesus is taken by the priests and the Nazarene's predictions are fulfilled. How long has he been with the Nazarene?"

"Almost from the beginning, I think, sir. Perhaps a few months later."

The next morning Deleig met again with Pilatus. He explained why he was headed to Jericho prior to going to Jerusalem for the Passover pilgrimage—where Pilatus and the Legion were always present in force. Pilatus was nodding agreement but paying more attention to the sheets of papyrus, the progress outlines of the Tiberium.

Thought Deleig, paraphrasing Juvenal, "Thank heavens Pilatus devotes more time to building his Tiberium than plotting to stir up the Judeans." Grandfather would be pleased I'd remembered his Juvenal, Deleig told himself.

The Prefect pulled himself away from the schematics on the table for an amicably animated exchange with Deleig.

"Describe the man's attack on the Pharisees you say intend to see him dead," said Pilatus.

Deleig replied, "The Nazarene takes Horace to heart, even if he's never heard of him: *Ridicule you'd best employ, If men you truly would destroy.*" Goodness, thought Deleig, I really must have Grandfather on my mind.

"I know you've told me before, but does the Nazarene really cure the blind and the crazed and possessed, and raise the dead?" Pilatus asked. "You know all about these things with your astrologer and sorcery—"

"Soothsaying," interjected Deleig.

Pilatus shrugged, "Is it honestly done, or a conjuring trick?"

"I have seen two cures," Deleig said, "or rather was present when the centurion's servant was healed. You've had my report on that. I've seen a blind man's sight restored. In both cases, because I was there, I had S'veyda's men subsequently spend days investigating whether these were bona fide 'miracles,' as they call them. No, no doubt in anything S'veyda has investigated, in these two cases. There is no indication that Jesus or any of his followers even knew beforehand the people who were cured. They came from all over.

"The centurion in Capernaum told me he'd heard of the cures and was convinced the man was a genuine healer. Such proved to be the case. Do people dispose themselves to be cured and simply await his word? Cure the mind and cure the body, cure the body and cure the mind? I think there's more to it than that, but what, I'm not sure."

"Tell me again about the men around him," Pilatus insisted. "You said one was a Zealot."

Quite so, Deleig told him, but with no allegiances to any current group or activity. "Former Zealot would be more accurate," said Deleig. "The others, fishermen and honest working men, and a tax collector—scarcely an honest man at one point—none have dubious connections. They are, like Jesus himself, what they seem to be."

"What does he seem to be, to you?" Pilatus asked.

"In his words, a man on a mission from God. Even while uncertain about the range and depth of his mission, in the religious sense, I don't doubt his belief in it, or in his God."

"But," said Pilatus, not yielding to Deleig's calm attitude, "he's had crowds of thousands. What if he doubles or triples that in Jerusalem? You say he's headed there for the Passover. A crowd of 15,000 or 20,000 suddenly on his side attacking the Pharisees and the priests—that could get nasty in a moment."

"He'll be preaching in the Temple. That's his goal. No more."

"I hope you're correct, Musan," said Pilatus. "You have been thus far. I don't want an insurrection. According to you, my popularity in Rome—never mind that, you know more about it than I do. But I'll still hold you personally responsible if there's trouble, or bloodshed."

"I understand," said Deleig, not in the least disconcerted. For whatever reason, Deleig had decided that while there could well be serious trouble, it would be a tightly focused trouble. It would take place in a small open circumference provided by a crowd in the Temple. The antagonists would be Jesus and Caiaphas, either Caiaphas directly or Caiaphas by proxy.

The following morning, Deleig left with S'veyda for Jericho. Formio would travel to Jerusalem with his mother and father as part of the annual shifting of the legionary force to the city at Passover. Pilatus always anticipated trouble and one year had tried to provoke it by having his soldiers dressed like the crowd and attempting to stir it up. The only long-term result of that had been yet another complaint from the Temple priests to the Emperor.

Myrmid delegated four guards to accompany Deleig, along with the servants. He of the bushy eyebrows maintained a sizeable private guard for Deleig in Jerusalem, but had never called it into service because Deleig's masquerade had never been penetrated. That changed with Deleig's public confrontation with the Zealots.

Meanwhile, Myrmid was to travel to Jerusalem with Pilatus because one of his duties was ensuring the safety of Claudia Procula and Formio when they were not in Caesarea Maritima.

In four leisurely days, Deleig and S'veyda traveled through Samaria to reach Jericho. From the far side of the Jordan, Jesus was also heading to Jericho. S'veyda was timing their arrival accordingly.

After a particularly comfortable night in the Winter Palace—why would the astrologer of the Prefect's wife not be treated as a most honored returned guest?—Deleig and S'veyda headed out. Jesus was due in the area this day or the next.

Two guards kept a good distance behind them as the pair left the city and turned up the road Jesus would have to travel to reach Bethany.

Behind the guards were two servants. One carried their light cloaks, in case they were still out that evening, the other struggled with two baskets of provisions, constantly reproving himself for not having rented a donkey to bear the load. The other two guards remained at the palace in case messages arrived for Deleig.

Deleig and S'veyda sat on the stump in a grove where a huge tree had once stood. The position gave them a clear view up the rapidly rising road that dipped down toward Jericho through the wadi. They'd barely begun to nibble on some dates when they detected a dark shadow cresting a distant hill.

It was a crowd of people, a light cloud of dust hovered above their heads. It would be an hour or more before they reached the grove as they were only now entering the cleft of the wadi into the valley. The warmth itself, Deleig suggested to S'veyda, would slow them down in a comfortable enjoyment—a moment of post-wintery bliss.

"They're more likely hot and perspiring already, dusty and miserable, and dismayed that the towers of Jericho seem so distant," S'veyda suggested.

"Oh S'veyda, to the contrary, the sight would have filled them with energy!" Deleig joked.

Deleig himself was feeling comfortably warm. He signaled a servant to spread out his cloak, lay down on it and within minutes entered a light sleep. In what he thought must have been at least an hour later, it was not a servant or S'veyda who woke him but a growing chorus of voices.

He opened his eyes, looked around and saw that a considerable crowd, perhaps three or four hundred people, had come up the road from Bethany and Jericho. Those numbers, added to the hundreds behind the Nazarene, meant there were possibly nearly a thousand people ready to attend to him.

Before long Deleig, seated on the stump, was looking again at the man he had last seen on a road outside Jericho. He was one of four men leading the motley band of intimates and followers. His clothing was the worse for his journeying, but not shabby—sandals sadly in need of replacement.

His animated manner, his hands gesturing, his constant turning around to address the people immediately behind him, made all else as nothing to him. He was talking to his followers, all of them. He was taking them along with him on several levels, regaling them with some story that their eagerness insisted he continue, taking their mind off the fact they were tired, weary, thirsty and likely hungry.

He slowed, and his entourage thickened around him as it came close to the newly gathered from Bethany and Jericho. Still not bedraggled, Deleig noted, still with the same quietly flickering smile. It was in some contrast to his intimates—they appeared solemn by comparison, as if they had recently been rebuked. Or had feared an attack by Caiaphas' organized forces.

S'veyda, who had walked up the road and into the mix of Jesus' followers, now reappeared and joined Deleig. From where they waited they could see Jesus rapidly enveloped by the crowd.

Deleig bent his knees and stooped in order not to tower over the others. He wanted himself and S'veyda to be just to two more men at the side of the road. Nonetheless, the advantage of height let him study the Nazarene, in whom he detected an uncertainty where he'd expected firmness of purpose.

No fear in his voice as he addressed the arrivals from Jericho, but a hint of hesitancy? He was telling them how to pray, repeating words he'd used earlier in his travels: "... Give to each of us daily bread as freely as you forgive our sins ..."

The people were respectful. Prayerful. Then, to their obvious delight, he plucked his words from his Scriptures, his experience, his passion and his imagination, and talked to them in parables. He repeated another apparent favorite from earlier in his journeying. Deleig knew of it, about the vineyard workers and the first would be last and the last be first.

Once more Deleig was finding the Nazarene a delight to listen to. Deleig was as captivated as the least educated of the man's listeners. It was only in part his voice; more it was his choice of words and phrases as he built pictures the listener put together.

But the voice? Confident, yes, as ever; despite what—an inner tumult? Deleig finally decided it was a deliberately damped down passion.

"Is he different from when you last saw him?" S'veyda asked.

"Perhaps a watchfulness not in evidence previously. Could it be because he is approaching Jericho—enemy territory, you think?"

"More possibly proximity to Jerusalem," S'veyda countered. "He is walking toward his death. From the demeanor of his apostles—apart from the one I mentioned, whom I just spoke to—the full import of what he is telling them still has clearly not registered. They are denying his words, I would say—I am saying this, my lord, relying on Judas' words—how can I know anything for certain?"

"Which one is the exception?" Deleig asked.

"Judas Iscariot? The man to the right, third on Jesus' right, with the cloth bag tied near the top of his staff. Dirty reddish bag."

Deleig looked at those closest to Jesus and identified Judas Iscariot. Again, Deleig was surprised. From what S'veyda had said he had expected Iscariot to stand out as a type. Deleig was expecting a follower, a somewhat broken man who would, with a favorable wind, run to the head of the procession, until the wind changed.

S'veyda described him as a man wavering in his allegiance.

Deleig realized he had conjured up a picture of the man shaded by S'veyda's words. In overall appearance Iscariot was little different from the others around the Jesus character. Dark, weathered, intelligent looking. He might be sad, Deleig thought, but he is convinced he is correct in what to be saddened over. A thinker who realizes he faces a serious dilemma? Possibly. He had taken his master's words as they were meant. The dilemma was he believed that his colleagues did not know what they meant.

Truly, the more Deleig watched Judas, the more he found himself disturbed by the man's subdued sadness. That was not self-confidence after all. He was consciously buoying himself up in order to continue. Underlying it all: anxiety? Or fear? Or regret.

Gradually the two groups of followers merged. The Nazarene and his intimates led the crowd, barely separated from the larger throng, those on the road and the new ones arrived from Jericho. They headed, slowly but relentlessly toward Jericho's walls, barely a mile from where Deleig and S'veyda stood and watched this assembly of walking believers. How many were true adherents of this "Good News"? To how many others did it appear, rather, a dangerous message?

As the body of the followers passed by, S'veyda and Deleig joined on at the end. If anyone noticed, it was not reflected in anything said or done. Such taggers-along, without a doubt, must be constant features of Jesus' progress through any countryside.

The people they were among were, from their clothes, of every class. There were many women who, from their clothing, appeared to represent wealth, widows possibly. They had manservants carrying their small bags of provisions and necessities. There were no travelers below the age of maturity. Sufficient dust stuck to all their clothes to suggest the people at the rear close to Deleig and S'veyda had been accompanying the Nazarene at least since he crossed the Jordan.

"How can we meet, Judas and I, without being seen or overheard?" Deleig asked S'veyda. "I'm so easily recognized." Not waiting for an answer, Deleig turned to hear what Jesus was saying, for he had begun to talk. But the Nazarene was now too far away. Within hailing distance, but not listening distance.

Then Jesus stopped. He appeared to be explaining something to his coterie, pausing in mid-sentence, in the road, to answer their questions. None of this exchange was audible. Deleig could tell the followers who shared these moments enjoyed them.

Deleig was giving S'veyda a chance to work out a plan. He was also glad Jesus had walked past because he did not want their eyes to meet. Not out of superstition, but because he did not want Jesus to know his face. Meanwhile Jesus' distant laughter appeared to smother his own cares.

The Nazarene and his followers, as they headed into the distance after the laughter, did so in a mood that seemed almost jaunty.

Deleig hadn't noticed S'veyda was no longer at his side. He presumed he had joined the motley to arrange a meeting with Judas Iscariot. Not all the local roadside crowd had yet drifted away. Deleig was now seated on the grass, his guards at some distance, watching. It was a half-hour later before S'veyda rejoined him.

"Judas will come to the Winter Palace tonight. I will wait at the gate at late dusk. He will not enter the palace. I'll send a messenger to you and suggest where in the shadows of the exterior walls we can talk in private. I will know where to take you once the messenger delivers you to me. You will be guarded—it will be night and we shall be outside the walls."

Deleig nodded. "Good."

The majority of the people walked toward Bethany. Others, probably disappointed the man had not performed any miracles—idlers seeking entertainment rather than salvation—headed to Jericho.

S'veyda and Deleig dined early alone, despite an invitation from their palace hosts. Later, not long before dusk, S'veyda left.

Deleig sat and read the latest batch of dispatches from watchers around the province. Though still light outside, the light inside was poor. One miserable oil lamp with two wicks.

The poor light irritated him. He could see no other lamps and did not want the bother of calling a servant. Instead, he wandered over to his cushions. He was more curious than ever about this man, Jesus, whose every move he had been following through S'veyda. Now S'veyda had added another man, Judas Iscariot, to the mix.

Deleig lay down on the cushions in the near dark, to think. Fitfully, half asleep, he rearranged the facts along with his new impressions and discoveries. At one point he sat up and in the dark, talked to himself. Jerusalem at the Passover is always turned into an armed camp, he said. Esteemed Prefect Pontius Pilatus was always delighted to have the army turn out in force. The annual military display was to remind the populace—as if the Judeans needed a reminder—they were a subjugated nation and Rome intended they remain so—by brute force if necessary.

Satisfied he had the rudiments of a flexible scheme in his mind, he returned his head to its cushion and immediately felt asleep.

It was still dark. It was S'veyda, not a messenger, who arrived at Deleig's quarters and shook his shoulder.

"Judas is outside, sir. The servant heard you talking in the dark. Then it was quiet in here. He thought you perhaps had someone in here with you, and he hadn't the courage to disturb you. Jesus and his companions will leave quite early from their rest at Bethany for Jerusalem. No one is quite certain when. My men will report to us. Jesus does not intend to spend the night in Jerusalem. He will travel back, this time to Bethany."

Deleig shook himself awake and left the cushions for the window area. The shutters had never been secured; the chamber was chilled. There was the customary pitcher of water and a bowl. As Deleig took care of his ablutions to jolt himself fully awake, S'veyda discussed what Judas Iscariot had told him of his own plans.

"You see, sir," said S'veyda, as they left Deleig's chambers to meet with Judas outside, "Judas wants to wait another day to see if Jesus either moderates his attacks, or changes his tack once he is actually in Jerusalem. If Jesus becomes even more inflammatory, Judas is prepared to assist the authorities in preventing Jesus' actions. He genuinely fears they will bring down the wrath of the authorities on the followers and their families."

"Repeat these thoughts to no one," Deleig paused, and then apologized. "Ignore me, S'veyda, I know you wouldn't. Look at this: Jesus has gathered as many as 5,000 devotees, or at least onlookers, at a time. In all, he has addressed many, many thousands. With those crowding in for the Passover, there are possibly 250,000 to 400,000 people in and around Jerusalem. Yes?"

"At an absolute minimum. Yes, sir. I might double those numbers, though I've no good grounds for saying so."

"That's almost immaterial. Take the lower figure. So how many of those pilgrims could be avid Jesus followers come for the Passover and ready to add voice, or presence, to his presence? If news of his whereabouts can travel like wildfire among those seeking cures, I'm sure it can do the same among those attracted to his message.

"Here's a scenario. Seneca could make a play out of it. Much of everyday Judea seems to know where Jesus is at any given moment, even if the authorities don't. Could there be 20,000 of the Nazarene's adherents in the city? 60,000? 100,000? The Nazarene sparks an unyielding and escalating confrontation, a biting and sarcastic battle of wits—he's well able to—with the Temple priests.

"Finally the Temple priests, tired of being humiliated before the crowd, and made a laughing stock due to Jesus' clever use of the Torah, call out the Temple guard. They order Jesus removed or arrested. The Nazarene's immediate people, those closest to him, protest, peaceably. The crowd understands Jesus' reasoning. It sees High Priest Caiaphas bringing in the guard to move against Jesus.

"Elements within the crowd are stirred into action by this miracle worker and healer being arrested. Stirred for a variety of reasons. They're primarily Pharisees. They know people who have been cured, or they have been cured themselves, by the Nazarene. They like what he says. They detest Rome and its Temple lackeys, but they can only lash out against the priests. You choose. A battle is joined between the Temple guards and Jesus' followers.

"Panicked, as the crowd moves into the fray, the High Priest calls on the Roman commander at Fortress Antonia to quiet the unrest. As the Roman troops come marching in, a genuine protest gives birth to a mob sensibility, attack for the sake of attacking. On both sides.

"That rapidly increases the numbers of Judean men prepared to join in the fray. The oppressed can be pushed into retaliating just as Pilatus can be pushed into a brutal response. It is the Prefect who is my prime worry at the moment. He'd welcome—he does welcome—any opportunity to play general rather than governor.

"The whole thing takes on its own momentum—riot, rebellion, insurrection. The governor of Syria has three legions. Pilatus calls on Syria and there's a bloody suppression.

"Or, taking the opposite view, I acknowledge there could be none of this. Perhaps Pilatus will—or has—repeated his past performance and insinuated hundreds of his men dressed in ordinary clothes into the crowds of Jerusalem. What say you?"

S'veyda did not answer. Deleig could imagine S'veyda scratching around in his bushy hair to stir up thoughts. But he didn't look.

"Forgive me," said Deleig, "if I deliver an oration on this point. To wit: One. What any Roman prefect or procurator of Judea knows—and the Judeans do not, fortunately—is that the Roman presence in Judea is actually insufficient, in fact totally inadequate, if it comes to having to quell a Jewish revolt or rebellion on any scale.

"The Esteemed Prefect is even now arriving in the city with his six hundred 'Iron Men' from Caesarea Maritima, leaving only about sixty soldiers behind. That bolsters the 2,400 legionaries in the Fortress Antonia.

"Two. At each Passover in Jerusalem, the military array in its entirety looks, and indeed is, impressive. Place 3,000 armed and armored men, backs to the wall to aggressively guard something, and the sight of the might alone is intimidating.

"But, three, it's a mirage. By no means could the commander of the fortress keep 3,000 men on duty. At most, he could have 1,500 men on twelve-hour shifts.

"Four. Fifteen-hundred Roman soldiers versus the 250,000-400,000 Judeans, residents and pilgrims, inside and outside the walls? These could overwhelm this military show. Considerable bloodshed would be the price, but there would be little doubt about the outcome. Slaughter.

"Five. If the Judean males in the population attacked, with anything from spades and pitchforks to chains and spikes, the

Romans would be outnumbered at least 50-to-1. Is there anything more aggressive, or frightening than a mob with its passions unleashed?

"Six, the peroration. If, further, it immediately spread, no serious widespread rebellion in Judea could be put down by the existing forces. Prefect Pilatus under duress would send rapid word to the governor in Syria. Four days to a week before reinforcements would arrive in any meaningful numbers. They'd arrive to see the results of a massacre—unless of course the Judeans decided to immediately bury the fallen. Any sequence of events such as these would mean open warfare. Caiaphas and the Temple priests and their Sadducee supporters and friends would prostrate themselves before any threatening Roman force. They'd side with Rome, say what they might in their private quarters about their hatred for Rome. Beyond those confines, they are mute and subservient before their occupiers and oppressors.

"Consequently, Judas Iscariot may serve me well."

S'veyda said, with a smile, "That was not a rehearsal preparatory for a bid for the Senate, was it?"

Deleig bowed from the waist, as S'veyda went on, "But to Judas: he is uncertain but not a man to dither. He is a man who can and will make decisions. While we cannot be absolutely certain what, he will take some action to thwart Jesus if Jesus intensifies his confrontations. Of that I have no doubt."

"Why does Judas speak so openly to you?"

"I think, sir, because after all these many weeks of my never asking questions, just listening, he does not notice when I ask a question. It is a normal part of our conversation. Of course, the reason he talks to me at all is he has no one else to talk to. He is dismayed by the other apostles' inability to perceive the obvious—at least the obvious to him."

"But what do you think of my speculating, S'veyda?"

"It scares the life out of me, my lord."

"And me," said Deleig.

They walked in silence out of the Winter Palace. S'veyda led Deleig into the shadows cast by the great portico at the entrance. They felt their way along the wall. A voice said, "I'm here. I can just make you out."

S'veyda guided Deleig toward the voice.

"Thank you for coming," Deleig said. "I shall be quite blunt. The risk for me in meeting with you is greater than for you meeting me. Therefore I expect you to mention it to no one." Deleig could not tell whether Judas had nodded in agreement but continued, "S'veyda tells me you need to contact Caiaphas, but you are uncertain how to achieve it. Is that correct?"

"It is, my lord," said the figure in the dark.

"What is it you would say—or have a messenger say to the High Priest?"

"That knowing he wants to restrain Jesus, I could arrange a place—or at least advise the High Priest of a place—where Jesus could be arrested without creating a major disturbance. That when in Jerusalem, he likes to go to the gardens on the Gethsemane Estate, or up into the wilder parts of the Mount of Olives to pray alone."

"Why would Caiaphas believe you? Why would he not think it is some sort of trap or trick? You are one of Jesus' chosen."

"I don't know." Judas was silent for a moment. "I could offer to do it for money. Caiaphas and his ilk are venal. He'd understand that as a motive. I also know Jesus' habits and preferences. Either on the Mount of Olives or in the Gethsemane gardens, Caiaphas and his men could easily overwhelm any group around Jesus if they chose—if it came to that."

"That's astute," Deleig said. "But what about your relationship with the Nazarene? He trusts you."

"Jesus knows everything before it's going to happen. He knows he is going to die. He knows where he's staying before a house is selected. He knows where the donkey with the colt will be when he wants to ride into Jerusalem. He and I were talking about how he'd make his entrance.

"This man knows everything. He knows of my concern for his followers. If I make contact with Caiaphas, he will know, if he doesn't already, that I will—in many eyes—betray him. Even though I regard it more as protecting the followers than a betrayal of Jesus. Do not think I lack love for the man, I do not. I admire him. And love him. I do. But he is still a man on his divine mission. It is this determined march to his death ..."

Judas stopped. He'd ended on a note of exhaustion. He had no more to say. Deleig was unmoved. He had greater concerns.

"Judas, are you afraid to die?"

"No more so than most. But I *know* the risk of being associated with Jesus; the others seem not to."

"Do you want me to see that Caiaphas receives your offer?"

"Yes, my lord."

"Then so I shall. S'veyda will report back on what steps were taken. I hope you and I will meet under less strained circumstances. You interest me. Remain where you are. Permit us to leave first."

Judas, softly, said, "Yes."

Following S'veyda, who acted as his scout, Deleig moved through the shadowed area of the wall. S'veyda signaled they could step out without being noticed. They re-entered the Winter Palace, only to turn around and stand in the shadows looking out. S'veyda said, "No one saw us, my lord. You have the facility to judge a person's character even from a distance. And also by their voices, as I just learned in the dark. What are your thoughts on Judas?"

"He is as you described him, S'veyda—afraid for the followers. Courageously foolish in the steps he may take, with our assistance. Which possibly makes us courageously foolish too, if we have helped hand over the Nazarene not to a temporary inquisition but something worse."

S'veyda said, "Yet Jesus intends to die no matter what? If you want to be ahead of the throng to see the Nazarene and Judas at a closer range than yesterday, we should leave early for Jerusalem."

"Jerusalem tomorrow morning for certain?"

"I am sure of it, sir," said S'veyda. "I have no idea what time or under what circumstances, and—as I said—he will not stay the night. Generally all arrangements, I gather from Judas, are as flexible as an eel's tail. But not this time. Let's wait for my man, Oller. What do you want me to do?"

Deleig did not answer S'veyda's question. They stood back in the great entrance, watched and waited for one of S'veyda's men, and chatted about the major characters Deleig's network depended on. The watcher, Oller, finally appeared, hurrying along the road. He reported that Jesus would head directly into Jerusalem tomorrow shortly after dawn.

Just after dawn, barely light, Deleig and S'veyda waited for horses to be brought. S'veyda said, "Sir, I have something to tell you that I hope will not upset you or ruin our friendship."

Deleig, in a warm voice, said, "S'veyda, nothing you could say or do would alter my feelings toward you. We are friends."

"Sir," he said, tremulously, "I feel called to join Jesus' followers. Permanently. I will not do that until I have trained someone in every aspect of my work and will continue to work with and for you until that time. Have I offended you with my disloyalty?"

"S'veyda, S'veyda," said Deleig, reaching out to his friend and placing a hand on each of his shoulders, "you must follow the call of your heart and viscera. That is the greatest discovery—the inner discovery. I admire you for it and envy you in the certainty of it."

S'veyda, relieved of a great burden, gave a sob. Then he said clearly, "You are a remarkable man, my lord. We should go, sir. The horses are coming."

Deleig said, "There is no need to train anyone. You have two able assistants even now running our trading enterprise. Talca can take over any other duties you deem necessary."

Off to Jerusalem. It would be an exhilarating ride at this hour, Deleig decided. The air was warm, yet with some crispness to it; the road, it seemed, not too crowded. The majesty of the surroundings added to the enjoyment. The bold escarpment of the Wadi Qelt cast its shadow.

Just over an hour later, the enjoyment began to wane—for the ride had slowed considerably. Dense crowds meant they'd caught up with the early departures from Jericho and the Jordan valley. These people had a full day's walk ahead to Jerusalem. The riders were not surprised at the numbers on pilgrimage. How could they be? The Passover was one of the three pilgrimage feasts to Jerusalem.

During Passover, Pilatus was always in residence at the Praetorium, where Deleig and Myrmid also had quarters. This time, Deleig was to stay the first night at Vasas' house—to make contact with Talca. Talca would be somewhere in the city now, checking in regularly with Morden, Vasas' guard, to learn if Deleig had arrived.

Upon entering Jerusalem, Deleig went first to the Praetorium to report to Pilatus. They sat in close quarters in one of the smaller rooms his entourage occupied. Deleig thought it odd as the Prefect enjoyed spacious settings. They normally walked straight through this room into the larger reception chamber, where they conferred. Was there someone in the larger chamber Pilatus didn't want him to see? Surely not a woman? No, not a woman. Herod Antipas? Not plausible, he hates the man.

Pilatus, without any formalities, asked, "Is this Jesus dangerous? Is he capable of leading of a revolt?"

"Why do you ask?" Deleig replied. He'd been briefing Pilatus all along on his perceptions.

"I realize you have told me, Musan, but tell me again. There may be more at stake here than even you are aware of."

"Certainly," Deleig said. "We must begin with his name"—which was precisely how he had introduced his last report to Pilatus—"Jesus, Yoshua, which means to the people he is the one in charge, he commands, he is victorious. Victorious in what? To answer we must see his movement from three perspectives.

"The first is the one that would rightly concern Rome the most. It is that all of his revolutionary rhetoric about setting the victims free, and his proclamation as the Messiah, is political: that he is indeed attempting to stir up a revolt against authority. I do not believe that.

"The second perspective is that all this has a deeply religious thrust as he tries to turn the leadership of the Jewish communities—the Pharisees, the Temple priests and their allied Sadducees—against him. He detests those religious leaders for what they are doing to the people: as he sees it, suppressing them in God's name. It is that oppression that he, as a religious leader, sees as a transgression against God's word.

"That transgression apparently has him on this mission. I do believe it is a fiercely determined mission—determined enough to get himself killed if the Temple priests have their way. I believe he wants the Jewish leadership to kill him. To stone him to death. In that way he would be a personal witness to—and victim of—the need for the Pharisees and the Temple to reform.

"His increasing vitriol, his wit, his scholarship and his—paradoxically—gentle character are aimed directly and exclusively at the Temple senior priests and the Pharisees' leaders. Along with that, he claims he is the Messiah. All his words must be bitter draughts for them, not least because he makes them swallow them in public. He is a most impressive speaker, orator, preacher—whatever it is he is doing. Courage personified.

"The third perspective is he could be both stirring up a revolt against Rome's occupation and simultaneously against the Temple. I find that incredible."

He looked at Pilatus, waiting for his response.

The Prefect said nothing. After more than a minute of total silence, he nodded his head up and down. Whether in agreement, or simply to acknowledge he had understood, Deleig did not know. He stood, nodded to his employer and colleague and said, "I will keep you abreast of events."

Pilatus looked at Deleig and spoke very softly. Deleig strained to hear him, leaned down, for Pilatus was almost whispering, as if he did not want to have anyone hear what he said next. Was there someone in the next room? Deleig wondered.

"My wife is troubled," Pilatus whispered. "I would be grateful if you would go and see her, talk to her. Give me a sense of how justified her anxieties are, and tell me candidly. She foresaw the arrival of this man you call Jesus—she is like that, seeing things. She sees his death. He is, to Claudia, just a good man teaching what he believes. He pressures no one, she says. His audience is present voluntarily, and his words please them. He is doing that, is he not? How does she know these things? Do you tell her?"

"I have never talked to her about the man," said Deleig, "though it sounds like a fair description. On another note, the Temple priests and their supporters, the Sadducees, have even enlisted the Herodians to their side. Or the Herodians are urging the priests on. Have you heard anything on your other grapevines?"

Pilatus stiffened when Deleig asked that, but he could not tell why. He continued, "On the surface little has changed since I saw you last—though the mutual animosity between Jesus and the scribes and Pharisees—has intensified."

"It is … so," Pilatus said, searching for words, "so, on the surface there is, nonetheless, trouble brewing?"

"For Jesus, yes; for Rome, no."

"My thanks. Musan, you will not forget to see Claudia, will you?"

"No, I shall send a message the moment I leave here."

"Thank you."

Rather than send a message, Deleig went straight to Claudia's quarters. She came into the corridor when summoned by a servant. She looked haggard. She spoke as if in a daze.

"It's the dreams, Musan. The cruelties. They won't let me sleep. Don't let them break his legs. Whatever happens. Not that. Promise me."

"I promise," he said, smiled. She believed him, sighed and relaxed. He left to head over to Vasas' house.

At some point during their assignments to Jerusalem, Deleig and Myrmid always walked over to the guards' quarters and introduced themselves to the captain of guards, in case he was a new appointee. These were courtesy calls scrupulously attended to. As an outsider, even though in the Prefect's entourage, Deleig believed official personal contact ensured that good relations were maintained.

He knew the garrison commander remained uncertain as to

precisely what authority Deleig had. As the commander was well aware of Deleig's fraternal connection to the imperial household, however, that was authority enough.

In Jerusalem, under Myrmid's command, there were six Parthian guards in the Fortress Antonia. Myrmid had auxiliaries, a dozen Scythians, billeted in the city, not in the fortress. These were part of his and Vasas' Jerusalem eyes and ears. The Scythians made weekly reports to Myrmid and effectively functioned as watchers for the entire Judean mid-section. They traveled as traders, peddling wares. Watching and listening. They were not dependent financially on their sales. They were, at some remove, employees of the Empire.

At the guards' quarters adjacent to the fortress's main gate, Deleig immediately spotted the centurion in charge of the watch. He was very tall, possibly within an inch of Deleig's height, though a more muscular man. He noticed Deleig, smiled and saluted. He nodded an acknowledgment to Myrmid, whom he apparently recognized.

"It is not often," Deleig said, "I meet a man almost my height."

"Nor I, sir," the centurion replied, easily. "How may I help, your honor?"

Deleig explained he was simply making a call to introduce himself, though he did have one request, which he outlined. The men chatted about their height. The centurion, too, admitted he felt like a freak as a youth, but once he'd donned a uniform, his height had been his advantage. It led to promotion because he was so easily recognized by his seniors.

Deleig laughed and said he'd probably have been promoted further had he not been so obvious, and so obviously an Easterner. Deleig asked the centurion to makes inquiries and to locate a particular type of soldier. He left it at that, and the centurion asked no questions.

TWENTY-FOUR

Morning was well established. It was a blustery day. At Vasas' compound, Deleig requested pen, sheet and ink be brought to the roof garden table. He made his way across the rear gardens and up the steps to the roof garden to look down. Within minutes, Talca had arrived. Deleig invited him to sit down and help himself to water or wine. He chose the latter.

The ink and papyrus were delivered. Deleig said, "Write as follows, 'There is a man in the retinue and service of Jesus the Nazarene' …"

"Yes, I have it."

" 'Who is prepared to assist the High Priest in furthering his aims. And this he will do by revealing which is the Jesus person in the group' …"

"Yes, sir."

" 'When in the dark of the evening the Nazarene goes with his companions to a remote place to pray. He does not yet know on which night this will occur.' "

Deleig paused to give Talca time to complete writing.

"Finished, sir."

"Talca, take the letter to the Temple. You will ask for High Priest Caiaphas. When the guard asks why, you will give him this note to deliver. The High Priest will be there at this hour." Deleig knew that because Vasas had left a note in his room to that effect.

"It is extremely likely Caiaphas will demand to see you himself, immediately, and equally likely Marianus will have you escorted first to him, and then the two of you walk to the High Priest's guest hall. Good luck."

Talca looked at him and smiled. He nodded and left. Spymaster Deleig spent a pleasant half-hour drinking wine, talking to Vasas and leaning against the parapet occasionally looking down, wondering how his latest ploy would work out.

There Talca was, battling the crowds. Momentarily, in an opening not pressed with humanity, a rare dry *khamsin* that had usually blown itself out by that time of year, caught the hood of Talca's cloak and tore it from his head to reveal black hair matted on one side with dried blood. Someone had assaulted him.

Talca disappeared into the passage. A couple of minutes later he was up the stairs to the roof.

"The High Priest?" asked Deleig. "He received you in person?"

"Unwillingly possibly, certainly begrudgingly, yet highly attentively. He was alone, entering from the far end of a grand hall with companions who immediately departed as I shuffled in from the other direction."

"Shuffled, Talca?" Deleig asked.

"One learns to play a role, Highness. I stood in silence. He asked, 'You have a name?' and I was alert enough guess he wasn't asking for my name but the man on the papyrus. Then he added, 'The man who might betray this Nazarene?'

" 'I do,' I replied. 'He will come to ask for money. The agreed sum is thirty pieces of silver.'

" 'You are liberal with my money,' the High Priest said. I replied, 'I do not myself speak to the man. I have someone closer to him do that. I relay only what I learn.'

" 'And this other, this someone?' asked the High Priest. 'How much money does *he* expect?'

" 'None,' I told the High Priest. 'He owes me a debt and this is how he is repaying it. I have no interest in seeing the money or determining the amount. If the man approaches you, that is the sum. If he does not, I have done all I can and all I am prepared to do. Like yourself, I am afraid of these people who have given their minds to this Jesus now approaching Jerusalem.'

" 'Like myself?' said Caiaphas, annoyed with me. 'Like myself?' he repeated. 'Who do you think you are to come into my establishment and suggest I am afraid of this Jesus?'

"I looked at Caiaphas and he looked at me. You, Musan, had told me to always respectfully hold my ground, to never be cowed, and that the safest way to do that was silence. Finally, the High Priest spoke again, 'The name of this man?' I told him.

" 'And when will he approach me, and by what avenue?'

" 'He will come to your palace and say he is the dissatisfied one. Whoever of your guards hears that is to notify you and bring him to your presence. If earlier, he sees you outside or in the Temple, he will approach you himself, there.'

" 'Why is he dissatisfied?' the High Priest asked me.

"I said I neither knew nor cared. I had delivered what I had promised. I told Caiaphas that I had a friend who knew I was there, and that if anything happened to me, he was to tell the world Caiaphas had had me killed. Further, he was to tell the followers of Jesus about Judas Iscariot and the High Priest—if anything untoward happened to me.

"The High Priest sharply stepped back, shocked. Shocked both to be spoken to like that, but also at the realization of what I had said, as instructed by you, Your Highness."

"The scheme is what, Talca?" Deleig asked.

"Judas Iscariot must make his approach to the High Priest. How, sir, will that be accomplished, if I might ask?"

"Go to Judas. Tell him—your head is bloodied, why?"

"As I was leaving, Caiaphas told his nearest guard to deliver me a blow for my impertinent manner, sir. The guard caught me with the hilt of his *gladius*. He knocked me to the ground and rubbed my face in the dirt."

"Tell Morden, Talca, to attend to that cut. There are too many flies to leave it unattended. You are a good man. Thank you."

Talca smiled at him and left. Deleig went down the stairs to sit in the cooler atrium, in the shade of the trees.

Ten minutes later, a breathless S'veyda came through the door. He looked around and saw Deleig.

"I've ridden in, ahead of them."

He seemed to Deleig shrunken, the way a fugitive might.

"The servant at the door is holding my horse in the passageway. Jesus—you've never seen anything like him. He entered Jerusalem riding a donkey like a mock king … ah, oh, greetings, I came because no one else would think to," said S'veyda, correcting the fact that in the heat of his enthusiasm he'd forgotten even a modest greeting.

"Jesus has been turning tables upside down in the Temple. He drove the moneylenders into the streets, scattering their coins. The street urchins loved it, and the moneylenders are now chasing them. It was chaotic."

"Water for my visitor, please," Deleig said to a servant.

S'veyda took it gladly as Deleig said, "Sit here," pointing to an ornate stone bench by the sputtering fountain. "Someone needs to get this fountain repaired," Deleig announced to the servants standing nearby.

To S'veyda he said, "What is the significance of what you have just told me?"

"He has never done anything like that. He has never disturbed the peace. Everything physical he has done has been to heal or embrace. I wonder if he's becoming deranged."

Deleig said, "Then we must go together to the Temple, S'veyda. Let us watch and discuss, and only then decide."

To a servant, Deleig said, "Take care of the horse, bring it into the atrium for safekeeping until you find stabling."

"Sir," S'veyda interrupted, "there's no point in going to the Temple." Deleig turned rather than continue to head for the door. "They have left for Bethany. I shall go to Bethany this evening. If Jesus is returning to the Temple, I shall send word ahead." S'veyda placed the water cup on the bench and stood up.

Deleig put his hand on his friend's shoulder.

"Be calm, S'veyda. Think of it this way. King David, too, approached Jerusalem on a donkey in prophetic ecstasy. Whether Jesus was or was not experiencing a prophetic ecstasy when he scattered the merchandise sellers and moneychangers from the Temple, I do not know. But this was certainly a double taunting of the priests and Pharisees. You know, with such public outbursts, of course, the curiosity factor will further attract the crowds. News like this travels fast, you certainly did, and there are certainly enough pilgrims wanting to change money that the word will spread."

S'veyda was only half listening.

"Oh, Myrmid," S'veyda stammered to his colleague, who had just entered. "Preacher Yaakov has arrived in Jericho and wants to hear Jesus. I sent word to him come here, to Vasas' house. I wasn't sure what to do. Yes?"

"I'll take care of it, S'veyda," said Myrmid. "Guards!"

He walked with Deleig and S'veyda as guards opened the recessed door. S'veyda patted the horse as he went past. Once in the alleyway, Deleig and S'veyda stopped while Myrmid positioned his Parthian guards in a protective cordon around them. All set, they headed to the Fortress Antonia, where S'veyda would be given a fresh horse to take him to Bethany.

Deleig told S'veyda he must take Talca with him and explained that now S'veyda was a member of the Nazarene's peripatetic community, he must withdraw as Deleig's contact with Judas Iscariot. Deleig said it was unfair to S'veyda to be placed in an ambivalent situation. Talca would act as the intermediary. S'veyda must wait at the fortress gate; Talca would meet him there.

S'veyda seemed not merely satisfied but pleased, as if Deleig had lifted a burden from him. He said he would glad to take Talca to Judas Iscariot in Bethany.

S'veyda returned to the events Deleig had missed. How an enormous crowd had followed Jesus to the Temple courtyard and how "as Jesus made his way he began flailing with a cord those who were buying and selling, sending them running—sacrificial doves were flying everywhere, as confused as the people."

S'veyda's voice contained his disbelief that such a thing could have occurred.

"But why now, S'veyda?" Deleig asked as they walked along. "The pigeon-sellers and market stalls and money changers have always been in the Temple courtyard."

"I don't know, sir, unless it was to bring more of the senior priests and Pharisees running. It did. It became the opportune moment for Jesus to taunt the senior priests and scribes, just as he had the Pharisees. The children were shouting, 'Halleluyah to the Son of David,' a claim to kingship under the Jewish religion if ever there was one. Forcefully, a senior priest asked Jesus, 'Can you hear what they're saying?'

"Jesus looked at them, sir, and I must say there was just the suggestion of delight in his eyes—quickly obliterated in order not to let them see he was mocking them again. He replied, 'Of course. And you've read, "Out of the mouths of babes is emitted the perfect praise."'

"Jesus turned his back on the priests and Pharisees before they had a moment to respond, and was out of the Temple practically before they had time to catch their breaths. Oh Musan, 'Out of the mouths of babes'—he really has insulted them. He insinuates that even children understand better than the Temple priests. He is so learned and clever and quick. I can quite see why Judas is alarmed."

"Why Bethany? I've forgotten, I know you told me," Deleig said.

"He has friends there, sir. He will stay with them and then move to the house of Simon the Leper."

"Why a leper?"

"Perhaps he is teaching by example, sir."

Deleig nodded thoughtfully and thanked S'veyda. To Myrmid, he said, "Where are we meeting Talca?"

"Guards' gate at the fortress," said Myrmid. "We may as well wait there ourselves—it won't be more than fifteen minutes."

S'veyda said, "While there's still a great deal of movement around the Bethany house where Jesus stays, I will introduce Talca to Judas."

"In that case," said Deleig, "I'll meet with Marianus. Myrmid, arrange things with Vasas as usual, please."

Following a brief meeting with Talca, who left with S'veyda for Bethany, Deleig made his way under Myrmid's guard to Vasas' house and was soon seated on the rooftop level, opposite Marianus, sipping wine, a servant with more hovering nearby. Myrmid said that with Claudia and Formio in residence, he had his hands full and must leave.

In the roof garden, after the customary courtesies, Deleig said to Marianus, "I'm growing ever more interested in this Nazarene. He has everyone upset it seems. But first, new rings. I've something quite startling for you, Marianus—the ring of the Chinese philosopher Confucius, it is said. From its apparent age and highly unusual design. Either they're correct, or it's an excellent copy, or an imaginative later original. My guess would be an excellent copy, notice the patina of the gold. Here's the symbol itself. These two sets of Chinese characters. Remarkable system of writing, isn't it?"

"When did Confucius live?" Marianus asked, noticing a servant had refilled his wine cup.

"Five centuries ago, give or take fifty or a hundred years."

"How amazing it has survived—if it is genuine. It *looks* worn enough, and beautiful enough. See the wear at the rear. But even if not, certainly …," sip, sip, "and even if not the original, certainly an ancient copy of it. Thank you, Musan …," sip, sip.

Marianus contemplated which of his many-ringed fingers could accommodate it. He decided on the third finger of his left hand, where it became the top ring of two. Marianus genuinely was entranced.

"I have to buy it."

"No, it's a gift."

Marianus was overcome by the generosity of it. Deleig laughed and said, "I still have that other one you may want to buy, until you hear the price. But this is no time for commerce, later when we adjourn." He asked him what the gossip was about this Jesus character.

Marianus bunched his lips together in a downward mock grimace. "Oh, the priests have become so preoccupied with his rantings and ravings. I've told my brother-in-law, Annas, 'Pay no attention.' Nephew Caiaphas has his own strategy: he wants to arrest the Nazarene somewhere the crowd won't witness it. Surreptitiousness is a Caiaphas strategy for everything, a most devious nephew ...," sip, sip, "in fact the only nephew I don't particularly care for, but the family is everything, isn't it? The last thing Caiaphas needs is to upset his extremely delicate balancing act vis-à-vis both the Prefect and the Tetrarch. I tell Caiaphas, 'If you let the Nazarene run his course, he'll disappear like the others.' How many messiahs and preachers have we had in the past ten or twenty years? Six? Seven? Twelve? At least six. What's one more? The others went away ...," sip, sip.

"The Romans are still shaking from the rebellion two years after Herod Antipas arrived—and of course Antipas shakes anyway. It was his first brush with insurrection, however minor. Yes, yes, there have been uprisings. I tell Caiaphas and Annas, 'There are always going to be uprisings, we Judeans are that kind of people' ...," sip, sip, "it doesn't mean all the Judeans are going to join in, most of us are happy to let things be. Yes, yes, I know the Romans are occupiers, but we had armed skirmishes before the Romans came. You know what they say, 'An Arab will argue with anyone, and if there's no one to argue with, he'll argue with the wind, and a Jew, seeing the argument, will instinctively join in and take sides.'

"We've always lived like that. We moaned at Moses ...," sip, sip, "we complain to God about God. Isaiah might talk about the lamb laying down with the wolf, that's easier than getting all the Judeans to lie down with one another—in the non-prurient sense ...," Marianus added hurriedly, with a laugh as he looked at Vasas to see if there was more wine. There was.

"Do the Romans even care about this Jesus character?" Deleig asked, in the least urgent manner imaginable—though it would be the most important question he'd pose during the meeting.

"That's the other thing. Caiaphas tells me the Prefect is concerned, though he did not tell me about what. More germane, Herod Antipas has been over to see Pilatus. That was one conversation a man of wealth wanting more—a man like myself—

would like to have heard. There is money to be made when kings conspire. But where? Eh? Answer that for me?"

Deleig was taken aback—Antipas had a role in this? The conversation drifted until Deleig asked, "Will Jesus be the cause of an insurrection—anything like that?"

"Sons and daughters! Certainly not! The Judean people don't care. It's a local show. Talk to someone from Herodium and they won't even have heard his name. This is bored Galilean fishermen needing an excuse to get away their boats and dangerous work, to wander the countryside living off the work of others. That's more their style …," sip, sip, "I daren't stay talking because I'll stay drinking and I daren't do that if I want to be able to enter my house on my own legs … You are, Vasas, the best of hosts with the finest wines and nicest friends and I'm on my way." He carefully struggled to his feet.

Once Marianus had descended the stairs, a servant on each side of him for safety's sake, Deleig said he would move over to his quarters in the Praetorium, now that Pilatus was in residence. Vasas nodded that he understood and walked with his friend to the gate where Deleig's guard waited.

Deleig had already decided he would report to Pilatus that the view from inside the Sanhedrin was there'd be no insurrection due to the Nazarene. He would not mention he knew about Antipas' visit—though Deleig was annoyed he had not been informed. He suspected Antipas' presence when Pilatus had insisted they talk in the small reception room and the Prefect kept lowering his voice. Myrmid's man in Antipas' entourage would probably have already confirmed that with Myrmid, or would before midnight.

Pilatus seemed pleased with himself as he cordially welcomed Deleig and they retreated to the customary comfortable salon. He listened to Deleig's report. Then Pilatus stood, bottom lip curled down. He tightened his lips, and he glowered at Deleig, peering into his eyes. Suddenly he shouted, "You met my wife in the middle of the night! Something has been going on but I don't know what. Until I do, stay away from my wife! Don't go near her again!"

Pilatus stepped right up to Deleig. Too close to hit me, Deleig thought, surprised he wasn't really stunned by the outburst. He took a step back so that they were an arm's length apart.

Icily, Deleig said, "How dare you, sir! How dare you defame your wife. How dare you suggest that my conduct with her has been anything but honorable. You have your other spies. Ask them. You know we are never alone together. I am appalled by your remarks, offended for her and disgusted with you. She came to me, with her servant remaining in the corridor—because she could not find YOU. YOU were not in your quarters or chamber. YOU were the one she wanted. She thought you might be with me—logically enough. Talk to her, to her servants, you disgusting man."

Deleig turned and started to walk out for he realized he was trembling. Pilatus said, "She said she wanted to talk to you about dreams concerning me and wanted my consent before she did so. I don't know what you two are doing together behind my back."

Coolly Deleig retorted, "You are vile. Further, you go behind my back meeting with Herod Antipas. Why didn't you tell me—I shouldn't have to rely on my spies for that."

"Who I meet and when is none of your business. I am the governor of Judea, not you."

Deleig left and went to his quarters. He went to bed and, once he was calm, slept soundly.

The next morning, Preacher Yaakov arrived, having been redirected from Vasas' house. S'veyda, too, arrived only minutes later, again in a state of high excitement, though not quite as extreme as the previous day.

After mutual greetings, S'veyda declared, "Jesus withered a tree, Musan, and now he is already in the Temple courtyard, or still on the steps, he may have moved, teaching, and I am sure he will soon be annoying the priests the way he was the Pharisees."

Deleig didn't know what tree withering was. He decided extreme calm was called for. So he said, quite slowly, for after all S'veyda was not at heart the emotional type, something had truly alarmed him, "Just take your time, S'veyda, and explain slowly, that I might understand all the implications of what tree withering is."

He said, "Early this morning we were walking into Jerusalem from Bethany and Jesus was hungry. He saw a fig tree, went to pluck some fruit and could find none—"

"Someone had already eaten it?" Deleig asked.

"No, sir—Musan—that is, apparently not. The Nazarene said it had borne none, and he was sufficiently angry to declare it dead and it withered up before our eyes."

S'veyda paused. Deleig asked Preacher Yaakov, "What would you say, Preacher?"

He said, "That we must be there at the Temple—to see and hear what new outrages he has planned."

But at the Temple what they watched and heard was not outrageous as far as Deleig was concerned. Jesus made brilliant theatre of it, theatre worthy of the finer playwrights. The word play was dazzling as he responded to the scribes and Pharisees. Hundreds more gathered close enough to hear. S'veyda pointed out a knot of some Pharisees and Sadducees. S'veyda whispered, "Those Sadducees are Herodians—a couple of officials from his court and others closer to the Temple but dependent on the Tetrarch's favor. The gathering of an unlikely alliance." Both Deleig and Preacher Yaakov nodded.

Jesus was speaking, but stopped. To the right of Deleig, as the three of them reached the front, the crowd behind the Nazarene was parting due to some noise being made. S'veyda whispered to Deleig, "Senior priests." Deleig had already seen them.

High Priest Caiaphas, priests and scribes entered the "arena" formed by the oval of people gathered to listen to Jesus. One of the priests immediately confronted him and demanded, "Who gave you the authority to teach these things in the manner you do?"

Jesus was unabashed and in a light voice of inquiry, controlled enough to carry to the crowd, replied, "I'll ask you one question, too. If you answer mine, I shall answer yours."

The priest nodded an agreement, and the Nazarene said, "Where was John's baptism from—Heaven or men?"

Deleig turned to Preacher Yaakov who quickly and quietly explained that other preachers quoted from the Torah to provide scriptural authority for their statements or interpretations—Jesus did not.

The Nazarene had the priests caught in a quandary. If the priests said John's baptism came from God, Jesus could ask them why they had not obeyed John. Equally, if the priests said John's baptism came from men, the people who considered John a prophet would murmur against the priests and inflame others similarly.

Yaakov and Deleig watched the priest confer with other priests. Then the priest said, "We don't know."

Jesus delivered the perfect riposte, "Then nor shall I tell you my authority."

At one end of the oval of Jesus watchers, Caiaphas, consternation written into his grimace, conferred with his priests. At the other end, Pharisees and Herodians had apparently agreed on an approach. One of them walked toward where Jesus was standing. The man held a small coin between his forefinger and thumb.

Jesus looked at him with interest and pre-empted what he apparently knew the man was about to ask.

"Whose image is that," Jesus asked, "and whose inscription?"

"Caesar's," the man said.

"Then render to Caesar the things that are Caesar's and to God those that are God's."

The man turned to look at those who had sent him, as if seeking advice. With none forthcoming, he walked disconsolately back to them. But already a scribe had entered the open area to succeed him as a questioner.

"Master," he said, politely, "which is the first commandment?"

Deleig felt someone firmly grip his shoulder. It was the preacher.

"Listen."

Jesus looked at those who disagreed with him, disliked him, perhaps feared him: the Sadducees, the scribes, the Temple senior priests and the Pharisees. Then he looked back to the gentle questioner.

Jesus was pleased with the question and answered gladly, "Hear O Israel, the Lord your God is God. And you shall love the Lord your God with your whole heart, whole soul, whole mind, and with your whole strength."

He paused and looked across the faces of the crowd. To them he continued, "The second is like it: 'And you shall love your neighbor as yourself.' There is no other commandment greater than these."

The scribe said to him, "Well, master, you have said in truth, there is one God and there is no other besides him. And he should be loved with the whole heart, and the whole understanding, and with the whole soul, and with the whole strength. And to love one's neighbor as oneself is a greater thing than all offerings and sacrifices."

Jesus, hearing him answer wisely, said to him, "You are not far from the kingdom of God."

The sudden increase in intensity of the preacher's grip on Deleig's robe made Deleig turn toward him again.

"Brilliant," said the preacher. "Unbelievably brilliant. Look at their faces." He indicated the expressions on the faces of Caiaphas and the others. They were in awe at what had transpired. They had obviously been silenced. Something had happened, but Deleig did not know what.

He loosened Preacher Yaakov's grip, and they stepped back through the crowd. "What did it all mean?"

"These men tested his knowledge of the Torah," Yaakov said. "What they have just realized is that Jesus knows the Scriptures better than they. To a degree that has silenced them. They are in the presence of a true master. It all hinges on the one word in Hebrew, pronounced *ve'ahavta*. I doubt it is in your limited Hebrew vocabulary. It means, in your Latin, and indeed Greek, 'and you shall love.' That particular word in Hebrew, with a personal direct object, is used only four times in the Torah: in the two passages Jesus quotes, Deuteronomy 6:5 and Leviticus 19:18, and in two which follow shortly after them and interpret them, Deuteronomy 11:1 and Leviticus 19:34 respectively.

" 'So, Preacher?' you ask. So this. It means Jesus has so memorized the Torah—think on that, an enormous challenge—that he can bring this obscurely used phrase to bear to allow the two passages, 'love God ... love thy neighbor' to be read in the light of each other as one commandment. Imagine: love God and neighbor as a single commandment, God and neighbor equal in every respect. God *in* neighbor?

"Much for me to think about—but these will ask no more questions of him. His learning has defeated them; their silence acknowledges it. They will hate him for it—even while admiring him. I am nigh speechless myself. I am returning home to Capernaum humbled by this man's intelligence, by the beauty of his thought."

With that, the preacher nodded to Deleig and departed. At which point Jesus stepped into the crowd and disappeared.

Deleig went to the fortress gate. S'veyda and Talca were already there. S'veyda said Jesus had left to pray in the garden and Caiaphas' men were headed in the same direction.

"Where?"

"The Mount of Olives."

Nodding, Deleig said, "We must leave."

TWENTY-FIVE

Under Myrmid's rule, when Pilatus' family was in Jerusalem, or anywhere beyond Caesarea Maritima, there was a watch system in place on Claudia and Formio. It wasn't enough that Pilatus himself was constantly guarded. It had fallen to Deleig, in the absence of Pilatus himself noticing the need, to see that his family was protected.

To Deleig, the simpler the system, the more effective. Servants are invisible. They wander at will doing whatever it is someone, somewhere, has ordered them to do. If they are carrying something, a sheet or a jug or fresh oil for the lamps, they can and do proceed unquestioned, for they are unnoticed except when needed. When Pilatus' court moved, the family servants moved with it.

When the family was in the Praetorium, Myrmid knew to have servants wander through Claudia and Formio's apartments at the rate of about twice an hour. That is how, on the evening of the Feast of the Passover, Myrmid learned that Formio was missing.

Myrmid quickly pulled together the six nearest servants and sent them to rapidly question other servants. Had Formio been seen? The answer came back almost immediately from the kitchens, from Fatima. Deleig knew the woman. She was the main soothsayer to the Fortress Antonia complex, and much in demand.

It was an older cook who had her son by the ear when Myrmid arrived down in the kitchens.

"Tell the master," she ordered.

The boy, about thirteen, said that "His Young Highness" had just left the kitchen after the boy refused to give Formio his tunic.

He said he wasn't going to do it again because his mother warned he'd be in serious trouble and lose his kitchen work.

"What do you mean, 'again'?" Myrmid asked.

"Let him use my clothes again, my lord—His Highness the Prefect's son," the boy answered, reluctantly.

"Again?" Myrmid repeated. His dark eyebrows seemed more threatening than his expression. To the boy it was obvious from the man's tone he must answer despite his promise, or was it oath, to His Highness, the young Master.

"He made me take an oath not to say anything." It came out of the boy's mouth tremulously, quavering, like a singer looking for the correct note.

"You are relieved of the oath by my authority," said Myrmid, eyebrows dancing. Whose authority he was revoking was no concern of Myrmid's.

"Two days ago, His Highness the Prefect's son came to me and ordered me to give him my tunic. If I did not, he said, he could have me severely punished. I asked him what I would wear. I couldn't work in my shift. I had to work in the kitchens—if I didn't, they'd find out what he'd done.

"He gave me his tunic. Saffron, silky. I said I couldn't wear that in the kitchen. He said, 'Wear it to go for another tunic.' It didn't occur to him I only had one tunic and he was now wearing it, for he'd dropped it over his head. He commanded me to bring him some olive oil.

"I wrapped the tunic around my waist like a skirt, went to the larders, but was looking for my mother on the way. Fatima saw me and went for my mother, who came to the larders and asked what I was up to. I explained. She raised her eyes, the way she always responds to a crisis, slapped me across the head for a stupid boy and told me to stay there."

His mother, standing there, raised her eyes and slapped him on the back of the head.

"I returned with my cloak for this stupid boy to wear," she said, "and a small flask of olive oil. Then I took the tunic and went to find a servant who could return it to His Highness's quarters."

"Then I took the olive oil to His Highness," said the boy, picking up his story. "He poured some into one hand, a lot, and rubbed it into his hair. He flattened his curls and made them hang down like rat's tails over his face and ears. He rubbed his hands together, rubbed his face, patted his hands on the floor and then rubbed the dust into his cheeks and across his nose. Then he had me take him to the entrance the servants use. As we walked, he made me take an oath I would not reveal what had happened. It didn't seem that long before he was back asking for his tunic. I told him my mother had given it to his servants."

By now, the kitchen boy was wide-eyed with fear. As Myrmid reached toward him, the boy cringed, expecting a blow. Instead Myrmid rubbed his head and assured him he was in no trouble. He asked how long since "His Young Highness" had left the building this time and what was he wearing.

The boy replied, "You walked into the kitchen just as he was going to the door. This time I told him he couldn't have my tunic. He handed me his clothes and left in his shift. His clothes are still behind that table in a box. I didn't want to get into more trouble."

That crafty young devil, Myrmid thought, as he recalled he had seen two figures at the servants' entrance, one he presumed was an old woman in a cloak.

Myrmid told the boy two coins would be sent down, one to pay for a new tunic, the other for his honesty. Myrmid ran toward the guards' entrance. With four Parthians to accompany him, he raced toward the Mount of Olives, uncertain where Formio was headed.

But Myrmid recalled Deleig had mentioned Judas Iscariot told him Jesus used the Gethsemane farm, as it was still referred to by older locals, for prayer. One of the Parthians told Myrmid Gethsemane was on the initial slope of the mount. It was an area where women laid their sheets across bushes to dry once they'd washed them.

As Myrmid later reconstructed the event, he said that Formio had known where to go by following Deleig, whose guards were carrying lamps on poles. That's why Formio was in such a hurry to leave the kitchen. Wearing just his shift, he'd run after Deleig, following the lamps. But Deleig had told the guards to wait while he went on ahead. Formio lost sight of Deleig and at a loss, veered to the left, still rushing.

A dozen yards later, he was set on by three men. They took his shift, obviously expensive because it was one piece in fine material, and sandals. At that point Myrmid and the four guards arrived. Formio was naked, but Myrmid grabbed a sheet from a bush and threw it around him.

What astonished Myrmid was that, despite his firm suggestion Formio return to the Praetorium, Formio was adamant in seeing what happened to Jesus. By that time the Parthian guards had captured two of the men, who lay unconscious on the ground, while one had circled around the dimly lighted area where Caiaphas' men were confronting and arresting Jesus.

One of Myrmid's guards spotted Deleig on the opposite side of the melee involving Jesus' arrest. The guard reached Deleig and told him of Formio's plight. In great long leaps, Deleig raced around the Jesus scene, which amounted to little more than a shadow play in his periphery vision. He was furious enough with Formio to consider reporting him immediately to Pilatus. He weighed against even as he ran because of its uncertain consequences.

Formio, horrified and fearful, saw Deleig racing toward him and squealed but froze. That squeal alerted the Temple priests' men and two of them lunged forward to apprehend the boy. They grabbed him by his sheet, but he squirmed out of it and, naked, fled.

Hurtling off into the black night, Formio suddenly decided, it seemed, that Deleig was the lesser of two evils—flight into the unknown or flight into his Parthian friend's wrath. He turned and ran into Deleig's arms. Deleig quickly wrapped the boy in his cloak.

Deleig saw Myrmid appear with Formio's shift and sandals. He left Formio with the cloak, telling him, "Put these on, go back to the Praetorium and remain there."

Deleig didn't wait for a reply but joined his guards—finally caught up with him—who urged him off in the direction Caiaphas' henchmen had taken.

As they descended the slight slope, Deleig realized Judas Iscariot was probably correct. Jesus' intimates and followers were nowhere to be seen, certainly not racing after the departing captive Jesus. They'd fled.

The guards and Deleig moved quickly through the dip that was the Kedron valley and on to the streets that led toward the Shoshan gate. They could tell from the animation of the people they passed on the street that they had been watching something go by.

The cordon of Parthian guards around Deleig pushed through the crowded steps to emerge into the bustling Temple courtyard. There was a hive-like buzz of excitement among these, the fortunate faithful of Judaism, come to celebrate and observe the Passover. Obviously the prospect of nighttime entertainment had spread quickly in the city. A spectacle was often preferable to prolonged religious observance, or at least an antidote to it.

Most of those looking around somewhat aimlessly were obvious visitors. The buzz was the prospect of something they hadn't seen before, whatever it was.

The many blazing torches around the walls gave the impression of a stage set for a theatrical performance. A death scene?

Moving in a dense pack like ants migrating, the leading curious reached the front of the High Priest's palace and arranged themselves in a half-circle around the Nazarene. Behind him were priests, Pharisees, Herodians, some of the Sanhedrin, Sadducees and other allies. Caiaphas strutted out of the palace in garments ornate and costly. A chicken in peacock feathers, Deleig decided.

Several of Caiaphas' colleagues moved toward him and flanked him as he joined the officials. Deleig saw Marianus to Caiaphas' right. The man on his left was probably Caiaphas' father-in-law, Annas, the former High Priest.

Deleig, given his height, wondered if there was sufficient light from the torches that Marianus could see him, too. In the space between the officials and the crowd, neither forlorn nor defiant, but badly bruised, was Jesus. The Nazarene stood there unafraid.

One of the priests, obviously appointed to the task, sounding more officious than official, called out, "Who has complaints against this man? Why is he here?"

Deleig looked toward Caiaphas. To the unknowing in the crowd, the High Priest could appear judicious, impartial—even innocent. He could posture as one called on to deal with something about which he had no prior knowledge. How clever. Testimony against the Nazarene was being shouted from the crowd.

At first Deleig was mentally complimenting Caiaphas on how quickly the entire scene, or charade, had been staged, accusers deliberately planted among the people. Then Deleig saw that the attempted subversion was becoming problematic—even farcical. The accusers had not been suitably rehearsed. They'd forgotten their lines as the charges leveled by one against Jesus ludicrously conflicted with testimony that preceded or followed.

This bizarre farrago threatened whatever Caiaphas' intentions were. Impromptu accusations were now heard from the crowd; the audience was joining in for a chance to be heard. Unwillingly, Caiaphas, as his staging began to unravel, left the security of his allies and stomped into the center not five feet from the Nazarene. It was some contrast. The serene captive. The agitated accuser.

Facing Jesus, Caiaphas stuck his hand in the air to signal silence to the crowd. The murmuring did lessen. But the High Priest had not thought about what to do next. So he returned to consult with two officials and then came back to Jesus. Ah, the benefit of height, Deleig thought as he watched the two officials slowly make their way around and into the crowd.

They convinced themselves no one was watching. Once in the crowd, they began earnest conversations with two of the apparent poorly rehearsed provocateurs. After several minutes, the two quietly resumed their place back among the other Sadducees, priests, officials and the few Sanhedrin members present.

Even with no action, the Nazarene simply standing there, torches making dancing shadows, the crowd was enjoying itself. Deleig heard a woman, probably a wife, urge a man, possibly her husband, to "get out there and say something—you're always complaining about these revolutionaries." He continued, against her will, to hold back.

Out front, the open space now accommodated only the Nazarene and Caiaphas. There was a detectable tremor of unease among Caiaphas' allies. The two men approached by the officials stepped briskly out into the open space. Amazing what money will do, Deleig thought, knowing well what it did because he utilized bribery so frequently himself.

Jesus was boldly accused of having said that he could destroy the sanctuary and rebuild it in three days. "Tear down the Temple," one man told the crowd. "He said he could do that." The other man stated this was the case. Jesus did not respond. Caiaphas was becoming increasingly disturbed. Deleig decided that given Jesus' previous willingness to speak out, the High Priest had probably not anticipated dealing with a silent Nazarene.

"Say something why don't you? Rebut what these people are saying if they are wrong." Silence. Caiaphas was breathing heavily, his exasperation mounting. His over-the-shoulder glances became more frequent. Did he realize his scheming was unraveling? Had it dawned on Caiaphas that he would now have to be the main accuser? Caiaphas had wanted to judge Jesus, Marianus said later, not prosecute him.

"I can put you under solemn oath," Caiaphas told the Nazarene. "I do so. Tell us, are you the Messiah, the Son of God?"

The Nazarene had been looking steadily at Caiaphas. His expression was that of a man who already knew how matters would play out.

He replied, "You have heard my words and not believed them. Why would you believe my answer?"

"Are you the Messiah?"

"You say I am."

Caiaphas, theatrically, jubilantly tore his robe as he yelled, "He is a blasphemer, we need no more witnesses. You all heard it! He is guilty by his own words. What shall we do with him?" The crowd was silent. Normally Judeans tear their clothes as a sign of mourning. Had that silenced them, Deleig wondered, or had they, too, regarded Caiaphas' actions as play-acting? Four or five officials tore their garments in a show of solidarity.

Fierce in expression, Caiaphas turned and faced his allies. His head moved from left to right, slowly. He stared at them, one by one. He was obviously demanding something from his colleagues they were reluctant to give. All Caiaphas was receiving from his supporters was evidence of their unease: shifting feet, averted eyes, silence.

"You all heard it?" he demanded of them. He kept examining their faces, one by one, as his head moved back to the left. The prosecutor before the jury. Willingly or not, there were murmurs of acquiescence as heads nodded.

"What is your verdict?" he demanded in an even louder voice. Several said, "Guilty." Caiaphas stared at them all, furious. Finally, a few others quickly uttered, "Guilty," as if anxious to be done with it.

Caiaphas was not done.

"The verdict is decided. What is the punishment for blasphemy?" Another brilliant prosecutor's trick from Caiaphas, thought Deleig. He was making his allies declare without declaring himself. From among his allies, a lone voice said, "He should die."

Caiaphas turned to the crowd, looking pensive. The tilt of his head backward, as if listening, was indication to the officials behind him he was willing them all to pronounce sentence. No one else spoke. He addressed the crowd, "You heard it: 'He should die.'"

Some in the crowd apparently finally remembered and misremembered their lines. They variously urged the accused should be stoned and impaled. This was also the signal for the guards and thugs who had apprehended Jesus to turn on him. As they spat on him, they slapped, punched and pushed him. He was ridiculed, thumped about the head.

This was all quite acceptable to the crowd apparently, thought Deleig, the expected entertainment once someone's fate had been sealed. The High Priest gave a signal. The Nazarene was led away. Caiaphas' expression showed he obviously was not pleased, but having to be satisfied with what he had. After a consultation with some of the others around him, they all entered the palace.

Deleig knew Caiaphas' dilemma. He next had to convince the Prefect that the man must die. Deleig knew his own role was to attempt to convince Pilatus that the Nazarene must not.

The crowd, knowing there'd be more to come at some point, resolved that loss of a night's sleep would be a small price to pay. They broke into smaller groups, talking, or went to the walls and sat on the huge flagstones, arms around their knees, waiting to see what might happen next.

Deleig decided nothing was likely to occur before dawn. He hurried through the crowd to the Praetorium and Pilatus' quarters. He was not leaving himself open to charges of dereliction of duty. Pilatus had retired for the night. Deleig was shown in by a servant with a lamp who set the lamp to one side on a table.

In the gloom Deleig detected the night odors of someone else's sleeping room. Pilatus from his bed said, "Speak." Deleig formally reported on the night's proceedings, but said it was a show trial.

"Caiaphas has determined the Nazarene is a blasphemer. The so-called trial was a travesty, just a rag-tag selection of the Sanhedrin and other members of Caiaphas' claque. Evidence was flawed, farcical; witnesses were suborned, people planted as provocateurs. The High Priest was judge and prosecutor. He attempted, mainly succeeding, in bullying his claque into accepting his guilty verdict."

"Good. Good. Well done," Pilatus said, obviously impressed Deleig was alert, still at work and determined to keep him up-to-date. In the dim light of the oil lamp, the Prefect nodded appreciatively until Deleig asked if Claudia's anxiety had receded.

"You should know," he said, nastily.

Deleig, deliberately, retorted, "You are losing control of your reasonableness in personal matters much as you periodically do in matters political."

Pilatus was rightly furious at this last dig, and Deleig knew it. The Prefect swung out of his bed and stood. "You—you fake, you fakir, you wizard in fancy dress, don't you dare address your Prefect—"

"I'm not addressing the Prefect, I'm talking to the man, Pontius, my once, and I trust, future friend."

In the darkness it did not matter that Deleig was red in the face behind his beard. He was red not because he was lying, but because he felt he was protesting too much.

Pilatus, surprised at the sharpness of Deleig's rebuttal, unable to think of anything to say, simply waved Deleig out of his sight. He left, willingly—not a little troubled. Pilatus was worried.

Deleig went to his quarters and wrote a brief note to Lydia. He called for Myrmid and had him dispatch a messenger to Caesarea Maritima so the note would catch the next transport to Rome. The endpoint of his association with Pilatus had arrived more rapidly than he had imagined. Deleig was not displeased, though he had to wonder whether that end was entirely unprovoked on his part.

It was with some trepidation, given the extremely late hour and his exchange with Pilatus, that he made his way to Claudia and Formio's quarters. He sent in word he wanted to see both, briefly. He realized he barely cared now whether Pilatus found out or not. As servants lit multi-wicked lamps in the reception area, Formio stumbled in looking half-asleep and singularly chastened. Claudia entered. The boy's hand hesitated as to whether it should reach out to his mother's.

Finally, he decided against it. Claudia told the servants to stand in the corridor, out of earshot but where she could see them if she needed them. Claudia did not look sleepily disheveled, just anxious.

Deleig asked, quietly, "Claudia, please tell me what has been happening. Why was Formio on the Mount of Olives estate? He could have been murdered."

"Musan, my dear Musan"—how Deleig loved to hear such words—"the dreams have been terrible, and constant—even if I close my eyes momentarily during the day. I needed to hear from someone else what this Jesus was saying. You were too busy for me to ask. Who else was there? I heard your messenger tell Pilatus that Jesus and Caiaphas' men were going up to the Mount. Formio had already been out once for me, to listen to Jesus in the Temple. I asked my son to hurry, to follow you, because you'd be sure to go. I wanted a report on what was happening. It was dangerous, but I was desperate."

Claudia protectively draped a hand on Formio's shoulder.

"Please don't tell his father, Musan," she said. "Please. Pilatus is in a terrible state of mind. I have no idea what he might do."

Despite her words, Deleig ordered, "Formio, come here."

The boy came.

Deleig leaned down a little and wrapped his arms around him. Releasing him, Deleig said as the boy stood close, looking up at him, "Going out alone was extremely courageous and, as you now know, extremely risky, therefore foolish. Your life was in danger. You are safe. Your courage does you proud. I need your most solemn word you will not leave the Praetorium again without my authority."

"I give you my word. Honestly, Prince Musan, sir. I am sorry. Please don't let this ruin our friendship."

"It hasn't," Deleig said.

Formio, ever the questioner, asked, "But how did the robbers know I was a Roman?"

"You were wearing Roman sandals."

"I'd never make a spy."

"Silly man, I hope you never have to, you should have been barefoot. Now, between the three of us, I am no longer in the Prefect's confidence. I am fairly certain I'll return to Rome within the next month or two—summoned by the Emperor. Claudia, I do insist, from the purest motives concerning the physical safety of both of you, that Formio be sent to Rome to be educated and that you accompany him. Please, Claudia, I beg you, take this course of action."

Claudia did not even hesitate. She said, "We shall leave for Rome. Of course, Formio and I will say nothing about this conversation. His education is a justifiable reason—a perfect excuse. I'm sorry I didn't think of it for myself." It was a phrase her husband frequently used, too frequently, Deleig felt.

Deleig gestured with his hand so that no more would be said on that topic.

"What do the dreams say?"

"That this man Jesus is good, he is just, he has been singled out. My husband must not proceed with this—whatever it is."

"Have you told him?"

"I shall tell him again. Once my servants tell me he is awake."

Deleig nodded. As Claudia tried to tell of her dreams she was tongue-tied, ashen-faced in the soft oil lamplight, shaking slightly. He walked toward her and held her hand, O delight, to encourage her to tell what she saw.

"Men stoning a figure I assumed was Jesus, hanging him and crucifying him with no head, with people dancing around screaming. Then everything went calm, and Jesus was just standing there, speaking, with no sound coming out, and all the people making no noise except for crying. Then men came with clubs and broke his legs below the knees, but he went up instead of falling down. His face agony. I've told Pilatus about it. He went white-faced and said not to disturb myself. He would do what he could."

"I don't know what it means, Claudia," Deleig said, releasing her hand.

"Don't let them break his legs, don't, don't."

"I said I wouldn't," Deleig replied. "I do think it right to be concerned about whether this man will receive a fair trial—or if he even expects too. As to what the Prefect will do, I have no idea. Everyone must now go to bed." He turned and signaled the servants to come in. To Formio he said, "Your hair still looks oily. I don't think your curls will ever recover."

They both smiled, harmony restored.

Back in Deleig's quarters, S'veyda and Judas Iscariot were waiting for him. Greetings concluded, Deleig asked what was happening.

S'veyda said, "Talca sent us here, Musan, because he said there were thugs following Judas Iscariot. Dangerous men."

"Where is Talca now?" Deleig asked.

S'veyda, somewhat abashed, replied, "I was not certain what to do, so he is outside the fortress walls, waiting."

"Which entrance, the guards'?"

S'veyda nodded.

"Wait here, I shall return quickly."

Deleig, accompanied by Myrmid, hurried across the Praetorium courtyard to the guards' entrance of the Fortress Antonia. Talca was standing just outside the fort, the twin torches on the arch illuminating his face.

Perhaps he had found his new S'veyda, thought Deleig. He did not give Talca time to refuse, or even consider, but said, "Go straight away to the Temple courtyard—I know it's the middle of the night. They've sent Jesus to the prisons. Commit to memory anything said if officials reappear. If the crowd moves, follow it. You'll have messengers and a guard with you."

Deleig looked at Myrmid, who nodded it would be done.

"You will be safe."

"Musan, I understand. Be not concerned," Talca said.

Deleig, returning to his quarters, asked Myrmid to waken Vasas and persuade him to get Marianus to his house. To help Jesus Deleig realized he had yet another role to play. Helping Claudia.

In his quarters he said to S'veyda, "Return to your friends, S'veyda. I shall miss you."

To Judas Iscariot he said, "I would like you to remain here."

S'veyda gave a little bow, which Deleig acknowledged, no strong farewells this time. S'veyda said to Judas, "You will be safe. Musan, I'll return if anything warrants it." And he was gone.

To Judas, Deleig continued, "I shall return in under an hour. Then I want you at my side for a while, to tell me about Jesus and his intimate circle. We'll do that as we walk over to the Temple. Please come with me that far. After that, you can leave if you wish. I have guards around me, so no one will harm you."

Deleig had spoken in Aramaic. He replied in Greek, "Yes, sir."

Myrmid came back, reporting that Vasas had sent for Marianus. Within fifteen minutes, Deleig was mounting the stairs in Vasas' residence to his private area. Marianus was en route—he really did come when Vasas called. To appease him for the late hour, Vasas had ordered up a particularly fine wine. Despite the hour, Marianus looked refreshed and pleased—even eager—to see them as he walked in. He was as voluble as ever.

The warm greetings were reciprocated. As Deleig lowered himself onto a divan, he said to Marianus, "You know that I serve various functions within the Prefect's household, but my questions tonight are not to satisfy the Prefect's curiosity but mine."

Marianus nodded. He smiled at Vasas, raising his cup to express his appreciation for the quality of the wine.

Deleig continued, "I'm sure you saw me tonight in the courtyard, as I saw you." Marianus nodded again. "I don't understand what actually occurred, as distinct from what I saw. We both saw witnesses being suborned?" He nodded. "We heard testimony that didn't make sense—or at least not to me—in that it did not amount to enough to find a man guilty of anything."

Marianus said, "The man didn't say anything to incriminate himself, I agree. You have to realize he was not found guilty of blasphemy by the Sanhedrin, because the Sanhedrin was not present ...," sip, sip, "his death was not ordered by the Sanhedrin, because that would have been against our law. Yes, there were some members of the Sanhedrin present, but not many of us. Whatever else went on, the Sanhedrin *per se* did not pass judgment. Nor could they ...," sip, sip, "under Jewish law, a man cannot be sentenced on the same day he is tried and convicted. The Nazarene was arrested and tried after sundown, but Caiaphas expects a verdict in the morning. The verdict uttered by the fool in the courtyard tonight counts for nothing.

"If Caiaphas wanted him dead at the hand of the Judeans, he should have had the man kidnapped on the road and taken care of …," sip, sip, "and repeating myself, if the Sanhedrin in the morning is pressured by Caiaphas to sentence him, it goes against the law—may I say …," sip, sip, "the majority of us present did not hear convincing evidence of blasphemy, nor would we say we had. We were silent until Caiaphas, with his clothes-tearing histrionics in effect told us to choose between him or betraying him to the crowd's derision. Silence …," sip, sip, "was the better part of discretion."

Deleig wondered what had been said among the Sanhedrin councilors but did not speak.

Marianus added, "Caiaphas wants the Nazarene dead. I can't blame my nephew, only his methods. This Jesus wants to tear the whole structure down, then where would we be?"

"What will happen next, Marianus?"

"Tomorrow morning he will be sent to Pilatus. There may be the same people around Caiaphas to convince the Prefect that Jesus has been properly convicted. My information, not particularly reliable and you'd know better, is that Pilatus and Herod Antipas are more interested in teaching Caiaphas a lesson than hearing a case against a would-be messiah."

"At this point, Marianus," said Deleig candidly, "you know more than I do. Thank you for your candor." Deleig stood and bowed toward Marianus.

To Vasas, Deleig said, "My thanks, as always," and left. For once, left before Marianus.

Back at the Praetorium in the dark, he and Judas Iscariot set off for the Temple area. En route Deleig told him who he was and what he did, and what was happening now as best he knew. He asked about Judas' background and how he had met Jesus.

"I am the only disciple who is not a Galilean," Judas said. "I was born not far from Jerusalem, to its south. An Idumaean, which means we are suspect in the eyes of more traditional Judeans, I was in fact synagogue raised. After my father died, his friend, a preacher, took me into his family. I was given an excellent education—the best educated of those around Jesus—we in the south tend to look on Galileans as simple country folk, though James and John are the most learned among them. Many of them were fishermen.

"That's a rough, tough and dangerous trade. The incidence of drowning during storms at sea, in their case, the Sea of Galilee, was real. Fishermen are scarcely known for being nature's gentlemen, you know, and can be a bit coarse. Peter, the chosen leader, had his own boat. His education is scanty, he's bluff, but he is honest and everything he is or thinks is right there on the surface. He's a good man and I like him, and a couple of the others. Some regard me as an outsider, a lesser breed of Jew.

"I'm younger than most of them; they gossip about me because I handle the money and they suggest I help myself. For what: more wine, women? You know even if I had the inclination, there's little time. I like to hear what Jesus is saying and try to anticipate what he'll do next."

Deleig and Judas were leaving the Praetorium now with the guards. Deleig could tell Judas was relieved guards were present. He examined the man. Ordinary, not a radical, medium height, black hair, square face, prominent nose, troubled dark eyes.

Rather than just walk into the Temple from the Praetorium, Deleig had chosen to walk around the city and re-enter through the eastern gate. He felt Judas would say more, and less self-consciously, if they were walking. He was also gambling on there being no fresh developments regarding Jesus during the night.

Judas did seem comfortable talking, and that put Deleig at ease. Judas was now the one on edge.

He said, "Jesus I like, indeed love. As I've said. You know—I went to him by accident really. I'm sorry I never heard John the Baptist, I would have liked to. His reputation is what started me on my journeying, but he was arrested just before I reached the Jordan. With no John to listen to, I was wandering and some people were going to listen to this other preacher John had admired."

Deleig and Judas were beyond the walls now, threading their way through the streets and alleys of the tightly packed residential area that ringed most of the city. Judas was talking freely.

"He'd gone back to Galilee, so I went to Galilee on my own and met him. There were only eight disciples then and I became the ninth. Like a lot of people my age I didn't mind listening to new interpretations of the teaching—I was well-versed in the Torah and the Psalms, the Psalms particularly."

"Where are we going?" said Judas, suddenly alarmed. He stopped and gripped Deleig's lower arm.

"I thought you said the Temple?" Judas was anxious, suspicious. Deleig didn't blame him.

He pointed to the guards and said, "We are, but by the eastern gate. I wanted the chance to talk freely without being overheard. People in the Temple crowd will look at me in my court clothes, wonder who I am and crowd in to hear what I am saying."

Judas was satisfied. They continued walking and Deleig said, "Tell me about Jesus. Who is he, what is he like, what is he doing? And why you wanted him stopped, particularly that—I know some of it from S'veyda, but I'd like to hear it directly from you."

Judas puffed out his breath through closed lips, as if cogitating about the best way to reply. He thought for a while—Deleig was consoled by that, for it suggested he was not intemperate.

Then Judas said quite cheerfully, which took Deleig by surprise, "Jesus is everything he says he is. Truly. He is this remarkable man, you know, who has some special relationship with God, but whose learning astonishes listeners. His insight into the teachings of the Torah, his interpretations of its words and phrases, turns everything around for the people to clearly see. They do see, when he speaks. They see him as the Messiah, but he sees himself as the Son of the Father in a unique way.

"Them, some, not a majority, want a messiah in the Davidic sense—sword and might and driving out the Romans. That's not Jesus. He is the Messiah, the anointed redeemer, but not to redeem Judea from the Romans, but individuals from sin. His death is the price of their redemption—a mystery to me, but knowing Jesus, I think it's bound to be a mystery.

"This idea of redeeming the people from sin requires Jesus to define sin, and he's using the failings of the Pharisees, the Temple priests, the scribes and the Sadducees to do that. The people recognize this part, and they have an inkling of the personal sin. But they can't interpret everything and weigh it against the Torah's full teachings—unlike the scribes—because they only know what they've been taught. Jesus doesn't like what he sees as incomplete teaching—that the Pharisees and priests engage in it is incomprehensible to him. Perhaps, or certainly, Jesus is the Son of Man and Son of God, as he likes to say—but that, too, is an astounding concept to have to absorb. Not even the disciples have been able to fully appreciate it.

"These are simple people. While his teaching is perfectly clear in some respects, he has the disciples mystified—not, you know, always able to quite grasp the significance. He's been telling us for months he is going to die in Jerusalem. The others hear it, they acknowledge, but it doesn't fully penetrate. It's penetrated me, I'll tell you that. I hear it. He means it, it's going to happen, and it's going to happen whatever I do or don't do."

They turned at the corner and were headed along the path to the wide steps that would lead to Caiaphas' palace. Judas didn't notice where they were. He had warmed to his topic, and—Deleig hoped—their arrival at where the crowd was now milling around wouldn't stop him prematurely.

"So here he is, you know, antagonizing all the Judeans—that is really an amazing development. He spares not the particular object of his barbs—the senior priests and Sadducees. It's amazing really. You know, just look at what's happening. The Pharisees and priests and Sadducees know what he is saying at one level, but not at the deeper level—just like the disciples."

Judas stopped, looking around to see where he was, but not paying much attention.

He said, "The *people* sense what he is saying at a deeper level but don't understand it, even though many of them accept it. Then there are the *disciples*; they're the ones I'm worried about.

"Jesus is going to get himself killed and the disciples don't see it, don't see that they are likely to be next. I see it, oh yes. I don't want it, but I don't particularly fear it. Every man fears death to some degree, but I least I know what I'm involved in, you know.

"So that's why I was prepared to gamble with the senior priests. If they easily had Jesus in a setting where the mob—or Caiaphas' men—didn't stone him or beat the life out of the disciples, then I felt Jesus was getting what he wanted. The authorities would be happy to have the man they wanted—peaceably—and have no reason to pursue the disciples. But something happened at the Passover meal, that was certain."

"What was it, Judas?" asked Deleig, fearful his voice might cut off Judas' train of thought.

"Well, you have to know that Jesus can see everything. He can look ahead and things happen. He wants a donkey and colt to ride into Jerusalem—he tells the disciples where to go for a donkey and a colt. Without ever having been there himself, or knowing the owner. This is the Passover. There are no rooms for the pilgrims to take the meal in, one of those few meals where the Judeans recline Greek-style rather than be seated at table. The city and all around it are overcrowded. That doesn't dismay Jesus. You know, he just tells the disciples—go see this man and you'll get the room. It was like that at the meal. And that's where it really hurt."

Judas looked bewildered, crestfallen even.

"At supper he tells the disciples someone is going to betray him. But doesn't tell them who, but after a while looks at me. He tells Peter that Peter's going to deny him. Peter protested, was offended, but I didn't doubt Jesus knew it would happen. With me, I didn't doubt he would see it as betrayal. I didn't see it that way. He was determined to die and so he would, no matter what I or anyone else did.

"Peter protested loudly because he couldn't even comprehend that Jesus might be right, that he might deny Jesus, and most of them had been that way all along when he—Jesus—was talking to them. It's not that they are stupid, but they were not alert. Until the meal, and even then, not at first ..."

Judas stopped talking. When he resumed, it was much more slowly than before.

"Jesus was speaking in such a way you could tell, or at least I could, that he was saying goodbye. He had everyone's attention. He took bread from the basket and said it was his body, and to eat it. I don't think they could fathom what he was talking about—eating his flesh. It was a vision, a concept, an allusion beyond them. Then he took the cup and said, 'This is my blood, the blood of the new covenant. I will shed it for you and the many. I will not drink again until I drink in the Kingdom with God.' "

Judas breathed out a huge, choking sigh, coughed and used the back of his hands to wipe tears from his eyes.

"Finally, finally, they realized. Blood they *could* understand. They'd bled themselves. As a group, they seemed to realize something serious was ahead. It had taken this long but now, at last they knew *he* intended to die. They still didn't know why. They were alarmed, and then frightened—was Jesus saying they were likely to die, too?

"In a way he was, and it was likely—whatever I did—that some of them might. What I realized for the first time is that I should have let events take their course, but it is too late for that. Even so, I, you know, realized it. Jesus continued talking, saying he would die but would be with them always, reassuring them that the situation would change but they would know he was there because he would send them a great sign in fire."

Again, Judas sighed and was silent. They began to head up the passageway. Then he continued, "Gradually we finished talking and by general agreement, though nothing was said, we were all standing up and getting ready to leave. Jesus and Peter went first, and when everyone had filed down the stairs into the street, I was the last. I went up to the Mount of Olives. I was hanging back. I discovered Jesus was praying in another area.

"Though Jesus was praying there, he kept coming back to where the disciples had fallen asleep while waiting for him. The wine helped. Finally, he roused them, and they headed toward the Gethsemane estate and the gardens.

"Soon, in Gethsemane's gardens, by following voices and a couple of lights, I caught up with Caiaphas' militants. One knew who I was. We were not far from Jesus and the followers; so I went up to Jesus so they would know which one to seize.

"Jesus said something to me, and to them, but I didn't hear it because I quickly turned away and left the area. I was going to go back to Bethany to think about what to do next. I was shaken at what I had done, unclear about what it meant, and a little unclear, you know, about what I would do next.

"I simply hadn't thought that far ahead, but I did want to throw the money back in Caiaphas' face and assure him the whole world would know of his perfidy. How, I do not know, but Talca, who had been watching me, found S'veyda—perhaps he had been watching it all, too—and he persuaded me to come to see you."

"I'm glad you came," Deleig told him, "and from the size of the crowd I think this is where we'll next see the Nazarene. My suggestion is—ah! there's Talca, headed this way—we find a space against a wall, sit there and try to sleep for an hour. The noise when they start again will awaken us if we are asleep, and no one—if I lead the way—will prevent us from going to the front of the crowd. Talca, we're going to rest a while."

"Thank the stars for that, my lord," he said. "I was beginning to think you never slept." He greeted Judas.

"Did anyone follow you?" Deleig asked. Talca shook his head.

"My guards are somewhere near," said Deleig. "Judas, sit by me. You are safe. Thank you for your candor."

There was a space that would allow two to be seated against the wall, but to much grumbling from those on either side, all three squeezed into it. Deleig had no difficulty in closing his eyes and going to sleep. The last thing he heard was a cock crowing.

TWENTY-SIX

Deleig awoke a half-hour later surprisingly refreshed. Judas was not asleep. Talca had left. The two men sat on the flagstones and leaned against the wall, ignoring their company on either side. No one spoke for quite a while, each lost in thought and tiredness.

The most peculiar thing about these past few days, Deleig decided, was the manner in which he felt they had aged him. Here he was, he told himself, barely into his thirties and beginning to feel like an old man. With his right index finger he scratched his hair above his ear. He smiled to himself, perhaps I'm finally beginning to truly mature.

Nothing matures like that first true test: being put in his place. He suspected it was by Marianus, but couldn't determine in what way. He admitted his testing could in no way compare to what Judas Iscariot was suffering. What would Judas do after this? Deleig asked himself, what would *he* do?

Judas spoke first. "What happened last night? I need to know."

Settling back against the wall, Deleig gave Judas a detailed account of what Jesus had endured. The disciple listened attentively, but did not interrupt, nor comment when Deleig finished.

It was several minutes of silence later when Judas said, "Jesus never wanted to be known mainly as a miracle worker. Yet each time he saw the people's plight, he took pity on them, and that's why he ended up curing so many of them—when he'd rather tell them about God's mercy, and justice, and forgiveness of their sins. Does this make sense to you?"

"Yes, it does," Deleig said. He nodded to indicate to this tense-faced man he was correct.

They stood. With the dawn the torches were being extinguished. There was a stirring in the crowd. Those not on their feet were beginning to stand. Deleig gestured that they should make their way with the crowd. People ambled, shuffled, the young and old, the alert and the exhausted. Most folks did not want to be too far back in the crowd and miss whatever might be worth watching.

Judas was describing the Sanhedrin role and powers in some detail to Deleig. He was supporting Marianus' view that the Caiaphas show trial was meaningless, that the Sanhedrin could not meet at night on a capital offense, nor pronounce guilt and a sentence the same day.

Given the crowd's size, it was relatively slow going. The crowd was an organism unto itself, forming and reforming and now spreading slowly, like spilled honey, oozing across the open space, with some remaining in place as the leading edge continued on. Deleig tugged on Judas' tunic and indicated they could go to the front.

"No," he whispered. "I want to be in a vantage point, but I don't need to hear what's said. I want to see where Caiaphas goes."

"Why?"

"I want to follow him to throw his money back in his face. To inform him I shall broadcast his treachery far and wide in my future travels."

"Where are you going?" Deleig asked.

"I don't know yet, but away from here."

"Do you need money?"

"Musan Deleig, I thank you, but I have come this far without money, and I shall go further yet. You are the only Roman I have ever met: a decent person, and a gentleman. You have been a revelation to me." And with that he turned and, as with Jesus in the past, was invisible as the crowd swallowed him—a fish entering darkened waters.

Oddly, Deleig suddenly felt bereft.

The crowd had gone silent. He saw why. Jesus was being pushed to a particular spot in the courtyard. He was unbound. With each faltering step he tried to hold himself ever more upright. The blood on his head and face was from last night's beating and buffeting; more blood showed through area of his tunic suggesting other wounds—he had been ill-treated beyond last night's public abuse. His captors stepped away from him.

The High Priest, senior priests and Sanhedrin members were coming in small groups, or arriving individually from elsewhere in the Temple compound. They gathered in their pre-ordained places. Soon the entire Sanhedrin council seemed complete because its members appeared to know who they should be next to and there was no shuffling. They waited only for two slightly decrepit elders being assisted into their places.

Caiaphas said nothing but stared at the Nazarene, who looked back at him without expression. In unison, as if to offset each other, both Caiaphas and Jesus turned to face the crowd, Caiaphas gloating, the Nazarene obviously in pain. Caiaphas simply stared ahead, but Jesus let his eyes run sympathetically across the crowd. Caiaphas turned toward the Sanhedrin. Jesus did the same.

A distinguished man, presumably the president of the Sanhedrin, said something loudly but indistinctly in Hebrew. Then, he repeated it in Aramaic. Not a verdict, simply a decision. He said the council ordered that the Nazarene be bound and taken to Pilatus. Deleig knew that meant to the Pavement, the large paved area in front of the Praetorium. As he'd anticipated.

He was about to turn and leave when he felt a firm hand on his shoulder. It was Myrmid with, a surprise, Formio, who told Deleig his mother wanted to see him. She would be in one of the offices to the left of the Praetorium's entrance.

Formio was staring at the bloodied Jesus, transfixed by the grim scene. Deleig thanked him, rested his hands on Formio's shoulders and physically turned him away from the sight, saying he must return to his quarters. Myrmid put his arm across the boy's shoulder and led him through the crowd.

Deleig, eager to reach Claudia, pushed his way through the crowd. He didn't like to do it and appear to be one more arrogant Roman. He laughed at himself and told himself he was arrogant enough as a Parthian. Once out of the crowd, he strode gracefully toward the Praetorium entrance, anticipation replacing his humor.

The Prefect's seat had already been carried outside the Pavement. Pilatus was still inside the Praetorium. Deleig entered, went down the corridor, and turned left.

Claudia was there, in the shadows. She rushed toward him, silently, like a lost thing fleeing something. She made no sound. Tears streamed down her face. As their hands touched, she pushed his arms open and wrapped hers around his lower chest and back, her forehead resting on his lower chest.

With one hand he gripped her to him, tightly, and with the other stroked her hair. She had come over to him. They were together. They would leave immediately for Rome, with Formio, while Pilatus was occupied.

Everything in him was melting, mind, heart, loins, viscera, soul. He was a trembling mass. Now he knew love, whereas he thought he always had. He touched her face, and she moved her head so the other side now rested on his chest.

One of his poems, written when he realized he had to contain his love and not be on fire all the time, came to mind. He softly told her,

Of my nights, imagined soft, your
Indiscernible footfall on carpets thick,
Tread muffled delicate unheard by
Any but me

Were footfalls of heart-hope mind-dream
That this night, O my soul, reveals,
Lightest force yet mightiest forged: the
Love bond, bonding,
Soulful souls full of gentle confess.
O my love

In that impersonal stone chamber, a tomb for love, they wept, clung together as tightly as they could. Then Claudia stiffened. It was a message; joy's death-knell rung loudly through Deleig's soul. He instantly realized that the moment they let go, as they would, they were letting go forever.

She had come not to him for himself, but for his consoling love and care, but he had misunderstood. O Ahura Mazda. He wept. Her hands consoled his face. He sniffed, looked at her, through his tears and hers, "What is it, Claudia, my love wife?"

"He will not help Jesus, not even as I pleaded and described the fearful dreams again. The brutality I've seen. Musan, Musan my love. Make sure Jesus, already unrecognizable, is dead so the soldiers don't break his legs. Do not let them further disfigure his dying bruised disfigurement, Musan."

"I promise. Will you then come away with me?" He'd finally asked. "Will you be mine?"

"I am. But I am not."

Fearing discovery, reality-shattering dreams—his if not hers—they mutually eased each other away. They searched each other's eyes in the low light cast through the archway. Tear-stained faces testament to the truth that lived in their hearts but would not be reflected in their lives.

She gave a startled laugh, a beatific smile, and held out her hands. He took them. "I love you, Musan Deleig." Then she was gone, a shadow in a darkened corridor.

Gone. Deleig looked in to nearby rooms. In the second he saw a water jug. He soaked his hands and rubbed his eyes and face, deliberately reddening his skin by rubbing it vigorously with his cloak so that his face would seem sun-scorched not tear-stained. He left the building, relieved Pilatus had not yet taken his seat.

There were three men in manacles against a wall to the left of the Prefect's seat. They were guarded. Jesus was not one of them. Deleig asked one of the guards the day's schedule.

Four likely executions, he said, if all those being charged were guilty. "And by the time they come before the governor, guilt is assumed, sir," he said with a laugh, "even if he does still ask them a few questions."

Deleig, fearing for the worst for Jesus—even only because of Claudia's presentiment—thanked him and headed to the fortress kitchens. Myrmid had Deleig's instructions if there was a guilty verdict. Deleig decided he soon must talk to the centurion commanding the crucifixion squad.

First, in long, straight-legged strides, however, Deleig went rapidly across courtyards and took shortcuts down into the kitchen to see Fatima, the soothsayer. He needed to quickly find something to eat. He could not remember his last meal and could not anticipate when he'd have the next.

Then it was rapidly back to the Pavement where, as he approached the crowd, he could already hear a trial underway. He stayed close to an archway in order not to distract the crowd's eyes from the proceedings. The Prefect had apparently just sentenced a robber to be crucified, and there was much wailing from a segment of the crowd. The man was returned to the wall as another prisoner was pushed forward to face the Prefect. Evidence was given on this man, a robber apparently in league with the first, and the same sentence followed the evidence with barely a pause.

He shuffled back to the shadowed wall with the first criminal. A third man was prodded toward Pilatus at the same time Jesus was being pulled from the archway that led to the cells. A guard gripped the Nazarene's shoulder.

Jesus was a badly beaten wreckage of a man. He blinked his bruised eyes against the sharp morning sun. Deleig could not imagine worse was yet to come, but Claudia had.

His hair was matted with sweat and blood, his face swollen on one side. Deleig thought of Claudia—a sudden pang, immediately dismissed—and wondered how accurate her dreams were. Thinking of her had made him tremble; he had not absorbed all that had transpired in those few precious moments.

Pilatus was dealing with the third man, apparently a violent robber. The Prefect wasted no time ordering his death. The man was taken to the wall with the others and Jesus brought forward. The Sanhedrin arranged itself to the rear of the Prefect, on his right; the senior priests and scribes made an informal group in front of them. Deleig moved over to the shadowed archways for a clearer view.

Pilatus surprised Deleig in his attitude toward the Nazarene. Pilatus ignored the Judeans and addressed the Nazarene. His questions were respectful, as if he were talking to an equal.

"Why are you here?" he asked, politely. When the Nazarene looked at him, not hostile, more curious than aggrieved, it was as if he was wondering what Pilatus might do to surprise him. Jesus made no reply.

Pilatus turned to his right and demanded of the Sanhedrin, Caiaphas and the Temple priests, in a particularly loud voice, "What is this man charged with?"

It was not the Sanhedrin councilors who answered, but one of the senior priests, "If he wasn't a criminal, we wouldn't have brought him before you."

"That is not an answer, or if it is, try him according to your law." Pilatus' face was thunderous at this breach of manners before a superior. That priest would be made to pay for his arrogance.

"Are there any charges against this man?" Pilatus demanded.

A panic of voices called out from the knot of senior priests and scribes, an anxious cacophony of "Blasphemy"—"Treason"—"He demeaned Caesar" ("demeaned," obviously one of the priests knew that word, thought Deleig)—"Claims he's the king of the Judeans" —"Refused to pay Caesar tribute."

"Enough!" Pilatus roared. "Guards, bring this man into the Praetorium."

Pilatus stood up and walked into the Praetorium as the Nazarene was led in behind him. The guard reappeared. This was not a situation where Deleig could follow; no one could be present.

After only minutes, Pilatus emerged and returned to his seat. Then the Nazarene was led out and brought before him.

"Answer me. Are you the King of the Judeans?"

"It is you who says so."

Pilatus, not facing the crowd, but instead turning to the priests, scribes and Sanhedrin, said, "I find there is no case against this man."

At this point a once again desperate Caiaphas spoke. Directly, clearly and in a voice almost as loud as Pilatus', he said, "For more than a year he has been inciting the people, in Galilee, across the Jordan, throughout all Judea."

"He is from Galilee?" Pilatus asked. Caiaphas said the man was.

"Then Herod Antipas must try him. He is in the city—take him to Antipas, he's Galilee's Tetrarch, let him deal with it."

With that Pilatus stood and walked into the Praetorium. It was not the entirety of the assembly that accompanied Jesus, well guarded, across the expanse of the complex and the Temple compound to Antipas' palace. Only Caiaphas, two guards, two priests and two scribes went.

Deleig followed Pilatus into the Praetorium. He found the Prefect resting his backside against the edge of a table, drinking something a servant had brought in on a tray. There was a second cup. Deleig took it—fruit juice, with honey. Most welcome.

He greeted the Prefect and asked, "What is likely to happen?"

The Prefect leaned his head down slightly and from that position lifted his eyes toward Deleig so they were slits. Deleig had seen him do it before when he was intent on something devious.

"Herod Antipas won't touch the case. He can no more find the man guilty of anything than I can. He will send him back."

Deleig nodded, for on the basis of what he'd heard, that had to be the case.

"And then?" Deleig asked, delighted that Jesus would, after all, be set free and Claudia spared her *suppressio nocturno*, her dreadful nightmare.

"I don't know!" he said, loudly. With that, Pilatus slammed his cup down on the table and walked past Deleig out of the room and along the corridor, deeper into the building.

Bewildered and disturbed, but not without a plan, Deleig placed his cup on the table and made his way to a quiet place to sit.

It was some time before the general noise of disturbances outside on the Pavement penetrated. Someone repeatedly called out the court was resuming. The Nazarene had obviously been returned by Herod Antipas.

As Deleig stepped outside, he saw Jesus standing in front of Pilatus' empty seat of power. The crowd had almost doubled in size and appeared particularly restless. Well-dressed newcomers had swelled the numbers. At first, Deleig assumed, wrongly, that many of them were the Nazarene's close followers, impatient for an acquittal.

When the Prefect re-appeared, the crowd, several hundreds strong, fell silent. He took his seat. Deleig was a short distance away to his left, more or less facing Jesus, though he could see Pilatus' face, side on. The Sanhedrin and priests had assumed their previous places. Pilatus looked as Deleig had seen him look on those occasions when he intended to pay no heed to anyone. He saw Deleig looking at him, knew he understood his mood. His look warned Deleig not to involve himself. They looked away.

Whatever powers of persuasion Deleig once had had with the Prefect had evaporated. Pilatus was staring ahead. He repeated to the prisoner the question he'd previously asked, "You say you are the King of the Judeans?"

Jesus was still slightly stooped from his injuries, but in control of himself and his situation. He did not answer. The Prefect questioned him again, but the Nazarene remained silent. Not defiant, resigned. But silent.

Pilatus addressed the crowd. "This man has done no wrong under Roman law. In my benevolence I intend to release a prisoner today. Shall I release the King of the Judeans?"

The roar of the crowd revealed that an orchestrating hand had worked its will. "Release Barabbas!" "Free Barabbas!" "Barabbas!" was the cry that rang into every corner of the Pavement, a barbaric howling by a chorus of Caiaphas' thugs—it could be no others'.

Pilatus had acquiesced to this? Pilatus had known this would happen, collusion of the most cruel sort, the type that suited him well in this mood, for he stood and called, "This man has done no wrong! What should be done with *him*?"

The evil chorus now sang a death chant, "Crucify! Crucify him."

The crowd had surged forward a little. There was a touch of alarm in Pilatus' voice.

"What wrong? What wrong has he done?" Even if Pilatus knew

it was a charade, he was not prepared for a show of forceful opposition. Deleig knew Pilatus was not physically afraid, but the Prefect hadn't experienced this before—a concerted mob effort threatened. It could light a violent conflagration in an instant.

Deleig studied Pilatus. He could see the man realized he had lost control of a situation he thought he was commanding. To lose control and be at the center of a revolt would mean Rome had lost control. If that happened and he survived, Pilatus knew he would be disgraced. Pilatus pointed to one of the three chained men against the far wall.

"Release Barabbas. Crucify the Nazarene. Affix a notice to the timber: Jesus the Nazarene, King of the Judeans. Crucify the King of the Judeans. Scourged and crucified."

Pilatus signaled an aide who brought a writing tablet, pen and ink. As Pilatus wrote, Caiaphas appeared quickly before the governor and stammered, earnestly, "You can't call him 'King of the Judeans.' What will the Tetrarch say?"

In a retort worthy of Jesus, Pilatus replied, "What I have written, I have written."

Pilatus was obviously furious at having been challenged and angrily waved Caiaphas away. When the High Priest hesitated, the Prefect stood up and stormed into the Praetorium.

Deleig, angry and almost losing control, stormed after him. Pilatus was moving down the corridor at a fast pace when Deleig called, "Pilatus! Stop! You just deliberately sent an innocent man to his death. That trial was a charade, a debacle of justice!"

The Prefect stopped, perhaps twenty feet between them. He wheeled around, his expression bordered on hatred—but hatred of Deleig or himself? Deleig wondered. Pilatus yelled, almost screamed, his voice echoing both ways along the corridor. "Don't—don't you dare, ever, ever, question my authority! Don't you ever question my understanding of the law. The man was obdurate. He refused to answer my questions. That refusal is treason, and treason is a capital offense."

Pilatus was glaring at Deleig, but Deleig was not about to yield. He shouted back, a yell as loud as the Prefect's. "Treason is a capital offense, but I doubt you can make the case that silence—even before a governor—is treason."

Pilatus now screamed. He seemed about to come undone and Deleig did not want that. He had seen it once and did not want a repeat performance. He must calm the situation—he knew what to do as Pilatus roared, "Are you presuming to tell me you know more about Roman law than I do?"

"No, I am not, Pilatus," Deleig said in an even voice dropped down loud enough to travel, but with a mollifying ring to what he was saying. "I am presuming to say I know as much about Roman law as you."

He continued, soothingly, "As one lawyer to another, I think you are incorrect. I shall go away for a couple of weeks into the desert and perhaps we can talk when I return."

"Go, and I don't care whether you return or not," Pilatus said, no longer shouting. Deleig was relieved. Pilatus wild was dangerous to everyone around him. When he lost control, it was as if he needed someone to lead him back down.

Deleig had skillfully maneuvered his way through similar scenes with him. The Prefect had calmed down because Deleig had. Now the Prefect said, "Come and see me when you're back. Stay away from my wife. She's the one who's filled you with all this nonsense."

Pilatus walked away. Deleig walked quickly to an intersection of corridors that would take him to the kitchen. Then he would go to the duty quarters of the crucifixion squad.

TWENTY-SEVEN

The part of the city to the north and west around the Gennath Gate area was a study in contrasts. The alleys and streets were as filthy and rank as any in the oldest parts of Jerusalem; yet the stonework, massive white-hewn blocks and occasional honey-colored slabs, only a decade or two old, gleamed a brilliance enhanced by the sun and heat's bleaching qualities.

The leader of the day's crucifixion squad was a veritable cube of a man, as broad as he was tall. He saluted as Deleig approached. He and Deleig would be together throughout the ordeal Jesus faced. The squad leader had been well paid, and knew his place.

The squad leader said that those to be crucified would be carrying their crosses through a smattering of watchers on both sides of the streets—generally, only people who knew the convicted, plus a few full-time crucifixion watchers who had nothing better to do. Them, and anyone who happened to be in that part of the city at that moment.

Deleig then realized that while the life and teaching and looming death of the Nazarene was of gripping importance to many, those many were few in the Jerusalem scheme of things.

"We crucify between five and thirty a week most weeks. It isn't a major event," the cube-shaped soldier said. "It's how we keep the criminal population down and stop the prison from getting too crowded. Nothing spectacular. Might get a few more curious today because it's the King of the Judeans we'll be nailing up."

His delivery of the phrase "King of the Judeans" was matter-of-fact; he was neither sneering nor believing, just giving the man the title he knew him by for this day's work.

They were waiting for the Nazarene to be brought forward; the two thieves due to be crucified were already en route to the hill of the dead. In fact, standing there, Deleig realized how little attention he had paid to crucifixions. What he knew about them was what any Romanized-Parthian might have accumulated. Early crucifixions on an X made of two tree limbs was cheap. The later cross made of a vertical upright and a separate crossbar had re-usable parts—if the nails didn't wreck the wood. The vertical posts, when the crosspieces were attached, were simply dropped in the post-hole.

Crucifixion's cheap utility had appealed to Cyrus the Great, and to Alexander the Great. The Greeks applied it, and the Romans inherited it—or appropriated it rather, along with much else that was Greek and Parthian.

There was no other method of capital punishment that touched it for barbarity—a slow, hanging death from suffocation in which the weight of the body itself, on the chest and the agonizing pull on the nailed hands supporting most of that weight, was a major contributor to the death. Cruel, humiliating, excruciatingly painful and fatal, as was its purpose.

If it was meant to deter others from crime or insurrection, the prevalence of it suggested that that aspect of its brutality failed almost completely. Despite the condemnation of Romans as different as Cicero, who saw it as "cruel and disgusting," and Seneca, to whom it was "a long-drawn-out agony," crucifixion by this time had, if anything, gained in popularity.

The actuality was worse than the description, for in Judea it was a two-part process, as Deleig was about to learn.

Jesus was dragged back into the open. He was no longer recognizable as the man Deleig had seen. This was nothing but a barely breathing mass of blood-sodden flesh.

"Why do this to a man?" Deleig asked the squad leader.

"Simple enough, sir," he replied. "You have to have the preliminary scourging. You have to flog the entire back and buttocks with a barbed flail."

"Why?" he repeated, stomach churning, sickened and horrified, but trying not to reveal his detestation to the squad leader.

"To gouge the flesh off. Get the right man with the flail, and we can almost time how long it'll take a man to die once we get him up on the wood. We flog them all so severe—not just the King of the Judeans—to have them bleed almost all their blood, so the loss will help speed them on their way. Can't have them hanging up there for twenty-four hours or more. Looks like this one's been given a bit too much flail; might not make it. He'll need a hand—or a shoulder more like," he said, with a laugh.

There was no particular malice in his remark. Deleig had to accept that to the squad leader this was simply one more execution in a lifetime of executions.

"When will he go for execution?" Deleig asked.

"Two ahead of him, about fifteen or twenty minutes."

Deleig nodded, left and ran to the officers' quarters at the Fortress Antonia. He stripped off his outer clothes, washed his face and changed into different clothes. He made arrangements for his discarded clothes to be taken to his quarters. He returned to Jesus.

He did not like what he saw on his return. The city might have been indifferent to the presence and fate of its messiah, the King of the Judeans, but perversely, the soldiery wasn't.

Soldiers of any nationality, when on duty but not fighting, are bored. Guard duty is one of the worst assignments among a boringly bad selection. Off-duty, at least there are brothels, fights, gambling and drunkenness. To be on duty and in total control over another is a temptation to some—an opportunity for imaginative, in a soldiering sense, sport.

Like any sport under such conditions, cruelty is the prime component. In the case of Jesus, it appeared that only official sanction had prevented the guards from killing this object of their blood sport.

Deleig looked at the benighted creature before him, this man a prisoner not of Caiaphas, not of the Tetrarch, but of the Romans. Disgust choked his throat, then receded, for he forced it to.

The Nazarene had difficulty standing even with a guard on either side supporting him. There was not an inch of his face that was not cut or bruised—and Deleig presumed the same would hold true for his entire body. Running blood was attracting flies. The squad leader must have seen the look on Deleig's face, but his was impassive.

There was nothing to say. Pilatus had decreed what he had decreed. The wreckage of what he had decreed was the barely-living human specimen before them. The Latin sign was now being nailed to the crosspiece Jesus would carry.

The soldiers, for their own entertainment and that of the small group of passing curious, had decided to heap a final set of indignities on their victim.

They were dressing Jesus in a purple cloak. Deleig saw the significance, the legionnaires were king-making. Next came a crown of woven thorns, jammed onto his head with every evidence in the soldier's eyes he enjoyed inflicting this cruelty.

In a perverted mimicking of courtiers, the soldiers paid Jesus obeisance by striking him with a stick, pushing and punching as they had done the previous day, while bowing and calling out, "King of the Judeans, all hail!" Some knelt in mock homage; others spat and buffeted his head to sink the thorns deeper through the thin flesh into the skull.

When there was not much response from the onlookers, the soldiers ceased their play, removed the robe, dressed Jesus in his own clothes and supported him to the crosspiece he was to carry.

They forced him to shoulder the crosspiece and led him to the street. They reached the Gennath Gate where the paved road of the walled city gave way to the rough-stone paved streets of a small a bazaar area, stinking and crowded. Beyond that the road became an uneven track.

The leader of the crucifixion squad cleared the way through the bazaar, brusquely pushed aside animals and humans with equal force. The crowd, banished to the sides of the street, paid little attention to the soldiery indignities and rough treatment, and almost none to Jesus. A few glanced his way; most didn't bother.

The slow journey further slowed as tortuously the Nazarene struggled ahead, only a half-step or less at a time. The problem was immediately obvious. Jesus couldn't sustain the effort. He collapsed.

"Hey you!" the squad leader said to a man walking in from the fields with his son. "You look strong enough. Help this man to his death, will you." The crosspiece had fallen to the ground. The passer-by—who could protest only at his physical peril—looked at the situation and told his son to follow at a distance, that everything would be all right.

He was a strong man, a farmer. He lifted up the crosspiece and walked around and behind the Nazarene. He placed and shifted the crosspiece around, so the bulk of the weight was on his right shoulder, and then gently lowered the other end onto Jesus' left shoulder. In this awkward configuration, the squad in the lead, they moved along the street away from the bazaar. The rear guard of the crucifixion squad, four soldiers plus Deleig and the squad leader, moved with them.

People on the street seeing this, one more crucifixion among the continual many, reacted variously. One man watched for a moment, squinted and peered at the face to see if it was anyone he recognized. A woman stepped in front of the Nazarene and wiped his face with a cloth. A woman with two sons who were eager to watch hurried them away. Most passers-by merely glanced disinterestedly and looked away again.

Deleig was not sure what he expected, but suspected he had falsely presumed that all those who had lined the streets to welcome their Messiah into Jerusalem only six days earlier would now be lining the streets in sorrow at his fate. That wasn't the case.

The onlookers were ordinary people going about their business. Deleig turned and looked behind him. Some twenty yards back, a group of perhaps eight or nine saddened, silent people, silent women actually, was following. No, not all women, there was a man to the side of them attempting to look inconspicuous. Talca.

The Nazarene fell again, almost pulling his farmer assistant down with him. The movement caused slightly more interest, and some onlookers peered closer at the blood-lust parade this crucifixion squad and its victim represented.

The farmer lifted the crosspiece up again, the expression on his face pleading that it wasn't his fault. A soldier delivered a couple of kicks to the fallen figure. Jesus forced himself to his feet, and the sad spectacle resumed. In time the street gave way to the dirt track.

They were moving out of the sprawling bazaar area into the wasteland and up toward an old quarry that included the mound of the Skull, its most permanent feature. The crucifixion site.

As they started up the short path to the top, the leader called on the squad to halt.

"That'll do, off you go," the leader told the man shouldering the cross. "He'll make it from here. Go on. Get out."

The little parade stopped as the dragooned farmer gladly relinquished his load. His son tearfully ran up to him, and the pair made quickly for the bazaar to be swallowed up in the safety of the crowd.

Alone with his burden, Jesus took several steps forward, then fell, the weight of the cross forcing him into an awkward position as it smashed his face into the dust, dirt and stones.

A soldier stepped forward, partly raised the cross and gave him a kick. "Get up." The Nazarene struggled to his feet. The soldier, not pleased at having to assist, lifted the cross onto the suffering victim's left shoulder and said, without irony, "Get moving, we're falling behind."

Whatever energy Jesus was summoning gave him sufficient endurance to make the remaining dozen or so feet. Deleig was trying to reason why: was it in order to end this ordeal—the actual crucifixion preferable to this excruciating journey? Surely not? Was it that a human pushed beyond the limits of normal or extraordinary endurance functioned as in a trance, not thinking, simply acting? He shook his head and ceased his wondering. Afraid to know.

Deleig showed no expression and inhaled a sigh to quiet his troubled *urvan*, his soul. There was no action he could take to end this. They struggled on. Deleig found his body almost mimicking Jesus' pained progress, Jesus' aches his aches. This was not good. He shook himself again and ordered himself to stop being stupid and to concentrate.

It was approaching noon as Jesus laboriously reached the worksite, the death site, where men were nailed to crosspieces, crosspieces attached to the vertical posts, then the entirety lifted and jammed into the permanent post-holes.

Despite the relatively late morning hour, there were two corpses from the previous day's executions stiff with rigor mortis. Friends or family waited with shrouds; others stood by two crude coffins. Where were unclaimed corpses buried, he wondered. He had no idea.

The men with the mallets and nails were waiting for the King of the Judeans. One idled by the vertical post lying nearby. Roughly the Nazarene had the crosspiece taken from him. As Jesus swayed, but remained upright, one man laid the crosspiece on the ground and another bound it to the vertical.

A soldier pulled Jesus' shift up over his head, leaving him naked except for a loincloth. Deleig knew that when the Judeans stoned their victims to death, the victims were always naked during the stoning, except the men's genitalia were covered. If a woman was sentenced to be stoned, though naked, she was covered both front and back. He had never heard that a woman had been crucified.

Another soldier gave Jesus a push and he fell down. Two more soldiers dragged him onto the cruciform shape. Three workers with mallets positioned first his hands, then his feet, raised their mallets and hammered home the nails.

Deleig did not look. He could not watch any more. He walked deliberately, head held high, the ten feet to where three workmen were waiting at an empty post-hole between the day's two other hangings, neither victim yet dead.

The area immediately in front of today's post-holes sloped rapidly, the land uneven. Four soldiers came up and stood behind the workmen, eyeing Deleig respectfully. He stood there, facing the hole, his back to the hands- and feet-nailing torture being inflicted on Jesus behind him.

Jesus cried out only once, but there were murmurs from his lips, indistinguishable, possibly unintelligible. The workmen were called over and soon re-appeared as part of a group that easily carried the cross and body up onto the higher ground. They raised it vertically to drop in the hole, hammered some extra wood in the hole and wrapped stout cords near the base to keep the extra wood in place.

That done, the workmen collected their tools and abandoned the area. All in a day's work.

The four soldiers at the cross jumped down to the lower level, sat on the ground and made themselves comfortable as one produced dice, another a board. The remainder of the squad lined up preparatory to marching back to the fort.

The squad leader came to Deleig, "Permission to depart for the fortress, sir." Deleig nodded. The cube of a man went back to the squad, called them to order and marched them down toward the northern wall in order to avoid the bazaar and instead arrive more directly at the guards' entry to the fortress.

Deleig turned back and now, for the first time looked at Jesus, eight feet away from him. The feet of bloodied broken bones shrieked a silent agony as Jesus tried to find purchase on the wooden block where his feet were supposed to rest. But couldn't. The block was so bloody his feet kept slipping off.

As Deleig approached, the height of the vertical, due to its positioning on slightly higher ground, meant Deleig's eyes were on a level with the Nazarene's knees. "Jesus the Nazarene, King of the Judeans," he said, softly. He was about to apologize for being unable to prevent his crucifixion. Words failed.

He was fixated as he watched Jesus' agonized, brutalized corpus attempting to deal with the pain wracking his body. The Parthian sensed movement behind him and turned. About twenty feet away stood the group of women from earlier. Talca also. But as before, off to one side to make it obvious he was not part of their group.

Turning toward the cross, Deleig saw the four soldiers. They were gambling to claim the Nazarene's bloodied shift.

Dutifully, Deleig was there for the three hours it took Jesus to die. His legs were not broken by the man with the pole.

Once Deleig was certain Jesus was dead, he left. The four soldiers stood as he departed. Deleig nodded to them then, after that, looked neither left nor right, though he knew the women were still there.

He walked rapidly along the route the squad had taken back to the fortress. There was much to be done, and more to be inquired about. Troubled, his mind alternately raced and seized up as he made his way in haste back to his quarters.

It might be some time before he saw Myrmid, who was dividing his energy between guarding Formio and organizing the desert journey. Deleig had already decided it was an excellent idea—as an antidote to the barbarity he'd witnessed.

In his quarters, in his bathing pool, he tried to cleanse himself of what he'd seen, to drown his sorrows by briefly resting his head underwater. Warmed, oiled of face and arms, leaning back, eyes closed trying to avoid the images of the past sixteen hours, he was telling himself he needed the cleansing the desert always provided.

Finally, he forced himself to dry off and change back into his Parthian clothing. He wrote first to Pilatus asking if he had no objections to Formio joining the desert expedition. A servant was sent with it to Pilatus' quarters. The next note was to Vasas, asking if he would like to join the desert expedition, and asking if he and Marianus might sup with him that evening. Deleig knew he would say yes.

The third was to Marianus, inviting him to Vasas'. Once he heard from Pilatus he would write to Claudia.

Pilatus entered unannounced.

"Musan, excellent idea, a kindness—taking Formio," he boomed, attempting a jocular tone to cover their very recent and very serious confrontation.

Deleig said, as evenly as he could, "The discomfort and adventure will do him good."

"Neglected him, in that respect. His mother will agree; wants him back in Rome. Education. Neglected him there too, should have paid more attention. Good idea. Well ..." His voice trailed off. He turned to leave, "Need supplies, men, take them, of course. See you when you return; um, sorry not going with you."

He still didn't leave. He stood there for a moment longer, looking vacantly into the distance above Deleig's ahead.

"Bad thing about that Jesus," he said. "Dine with us this evening." Then he left.

Dressed in finery to make himself feel better, Deleig went to Claudia and Formio's quarters. With a dinner invitation offered and accepted, he didn't need to write to her for an appointment. He was shown in. She was standing, two attendants with her, one fixing her hair and others fussing, showing her some clothing. He briefly gestured with his hand so they would continue.

"It is done," Deleig said. She nodded, her face solemn.

There was silence for a while.

She asked, "Was he in pain?"

"Excruciating pain. Until the very end."

"Was he the Son of God?"

"Son of God? Yes. I can say that because I think Zoroaster might well have been an older son. I am convinced his God is also my God, Ahura Mazda. These are mysteries that are beyond me. The interconnectedness of all this is beyond mc—just as our disconnectedness, you know what I refer to, is beyond me, though I accept for your sake. You need to know Formio was very brave. The shock of seeing a man beaten and bloodied as he was led out to his trial—those images of cruelty will stay with him for a while.

"I've come, Claudia, to ask if Formio might explore the Arabian desert with Myrmid, and my friend Vasas and me. Usual guards and servants. Two weeks. A day or two either way, depending on weather and travel conditions. Myrmid has heard of an abandoned caravanserai in the southeast. That's where we'd head.

"Pontius has agreed, but I wanted to ask you. It will be more arduous than dangerous. Just what a boy his age needs after the events of the past few days. It would be good for him to experience the desert again; he'll get more from it this time."

"You've seen Pontius, then?"

"He came to see me, Claudia, after I sent a message to him. He appears to have taken Jesus' death … he appears uncomfortable. Discomfited … distressed, even, over it."

"Well he might be, Musan," she said, softly, "well he might be. He has agreed that Formio and I return to Rome to see the boy to his education." They were speaking in Greek, the language of her servants and Pilatus' household. Claudia was looking at her two attendants who, though working, she knew were also listening.

She said, "You know my servants speak only Greek. That said, I remember Formio telling me that you and your grandfather would toss Latin phrases, quotations and law maxims at one another, and who ever could keep the 'conversation' going longest won. As for my husband …" She continued in Latin,

> "*Mel in ore, verba lactis,*
> *Fel in corde, fraus in factis.*"
> (Honey in his mouth, words of milk,
> Gall in his heart and fraud in his acts.)

She paused briefly and added, "*Te amo,*" which surely needed no translation.

Deleig, suddenly flushed with joy, said, "*Amare et sapere vix Deo conceditur. At spes non fracta.*" (To love and be wise is scarcely granted to the highest. But hope is not lost.)

Claudia began, "*Patientia et perseverantia—*" (Patience and perseverance.)

"No," Deleig called out in Greek, interrupting her. Then in Latin he said, "*Aude aliquid dignum—*" (Dare something worthy.)

But Claudia cut him off. "You must understand," she said in Greek. She was shivering, but she continued the game. "*Ille dolet vere, qui sine teste dolet.*" (She grieves sincerely who grieves unseen.)

"But Virgil," he protested, "*Omnia vincit amor, et nos cedamus amori.*" (Love conquers all, let us yield to love.)

She knew the phrase ahead of his completing it and was already shaking her head.

She dismissed her attendants with a gesture of her fingers. They had barely left the chamber when she was in his arms, pulling his head down to her, kissing him, murmuring, her tears running down his face.

Then she was gone, running to follow the servants. At the arch that would take her away, again, she stopped and turned. She was still crying.

"It cannot be. Ever. That is even more the case now Jesus is dead. I understood, you see." She stopped crying as more practically, she added, "I'll tell Formio about the desert. He'll be ecstatic. I understood Jesus. He had touched me."

Deleig never erased that momentary leap of hope when Claudia had volunteered, "*Te amo.*" He looked around the room. There was a water pitcher and cups. He plunged his hand into the pitcher and used the wetness to wipe his eyes and face which he dried on fabric draped across a chair.

As he was leaving her quarters, S'veyda was waiting. Deleig, glad of the diversion, went to greet his friend. Formio, however, came running out of their quarters filled with excitement. He stopped a short distance from Deleig, uncertain whether he was truly back in his Parthian friend's good graces.

"Oh Prince Musan, sir, a final desert expedition before we leave for Rome. How marvelously kind you are. Thank you. But Jesus' death ... what a cruel country filled with cruel Judeans. I'll be glad to leave."

"No, Formio, you have to make distinctions. Not cruel Judeans. There's a story of a man entering Greece, stopped by a guard, who asks his nationality. 'I am of the rich,' the man replied. The guard admitted him. Think in those terms of the powerful, emperor, king, or the ruling elite, like Caiaphas' court. Like my own family. I am of the powerful, they don't have to say it most of the time. It is too obvious. The wealthy generally all act in the same manner."

Deleig stepped forward and rested his hand on Formio's shoulder.

"So do the powerful. They are more alike than not. So it wasn't the people of Judea who killed Jesus, it was the powerful whom he threatened—and their followers. The wealthy and the powerful always have followers. They are a populace to themselves in time and history."

"I think I understand, sir," Formio said.

"Rome is cruelly administered. People are ordered killed, arbitrarily killed by emperors, fearful men who can also act justly. Yet some of the finest people I know are Romans, Brutus and Prosperina and their family, or Judeans, Elph the ferryman on the Jordan and his wife and friends. Alas, in my own country, I've never had the privilege of meeting everyday people. Just Vasas, who is scarcely ordinary.

"Your country and my country have killed men as brutally as Jesus was killed. He was killed by the powerful who did not want their power taken away from them. Off you go, I'll be with your family for dinner."

Formio smiled sadly and left.

S'veyda stood there, listening, head down, silent. Deleig went to him and placed his hand on his shoulder. This man who was his friend and once constant companion—he was saddened seeing him so abject.

Deleig said, "Another unnecessary death."

"You already know, then?" S'veyda asked in surprise, looking up. His face was Tragedy's mask.

"I was present," Deleig said, "until the very end."

"When Judas died?" S'veyda asked, incredulous.

It was Deleig's turn for shock.

"Judas? Murdered?" He stiffened with rage. "By whom?"

"He was found hanged."

"Caiaphas!" Deleig roared.

S'veyda stepped back, startled. "No, Musan. No. Judas was not murdered. Judas took his own life. He came to me and told me he had played God. That he had been wrong. He said we would not meet again. I thought, of course, he was going away. But I honestly do not believe he was murdered."

TWENTY-EIGHT

Vasas was in fine form. The idea of leaving on a desert outing into Arabia appealed to him as much as it did to Deleig. Shorter than Deleig, trim and fit, Vasas always exuded an easy generosity, offering to equip the desert party. It was a generosity Deleig knew he took constant advantage of, but not this time.

Vasas said, "Wait a minute, Musan, all that noise and activity in the atrium can only mean one thing."

Marianus, the ebullient and non-stop monologist, but likeable in the extreme. Deleig hoped that from Marianus he could piece together Caiaphas' role in all that had transpired. He was to be satisfied. Marianus, greeting them both effusively, spoke as usual, seeming to never need to stop for breath, only wine.

"Caiaphas was inconsolable during the attacks leveled at him, could not be restrained in his determination to rid himself of this pest. Thank you, Vasas …," sip, sip, "oh, rather good, this one, don't you think? …" sip, sip, "disturbed by the fact that there may be some justification to at least a few of the Nazarene's claims—doubtful when one considers the Nazarene died just like everyone else—except not like anyone else. I hear, though I did not attend, the sky darkened …," sip, sip, "but it is my impression that people become quite gullible when faced with uncertainty—and this man had made them uncertain. He had not committed any crime for which the Sanhedrin could possibly convict him on the evidence …," sip, sip, "even while Caiaphas was privately pushing every one of us to do precisely that. We couldn't, of course, that night …," sip, sip, "the next morning," sip, sip, "delectable, Vasas, our source of all knowledge, delectable, Vasas, as ever."

Marianus barely paused between great quaffs of the pleasing liquid. "Before the Nazarene was sent to Prefect Pilatus, Caiaphas said if the Sanhedrin didn't support him, the Temple would be ridiculed by the populace. Personally I couldn't understand what the man Jesus was saying. I do think that the Prefect—your Governor Pilatus—took a nice public slap at Herod Antipas and Caiaphas giving the Nazarene messiah—some messiah—that title, the King of the Judeans. I gather Pilatus and Herod Antipas had worked that out in advance to put Caiaphas in his place."

Deleig interrupted Marianus, always a risk but one he felt impelled to take, "What was this agreement between Pilatus and Antipas?"

"Antipas wanted the Nazarene dead. Don't forget Antipas was literally a haunted man ...," sip, sip, sip. Deleig sensed the man was drinking more than usual this night. He wondered why. Was he hiding something? Guilty feelings? But why guilty?

Marianus continued, "He had some tangled notion the man was sent by John the Baptist or was John the Baptist bent on revenge, or was Elijah, and whatever the case, the Nazarene boded ill for him. Haunted and superstitious, that's Antipas the man, as you undoubtedly know. Pilatus did not care whether Jesus lived or died, though I hear that his wife did."

Marianus, Deleig readily understood, had good sources too. Deleig shook his head in astonishment. So he should as the Judean spy chief working out of the Temple. He's outwitted me. He's been getting as much from these impromptu meetings as I have—simply by checking out what my latest interests were.

Deleig delightedly admired Marianus' craft—even though it was a delight at his own expense. He'd been naïve, he told himself. Marianus running the Temple spy system while watching Deleig run one for Pilatus, and he thinking Marianus a bumbler. Who was the bumbler now?

Marianus was droning on, not drunk, but less crisply than usual.

"The agreement, as I understood it, was that the Prefect and the Tetrarch would work in closer agreement and greater harmony to isolate Caiaphas from some of his power by finding ever fresh ways to deprive him of more of his authority. What I hear is that the desire for Caiaphas' ouster, if that's an accurate and adequate description of their hopes, makes it likely the Prefect ...," sip, sip, "joined undoubtedly by Antipas—will move against—do something—to expose Caiaphas' weaknesses or unsuitability in office."

No matter how much longer Marianus talked, that was the

extent of the information. In time, Marianus and Deleig left together, Deleig linking arms with the man because he seemed unsteady. Outside, Marianus' guards awaited him. As the two men stood there to bid each other good night, Deleig said, "You are very good at what you do, Marianus. Extracting information from me by giving me so much. I'm deeply impressed. All honor to you. I know of course you control the money lending and international financial transmissions."

Marianus drawled, "Do not take it too hard, dear presenter of beautiful finger-rings. You have six years of working for a conquering power. Survival is a far better teacher than superior power. One's wits are honed sharper under oppression, that's all. I have decades of experience working for a subjugated nation. We Judeans have to be craftier than you Romans. You, Deleig, have had your initial run—you've been successful organizationally. Your dealing with the Zealots was masterly, expertly so. I—quite honestly—was envious. You are not, however, born to it. I was. I am. And will remain so. Despite my misgivings. And my apparent bibulous failings."

They parted with an embrace, knowing they were not likely to meet again.

Suddenly Deleig wasn't done. "But Marianus, what about the time I had your spies in our quarters bound and dumped in the High Priest's palace?"

He simply grunted an acknowledgment. Marianus obviously didn't want to be reminded of that. He waved his hand and with a shake of his head indicated to his guards they should leave.

As they walked away, Deleig accepted that Marianus probably already knew, somehow, that he was returning to Rome.

"Marianus," he called, "you're the better of the two of us."

The man turned. He beamed a sad smile and called, "O Musan, Musan, source of all knowledge."

Goodness, Deleig thought, "source of all knowledge"! That's the expression Marianus had used earlier to described Vasas. He felt as though the Fortress Antonia had hit him across the back of the head to wake him up—it was Vasas who was the spy, the spymaster. For the Judeans. Not the Temple Judeans, no, spymaster for Judea's wealthy. But why? What did *they* want?

Deleig did not hear the rest of Marianus' farewell, for, blushing so much he feared the veins in his face might burst, he was banging on the wooden door to Vasas' compound. He was admitted, hurtled across the atrium and raced toward Vasas' quarters. As he burst into Vasas' huge reception area without knocking, a smiling, companionable Vasas said, not judgmentally, but admiringly, "You've worked it out, Musan, everything but the 'why.'"

The two men, contemporaries, familiars, stared at one another, and burst out laughing. Vasas ran forward and threw his arms around Deleig. Deleig, in return, enfolded Vasas in a great hug. As they released one another, Deleig asked, "Aren't I the slow learner? So, what is the 'what' and what the 'why'?"

As Vasas indicated they should sit, he twisted his fingers in the air. A servant started across the room with a tray with wine and goblets. He poured and left the room.

"You've learned, Prince Musan Deleig of Hatra and Dura-Europos. Grandson of Deleig of Deleig of Carrhae. You've learned. Your initiation into the craft is complete. Trust no one."

They gestured a toast to each other as Vasas said, "The 'what' and the 'why.' My grandfather was a general unlike yours. He looked to King Herod after we Parthians were pushed out of Syria. He wondered what lessons could be learned from the defeat. In studying it he became close to a sort-of fraternity of very wealthy Judeans who needed a back door to fund the Zealots. These Judeans, only loosely connected to the Temple—like Marianus a generation later, observant, perhaps, but not necessarily devoutly so—saw the Zealots as the means—if any existed—to overthrow Rome, or at least to make the province so troublesome Rome might just walk away. My grandfather was close to Marianus' father through a business arrangement.

"After that final Dura-Europos winter, Marianus and I were sent together to Greece simply to give us a mutual broader perspective on the Mediterranean countries and Rome, and in those two years, the close bond we have was formed.

"We both thought, and feared, when you intentionally learned from me of the Zealot plot that we'd be discovered, that Rome would learn of our work and take action against us. We had to take the risk, but we hadn't expected your non-violent style. We couldn't see how you'd subdue the cell without bloodshed. We witnessed your brilliant ruination of the cell, the three cells, and their works—without a blow being struck. Only then did I realize what it had meant when you wouldn't strike the street boy in Dura-Europos who lost my dhow for me. You dislike violence. Our spies in the Prefect's palace, bundled up and dumped on Caiaphas' floor—Caiaphas didn't even know we had spies in the Prefect's palace! We howled with laughter, Marianus and I. We also trembled at your skill, not knowing when we'd be unveiled. That's been the situation ever since you arrived—anxiety we'd be discovered. The urchin in Dura-Europos with the dhow! You remembered that?"

As if reading from a page, Vasas recounted the event, the several boys—from socially and militarily important families like theirs—sailing their homemade model dhows on the river's edge at the end of long, fine cords. Some city urchins crowded near them to watch. One came close to Vasas and in doing so, stumbled on a loose stone and banged into Vasas' shoulder.

Vasas had dropped his securing line. Everyone watched his model dhow find the wind on its own and sail majestically down river. Vasas, who'd spent two weeks fashioning his dhow, was furious and turned on the urchin, prepared to beat him. Musan had stepped between them. He said, "Have my dhow, Vasas," and handed him the cord wrapped around the stick that kept his dhow tethered. Vasas accepted with thanks. Musan asked the urchin his name. The boy, probably a year younger than Musan and Vasas, wouldn't speak. Musan convinced him to. It was Fuad. Fuad was brought to their quarters to learn how to help craft another model dhow to replace the one he'd caused Vasas to lose.

Fuad did not become their friend. But there was no animosity toward him as he watched them fashion a dhow, shave the wood and with a needle and thread, make the dhow's sail. Copying them, Fuad, the street boy, modeled a dhow to present to Vasas. Vasas later thanked Musan for his calm way of dealing with the crisis of the lost dhow. The result was they'd maintained contact all their lives.

"Why are you so opposed to violence, Musan?" Vasas, relaxed in his Jerusalem quarters, feeling in charge of the conversation, but uncertain why.

"I can't hate. My sense of enmity is nonexistent. My opposition to violence is instinctive, innate and reinforced. My first day in Rome I killed two men."

He told Vasas about the Egyptian dancers' lessons, about Sejanus' wish to harm him, his attack on Sejanus' guards and how his blows had killed them. How he'd had to defend himself entering Judea and had softened the kicks and blows. Vasas shook his head in wonder, but said nothing. They sat in silence, companionably. Ten minutes later the men parted.

Early next morning Deleig sent for Formio. When the boy arrived, Deleig said, "I want you here because Talca is coming. He witnessed Jesus' death and I would like you to hear his account." The two of them chatted until Talca arrived.

Talca was eager to describe the setting to Formio, how he'd joined up with the group of women following Jesus, but stayed apart from them at all times. He suspected, he said, from the little bit of conversation he heard, that one of the women was the Nazarene's mother.

It was a scene, he said, populated by a dozen legionaries and a centurion, soldiers and workmen, the women in the distance. A scene dominated by Jesus nailed to the wood, as workmen assisted by soldiers positioned the cross in the post-hole. The stark outline was the dying Nazarene flanked by two other crucified men.

The workmen and the majority of the legionaries left. Four soldiers and a centurion remained. He described how the soldiers sprawled on the ground and played dice for Jesus' clothing, laughing and joking, gambling after that with pieces of gravel in place of money, simply passing the time until the three men were dead.

After an hour or so, said Talca, Caiaphas and other priests arrived, each trying to outsmart the other with jokes about the King of the Judeans who could tear down a Temple but not save himself. Jesus was dying, not yet dead, but beyond paying any heed, consumed by pain as he sank deeper into his agony, close to his end. The High Priest and his acolytes, bored finally by the inactivity, left.

"The morning became noon, and as the day stretched on, the life seeped away," Talca said, poetically. "Then Jesus rallied and he seemed to pull all the remaining strength from his physical body as he shouted, '*Eloi, Eloi, lema sabachthani?*' "

In great earnest, Talca said that cry of "My God! My God! Why hast thou forsaken me!" rattled him. The soldiers looked up, but it was the centurion who moved. He bent down and picked up a long stick. Snapped his fingers and a soldier stood and gave him a sponge and a small gourd.

"The centurion poured the liquid on to the sponge and raised the sponge on the stick to Jesus' lips and offered him the drink. Jesus sucked on the sponge. He then cried out, perhaps in greater pain, perhaps in release of life, and was dead. The sky darkened.

"Really, it did. The centurion was still the only one to move or comment. He turned to those who had witnessed the death, the women, myself and five or six others who had drawn closer from below—the soldiers unconcerned. 'On what grounds would you doubt this was the Son of God?' he asked as if hoping someone could answer the question—or confirm his statement."

Talca continued that then, in a perfunctory manner, a soldier came and stuck a spear in Jesus' side. Two of the earlier workmen returned to the site about a half-hour later carrying poles. With a pole one broke the legs of the man on the first cross. The soldier with the spear waved it to catch the workmen's attention and told them the third man was dead. The centurion called, indicating Jesus, "This one's gone." The workmen left. The soldier with the spear said to the centurion, "We can go, sir."

"I watched," Talca said, "as the centurion marched away. I watched them at some distance, until they disappeared over a brow of the hill."

It was an impressive and moving account. Deleig was touched on hearing it so plainly delivered. Formio was tearful but did not cry. Deleig said to him, "I can vouch for the account's accuracy."

Two days later the expedition party left for Jericho and the southeast wastes. The wastes beyond the trek up Perea's mountainous road to beyond Philadelphia in the Decapolis, and out, out, out into the high desert until they reached the caravanserai Myrmid wanted to show them.

TWENTY-NINE

Rome, 81 CE. Musan Deleig stood at the western balustrade of the garden atop his Janiculum Hill villa, his elderly eyes, with difficulty, scanning the city. His hands rested lightly on the stone parapet. Even in age the elderly Romanized Parthian was still taller than most Roman males.

His pointed beard was marked only by flecks of gray. His dark hair still rushed back in abundance from his narrow face that in profile was now as sharp as the image in a shadow-play: the axe-head forehead with axe-head nose below. Gentle, smiling eyes remained the saving grace of what could be a fierce mien.

He gazed because he was trying to avoid thinking about the letter on his table. It had arrived the previous day, from Antioch. He was also attempting to stop reviewing his life. He felt he was in the grip of old man's remorse: the people he hadn't thanked sufficiently, the people he hadn't thanked at all who'd truly deserved his gratitude, the ones he'd slighted, the ones he'd failed to praised properly. They were all marching across his inner mind, shadowy but real.

The letter. The writer was Formio, though it was signed "Pontius Cletus Formosus." It opened *My dear mentor, guardian and chosen father, Prince Musan.* Formio was now a man in his sixties. After the normal salutations and family details, travel plans and health, the letter asked:

I have pressing questions, Prince Musan. They all affect my future. We need the information to show that I really am who I say I am, and that you are who you say you are. I need to reveal your own assessment of—might I say your deep feeling for—this Christ in whom you do not believe. You understand why. Also, on a far more personal level:

How, these decades later, do you now judge my father?

How, this half-century later, given all that I have forwarded to you since my exile, and the people I have sent to meet you, especially Marcus, do you now view the Nazarene, his work and who he actually was? Did you know that you and Jesus were born in the same year?

Who murdered Jesus the Christ?

The most fraught question of all. A half-century ago I asked you why you were given the name, Musan. You told me you would tell me later. By my reckoning, a near half-century is later. Explanation please.

The Parthian forced himself to stand erect. He steadily walked back to his writing table and sat down in his wooden armchair. Crows were arguing in the distance—as always. He slid a sheet of papyrus from under a carved stone weight, selected a pen, dipped it in the stone inkwell and wrote, regularly pausing for more ink.

Villa Dura
Janiculum, Rome
The First Year of the Esteemed Emperor Domitian

To the Most Honorable and Esteemed Pontius Cletus Formosus,
   Greetings from the Land of Retrospect, where people my age live!
   "Who murdered Jesus?" you ask. Even that could not offset my joy at the happy news you are soon to return to Rome from Antioch!
   What a delight after such a lengthy exile. You were right to leave when you did, even I could not have protected you and your family from the crazed Nero much longer.
   We were young then. You would still recognize me, I am as erect and dark-haired as ever, but my hearing is poor, and one eye sees only close up objects and the other, distant images. I still ride, and lament every jerk and jog, but refuse to give it up. I still have my eyes on the desert, my Bedwani encampment alongside the pool at our El Qassassin oasis, the place to end my days.
   I need my horses to keep me fit enough to ride camels for when that time comes. It will not come before you have arrived back at this villa, which is deeded for you and your family in perpetuity, my emotionally adopted and almost son.

Where to begin? He would draft a separate letter to satisfy the demands of some authority who wanted verification of who

Formio was. He must, however, answer the personal straightaway. Deleig rested his pen in its holder and wondered, how much detail did Formio want? How much was necessary? Some things he dared not say, he supposed. He retrieved his pen, dipped it in the ink.

Post-Judea, post your father's Judea, so to speak, Caligula exiled Pilatus to Vienne, on the Rhone, in Gaul. Emperor Claudius exiled Herod Antipas to Lugdunum on the Soane, twenty miles north of Vienne.

I urged Claudius to let me bring together to Rome all the principals and participants in the events that led to the trial and slaughter of Jesus the Nazarene. I thought Claudius would agree because he loved to sit in judgment—meaning in judgment to exercise his extensive legal knowledge.

Never explaining why, Claudius, he was my closest friend in Rome after Lady Lydia, refused to do that.

Now to your father. My trusted Formio, your honorable father, Pontius Pilatus, was two men in one skin. Concordia discors, *"the dissonant harmony," existed under that skin.*

*Interpreting what drives another to certain actions is a perilous exercise. We can subject your father to Ovid as Ajax—*Spectemur agendo, *"let us be examined by our conduct." Examining his conduct produces no stranger variant than your father.*

Deleig was restless. The day was becoming overcast—it suited his mood. Up from his table he meandered about in his rooftop garden, unable to settle. Each step revealed an inner irritability, a slight purse-lipped stamping of the foot. He was finding Formio's questions increasingly difficult to deal with. Because he was dealing with much inside himself as a result. For one thing, though he hated to admit it, Deleig knew he had always felt ambivalent about being a Roman for he was, at heart, a Parthian.

If he was conflicted, he decided, he was also haunted. Throughout his almost sixty years of service to Rome, haunted by those mere twenty-seven months in Judea. The sodden mass. Staring, horrified, as he still did in his dreams, at the dying man's twisting nailed feet.

From the first day he heard of this messiah, twenty-seven months of increasing foreboding. Culminating, in that single twenty-four-hour period, day-night-day. Each day occupied with it, and with the desire, the need, the essentiality, of bringing these criminals—Pilatus foremost—to trial. To trial, finally, even in absentia, even if the trial results were only privately circulated. That sodden mass of what was once a man, once a living Nazarene—the trial was Deleig's private vow to himself.

Questions, questions from Formio. It was just the same when the boy was fourteen: questions, questions. Painfully difficult.

Deleig didn't want to further disturb that period of his life, it was disturbed enough. Everything was geared, rather, toward his final retirement to Parthia, to his oasis, to await each desert night, and the next night, until no more.

It was turning chilly. He had the desk moved inside the lower room. For several more minutes he sat back down at it, satisfied the light from the windows and open doors was adequate. Then he reached for his pen, dipped it in the stone inkwell and wrote.

Formio, unbelievable though it seems, I was the man who murdered Jesus the Christ.

I was the centurion on the Hill of the Skull because I had promised your mother Jesus' legs would not be broken. How I did it came fully formed to me when I met that exceptionally tall commander of the guard.

With his collusion and wearing his uniform—he was not about to quarrel with a member of the imperial family, so to speak, a counselor to the Prefect's wife, no less—it was done.

I was the one who held the sponge on the reed to Jesus' mouth that brought about his end. The sponge from which he sucked contained not wine or water but a concentrated tincture of the wolfsbane and rapidly acting mineral poisons I had Fatima, the soothsayer in the Fortress Antonia kitchen, prepare for me.

I carried the small gourd of Fatima's poison with me to the mound of the Skull and had a soldier mind it for me until I was ready. That was the small error in Marcus' crucifixion account. It was not the soldier who raised the sponge to Jesus' lips.

It was me who asked, "On what grounds would you doubt this was the Son of God?" You said in your opening, the Christ in whom I do not believe—you are half correct. On the Hill of the Skull I was caught up in the horror of the magnitude of this self-sacrifice. I fleetingly, momentarily, knew I must acknowledge this was the Son of God. It was true for me emotionally and in my head.

In my viscera I clung to Zoroaster, however, as my path to the one God. Perhaps, I reasoned on that hill, Zoroaster is an older Son of God, the brother with the lesser mission. Not called to the same level of sacrifice. But if one Son, why not more? Why not daughters? My mother was much nicer, kinder, more gentle than my father or brother, your mother similarly a better person than your father. But such speculation was, is, beyond my power to reason. My mind does not stretch that far.

Back to my key preoccupation.

In actuality, four people, or two—depending on which Roman authority sat in judgment—murdered Jesus the Christ.

Deleig stopped writing. Who was he to be sitting in judgment on others? From what lofty pinnacle could he look down? What had he accomplished, achieved, for himself? He had great wealth, though apart from the Janiculum villa he had never spent lavishly. Wealth untouched, and too late now spend it on good works. He hadn't earned it. What wealth he felt he had was the friendship of people he'd met.

I searched for mitigating circumstances for your mother and myself to absolve us of any responsibility—she did not collude with me, but influenced me greatly.

Fortunately I could consult Rome's most learned jurist, a woman—it may surprise you to learn—my early colleague and sometime dining companion, Rubecula. A learned colleague whose husband was equally learned. I have willingly accepted her decisions.

To repeat: the legal decisions in what follows are Rubecula's decisions. Mine might have been otherwise.

Here is my main contention. Jesus was not lawfully executed by an occupying power for having broken its laws—he was murdered. You must have heard me say that in a conversation with others, but I can't recall where or when that might have been.

Jesus was in fact tried and judged under Roman law, as in a Roman court, as if he were a Roman citizen. That it took place in Judea, in a military setting, and Jesus not a Roman citizen, is immaterial.

I say this on the basis of Pilatus' conduct. Who knew your father better than I did, his moods, his mental state, the manner in which he saw his failures and successes, his poses and preening?

I say it because he conducted himself and the trial as if he were sitting in judgment in Rome, in a civilian setting. He transported himself into that state of mind—I witnessed it: judging under Roman law as in a Roman court and of a Roman citizen.

Pilatus was, in action and attitude, the civilian jurist, not the military general. It was as if, when he took Jesus into the Praetorium to hear him in private, Pilatus saw himself among the legal great of Rome. Something he was quite capable of doing. He was a poseur who accepted his pose as legitimate.

He had reverted to that role. Of that I am certain. The consequence was, as I say, repetitive though I am, he tried the Nazarene as he would have tried a civilian offender, himself the civilian judge.

That was his attitude until he referred Jesus to Herod Antipas—who sent him back. I am convinced your father had convinced himself that Jesus would go free, despite any arrangement between your father and Antipas. Antipas' "no case to answer" jolted your father.

So now Pilatus had to try Jesus a second time.

The mob destroyed Jesus' acquittal.

So where does guilt rest?

Under Roman law in murder cases, intent is everything. To intend a man's death is sufficient for a verdict guilty.

What about Judas Iscariot, you may ask? Let's go through them.

JUDAS' GUILT: Judas accepted Jesus was going to die. Judas knew there was nothing he could do to prevent it. He did not know when. He facilitated Jesus' arrest, no more than that, out of his concern for the others. He could not be certain—nor would he have wanted certainty—that this was the occasion that would lead directly to Jesus' death. Only Jesus knew when he was going to die. Judas did not murder Jesus.

CLAUDIA'S GUILT: Claudia did not want Jesus to suffer. If he had still been alive when the workmen inspected the day's crucifixions, they would break his legs—more excruciating agony than he was already experiencing. I knew that for a fact; your mother knew it from a dream. Your mother had even sent a final message to your father while he was conducting the trial to urge him not to pursue this case. I killed Jesus because I knew the leg-breakers would, at some point, arrive.

Here I was particularly delighted that Rubecula wrote: "For someone to be found guilty of murder, there must indeed be a guilty intention, dolus. But there must equally be an actus reus, a killing or an attempt at killing. Claudia had nothing to do with either sentence or execution. She was not your accomplice, Musan; she provided nothing concrete, she made no concrete suggestion. An accomplice must hold the ladder, or tell you where that ladder is kept."

So, under lex Cornelia, though a mercy killing is murder, your mother was not involved. And in any case, any court, given the man's death was imminent, would refuse to hear the case against, or dismiss it immediately.

MY GUILT: In the law of delict, under the lex Aquilia, Rubecula wrote, "Such a hastening of a slave's—or horse's—death might impose a share of liability, where an owner is wanting to recover the full value of his property. But no criminal court would be bothered with hastening a person's death by an hour or so. In other recorded executions, people did give drugged wine to the victims, and this was ignored by the authorities; it's too trivial, or seen as natural, humane. You, Musan, must acquit yourself. (The kitchen soothsayer, Fatima, who supplied the potion, is guilty of being an accomplice, but must similarly be acquitted.) You can wallow in guilt if you wish, but you are simply indulging yourself."

ANTIPAS' GUILT: Antipas was innocent of murder, Formio, a pity in a way, because Antipas deserved to be included in my list of murderers. The evidence, however, is simply not there. The man was a liar and a fraud, deceitful and shallow enough to let it be thought in Jerusalem he was colluding with your father regarding Caiaphas and Jesus. He was attempting to build up his own importance. There was no evidence of collusion—despite what Marianus told me. And Marianus had his own reasons for sowing misinformation. Your father laughed at the idea of Antipas being anything but a Roman puppet.

CAIAPHAS' GUILT: Under lex Cornelia *the one who orders the killing is a murderer. The motive is irrelevant. Caiaphas certainly murdered Jesus. He had murder in his heart and murder on his lips.*

Ruled Rubecula: "Caiaphas is more difficult. Did he make a false accusation? Not if he truly believed Jesus guilty of blasphemy. Abuse of procedure, yes: night meetings, tearing his vestments—which the High Priest was not allowed to do—bullying his colleagues into acquiescence, giving sentence at the same meeting as the accusation. All these, yes. Whether, in Jewish law this should lead to Jesus' release, or just to a renewal of the charge, I do not know. Morally, to say that Caiaphas was no better than a murderer might be justified, but not legally."

PILATUS' GUILT: Finally, your father murdered Jesus. If someone's death occurs because a magistrate is bribed to bring such a verdict, that is murder.

What was the nature of the bribe? Caiaphas' control over the mob. That was the bribe: Convict Jesus or the mob will erupt.

I make no appeal to precedent; I believe the bribe/coercion applies.

Pilatus was morally a murderer.

On this point Rubecula was also quite firm: "Had Jesus been a Roman citizen, it is certainly possible that Pilatus might have been held legally responsible for his death. The development of the lex Iulia *was extended from financial extortion to abuse of official power. It covered taking money to give or withhold a judgment, and taking any sort of bribe to do more or less than one's duty; the pressure brought by Caiaphas might amount to a 'bribe.' There were overlaps with the laws on treason* (lex Iulia maiestatis) *and violence* (lex Iulia de vi) *in bringing about the death of an innocent man.*"

So, there we have it, Formio.

My dear almost son, I accept all Rubecula's points, and welcome them. I would still attempt to argue my case against Pilatus—if only to bring it before the Roman people.

Am I so passionate about this because I witnessed the cruelest death—that mass of sodden flesh, once a man, a man I regard as a direct Son of God? The Son of the one who is God of us all. I do wonder if the older son was Zoroaster. For this God, my God, the Judeans' God, Marcus' God, your God, is God.

Oh yes. I would press my legal case against your father, even though I might have to depend more on my rhetorical skills than legal references. As you know, I'm quite a performer in public, and a trial is a performance.

Yes, I'd need the oratory of a Cicero ahead of the poetry of a Zoroastrian. "How far will you go to abuse our patience, O Pilatus?" I could never parody Cicero, but perhaps I could paraphrase him. Or continue on, not from Cicero's oration against Catiline, but that from Licinius Archias, the poet, arguing "… also with forensic speech, as I plead at the bar, you may grant me in this case that indulgence."

I know, Formio, I can hear you say it, "You are a dreamer, Honorable and Distinguished Musan Deleig, still a Parthian even if a Roman citizen."

Of course it cannot happen.

But oh! for the chance to argue before the Senate, appealing to their knowledge of men's minds and not merely men's actions. If easing the death of a victim wrongly accused under Roman law and wrongly sentenced by a Roman magistrate is insufficient a defense, then none of us is safe. But what about undertaking it to ease the death of that victim to preserve the honor of the law? To preserve Rome's honor as an Empire under the rule of law? A lawyer such as I would be willing to argue that.

I rested my case, my dear Formio. Even if I have lost it legally, I have proved it morally. I believe. It was a decade or more before I realized that while the Nazarene wanted justice for the poor, he understood all he could offer was love.

The Parthian Empire my family and I had known is no more. The Roman Emperor appoints the king. My family is safe, and very wealthy—from the trading empire I turned over to my brother. My family bows to Domitian, as I do myself—or would if required.

The Judeans did rise up against the Romans. What a price Judea paid. The Temple is no more, King Herod's monumental fortresses are mainly in ruins—though I note Caesarea Maritima and the Winter Palace have survived.

Not for the first time have the Judeans been homeless.

I was able to render the Judeans one final kindness. I was in Judea with Vespasian during his campaigning to rid the land of Judeans. He had asked for me, as historian, to record the events—knowing I knew background, terrain and people. Everything in Jerusalem was in disarray. The Judeans had obviously vowed to fight on to the death.

Then, quite out of nowhere, a preacher appeared at the main encampment and asked to see Vespasian. I volunteered to meet first with the preacher, given my knowledge both of Aramaic and Judea.

The preacher's name was Yochanan ben Zakkai. He was the Pharisee leader in Jerusalem. But he had no wish to remain in the city with his followers with death as the inevitable outcome. In a ruse, his followers reported he had died. His purported funeral was the means for rushing him out of Jerusalem in a casket.

He had come to plead with Vespasian. Ben Zakkai told me it was because he was eager to create a yeshiva in order to perpetuate the teachings. He asked me if I could intervene with Vespasian to gain permission for a yeshiva, perhaps at Yavneh.

I smiled and realized that for perhaps the final time, the answer lay in my astrological, soothsaying and superstition-collecting past. I knew sufficient about the Hebrew Bible to know that all its prophecies began with "If."

I knew also Vespasian was susceptible to predictions. I suggested to ben Zakkai that he tell Vespasian that "if" Vespasian gave permission for the yeshiva, then one day Vespasian would be named Emperor. My Roman contacts were paramount here—I knew the prevailing whisper in Rome was to have Vespasian succeed Vitellius.

Alone, I went to Vespasian and explained part of the predicament and nothing of the plot. Then I accompanied ben Zakkai to meet with Vespasian and make the case, and have him utter the prediction himself. The commander listened and granted the request. The next year, Vespasian was Emperor. His son Titus augmented the siege. When Titus triumphed, an arch was built to commemorate his eventual victory over the Zealots, and all Judea. An arch? When I saw it I thought of your father. He so wanted one.

Your fourth question: my name.

THIRTY

Thank the stars for a reason to switch to something light enough to be hilarious—if used to sit in judgment on men. It is an involved story, and as silly as any other I've ever told.

My maternal grandfather, King Phraates IV—he died the year before I was born—in a generous gesture to Rome once the Pax Romana became an actuality and persuaded by my paternal grandfather, returned to Rome the Legionary Eagles he, General Deleig of Deleig, had, as a young officer, daringly seized in the deadly tumult at Carrhae.

In response, as a token reciprocal gesture, Emperor Augustus sent Phraates an Italian slave girl. She was called Musa. She may have been very young and obviously was beautiful. Trained to please. Very well trained.

As she entangled my maternal grandfather—and he no doubt wanted to be entangled—she revealed herself as an arrogant and ambitious young woman who soon bore the king a son.

As an aside, my mother was not born to Musa, but to Phraates IV's first wife, the one before Musa. My mother, Farida, was the king's youngest daughter.

Though Phraates IV had other sons, the Italian harlot, Musa, persuaded him to make her child his heir. Then, at Musa's bidding, Phraates IV sent his other sons to Roman territory as guarantors of Parthia's intention to keep the peace. Once that son was the new heir, and as Musa's son reached his teenage years, mother and son—or certainly the mother—poisoned Phraates.

So now we have Musa's boy on the throne as King Phraates V. Musa then brought about her own downfall. First, she declared her name sacred and reserved only to her. She ordered a shrine built to honor her rule and endorse her decree. She ruined this triumph for she then married her son. She became his Queen Musa.

That was too much, even for Parthians, who only moved against the rulers when there was no other choice.

Led by my grandfather and father, they killed mother and son but told the populace they had been sent into exile in Roman territory. As a short-term measure, they placed on the throne one Orodes—who barely lasted a year before they kicked him out.

I was born during this period. My father used my arrival to his own purposes. He was delighted to have a second opportunity to assist in upsetting the claims of the usurping Queen Musa. She'd declared her name sacred.

He said, not so. He named me Musan to abolish any vestige of her authority and tore down her shrine to herself, which had been started but not completed. My father certainly never thought I was sacred.

Speaking of names, I now do something, Formio, that I have never done. I address you by your formal name.

My dear Cletus, I congratulate you on your appointment, the reason for your pending return to Rome from the East.

With open arms, I remain your welcoming father and you my beloved son—even if not in the blood. With arms closed around her, if only in my mind, Claudia remains my beloved love-wife—in those realms where such love is possible.

Completed under my seal in the first year of the reign of the Esteemed and Revered Emperor Domitian.

Musan Deleig

Cletus, Bishop of Rome, was Christianity's third pope.

ACKNOWLEDGMENTS

My good friend Allen Coven was my key to unlocking matters Judaic and Judean. Thank you, Allen.

The quality of the legal argument in Chapter 29 is due entirely to Olivia F. Robinson, Professor Emeritus, School of Law, and former Douglas Chair of Roman Law, University of Glasgow. Thank you, Olivia.

Mentioning Professor Robinson immediately conjures up memories of a fine Robinsons-Joneses meal at the Glasgow restaurant Two Fat Ladies at The Buttery. What an evening!

Every author needs tough early "readers." In Professor William Bettridge, retired head of the English Department at the University of Maryland, Baltimore County, and his wife, Patricia, a retired high school English teacher, I had the best. Thank you, Bill and Pat.

Any errors in the book are entirely mine.

Artist Carol Davisson's paintings beautifully illustrate the book's two themes. Carol, thank you for the superb cover artwork. Kudos to photographer Kosta Viennas for work on an earlier cover idea.

My daughter Chris edits dance books. As my production editor, her cover design decisions, typeface selection, layout and proof supervision make this the most handsome of my many books. Thanks, love.

To my wife, Margie, who saw "her" book once more delayed, thanks, love. I promise its rewrite will begin January 1, 2020.

My children and grandchildren, working through the family's Capparoe Books, will utilize all the 21st-century marketing skills their father/grandfather lacks. Thank you all so much!

ABOUT THE AUTHOR

Arthur Jones' dozen previous books include three biographies: *Malcolm Forbes: Peripatetic Millionaire* (Harper); *Pierre Toussaint* (Doubleday); *The Road He Travelled: The Revealing Biography of M. Scott Peck* (Random House/Ebury UK) and its U.S. version, *Boomer Guru: How M. Scott Peck Guided Millions, but Lost Himself on the Road Less Traveled* (Capparoe Books, USA). See more of his books at arthurjonesbooks.com.

Printed in Great Britain
by Amazon